The Schwarzschild Radius

DIANA E. SHEETS

SIGNALMAN PUBLISHING

The Schwarzschild Radius
Copyright ©2024 by Diana E. Sheets

All rights reserved. This book may not be reproduced in whole or in part, in any form (beyond copying permitted by Sections 107 and 108 of the 1976 United States Copyright Act, and except limited excerpts by reviewers for the public press), without written permission from Diana E. Sheets who may be reached via her email, dianasheets@hotmail.com.

First Draft2Digital Original Print Edition, 2024

ISBN-13: 978-1-940145-94-5
ISBN-13 (ebook): 978-1-940145-95-2

Diana E Sheets's website, www.literarygulag.com
Diana E. Sheets's University of Illinois IDEALS website, https://www.ideals.illinois.edu/collections/459

Cover image design by Sasha Rubel, website: https://www.sasharubel.com/About

For Stephen E. Levinson and those scientists, engineers, physicists, mathematicians, and computer scientists who advance the frontiers of knowledge and, we hope, provide the scientific and technological innovations to sustain our future.

About the Author

Diana E. Sheets lives in Champaign, Illinois. She has two earlier published novels, *The Cusp of Dreams* (2010) and *American Suite* (2010). *The Schwarzschild Radius* (2024) is her third work of fiction. Her fiction is available at Amazon, Apple iBookstore, and Barnes & Noble. *The Schwarzschild Radius* is also widely available at many major bookstores.

Diana has published a nonfiction book of literary criticism with Michael F. Shaughnessy entitled: *The Doubling: Those Influential Writers That Shape Our Contemporary Perceptions of Identity and Consciousness in the New Millennium* (Nova Science Publishers, Inc., 2017).

Diana's published articles in collections offered by Nova Science include the following: "The Great Books and Cultural Identity: "The Rise and Fall of Western Memory and Its Implications for Our Time" in *Reading in 2010* (2010); "Reading and Thinking Critically in the Age of Disputation," in *Critical Thinking and Higher Order Thinking: A Current Perspective* (2012); "The Humanities in Crisis: What Went Wrong and How to Restore Their Centrality in our Daily Lives," in *The Humanities in 2015* (2014).

Diana's published a case study about STEM education and iFoundry at the University of Illinois, "Transformative Initiatives: How iFoundry Reimagines STEM Education for the 21st Century," in *Transforming Institutions: Undergraduate STEM Education for the 21st Century* (Purdue University Press, 2016).

Diana's essays on literary criticism and political commentary between 2007 and 2016 appear on her website, www.literarygulag.com.

Diana's book *The Doubling*, her essays for Nova Science and Purdue University Press, her criticism and commentary posts on her website Literary Gulag, and her Ph.D. thesis *British Conservatism and the Primrose*

League: The Changing Character of Popular Politics, 1883-1901 (Columbia University, 1986) are all available under her name and the relevant titles on the University of Illinois public access website IDEALS, https://www.ideals.illinois.edu/collections/459.

1

Just as a dying neutron star can contract no further than its Schwarzschild Radius without collapsing under extreme gravitational force into a black hole that devours everything around it, so too those civilizations whose capacity for conscious thought diminishes sufficiently will implode under the crushing burden of their own primitive minds.

ChandraX

Emoja has been circling the event horizon of Cygnus X-1. Around and around and around she goes. One Emoja, two Emojas, one hundred Emojas in all, orbiting around that black hole. One hundred cyborgs sent from the planet Oturi. Partly Oturian, partly robotic—computerized, modern, blinking—a mass of circuits generating 0s and 1s.

Outside the event horizon are gases—hydrogen and helium, mostly. Extreme temperatures have stripped electrons so that only charged particles cluster amongst the gases. Gravity, so intense. Heat, so extreme. This swirling mass of particles and gaseous clouds looping around the perimeter.

Inside the event horizon beckons Cygnus X-1. From without—extreme radiation. From within—darkness and the void. Other universes? Perhaps. But to know this requires entering the black hole with little prospect of return. Only the smallest sub-atomic particles have been retrieved. Thus, for most organisms entering Cygnus X-1, assuming they could reach that destination, the outcome is terminal—the cessation of life as we know it.

Why are all those Emojas sandwiched between the gases and extreme temperatures, on the one hand, and the dimension of zero gravity, on the other? They defy the logic of space and time, of physics as it is understood. Emojas circling in suspended animation, around and around. While the reader watches and wonders.

But not for long. See the rocket speeding toward them? A living, breathing fireball emerges—the Galactic Kid (GK). The rocket then falls into the black hole, although it appears as if it is hovering at the event horizon because the light reflecting it escapes ever more slowly as the vessel approaches the event horizon. But physics is not our concern here. Back to GK He's tumbling, bouncing, and rolling before colliding with Emoja. The shock of their impact is jarring. They twist and turn. Become entangled. Shimmy and swish. Swash and swoon. He, mostly Oturian, though upgraded for the Virt and the cosmos. She, more robotic than biological because of her vast array of electronic and electromechanical infrastructure. Her exterior is fashioned out of the latest plasidium chromate metal, softer now, although more impenetrable than in the days of the Hercules-Corona Borealis Great Wall exploratory probes, an era that seems like eons ago. Her muscular apparatus comprises atomic motors to ensure strength and longevity. Her epidermis is the darkest of hues, consisting of the most durable polymers. Her hair, the reddest of reds, complements her crimson eyes. Her ebony skin-tones, her flaming tresses, her blazing eyes—all telltale features disclosing her Vargusian origins.

She appears female. He recognizes that. He's definitely male. She registers that. Our GK is long of limb and slim of build. Notice his mulberry-magenta streaked hair and blazing chartreuse eyes. A bolder, brighter, brasher signature than was characteristic of his fellow Neuro-Typicals (N/Ts). He signals to her in what he hopes is universally understood signage, motions that any Oturian from the third millennium would have immediately understood. Watch as his thumb and index fingers form an oval on his left hand. His right-hand pinkie now penetrates that interior. In and out, in and out. Again and again. Like a piston lubricated and enhanced, designed for performance. GK, that primitive, has propositioned Emoja in the crudest manner. Well, what is to be expected? All that testosternet. Been traveling for what seems like eternity. So he does what males of his species have been wont to do: He makes his move. Presses against her. Attempts penetration. Thrusting, pushing, grabbing.

That's when she zaps him. No emotion, no tears, no anger, just 560 volts of prime wattage that send him ricocheting. Around and around, like a top he spins. When he stops, he's facing her. Undeterred, he tries again. Again, she zaps. Like a pinball, he moves. Here, there, everywhere. On his third approach he alters his strategy. He's inquisitive, less the hustler than the disoriented traveler. Speech, when all else fails, attempts to bridge the divide.

"Where am I?" he asks.

"Don't know," she replies. *Just how long have I been here?*

"Who are you?"

"Emoja 96 Excel." *As if my name explains things.*

Falteringly, they attempt this endeavor called communication.

"The Tribunal," he continues, "sentenced me to space colonization. The cosmos is where they send you to die."

"Your crime?"

His laughter is bitter, ironic. "Only one?" *Just like a borg.* "Bitch, get real. The Tribunal convicted me on charges related to embezzlement and thirty-nine assassinations in the Virt. Plus a lot of misdemeanor prac that I committed in the Desolation of the Real: thefts, muggings, detonations, same old, same old, LCD tshi. Not exactly the requisite M.O. for N/Ts."

The talking is enough to spark his Memory Well of all that. Back to planet Oturi circa 3460 Anno Oldem (A.O.). Continent—Artun, where he resided in its largest city, a metropolis called Atmos Legosa that everyone called AL. A sprawling, featureless, smoldering elzhar-ole. Where, if the electricity flowed, the city was bathed in iridescent neon. Those reds, those blues, those orange swells of color embedded in a carbonaceous haze. Provided the place was stoked. But "leakage"—a euphemism for constant power shortfalls—frequently dimmed the skies to a charcoal gray rinsed in jet-black. A fitting noir backdrop for the specter of a metropolis on life support. Along the streets trashed vehicles, with their fuel gauges tripping past empty, were desecrated and abandoned. AL, as with most of Artun, was engulfed in detritus. The air was blanketed in smog. The water, when it could be coaxed to drip from the tap, sputtered sewage embedded with carcinogens. Graffiti, spewed on dilapidated buildings, was caked with excrement. These micro-missives warned of the commonplace environmental hazards: "Can't see! Don't breathe! Mustn't drink!" The autobahns and supersonic runways that functioned were exclusively for the military—the Waja robots and androids—and the privileged—those gorgeous Artunian specimens known as the Enhanced.

Constituting less than .00001 percent of the population, the Enhanced were the essence of celluloid perfection. With skin so pale it cast an alabaster sheen, with eyes so penetrating and cerulean irises so blue, with hair the silky sheen of pewter-albumen, the rare visitor or dignitary dared not gaze too long or risk becoming entranced by their sublime beauty.

What of their genetic code or NAD? Modified to include the very latest bio-organic, semi-conductor molecules. This silicon-based biochemistry overlaid the preexisting carbon-based molecular structure. Thus, electronic circuits, not organic proteins, regulated key sensory and neural pathways. This dramatically improved visual and auditory acuity. It also boosted numerous other capabilities including the ability to capture, display, and alter imagery, the potential to invoke real-time global positioning, and the facility to employ sophisticated computational measurements augmented by vastly enhanced memory capabilities. That, in turn, allowed for the storage, retrieval, and processing of dynamically compressed data bases, as well as the concomitant integration of these knowledge resources across a broad-spectrum of cognitive applications. Because of the latest advances in science and technology, this silicon-based biochemistry had been genetically integrated so that it was encoded into the NAD and capable of being transmitted from one generation to the next, thereby enabling the possibility of evolutionary advances achieved through natural selection.

By contrast with the Enhanced, the N/Ts might be characterized as primitive cyborgs. They had plugs and external circuitry enabling connectivity directly into their brains, thereby transmitting the source data throughout the central nervous system via neurotransmitters traveling synaptic information highways. Source codes from the Virt stimulated the pleasure/pain center, the appetite/cessation domain, the thirst/quenching sphere, the sexual and hormonal receptors, and the wake/sleep pathways even as they subtly altered those areas of the brain associated with consciousness. However, although the N/Ts perceived that they were feasting and drinking and f<>#ing and sleeping and partying in the Virt, they were actually in various states of atrophy known to trigger appetite suppression, dehydration, sleep deprivation, and, in the most extreme cases, actually culminated in the cessation of all major bodily functions as flatlining ensued. And yet, the perception persisted, against all evidence, that only in the Virt were N/Ts truly alive.

Both the Enhanced and the N/Ts considered the LCDs to be a sallow, sub-Artunian tribe. A single glance from those most privileged was all it took to sanctify righteous condemnation.

"Grotesque abominations from the sub-strata!" the Enhanced would exclaim.

"Gory-Gory Helishow! SMK!" became the rally cry of the N/Ts.

Alas, those LCDs. Their skin so icteric, their eyes the chromatic aberration of burnt cadmium, their hair a listless flaxen hue—all demonstrable proof of their innate inferiority. Biologically they lacked the semi-conductor, molecular advantages of the Enhanced or even the basic electronic and external circuitry that defined the N/Ts. Though that was hardly a surprise given that the LCDs came from the most disadvantaged sectors of the community and, as such, no effort had been made to modify or improve their performance. Certainly, there were always a few renegades from the N/Ts who became "unplugged," thereby being subsumed into the ranks of the LCDs and potentially susceptible to joining the Resistance. And there were persistent rumors that among the LCD underclass there were a few eggheads, the Rajakians, who eschewed modern circuitry and electronic wizardry for the Byzantine pursuits of scholarly knowledge reputed to be contained in the vestigial remains of the Rajakian Archives.

But the thoughts of GK have digressed. Let us stimulate selective neural pathways within his Memory Well to have him return to the subject of the Enhanced. They lived luxuriously in their high-tech fortress up in the clouds. Venturing outside the compound was perilous, requiring its inhabitants to ride in AmphibiRovers resistant to ambush from insurgents attacking by land, air, and sea.

But should their enemies suspend activities long enough to glance intently at the Enhanced, they, too, might be mesmerized by the celluloid perfection of these majestic Artunians. Beautiful and intelligent, the Enhanced possessed exceptional grace and bearing. They scarcely aged. Their minds never dulled, although they scarcely had to think about anything, so they might have been characterized by impartial observers as Zbies. Children, though few, resembled the near-perfection persona of their parents. Nevertheless, despite that charm, that beauty, that poise, the Enhanced were a predatory tribe resistant to miscegenation. Outsiders were rarely admitted within their ranks. The N/Ts and LCDs might lay siege to the fortress; they might try their hand at murder or theft or espionage, but marriage among the Enhanced was prohibited. In any case, those less privileged lacked the lingua franca of the most exalted. For the Enhanced conversed in elaborate sentences. Florid paragraphs.

Tenses and declensions that evoked the spectral remnants of their illustrious heritage, seemingly light years removed from the squalid existence that was the lot of the N/Ts and LCDs.

The Enhanced were blessed with an awareness of time. Their perceptions of past, present, and future were enforced through their spoken and electronically inscribed language—those tenses and declensions linking together obscure cultural references—enabling them to envision a string of causal events moving along a linear continuum influenced by dimensions of spacetime. Their perspective—Action Equals Change Over Time ($A=C/T$), when coupled with the nominal exercise of free will it engendered, helped to preserve a flicker of consciousness.

By contrast, the N/Ts and most of the LCDs were locked in the atemporal limbo of the eternal present. They had no perception of what came before or any expectation regarding the future. Nor were they cognizant of the cultural heritage they had once shared with the Enhanced. The vocabulary of the N/Ts and the LCDs was limited to a maximum of eight hundred words, and all communication was conducted in the present tense.

However, the N/Ts, unlike most LCDs, could understand and convey brief phrases of electronic text. *Reader, you may have surmised that our GK, rebel that he is, read surreptitiously while on Oturi and extensively during his sojourn through space and, therefore, has developed a relatively complex syntax, unlike most N/Ts. But let us return to GK's thoughts.* Being was all, everything, the NOW. All else, irrelevant. Whatever occurred in the Virt or on the monitors throughout the Desolation of the Real was TRUTH. TRUTH was always in the NOW. There was no past TRUTH in opposition to the present. For that required memory, an awareness of how previous events might influence the NOW and guide the future. Because of this loss of temporal perspective, there could be no perception of consequence. And without consequence, there could be no culpability. Ergo, no free will since the ability to choose rests upon awareness that the past might alter the present and impact the future. Consequently, the behavior of N/Ts was motivated by a rudimentary pleasure/pain stimulus.

The LCDs occupied the lowest socioeconomic strata on the social spectrum and were, for the most part, illiterate. However, because they were prohibited from accessing the visually frenetic domain of the Virt, their ability to express themselves verbally was comparable to the N/Ts. But that was the extent of their similarity. For the N/Ts, day-to-day existence was abject misery. They lived on the streets, in the corridors of abandoned buildings, and in the sewers. They survived on handouts, resorted to theft, and rummaged through garbage. Their moment-by-moment existence was lived beyond the pale.

The circumstances of the LCD renegades, who were either more resourceful or allied with the Resistance, was marginally better than the rank and file, although their stature would hardly have enabled them to elevate their social standing to join ranks with the N/Ts.

Only those members of the LCDs known as the Rajakians were said to live in relative comfort. Where and how they accomplished this feat, however, was never disclosed. Still, the rumors and innuendos persisted. The Rajakians were said to be engaged in "Time Restoration" or the recovery of their ancient culture and its importance in Artunian historical destiny by means of restorative tools. These included the study and understanding of antiquity, the use of complex tenses, the appreciation of the consequence of actions when analyzed along a linear time trajectory, and the imposition of free will.

This "Deliverance" for Rajakians was the pursuit of learning in search of wisdom or the "Divine." It was to be obtained, in part, through the restitution of the lost Rajakian Archives, a written repository of the intellectual and cultural achievements of all Oturians. Thus, historical knowledge equated with wisdom for the Rajakians and was regarded as the source-code for enlightenment. And with enlightenment came the prospect of a restored and vibrant consciousness—the apogee in their quest for "Redemption."

But the pursuit of consciousness by the Rajakians through the acquisition of knowledge necessarily made them the enemy. For if there was one thing everyone else in Artun agreed upon, it was that CONSCIOUSNESS=PAIN. Pain was to be obliterated and replaced with Bliss. Bliss was purported to be the path to the Divine. The attainment of Divine Bliss (❁) brought about the eradication of pain, the end of meaninglessness, and the removal of adversity. ❁ was all.

However, the state of was realized in different ways for each of the three social classes or tribes. For the Enhanced, it was a state of grace that enabled them to live a life in abundant comfort free of pain and exertion. For the N/Ts ❁ was to be achieved in the Virt through gaming. The Big Win could beget a Bigger Win, which would lead to the ultimate win obtainable only by participation in the Memory Palace (▦): A Game of Omissions. The prime directive of gaming in the ▦ was employing the tactics of warfare that emphasized triumphing over others—destroying them if need be—in order to ensure one's hierarchiary in the ▦.

This was obtainable only by stratagems of violence comingled with bravery and hints of sagacity. Winners inhabited the inner sanctuary of the ▦. Losers were banished to the periphery and suffered the dire consequences. Only N/Ts were Gamers in the Virt.

The Enhanced were forbidden to play and only under exceptional circumstances were granted access to the Virt. The LCDs were off-the-grid and nearly all of them knew only squalor and misery. For them, the ❁ could only be achieved through theft and insurrection, except in the case of the Rajakians.

So that was Artun, a continent where social class was maintained with a vengeance. The Enhanced never spoke to the N/Ts, who never interacted, except at great peril, with the LCDs. And if there was one thing that most Artunians were agreed upon, it was death to all Rajakians.

"Tell me about the N/Ts," she asks.

GK pulls himself out of the Memory Well, a flood of pulsating images with crawling text that, for him, represents the horror of what was. A ceaseless recall of the trauma of survival that some called living. Emoja is looking at him. Expectant. Waiting. The object of his desire. So he attempts to explain.

"N/Ts live in spaces we refer to as cubicles. Each cube is self-contained. It has a toilet, a bed, a table, and provides access to the Virt. N/Ts immerse themselves in the Virt. Everything they long for is there: gaming, adventure, sensate pleasures, and the community of like-minded egoists' intent on pursing the visceral thrill of living beyond the Desolation of the Real. It is the dream of dreams. I was an N/T, a gamer. The very best of the best."

Just saying the words catapulted him back to his former cube. Back to the smallest confines of nothingness called living that perilously approached the null. Like most N/Ts, he preferred the Virt to the Real because that was where life seemed tolerable. In the Virt, there was Hustle, which stoked emotions and spiked the pleasure/pain center. Vertical ascents alternated with G-force plunges. Exciting, vibrant, infinitely preferable to the insufferable claustrophobia of life lived in the Desolation of the Real where it wasn't safe to go out, where there was no place to go, where only chalky gruel and liquid nutrients passed for sustenance, where one necessarily lived one's life alone for the count. In the Virt, if you were ascendant, there were perks. The better your performance, the greater the activation of your pleasure centers. More stimulation, More tasecsy, and always the possibility of MORE! So what if it was virtual. It felt real. Better than the Real. For a while, anyway.

He spins a tale for Emoja. Of that wreckage called life. Hear that swell of music? So sorrowful. See GK with his eyes cast down; notice his look of pain? Out pops his question, "Want to f<>#?"

She neither laughs nor cries. Neither attracted nor repelled. "I'm not designed for intercourse."

Bitch. Whore. No big deal. "I know a line when I hear one. Been turned down by Borgs, Bots, and Babes sexier than you." *Sort of. Twelve rejects in the Virt, 107 smacks from Bitches in the Real. Be cool, dry ice, even if the loins throb.*

"GK, I..."

What? How does she know my name? The Bitch is telepathic??? She intercepted my thoughts. She already knew what I was thinking about the N/Ts before she asked me to explain.

"I analyze brain-wave patterns. It prevents miscommunications."

Every f<>#ing thing. Every obscene inclination. No way to edit all those thoughts. Not that I wanna.

"GK, I'm not designed for intercourse, for the interchange of fluids between male and female Oturians. Emojas aren't designed to breed. We can always generate replicants. Their composition can be altered to provide for greater variability than our present configuration. Put simply—we don't need to mate.

"When you come right down to it," she continues, "your KY chromosome is a genetic nightmare. It barely embraces the XT, and then only at their tips during initial cell division. The limited opportunity to recombine hampers its ability to repair. The mutations keep growing. The KY chromosome gets sicker and sicker. Even though it has some internal recombination going on, that doesn't guarantee that gene conversion will reverse the damage. Your KY chromosome is a genetic graveyard."

"Bummer! I'm slated for extinction! That's what repels you? Not my bod, my bodacious attitude? When you zapped me, I thought it was because you found me physically repulsive! But now I know it's just my obsolete NAD. To elzhara with borg-isms. Let's F<>k!"

He leaps forward. She pushes him back, gently, but firmly. "GK, I was sent here on a mission. That mission overrides everything."

Emoja's resistance has the unexpected consequence of generating a stream of associative memories, thoughts reconstructed from her Core Memory. Perhaps that is why they are so transitory. Must have been damaged in some system malfunction. Nonetheless, the fleeting images persist. Of the Institute in Artun tucked away in the Oasis of the Real. Where scientists gathered from around the globe. Nominally, they were part of the Enhanced since they lived in the rarified domain of the privileged.

But scientists engaged in research—an endeavor that was always suspect. Their knowledge extended back to antiquity and continued to press forward insistently into the distant future. Political stratagems never held much appeal to them. They wanted to understand the cosmos. They sought Truth, even when the mathematics suggested dismal societal outcomes or failed to prove the economic theories propounded by the Enhanced.

Therefore, scientists were not to be trusted. They weren't interested in preserving the established order. They disdained stratification. If someone demonstrated scientific genius, they didn't care if that individual had come from the N/Ts or the LCDs. Nor did they erect barriers between themselves and colleagues from other continents. To the scientists at the Institute, these restrictions were parochial. Their lives were focused on 0s and 1s, and they welcomed researchers from around the world with whom they might confer.

Given this egalitarian predisposition, the scientists, like the Rajakians, were considered dangerous. They were constantly under surveillance. But the Enhanced needed the scientists to maintain their privileges. Indeed, Artun was dependant upon them to sustain the technological and military advantages vis-à-vis the four other continents: Zhinboya, Sirus, Catalla, and Vargus. Of these, only Zhinboya posed a significant threat. Sirus had become almost entirely radioactive from the N-Deluge. Catalla, once a bastion of civilization, was besieged with Sirusian refugees. It was buckling under the strain of ethnic conflict, scarce resources, and a lack of resolve. These were the unintended consequence brought by the erosion in Catalla of cultural, political, and economic memory. Vargus, deep in the heart of Oturi, was a molten core of deprivation, an incandescent heat.

Despite the necessity of relying on the scientists at the Institute, the Enhanced never trusted their forecasts. In part, this was due to the fact that the scientists' prognosis for the future of Oturi was dismal. Their scenarios were relentlessly pessimistic and founded upon the premise that there were too many Oturians and insufficient resources to supply the needs of the citizenry. Shortages would result and all the associated woes—starvation, diseases, and a dearth of drinkable water, which, in turn, accelerated the crisis. Only the perpetual War of Hegemony between Artun and Zhinboya convinced the Enhanced of the importance of continuing to employ the scientists, whose skills were deemed essential for Artun's planetary and cosmic victories.

Thus, the scientists at the Institute played an essential role in the conceptualization and execution of military strategy. They agreed to build the space stations, the bombs, and the laser systems designed to eradicate enemy warheads. Whatever was asked. Whatever was required. Provided their fundamental research would continue and that it would have as its overarching goal the establishment of a space colony comprising a new breed of Oturians based on advanced cybernetic concepts.

The Cygnus X-1 Mission, known as The Emoja Project, was the third such planetary attempt to colonize outer space. The first ship, with a crew from Artun consisting of eighteen robots, blew up when it hit an asteroid field as it approached the gravitational field of Gamma Cyg. The second vessel was sponsored by the Zhinboyans. Their astronauts totaled thirty-four cyborgs, half male, half female. That mission failed when the ship disintegrated as it entered the heliopause at the edge of the Deneb solar system.

Naturally, a great deal of anticipation surrounded the third venture, undertaken by Artun, to send a team of robots and cyborgs to the event horizon of Cygnus X-1. So risky was the mission that a decision was made to recruit Strangelets, the young female waifs wandering the streets and tunnels of Vargus, the most impoverished territory on Oturi.

Located at the core of the planet, Vargus was a blazing inferno. So interminably hot, so forlorn, so devoid of possibilities. With its hardships, its scarcities, its lack of natural resources, and its diseases, life in Vargus seemed but a momentary reprieve from death. Despite insurmountable odds, however, the Vargusians—those that remained—were a majestic people. Of stunning beauty with their noir complexion and their crimson hair. To witness their carriage, their bearing, their manner of speaking was enchanting. So exquisite were they that it was hard to fathom at first glance that the Vargusians were desperately struggling to survive. And most at risk were the Strangelets, those female pre-adolescents abandoned during infancy to fend for themselves.

With so much at stake, it was hoped that the one hundred Strangelets, age nine or ten, who had been selected for the mission, would agree to participate. And indeed, so dismal were their prospects that none refused. Nor did any authority intervene to prevent their departure for Artun since Vargus was in a state of anarchy.

Having already performed a series of highly complex modifications—both mechanical and computational—on aquatic, reptilian, and mammalian creatures, the scientists at the Institute began enhancing the Strangelets. Given the experimental nature of their project, the process wasn't as simple or flawless as the scientists had hoped. It took years, in fact. But at the age of eighteen, after numerous modifications, Emoja 96 Excel was selected over the ninety-nine other cyborgs for the space mission.

And what were her attributes? Emoja was tall and athletic. She was agile, both with respect to her body and mind. Nothing intimidated her, and she was infinitely curious. Her computational and scientific-reasoning capabilities tested off the charts. Having surmounted daunting challenges, she welcomed adversity. Her outlook on the Zfacto Assessment Scale topped the charts at 180. She was probing, skeptical, assertive, inquisitive, intelligent, and insightful. Though few would admit it, many of the scientists—both male and female—were enamored with Emoja. Not surprisingly, given that she was their designated emissary to venture forth into the cosmos, their best hope of transmitting all that was deemed worth salvaging from Oturian civilization.

Having determined that Emoja was the best cyborg the Institute was capable of deploying in 3458 A.O., it was decided that she should be cloned. A total of ninety-nine other Emojas were created as a symbolic homage to the cyborgs remaining to assist the ongoing research at the Institute. From then on it was desided that Emoja 96 Excel would be referred to simply as Emoja while her clones would be identified by their specific Emoja number (1-99). Emoja, her clones, and a storehouse of potential replicants would travel to Cygnus X-1 along with the seventy-five robots, model Artun85.

That was the genesis of the Emoja Project, which she explains to GK.

"And the robots," he asks, "What about the bots?"

"The Artun85s possess all the technological advancements of the Emojas. Their computational abilities exceed the latest generation supercomputers, the SC6800, at the Institute, and their kinetic abilities surpass all previous generations of robots. Like the Emojas, they possess dual processing capability; namely, they can solve complicated equations both in parallel and sequential modes.

"However, the Artun85s," she continues, "were designed to be fully conscious, but devoid of qualia. For this reason, the Artun85s subsequently challenged existing interpretations of what it meant to be fully conscious."

"What the f<>#　is qualia?"

"If you were to consider the property of 'redness'..."

"As in your red hair?"

"Well, the property of redness as distinct from the object under consideration. That is to say, if we examined your subjective response to visualizing the essence of 'red,' the feelings induced would be characterized as qualia. Think of qualia as the sensations triggering your emotive response to the perception of objects or individuals or places. The burst of citrus flavor that you smell and taste as you bite into a piece of fruit; the anger you feel when an injustice has been committed against you; the bitter-cold sensation caused by plunging headfirst into a mountain stream. That sensate pleasure, that explosive rage, that cataclysmic paralysis, that swell of emotions you experience in response to stimuli is referred to as qualia. Scientists at the Institute believed that these emotions inhibit the machine capabilities and, consequently, elected not to build qualia into the Artun85s. Naturally, they have indicators to warn them of risks and dangers, but the emotional triggers influencing behavior were deemed irrelevant."

"You have them."

"To a degree, yes. I'm responding to you emotively because that's your operative state. I have other modes of being."

"All bitches do. Damned if I know what they are."

"Sure you do. Much more that you're admitting. Anyway, that's my story."

"Wait, wait, wait. This qualia. It's not biological. It's spiritual. There's biology and then there's this higher state of consciousness that stands apart from the mechanics of living, call it the Oturian soul, if you will."

"What you refer to as soul is little more than the pattern of synaptic connections and neural firings that result in predictable responses to a wide variety of stimuli. Nothing more."

"Perhaps for you, but as for us Oturians . . ."

"I'm Oturian, and I'm telling you it's not necessary."

"You're no Oturian. You're some kind of freak. You were genetically modified and sent here as part of the Institute's preposterous mission for survival."

"Whatever your thoughts or feelings about my existence and purpose, there can be no denying the fact that I'm here. Just as you are."

"Just two bloody mistakes who were catapulted into space to die."

"GK, you've been given a second chance, just as I."

"You're nothing more than a creature drawn from the purgatory we call Vargus and artificially reconceived as some experimental nightmare. You're scarcely Oturian. You're barely alive."

Maybe that's why she kisses him. For underneath his tough, brash, cruel persona is an inquisitive soul. An Artunian filled with pain. A fighter. A warrior. And now a celestial explorer. So she reaches out. A kiss with tongue. Cyborg greets Oturian male.

"Our quest has only just begun," she mutters.

And so it has.

2

Cultural memory is the bedrock of a civilization. It is the air we breathe, the dreams we share. Without it, there can be no past and no future. Instead, historical events are replayed continuously, each recursion becoming ever more farcical. Without a past that evolves into a future there can be no prospect of advancement. Cultural amnesia has us spiraling down the evolutionary ladder. We regress to our primal antecedents, thereby closing the book on our story.

ChandraX

Emoja and GK continue circling round the event horizon of Cygnus X-1—first, side-by-side; then, front to back; later, up and down and every which way; sometimes, alongside or between all those other Emojas. There's a seduction in play, although the outcome is far from certain. Emoja says GK's actions stem from the male territorial drive to possess. GK insists their connection, consistent with the theosophy of Nezoat, has been ordained from the very inception of the cosmos. Emoja points out their union can have no physical culmination. GK says he prefers to live in the moment. It's ing and ang with a new melodic twist. Given the mechanical constraints, discourse must necessarily take precedence, for now, over biological fulfillment of carnal desire.

The collision and subsequent interaction between Borg and Kid help restore much of Emoja's memory. Together, they set about to reactivate the functional utility of the Memory Well and its storehouse of memories in the other Emojas. Details of the mission return. The Emoja Mission was to harness the energy source of Cygnus X-1 so that it could be used to establish terraforming on designated planets with the possibility of sustaining life and nurturing viable colonies in space. Periodic updates were to be sent to the Institute.

Arrival at the event horizon must have been rough. Perhaps, that explains, in part, why the Emjoas developed amnesia and were aimlessly circling the event horizon of Cygnus X-1 when GK encountered them.

But the robots? Where are they? The Artun85s had been instructed to explore the major constellations of the Milky Way from Cygnus to Sagittarius while the Emojas developed the fuel reserves necessary for continued exploration and habitation in space. Communication links were to be relayed between robots, cyborgs, and scientists by means of the spaceship Nexus. Indeed, it still orbits just beyond the perimeter of the event horizon, absorbing and redeploying energy to deflect the gravitational pull of Cygnus X-1.

With her telepathic powers magnified for messaging, Emoja checks the flight recorder, the log, and the computerized database. Nothing. Either from the Institute or the robots. Something has gone terribly wrong. She explains the situation to GK.

"Let me help," he says. "I'm a quick study." And so he is. They transport to Nexus and begin poring over the records. So much is indecipherable. Emoja dispatches text messages by means of Advanced Protocol Hyper-Cosmic Speed to the Institute. Not one word of response. Consequently, GK and Emoja begin building and reconfiguring the damaged hardware in an attempt to rescue lost data.

But it is an arduous task. The ship's command station appears to be malfunctioning. Both input and output communication links have been damaged. IG [intergalactic] text, meant to be preserved on an internal disk, is garbled. There is no reliable backup. So they search the records, trying to discover how to retrieve information while simultaneously rebuilding the hardware and debugging the software. They troubleshoot the pathways, the directories, the filters, the memory tree.

"It's all there," he says. "You just have to figure out how to access it."

Assuming there's a compatibility issue, GK tries to extract data from the substrate command. The log notations appear, but no messages. He examines backup systems.

> backup [drive zx:][path:rwq] [access: comlog/messaging] [/m:72][/a] [/f:size][/d:all]

Nothing. He investigates breaks in the data flow where stoppages occur, but discovers no recondite traces. Still, he persists because the outcome necessitates explanation. He checks the error messages. Nothing abnormal. He troubleshoots the clock and finds that it's not displaying. Perhaps it was damaged during a meteor shower. The autoexec function is also malfunctioning. He repairs both and begins making adjustments to the Search & Retrieve Command.

GK is a whiz at all this. At analyzing, debugging, and rebuilding code. At source lines and mapsym protocols, be they numeric or symbolic. All linkages have to be restored. He reassembles the /segments option that executes the X++ fulfillment code. Forty-five days later, as measured in Artun time, GK has managed to restore several critical messages from the Institute. From these he concludes that the damage to the ship's communication system was caused by extreme radiation emanating from a star that went supernova. It seems that the gamma rays damaged Nexus and erased the memories of the Emojas. After filtering and boosting and reconfiguring interpolation algorithms, a few key messages from the Institute are retrieved.

> Log 3463 MS. 33—Inst. Heavy meteorite shower. Damage to Nexus. Emojas at the event horizon. Unable to est. communication.
>
> Log 3464 MS. 66—Inst. No communication from Artun85s.

Sent communication to Artun85s.

Sent communication.

Sent communication.

Log 3466 MS. 67 Inst. Sent communication to Emojas.

Sent communication.

Sent communication.

Sent communication.

Log 3468 MS. 48 Inst. Artun @ war with Zhinboya. Fuel stoppages. Water shortages. Massive casualties. Air quality—dangerous. Planet status: Critical and hostile to life. Sirus no response. Ditto Vargus. Communications only from Artun and Zhinboya.

Log 3470 MS. 99 Inst. We've been hit. Computers crashing. F<>#!

The last recorded communication occurred at 21:00 hours in the year 3470 A.O.

"No way," GK mutters. He's perspiring. Pacing. Angry. "The enemy just doesn't up and die. I was going to take 'em out! That was my mission."

"It's over. The Oturian adventure is over." Emoja says it softly. Though a cyborg, it seems a tear rolls down her cheeks.

Space is so vast. So empty. So seemingly devoid of life.

"Cosmos," GK mutters, "You are huge, and we are miniscule."

Our hero and heroine embrace. To watch them is to witness the last remaining biological Oturians huddling together, seeking comfort. Then, at precisely at 12:23.14 Artunian time, Borg and Kid fall asleep entwined on the captain's berth of the Nexus spaceship as it continues circling the event horizon.

3

Time is relative, less than absolute. The closer an object is with respect to a black hole, the more times slows. Once inside the event horizon, time ceases. At the center of the event horizon is the singularity where the laws of physics are suspended. Outside the event horizon, the rotation of particles creates an accretion disc that heats up in excess of one billion degrees Fahrenheit as it sucks everything in. All that heat, that radiation, that transmogrification of time.
ChandraX

Though not visible to the naked eye, Cygnus X-1 is detectable by virtue of the x-ray frequencies emitted as the massive gravitational field pulls gaseous particles and dust into its midst. That force is so powerful that its orbiting companion, a blue supergiant, is shedding its outer shell. From a distance the clutter of debris gives the black hole the appearance of a celestial halo. Ah, the majesty of extreme gravity at play.

But binary systems need not be a single star coupled with a black hole. More typically, they are two stars positioned so close that they share an orbital path. As with Emoja and GK, who appear inseparable as they circle round and round, plotting their destiny.

Eventually, their plan takes shape. Emoja and GK prepare to return to Oturi in hopes of discovering exactly what happened on their planet and what may have caused the systems failure at the perimeter of the event horizon of Cygnus X-1. They also intend to learn why the robots failed to maintain contact. Our heroine and hero are busy enhancing the capability of Supernova Time-Leaps (STL) by Nexus in order to expedite GK's ability to travel back through time.

His reasons for returning are many. He wants to understand the now distroyed civilizations of the five Oturi continents, as well as understanding why they perlished. To do this, he has decided, he must walk among the Enhanced and the LCDs and, once again, experience life in the Virt. Most of all, GK wishes to gain access to the Rajakian Archives, documents that, he is convinced, will answer many of his questions and enable him to comprehend the underlying factors shaping the destiny of the planet. Assuming, of course, that they actually exist. And if, along the way, GK inflicts retribution, he feels, so much the better.

Emoja's reasons for returning to Oturi differ from GK's. Her primary interest is in gaining access to vital information at the Institute and discussing its ramifications with her former colleagues. She would like to obtain all relevant data regarding the design specifications and operational procedures pertaining to both the Emojas and the Artun85s. Her goal is to discover what went wrong with the mission and set it back on course.

Emoja is virtually certain that everyone on Oturi is now dead. But what if she is mistaken? Might she change the destiny of life on that planet? Yet how much, if anything, could she do to alter the outcome? Emoja dreams of returning to Vargus. She longs to experience it, taste it, smell it, touch it, live it. She knows such a visit entails tremendous risk. Nevertheless, she must revisit her homeland. It is a journey she intends to make.

Then, assuming there is time, Emoja is considering asking scientists at the Institute about the possibility of being reprogrammed to have intercourse with GK. He wants it. He insists. And since GK is also prepared to make this perilous journey, she feels she must explore that option. Then, there is the issue of offspring. Afterall, why be programmed for intercourse if there is no possibility of procreation? She has decided not to mention this scenario to GK. He has enough concerns regarding commitment, why burden him with issues associated with progeny?

In any case, Emoja's not sure that a committed partnership is a prerequisite for raising younglings. The central issue, as she sees it, is whether there will be any cosmic benefit to coupling their NAD. And should she discover when she returns to Oturi that everyone on the planet will die, would that alter her decision? Would she and GK, then, have a moral obligation to combine their nomeseys? She considers this issue warily. After all, the Emojas were never conceived as reproductive vessels and their mission requires that the prime directive—colonization—takes precedence over everything else. Progeny would complicate matters and risk diluting the focus away from pressing issues to the most primitive and prosaic considerations.

But serendipity is a strange phenomenon. GK ended up here, at the edge of the event horizon. He bumped into her, inadvertently paving the way for the restoration of her memory. If not for his intervention, Emoja suspects, she and all of the other Emojas would not have been able to reactivate their memories and pursue their mission. But was his appearance serendipity or fate? Could destiny be a factor in a universe generated by 0s and 1s?

The questions kept on coming. Would she have a moral obligation to perpetuate GK's nomesey? Must he be informed of her decision? Fortunately, Emoja reasons, she needn't discuss this with him at present since the issue of offspring could only, as of now, be theoretically postulated. In any case, it's far from certain that she or GK will survive the voyage to Oturi, let alone their journey back to the event horizon of Cygnus X-1. And with these dangers in mind, the remaining Emojas must be fully updated on the mission and how to proceed before she and GK depart.

Then, there is the issue of how Emoja intends to return to Oturi.

After numerous calculations and estimations, she has determined that her best means of traveling back through time is to enter Cygnus X-1. She's convinced not only that it can be done, but also that her travel to Oturi will be quicker and reentry far more precise by means of Cygnus X-1 than by spaceship. Her preliminary data suggests that there is critical information contained in the black hole that will assist her in obtaining the precise coordinates she needs to arrive at the Institute and, hopefully, provide the source code enabling her to return to the event horizon of Cygnus X-1. Though risky, this journey would assist her in learning more about black holes—one of her prime directives—since capturing energy from black holes and redirecting it toward planets that were to be colonized would sustain the mission. Emoja recognizes the importance of having GK travel separately in order to increase their respective odds of survival. In any case, he isn't equipped to enter Cygnus X-1. He'd never survive.

Given the inherent dangers and the possibility that either or both of them might perish while trying to complete their respective missions, Emoja and GK have agreed to reunite on Oturi to share their discoveries before attempting to return to the event horizon. They intend to communicate by means of an obscure cipher, the Biterbi code based on a twelve-node trellis. They have meticulously set their rendezvous for 3467 A.O. at the precise moment that the star Zepora enters the orbital flight path of the star Aaron. That is just six months after Emoja has arrived on Oturi and four months after GK's projected landing. And just days before he was once designated by authorities to be rocketed into space to die. Both have agreed that should either fail to return to the event horizon of Cygnus X-1, the survivor will provide the other Emojas with all the pertinent information obtained while on Oturi. Indeed, by now the Emojas have already received the most recent data downloads so as to ensure they understand the intentions of Emoja 96 Excel and GK in case neither returns. In truth, the mission is almost impossible, just as success is deemed essential.

Emoja tells GK of her intention to time travel by means of Cygnus

X-1. After learning of her plans, GK is sullen. He's convinced she won't survive. His anger and anxiety are largely manifested through physical motion. He keeps bumping up against her. Angrily, tenderly, bitterly, sweetly. He doesn't appear worried about himself. He tells her that in his brief life he has already experienced a thousand deaths. What's another "system failure" for him in the scheme of things? Emoja reminds him that failure in this instance would be real, not virtual. The outcome, she emphasizes, is permanent. GK is unconcerned. He insists that it's Emoja's safety that is paramount. She must be protected from unnecessary risk. After all, he brought her back to consciousness. Why throw her life away by plunging into a black hole?

Weighing on GK's mind is the possibility that she might even be *The One. The One . . . . The One . . . . The One . . . .* He can't even believe he's considering this. *After all, I'm just the Kid. I'm not reliable. I'm not even stable. She must know I'm not to be trusted. F<>#ing bitch! She reads minds. She'll discover I'm fickle. Protective, domineering, and fickle. Really pathetic.*

"I love you," he says as he bumps up against her. *Why should I care if she knows what I'm thinking? I love her now. Isn't that enough? Besides, who commits for eternity? No one, that's who! Some days, just a few hours is more than enough. Anyhow, we haven't had sex. No way am I committing to this Borg when she hasn't even delivered. Gotta know the goods. Nobody buys a product without testing it beforehand. No one.*

"I trust you, GK."

"How can you trust me? You know my thoughts. You know too damn much." His current state of qualia could be characterized as anger tinged with a hint of liquid sorrow.

"I love you, GK." She leans over to kiss him.

Oh, but that Borg can kiss.

4

Waging battle against cultural death is futile. These efforts succeed only in slowing the rate of decline and in enervating those individuals who still have the capacity to advance. Their efforts are expended on the sands of useless toil while averting nothing. Better to gather up the remnants of the cultural artifacts and move elsewhere.
ChandraX

And so Emoja and GK begin their preparations. They devote a great deal of effort to downloading information into GK's Foundational Memory and enhancing his connective linkages and speed of retrieval. He's also been given significantly greater capabilities to store information within his Functional Memory. GK's computational powers greatly improve as do his abilities to compensate for the effects of weightlessness in space and tolerate the enormous physical forces that are anticipated during reentry into Oturi's atmosphere.

Emoja reviews the available information on black holes. Despite the tremendous gravitational pull—so strong that no light is emitted—nonetheless, she notes evidence for the existence of virtual particles that escape from black holes as a result of quantum effects close to the event horizon. This spontaneous release is equivalent to black-body radiation. Should this phenomenon occur sufficiently outside an event horizon of any given black hole, it would cause a corresponding loss of mass from within. The greater the amount, the greater at risk that black hole would be for evaporating. If this occurred, there would be a final brilliant burst of radiation before it vanished. But that time horizon, particularly with respect to a significantly sized black hole, is estimated at trillions of times longer than the existence of the Milky Way. Nevertheless, it is regarding these spontaneous releases of virtual particles that Emoja finds herself thinking about.

The closer Emoja and GK get to their departure, the greater their intimacy. To look at them circling the event horizon is to comprehend how entangled they have become. Often not a word is spoken. A gesture, a look, a touch says it all. Naturally, this closeness has its difficulties. They are already experiencing the emotional stress associated with their impending separation. The uncertainly of their future together weighs heavily upon them. They rehearse over and over the details for their rendezvous—that propitious moment in 3467 A.O. when the star Zepora enters the flight path of the star Aaron. There are risks. What if one of them fails to show up or arrives late, after the stars are out of alignment? What will be the consequence? So painful is the subject that neither has the heart to broach the matter.

The other Emojas shield the pair as they orbit the event horizon. It's been tacitly acknowledged that Emoja 96 Excel and GK are special. Their successful completion of the journey to Oturi is deemed critical. Their courage is admired. The support of all the other Emojas for our heroine and hero is clear. See them traveling in elliptical rings around them? Their dance resembles the tribal steps the Strangelets performed back in Vargus all those years ago when every moment lived was fraught with danger. As the Emojas glide and pirouette and chassé through space, they sing **"Song for the Journey."**

Twisted Pair
Uncoupling now
In search of memory.

Time's eye regress
To Continents Lost
And Oturi lives erased.

Dance, then, those fateful steps
Near nested globes so perfect
For there 'twas sung "Song for the Journey."

    Ascending voices coalesce in a spiral spin. We watch the dancers weave this collective farewell. Memory traces rutted in filaments and etched in residue as Emoja and GK bid adieu.

5

Outside is a cosmos subject to immutable laws. Perhaps less than absolute, but definable, scalable, with universal points of reference. Within lies the possibility of infinite dissonance. Tonality, with its hierarchical order and central point of reference, is shattered. In its place is the frenetic possibility of all. All sounds, colors, tastes, smells—sensations replete with the possibilities of all worlds, all time. Or no time at all. To find one's place in this rush of entropy, one must choose and act accordingly. That is the key to finding your way. Heed my instruction.

ChandraX

Once inside Cygnus X-1, Emoja feels as if she's swimming in a vast primordial sea. Thick and gooey with the infinite wash of colors flooding to black. Breaststroke, sidestroke, backstroke, freestyle stroke, all with, not against, the flow. Resistance appears futile. She wants to survive. Conserve her energy so that she may reach Oturi. She dare not taste, or she may drown. She denies her sense of smell. She touches only when she must; she swims on through. Sounds flood in—a cacophony of atonal registers threatening to lay waste to "**Song for the Journey.**" Swim, swim, stroke, stroke. Persevere. She pushes on through.

Then, she hears ChandraX's words of instruction, **"To find one's place in this rush of entropy, one must choose and act accordingly."**

"Who is speaking?"

"'Tis I, ChandraX."

"And just who might you be?"

"It is enough that you should know my name and heed my words."

Then silence. ChandraX speaks no more.

This cosmic presence, ChandraX, has said that I must choose. But who is she? Why should I heed her instruction? Should gender be assumed from a disembodied voice? What is the intentionality underlying her words? All these thoughts, Emoja has, as she swims, swims, swims.

She hasn't prepared for the movement, the force, the resistance within Cygnus X-1. Swimming, who would have thought that this, of all modes of traveling, would be her means of returning to Oturi.

Perceptions of journeys—bedazzled with new beginnings—leads Emoja down the Memory Well. Back to Vargus that blazing inferno. Back to when she was a child, one of the Strangelets. Back to memories of the sky afire, so blazingly hot. Memories of the tunnels where she fled for refuge until the cooling temperatures of night made it bearable to walk the streets. She and the other Strangelets were gathered deep within, each pursuing her own quest for survival.

Those tunnels were fraught with danger. Primordial ooze she called it then. Now, it held associations with Cygnus X-1. Back then, Emoja had to walk, wade, or swim through murky waters comprised of sewer runoff. "Don't drink!" Whatever she did, she never drank from those waters without decontaminating them first. "Don't look!" She never opened her eyes while immersed in those waters unless she applied protective eye-drops and wore googles. Whenever possibly she kept her head above water.

Those tunnels were no sanctuary. Crimes were committed by adults, primarily male Vargusians: murders, rapes, seemingly random attacks. To survive, she sought a domicile far from prying eyes. A private refuge, some dry place where bits of food and drink might be stowed along with the few possessions she called her own. Emoja quickly learned never to place even the smallest morsel near her bedding. For the stra, those diseased stra that bit and gnawed, presented one of the greatest perils of all. So many Stranglets succumbed to the disease carried by the stra, a disease that knew no name.

The Memory Well recedes. Emoja is, once again, conscious that she's swimming. Swimming through the primordial sea of Cygnus X-1. She must choose; she must choose; she must choose. But what does it mean to choose when the choices aren't even clear? "At least, my strokes are rhythmic, strong, and my breathing effortless," she tells herself. Yes, Emoja could swim, if need be, for a long time.

Swimming along, swimming, swimming, swimming, she imagines that this primordial sea is no longer black. Consciously, she begins parsing colors until the black fades away. Remove those browns; limit those greens; highlight those yellows. Don't omit those blues and reds, let them shine through. Emoja thinks about color, nothing but color. Eventually, she succeeds in restoring hue. At first, there's just cobalt blue, but later she identifies iridescent orange and dusty rose.

She's so grateful for the colors. It is easier to swim with this assortment of hues. With the proliferation of light, glowing ever more iridescent, she now understands why she initially favored breaststroke. Under the cloak of darkness, she preferred to look ahead in search for light. But now, with all these striations of hue, there is so much to see. Above, below, left, right. The more intent her gaze, the greater the variation.

She rolls over, backstroke, the better to look up. Up, up, up. Now, she understands. Each color above her is a demarcation—a choice, a path taken, or not. Other universes, perhaps. All coded numerically and by color. Why hadn't she noticed all this before? All these universes in space. If she has the inclination, she might visit them. Given the absence of time within black holes, she might journey through them all, accomplish her mission, and still return to the other Emojas circling the event horizon of

Cygnus X-1, having spent fractions of nanoqs away.

This realization should have brought relief. Instead, it heightens Emoja's anxiety. For the sheer thrill of it all, the opportunity to explore all universes of time and space, seemingly the greatest freedom of all, an experience akin to an immersion into the infinite—a prospect heretofore only theoretically imaginable—here represents a new kind of tyranny, a limbo of endless possibility.

What might she gain in traveling to other galaxies? How would that help her save Oturi? She has a mission to accomplish. She repeats ChandraX's admonition: "To find one's place in this rush of entropy, one must choose and act accordingly."

"I must choose. I must choose. I must choose," whispers Emoja.

And so our heroine adjusts her body, again, so that she might see other vistas. Instead of up, she rolls over and begins swimming freestyle while peering down. And what does she notice? Wormholes, lots of them, labeled numerically, keyed by color, as if for ease of use. Where do they lead? Surely there is one that would speed my way to Oturi? But the code is so difficult to decipher. All those possibilities, a swirling multitude of choices.

She thinks of GK onboard Nexus journeying toward Oturi. Their last kiss, the touch of his body against hers. The exhilarating contact of Kid and Borg. She will arrive at her destination much more quickly than he. He is traveling, after all, on a spaceship that can only surmount the speed of light by means of STL. She has calculated it will take two months, as measured in Oturi time, for GK to return, whereas she's traveling expeditiously through a black hole with the potential to arrive almost instantaneously. But now, as she labors as if suspended in Treacle Time, her voyage seems excruciatingly slow. Would she ever arrive?

Emoja rolls over to her left side, swimming sidestroke. She might travel forever this way. "Time and color," she whispers, "give me a window for Oturi." And then, she sees a wormhole flashing burnt orange with the notation **"Oturi, odd years only"** cascading back though time. Rolling over to her right side, still swimming sidestroke, she notices **"Oturi, even years only"** spiraling back through time. She enters this wormhole. Spinning, spinning, spinning—back, back, back. She sees an indicator designating **"the Institute"** aglow in purple. "It won't be long now, not long at all. I'll find the EXIT portal and proceed from there."

6

When historic circumstances take an unfortunate detour, one must intervene, if necessary, to set things right. Though it must be remembered that intervention, in and of itself, does not ensure the optimal outcome.
ChandraX

GK is headed in the spaceship Nexus back to Oturi, which orbits the star Kepler-186 in the constellation Cygnus. Assuming the spaceship Nexus will take two months to reach its destination, despite enhanced STL, he has a lengthy journey. Not that GK gives much thought about how he will utilize this lengthy time on board. In truth, he's a bit of a slacker.

As with most Oturians, his brain is comprised of six concentric rings of nested memory sites—Lianitper, Core, Freebasing, Subcam, Sequencing, and Cereumla—with the most primitive (Lianitper) at the creation nub and each subsequent evolutionary advancement layered on top of its processor. Thanks to the multiple cortical upgrades administered by Emoja before his departure, the Kid's ability to process Foundational and Functional Memories, located in the Core and Subcam, respectively, have vastly improved. More significantly, his capability for analytical, scientific, and mathematical reasoning in the Celeumla has risen by a factor of 10^{24}. Indeed, GK's computational skills have increased so markedly that the Qutoseq portion of his Celeumla is now capable of calculating the probabilistic trajectory of Nexus utilizing an automatic number sequence framework.

As for Freebasing, that domain known for its Associative Memories, has also been upgraded. It is in this region that GK's synaptic combustions trigger his desire for social and political revolt. Our hero has always prided himself on his capacity for creating mayhem. As he himself noted, "I'm the Butcher Lord Suzerain of Destruction." Yes, the Kid has been and intends to remain the "King of Carnage," exerting his powers above and beyond those exercised by the LCD and N/T in their respective dominions so that he might enter and triumph over the Enhanced in their realm, the demesne.

What of the other areas of GK's brain? Sequencing is focused primarily on integrating and arbitrating the decision making part of the brain associated with the senses—vision, speech, hearing, touch, as well as movement, and interpreting the response to pleasure and pain. The highest and most modern sector of the brain, the Celeumla, is the most analytic and rational, the area most likely to enable GK to understand and to relate to Emoja. Nevertheless, the Celeumla is potentially at odds with the Core, which houses those emotions that form the emotional basis for moral reasoning and, conversely, the visceral instinct to fight or flee.

GK has determined that, in order to enhance his prospects for survival when he returns to Oturi, he needs some contextual backboning in order to stay on top of his game. That refresher training, he estimates, will take seven days to complete.

And so it does. The Kid's proceeding on schedule. He's scanning every electronic file available, focusing, particularly, on infrastructure, leadership, and control implementation, as well as studying the social patterns of the Enhanced, the N/Ts, and the LCDs. Not that he spends a great deal of time focusing on the N/Ts since he was once one of them. But he examines carefully the behavioral patterns of the Enhanced and the LCDs since he doesn't intend to take another "bullet," his lingo for death through "banishment" in space by an Oturian rocket or spaceship.

Nevertheless, one week into the voyage, our GK is getting bored. "That's the problem with voyaging in a junkyard 'borg & bot' ship," he mutters. "No fun. No sex. No comics. No games. No junk food. Nothing to do. I'm sooooo booorrrreeeeedddddd. . . . There's only so many times the Butcher Lord Suzerain can jerk off. No pinups. No porn. F<>#!"

But GK's nothing, if not resourceful. He scrounges round, looking for bits of hardware and software. Here, there, everywhere. Builds himself a Virtual Babe (VB): stacked, sexy, wild, and deliciously naughty. Redheads are banished from the spectrum since, he growls, "even in the Virt they're treacherous!" GK gets laid a thousand times. He tinkers with the stimulus response to peak his arousal levels. Retooled that a dozen times. His VB is programed to initiate sexual seduction by means of strip tease—slowly, seductively, enticingly. GK creates thirty subroutines. Occasionally, he has her resist his advances, but later scraps that scenario since he "burns hot" when she refuses.

Eventually, GK succeeds in perfecting the optimal design criterion for VB—blue spun hair draped seductively around her dark-bronze limbs. VB is long and leggy with a body so trim and firm, a stomach so flat, hips so narrow, breasts so full that she embodies his ideal slut bitch. Yeah, the Kid likes his Babe. At first, he has her scantily clad. But after a while he prefers her nude, floating there, legs spread. He can't quite actuate VB in full 3-D, nor does he succeed in having himself fully materialized with her on the Vid screen. "Bummer that!" he cries. And GK tries never, ever, to think about Emoja, despite his nagging doubt that perhaps the VB has acquired some of her features and characteristics.

He builds games. Virt battleship sims that predict how Oturi self-destructs. He reconfigures the design and the cataclysmic outcome again and again. Sometimes, he has the Enhanced win, sometimes the LCDs, but he makes sure the N/Ts lose every time. Perhaps, because that's how it was for N/Ts in Oturi. No hope, no victory, no life. Just like the stra scurrying to and fro, frantically seeking that small morsel that staved off the inevitable.

Despite his best efforts, GK never succeeds in actualizing the Rajakians. They always appear as if they're automata, more silicon than carbon. Somehow, he hasn't captured their aura. GK acknowledges he can't begin to imagine their thoughts and actions. As for the scientists at the Institute, GK never creates scenarios involving them. Why bother? Let Emoja suss them out.

"I'm sooooo booorrrreeeeeddddddd!!!!!!!" He must have screamed that sentence 777 times. Is it any wonder? When the Kid rocketed into space previously, his preoccupation was staying alive. Now, given his improved capabilities and the lack of imminent danger, GK has the perception that time is infinite and interminably slow.

What to do; what to do; what to do? How can existence be so BORING? Who could possibly sleep another minute when, with just a little imagination, I could metamorphose into the Knight-Bong of Nexus, the squire dude who bounces off walls. Look at me! See, a single-finger handstand. Watch me roll from my feet to a handstand and back again. Now, I'm bouncing, bouncing, bouncing. Notice as I somersault into a one-and-a-half pike launched from the ceiling from which I land on the floor before performing a double twist off the starboard wall. Wall to floor. Wall to floor, then, up to ceiling and down again. Bouncing and bouncing and bouncing.

GK is bonkers. Like a veritable rouge pinball in an arcade game. There's the flipper bouncing between the tap pass, the flick pass, the alley pass, now nudging, and then watch as the pinball is caught and "saved" by a "bang back." GK is punch-drunk, drug crazed—crawling and flying and flipping around the cabin. So bored that he wishes he'd made a Vid of Emoja. Just so he might hear an Oturi voice, even that of a bitch cyborg. Now, finally, he comprehends the madness that threatens so many solitary space travelers. He marks the days, hours, and minutes preceding his arrival on Oturi by scrawling a graffiti calendar laced with obscenity on the walls of the ship. With six weeks remaining, GK is experiencing a systematic systems error, what is known as "a head crash." It's bringing him down, down, down.

"Reader, this is ChandraX speaking. Forgive me for intervening, but the Kid's losing it. His intellect is atrophying. A few more weeks of solitary space confinement and he'll barely be able to calculate the simplest of problem sets. The Nexus has become a cesspool. The Kid has ceased all analytic thought. In the Nexus, his tightly constrained universe, waste clumps litter the atmosphere like a cluster of death stars. Need I say more? The spaceship has become a crap hole since the Kid's addiction to porn.

"In its current state, Nexus is compromised. Its hull and navigational capabilities have been damaged from the stresses incurred in space-travel. The fuel is now spent, and liquid and granule consumables are nil. If our hero is to survive, I must intervene. No cause for worry, cosmic readers. My action will be but another swerve in the Kid's cosmic destiny. After all, it was I who propelled his rocket toward the outer perimeter of the event horizon of Cygnus X-1. Now, I must intercede again on his behalf.

"Notice as the Kid stares at the Vid monitor. He's so transfixed that he no longer checks the instrument panel or records the progress made in the ship's log. The moment is propitious for my intervention."

Sheit! *Something's wrong. F<>#! Look at the gauges. They're in the red zone. Plummeting. Now zero. Slipping into negativity. Who survives this? Feels like wind shear. Down, down, down, spinning like a top. Gotta access those celestial charts. Those external readings. Damn, nothing! F<>#! Switch to voice activation. There, I've flipped on the manual switch. Please, oh f<>#ing, please.*

"Location, please." *F<>#!*

GK's nauseated. He's never been ill in space before. But something has changed. The ship is not proceeding on course.

"Overriding autopilot," he commands. "Reverse operation." *Squat.*

"I command you. Reverse Operation." *Zip.*

GK tries to flip the kill switch. *Nada.* He tries to reboot the system. *Zilch.* He checks the auto-log. All the flight data has been deleted. Where once he was bored, bored, bored, now his nalineadre is stoked.

"Am I about to die? No way. I'm not flatlining. Not yet. Not if I can help it."

He glances out of a window. He sees nothing. Just the black swirl that reeks of nothingness. *The ship's rotating. F<>#, I'm rotating. Feels as if I'm being sucked into a maelstrom. Spinning down. But down into what? Can't read the instruments. Bloody hell. What a pathetic way to die.*

"GK, you're in a wormhole. Prepare for destination Oturi."

A *female voice. Authoritative. Matter of fact.* "Who are you?" he asks. Too *many f<>#ing broads telling me what to do.*

No answer. Lots of suction. Spinning on down. F<>#! Must be hallucinating. I'm about to die and yet another bitch yelping orders at me.

"In fifty-two q-units you will emerge from the wormhole. You will be ejected from your ship and parachute to Oturi. Put on your spacesuit. The Nexus ship will obliterate. Take what you need with you."

GK suits up in twenty-nine q-uints. He grabs his communication equipment, his digital recorder, his log. They fit into his slim hip pocket. Micrometically slim electronics.

"Who are you?" he hisses.

"I am ChandraX. On your last voyage, I diverted your rocket through a wormhole in order to ensure that you would arrive at the perimeter of Cygnus X-1 and coated your extremities for additional protection. Now, I'm intervening again."

"You're lying. If that happened, I would have remembered."

"It wasn't necessary for you to remember."

"But I don't understand. Who are you? Why . . ."

Nexus crashes through the stratosphere. The impact is intense. GK was seated at the console. Strapped in. Secure. But now he's ejected. Our hero is parachuting. He hears a tremendous explosion. Looking up, he sees Nexus reduced to shrapnel. Nothing to return to. No going back.

Meanwhile, the Kid's floating. Floating down to Oturi.

7

A civilization is either expanding or contracting. An expanding civilization has a burgeoning culture in which the arts intersect with innovations in the sciences and technologies. Failure to advance along the enlightenment continuum necessarily risks a regression toward superstition and alchemy, the harbingers of civilization's destruction.

ChandraX

Emoja spots EXIT portal 3466 A.O., destination Oturi: **"the Institute"**, though it feels as if the portal finds her. Emergence, a state of passing into and through the portal to her destination, resembles an antechamber, a rectangular vestibule with translucent walls and a radiant ceiling, all of which are encoded with numbers and letters and formulas. So many equations expanding and contracting throughout this rectangular space—burnishing neon, then, dimming to a soft luster before radiating again in neon highlights. Above, she notices the designated codes to return via this portal. Next to these codes are mathematical formulas that would strengthen GK's exoskeleton, permitting him to enter Cygnus X-1.

Emoja now realizes that GK is to return with her rather than by means of the starship. She mentally denotes "**Critical**" to this important information, consciously directing this information via a priority stream to her Foundational Memory moments before she dematerializes.

As Emoja dematerializes ChandraX temporarily overrides the laws of physics, thereby permitting our heroine to depart safely from Cygnus X-1 and arrive on the very steps of the Institute.

Emoja cries out in joy. She's returned to the place where she—as cyborg—was created. As such, it represents her intellectual foundations, a kind of homeland, although far, far removed from Vargus, her native birthplace. It's always assumed that cyborgs are more mechanical than biological. That their emotions are minimal. That silicon and mathematical equations define them, rather than carbon and metaphysics. But that's only a partial explanation and far from illuminating. For our heroine has never really anticipated returning to Oturi. She never imagined the swell of feelings she might experience at the prospect of meeting with Dr. Zavorsky again. So much to do with scarcely a moment to spare; yet, these emotions persist.

Emoja strides briskly up the stairs, into the atrium, passing by sensors that scan her retina, fingerprint, and voiceprint. She takes the transporter to the fifth floor. Emoja passes down a corridor, all so familiar and yet remarkably different. Aniha, Cyborg 37, passes by. She was one of the 99 considered and then rejected for space exploration. She and the others cyborgs remain engaged in research here at the Institute. Aniha nods her head in what passes for a perfunctory greeting.

"That's odd," Emoja says to herself in encrypted thought so as not to be overheard by Cyborg 37. "It's been years since I've seen Aniha. No surprise, no astonishment, nothing! Then again, she's never paid much attention to events that pertain beyond her prevue, and I believe she's now assigned to general research. Her response, I suppose, is one reason she was never selected for space colonization."

Emoja then approaches Dr. Zavorsky's office. Someone's inside. She waits until the scientist leaves. Knocking briefly on the open door frame, she hears, "Enter."

Leon's at his desk. Intently gazing at the Sim monitor.

"Dr. Zavorsky . . .," she hesitates.

"Emoja, you know the drill. Call me Leon. We're strictly first names here. No titles, except when in the presence of visitors and dignitaries." He's fixated on the screen. Scarcely aware of her presence.

Slowly, her words penetrate. Leon turns away from the monitor and stares at Emoja in disbelief. Those eyes of his—thoughtful, compassionate, penetrating—a gateway into his consciousness. She watches as a rapid swell of emotions alters the muscular dimensions of his face, modulating from distraction to warmth, followed by excitement that shifts to concern. It's the concern that prompts him to rise from his chair to greet her.

Not a hand shake. Oh no, not that. Theirs is a full embrace. His watery eyes. That quiver in his voice. "Emoja . . ."

The father she never knew. A friend, always, when needed. Her mentor, although they refused to be confined by the limits of professional boundaries.

"I promised I'd return." Emoja says these words lightly, with only an undercurrent of emotion.

"Emoja, I should have realized." Leon hands linger on her shoulders before he drops them to his side. His maintains his gaze, as if convinced she'll disappear. Emoja experiences his warmth, his touch, his concern. "How," she asks herself, "could I have suppressed all that?"

"Where are my manners? Have a seat."

Leon gestures toward a chair before moving his from around his desk. Then, he steps away to close his office door before sitting down next to Emoja. He reaches out, grasping both her hands with his fingers for a suspended moment or three. Reluctantly, he lets go. He still has trouble believing she's here.

"Emoja, we lost communication with Nexus three years ago—3:33.03 in the year 3463 to be precise. We have continued sending messages." His voice choked. "We thought you were dead."

"A star went supernova. The gamma rays damaged the ship and wiped out my memory, as well as the memories of the other Emojas. We had been circling Cygnus X-1 when it happened. In all likelihood, we would have remained circling forever had it not been for a renegade from Artun, the Galactic Kid, who penetrated our boundary. He helped restore our memories. However, despite his and our best efforts to recover our memory and all the necessary data linkages, there remain significant omissions that compromise my ability to carry out our mission. The situation is exacerbated because radiation has destroyed most of the ship's records, including the communication log. As best as I can determine, the Artun85s have left to explore the galaxy and have made no effort to contact us. Nor does it seem likely that they will in the future. Since the collaboration between cyborgs and robots is critical to the mission, I returned to restore my memory and to ensure I have the information necessary to resume communications with the Artun85s. The last entry in the ship's log appears to have been made at 2100 hours in the seventh month, third day of the year 3470. That's my summary status report."

Emoja doesn't tell Leon that the last message decoded on the ship's log indicated that before the end of 3470 global warfare will have ensured and that everyone on Oturi will have likely perished. How could she?

A momentary silence follows. Leon realizes Emoja has time traveled from the future back to 3466. No Oturian has ever before accomplished this feat. The Nexus wasn't designed for time travel. The existing technology couldn't support it. *How the hell did she get back?*

"I came through Cygnus X-1."

He's excited now, pressing for details. Unfortunately, there's so little scientifically that she can tell him. Except for the obvious: She's here.

"And I intend to return the same way I came."

There are tremendous risks, he can't help thinking. *Once—call it a miracle. A second time—impossible! After all, a complex life form has never successfully been documented emerging from a black hole. And to accomplish this twice? Inconceivable. Only the smallest particles have been retrieved. The science doesn't support . . .*

"So much for technological understanding," Emoja says softly. "I'm here. That's evidentiary fact. GK and I intend to return to the event horizon via Cygnus X-1. But there's so much to be done before then. In the meantime, he's piloting Nexus back to Oturi."

"The person who restored your memory and the other Emojas?"

"Yes, the Galactic Kid, known to the Emojas as GK. He was sentenced to space colonization via rocketship in 3467. The Nexus traveled to Cygnus X-1. His arrival at the Schwarzschild Radius suggests someone who might be characterized as a Cosmic Wonder."

"A criminal? You're having a renegade outlaw attempt to pilot a starship back in time? Impossible. The Nexus wasn't designed for time travel. The science isn't known; the ship can't possibly be equipped for such a journey . . . . Pure madness. He's certain to fail."

"GK saved my life and the lives of the other Emojas. He restored our memories: What could be restored at that time, anyway. I'm convinced he'll succeed. In any case, isn't this entire endeavor a gamble?" Emoja emphasizing her point with a wave of her left hand.

"In the meantime," she continues, "Leon, I need your help! I can't accomplish my mission without your assistance. I've got approximately six months to get everything done. That's such a narrow window. May I count on the support of you and your team here at the Institute?" Emoja flashes him a smile. Her warmth, her courage, her spirit melt his crusty demeanor and his reservations. He was never able to resist her entreaties. Indeed, why should he? Leon laughs. "A rogue cyborg that refuses to operate within parameters. How could my colleagues have ever questioned your abilities? They were convinced that you lacked initiative. 'Not a chance,' I said. 'She's tougher than plasidium chromate and smarter than all of us put together.' So yes, Emoja, how may I assist you?"

8

Destroy a culture and its historical antecedents. Substitute in its place a perversely decadent simulacrum of what was. Let everybody celebrate its virtues. This is the ghostly specter of the Desolation of the Real. In place of culture and wisdom is a grotesque parody of knowledge that dons the cloak of false virtue portending to be truth and beauty whilst all that was once cherished has long since been forgotten.

ChandraX

Four weeks ahead of schedule, GK returns to AL, the city of cities in Oturi, the perfect manifestation of the Desolation of the Real. The stress of reentry has been difficult for our hero. His landing suit is in tatters. His hardware—primarily communication equipment—all destroyed. And our hero's state of consciousness? Let him speak for himself.

"F<>#! All my communication devices—Useless! Nothing to be done."

GK studies his surroundings in the Now. AL is the same, only more so. That charcoal-gray rinsed sky shadowed with jet-black streaks. For the moment there's an absence of neon due to leakage. The air so hard to breathe due to the toxic ozone, the carcinogenic particulates, and all the rest. The landscape is gutted with desecrated buildings. Occasionally, an LCD appears. Bastard/bitch or some confab of the two—no matter. He/she/it comes as scavenger or beggar or thief or perpetrator. In AL one is either horrific victim or maniacal attacker. Then, there are the Waja, always cruising the skyways and city streets. Searching for their next target. The adrenaline rush associated with surviving in the Now returns to GK in one tsunamic rush.

But it all feels different somehow. His cosmic journey has altered his perspective. Perhaps, his outlook is influenced by the memory downloads Emoja administered. Or, maybe, all those electronic texts he scanned while journeying back to Oturi onboard Nexus. Perspectives change. For GK in the Now of the Desolation of the Real what was represents a lifetime ago.

Things aren't the same; he's not the same. The dimensionality of time keeps intruding. The perspective of what was or what might have been has begun to form a dialogic interface with the Now. Consequently, GK functions not just in the present, but bifurcated between then and now. What was. What is. A commingling presence propelled toward a future that proceeds along a linear continuum.

One of the challenges for GK is that his vocabulary isn't what it was. Ever since he was rocketed into space, new words with layered meanings keep surfacing within his consciousness. These developments—his burgeoning vocabulary, his broadening perspective, his desire to assess his life as progressing diachronically through time, these developments suggest consequences. He could no longer just exist in the Now.

Events—past, present, and future—are converging. The result, not surprisingly, is that GK is increasingly compelled to alter his actions in anticipation of what may come to pass. Is this how agency is born? If you have a past, a present, and an implied future are you then going to take actions that make you responsible for your actions? The word "culpable" ricochets through his Subcam. All these pulsing thoughts give him a massive headache. Would his head explode? Implode?

The Now intrudes. GK looks around. That garbage, that sewage, that stench in the air. GK watches as an N/T approaches. The Zbie is not really extant since he's Zoning in the Virt. Usually, N/Ts have enough sense to avoid the Real when they're fully connected. For their *virtualosity* places them at risk. They become the perfect target for the LCDs who will rob them, attack them, kill them as they ghost the boulevards, oblivious to their surroundings. GK watches the unfolding events as if he's gone spectral. As if he were seeing it all for the first time.

Look at that N/T nimrod! Slacker grunge is attired in synthetic, a silvery black polyvinyl coating that clings to his skin. The dude's HUGE, with tires of fat. His mohawk spike is a black echinated mass of fimbria pilus. Slacker Grunge continuously points at himself. As if he's hallucinating, but, actually, he's connected to the Virt. His universe, even as he ventures out into the Desolation of the Real. Slacker Grunge shouts while tapping his index finger against his chest, "F<>#, don F<>#, Se? Less U die. Me King. Me. Me. Me. I. I. I. I. I. Me. Me. Me. Me. Just Me & objects 4 me."

Idiot. Slacker Grunge is referring to his "objects of consumption," those material items that he regards as extensions of himself. Sub-par, grotty, worthless turd. So devoid of vocabulary that he's distilled language down to a senseless patter associated with some feeble gestures. This realization is disquieting to GK. Is there nothing left except Virt lingo? Are all N/Ts really that stupid? Can't believe I was once one of them. Why aren't I now?

Slacker Grunge won't shut up. He's gaming in the Virtworld of the Memory Palace. "Hear me? Don f<># Me! Don! Don f<># Me! F<># Me & I kill U! Dead. There, U dead. Ha Ha Ha Ha, U dead! C don f<># me!!!!!!"

GK listens in agony. That's it? That's the best Slacker Grunge can do? Don f<># Me! Don . . . f<># . . . Me . . . is . . . ALL . . . ALL . . . ALL???

Then, GK watches as an LCD approaches. The guy's clothes are tattered rags. His face is smudged black, furtive, almost invisible in the jet-streaked soot of day. GK watches as the LCD rolls Slacker Grunge. Takes his ID. WOW. Your ID is everything. GK reaches into his ziplock, checking. Good. Still there.

"Sheit," he mutters. "I'm still wearing my spacesuit. Ditch it." He does.

GK can't believe the LCD boosted Slacker Grunge's I.D. Your I.D. is all that you are—your assets, net worth, portfolio, the documentation to gain access to your cubicle—conveyed via the endless stream of data that represents the total sum of your identity, all encoded onto a nanochip. Nimrod is f<>#ed! Just wait until he tries to enter his building. He'll never return to his cubicle. He's TOAST.

GK laughs. He shouldn't since Slacker Grunge is now effectively liquefied. He might just as will have been vaporized by the Waja. What's his fate? The Dude will die of starvation or be dismembered in a street altercation or succumb to some contagion. If he's lucky, he'll become incensed and join the LCD resistance. GK puts the odds at 99 to 1 that Slacker Dude will expire curbside still connected to the Virt. Maybe the Kid should care. Perhaps he should feel something. That emotion called empathy? But he doesn't. Slacker Grunge deserves his fate. More power to the LCD. This realization surprises GK. He hasn't realized how far he has distanced himself from the other N/Ts. He mutters *sotto voce*, "I'm no longer one of them."

GK shrugs, as if to say, "No matter. What was, was. What is, is." Heads to his domicile. It's an older building, only twenty floors high. Built when they still had lobbies and Artunians thought it appropriate to congregate. GK arrives. IDs himself in. WOW. Still works. Why does he have it? Wasn't it confiscated before he was rocketed into outer space? Even if it had somehow slipped through security before he was banished to outer space, how did it survive the extreme gravity of the event horizon or planetary reentry?

"I thought you needed it."

That disembodied female voice again. F<>#. He had heard about this. It's what happens to you when your brain silts to sheit. A loss of consciousness—Mental Flatlining—they called it. You're so used to the visuals and the voices intruding that you no longer have the capacity for autonomous thought. Some message is always broadcasting in your head, and it's only a matter of time before you do exactly as instructed by the Voice. "Go to the X domain. Target"—another name for kill—"the Actuator"—the controller of that domain. And you do it, no questions asked, because the Voice ordered you to. "F<>#," says GK. "I've returned to Oturi to become a Zbie, one of the walking dead. Well, I'm not giving in that easily. I'll . . ."

"If I had wanted you dead, I would have let your ship remain on course. You never would have made it back. There wasn't enough fuel or food on board. Nor did you have the resources to survive time travel."

"Emoja and I did the calculations."

"Your calculations were wrong. The fuel gauge was false. It was damaged by the Artun85s. They took most of the propulsion fuel with them. The supplies of food and water remaining would have only sustained a cyborg. You required three times that level of nourishment. Then, there's the issue of Time Travel. That requires a special travel cloak far more enhanced than your spacesuit."

"Why should I believe you?"

"Because it's in your best interest to do so."

"I'm not in the business of following instructions. From anyone."

Silence. She was gone. She, it, the force, whatever.

GK tries to enter the transporter. It doesn't work. "Natch," he mutters, "why would it?" AL Power Consolidated is always guilty of leakage. Same old, same old. He climbs up and up the stairs. He had chosen the top floor in what seems as if a lifetime ago so that he might have access to the roof. Sheithead!! The Penseurs (🐾), those thought police, regard venturing into the Desolation of the Real as evidence that you're either so immersed in the Virt that you don't notice anything outside that domain or you're at risk of gaining consciousness. Either way you're likely to become one of those Transitionals (　) that eventually become the Disappeared (　).

Yeah, he forgot about the 　. One day a person, seemingly a regular N/T, furtively walks the streets of AL. Then, that individual is grabbed by the Waja and suddenly gone.

Who knows where. Maybe they're working the streets, reborn as a scrounging LCD. However, if that individual is genuinely subversive, the 　transport the person to Vargus where the odds of surviving are infinitesimal. That's the chatbuz. The most notorious cases—GK was one of those—well, the Tribunal convicts the person of "Crimes Against the State." In that instance, the person is either sentenced to death (and joins the 　) or, as with extreme politicos and dangerous social outlaws, are blasted into the cosmos. Colonization—that euphemism for death.

GK arrives at his floor. Walks down the dark hallway. Opens the door to his cube. Nothing's changed—bed, desk, Virt monitor, chair, and urinal—same 'ol, same 'ol. Stuff still here. Good. Everything jammed into seven cubic feet. GK gets comfy. Natch!

"How come the monitor's on? Dude," he mutters to himself, "it's always on." The N/T green light for entry beckons.

"Gotta upload," he says, as he materializes into the Virt.

9

As society modernizes, tools are introduced to assist in routine tasks. Mechanical and then electronic machines capable of solving increasingly complex equations are later developed. However, in order to be truly useful, they must have the ability to manipulate their environment—hence the creation of robots.

ChandraX

It's wonderful being back at the Institute. Emoja had forgotten how much she missed it, how exciting it had been collaborating with Leon.

"The Memory Spectrum Analyzer will access the extent of your cognition loss," Leon says, as he begins attaching the probes to her scalp in order to conduct a series of tests.

The analysis is fairly complicated given the dual processing capabilities of cyborgs that combine the nested brain structure of Oturians with the vertical integration of machine architecture characteristic of the Artun85s. Consequently, Emoja has the same Lianitper capabilities as GK when it comes to primitive emotions—fear, anger, surprise, delight, and the entire range of emotive responses—governing this primary pleasure/pain center, although she possesses far greater general functional capabilities than Oturians (10^{30}), as well as boosted speed (10^{50}) and versatility (10^{77}) in the five outer memory rings.

In Emoja's nested memory, Clustering, which is dominated by numerical reasoning, has replaced Freebasing. For not only does Clustering operate associative memory functions characteristic of Freebasing, it has a highly correlative interface between Oturian and machine cognitive processing that enables her to access her machine memory architecture that emulates the Artun85s hardware and software capabilities. It also has boosted accelerators for multitasking (10^{99}). Thus, Emoja's capabilities far exceed Oturians, even GK's recently enhanced capability.

Leon's battery of tests are far from conclusive. However, they indicate that the primary deficits are in the Core and Subcam sectors as they interface with the Register and Core sectors contained in the vertically integrated robotic column of her brain.

"If necessary," Leon says as he shakes his head, "we'll perform a complete system reboot, although I don't understand the cause of your system failure. The data suggests that all the information is intact. Apparently, what has been lost are some of the connective linkages that facilitate your dual processing capabilities. This interface should have been infallible. It was designed so that should a catastrophe occur, the backup memory modules onboard Nexus could easily have restored your functionality. Your memory should have been reactivated by the Artun85s as part of a restorative cortical download, that is, unless they also lost some of their cognitive functions and, therefore, were unaware of the resources available.

"Of course," Leon continues, "this raises a more troubling question. Why did they leave? Given that their mission was a collaborative one, why wouldn't they have remained at the event horizon until you were fully operational? Their response doesn't make sense.

"Obviously, our failsafe mechanisms were insufficient. We'll have to implement additional protocols to ensure that you automatically receive cortical reboots from within your cybersphere should you fail to respond to internalized signal-response queries. That should ensure that you'll never again have to rely on an external assist. The process should be self-restoring wherever you may be and, hopefully, whatever the circumstances. Naturally, I'll also make sure these upgrades are available to all the Emojas.

"Because, although it's wonderful to have you here, we can't be sure that we'll be able to collaborate next time," Leon adds with a smile.

They laugh, masking an implicit acknowledgment on both their parts that the likelihood of a future rendezvous is almost nil. Together, they walk down the hall to the Robotics and Cybernetics Restitution Lab where Dr. Kuang Hu, the Institute's top robotic and cybernetic expert, instructs Tsolisa, Cyborg 48, to perform the necessary tests on Emoja.

The diagnostics concur with Leon's preliminary findings, suggesting that only a modular restitution will be required to restore the connective linkages that will permit Emoja to resume fully her dual processing capabilities. The repairs are performed forthwith. Kuang begins to assemble a team of scientists and cyborgs who will collaborate with him to develop additional safeguards that will be patched in over the course of the next few weeks to ensure that Emoja will not experience this malfunction again and that reboot mechanisms will be embedded into her endoskeleton with duplication capabilities for distributing to all the other Emojas. Having completed the restorative process, our heroine has begun setting up her office with all the prerequisite data links, system hardware, and software interfaces. She places a sleeping cot in the room to allow for brief naps, thereby maximizing her work schedule.

Emoja is now able to begin a detailed review of her mission. She remembers all the data associated with the mission including the proposed flight plan of the Artun85s to explore the major constellations of the Milky Way, extending from Cygnus to Sagittarius with prospective visitations to Vulpecula, Sagitta, Aquila, and Scutum. While calculations based on estimated speed and elapsed time since the arrival at the event horizon might be made to ascertain the location of the Artun85s, there could be no guarantee they pursued this course. If they strayed, only statistical approximations of their possible trajectories might be derived. In summary, there could be no certainty of their whereabouts.

Emoja is sitting with Kuang and Leon discussing these details.

"If the gamma rays had done sufficient damage to your hardware," says Kuang, "and the Artun85s determined that the Emojas had critically malfunctioned, then, they must have opted to continue the mission on their own. This postulation assumes that the backup memory modules on-board were malfunctioning, that the communications system on Nexus was damaged, and that there was no means of either transmitting or receiving instructions from Oturi. Such a departure would have necessitated taking most of the ship's fuel reserve in order that the Artun85s might have enough energy to continue traveling to the nearest planet suitable for developing a geo-fuel generating station."

"But I checked," says Emoja. "The fuel gauge read more than half full."

"There are ways of depleting the reserve without affecting readout," replies Leon.

"Really? So in that case the Nexus wouldn't have the fuel necessary to return to Oturi?"

"Assuming, the Artun85s siphoned fuel in order to assist them in planetary exploration."

"And if they didn't?" asks Emoja.

"Then, in all probability, the robots were destroyed."

"You're suggesting that I should assume that either GK or the Artun85s are inoperative?"

"Either—or both—is possible," Leon says softly.

"Then, we must change the mission plan. The Emojas must now be responsible for fulfilling the prime directive."

"A useful assumption, although you would want to retrace the projected route of the Artun85s in hopes that they are, in fact, carrying out their mandate and that you might be able to resume working with them. I wouldn't write them off—not yet, anyway."

Emoja realizes that Leon is tactfully suggesting that GK is dead or likely to expire shortly. Perhaps even the physical act of pushing away from the extreme gravitational forces at the event horizon would have been enough to deplete the remaining fuel reserves. But Emoja can't think about that now. Her mission overrides all personal considerations. Even if she could locate the Kid, there would be no guarantee she would be able to rescue him. Nevertheless, the knowledge that she might have been responsible for the death of even one Oturian causes her great pain.

Leon must sense her distress since he says in thought, "You couldn't know, Emoja. Don't blame yourself. Your memory wasn't fully operational. In any case, you can't be sure exactly what has happened. You may never know."

His reasoning fails to reassure her. Culpability is a terrible thing. The onus of responsibility doesn't operate as binary code. The gray-scale tabulations of doubt always intrude on the memory circuits.

"There is another scenario," says Kuang. The Artun85s may have felt it optimal to proceed on their own. They're fully capable of operating independently. With the Emojas and the ship rendered useless, they may have entirely revised their mission and proceeded accordingly."

"Are you suggesting," asks Leon, "that they might no longer be amenable to a collaboration?"

"It's certainly possible," replies Kuang. "Their orientation is founded on mathematical probabilities, rather than sensorial qualia that influence Oturians."

"Well, let's hope you're mistaken," says Leon. "Your conjecture posits an entirely new area of investigation. Our operative strategy was founded on collaboration, not conflict. Indifference and possibly even hostility must be now factored into our model, which significantly alters the methods and means of optimizing the strategic framework."

With the intent of minimizing Kuang's troubling assertions, they begin discussing other issues.

10

Once machines are capable of judgment, it is only a matter of time before they become self-conscious. The question then arises: How will this evolutionary development shape civilization?
ChandraX

In her efforts to reexamine the nature and scope of her mission, as well as the best means of implementing its desired objectives, Emoja decides to begin by scanning the electronic archive for information relevant to the history of machine intelligence and the causal factors influencing this development. This research has the additional benefit of elucidating the social transformation of Oturi over the course of the last five hundred years. While Emoja is familiar with economic and societal developments throughout this time span, she is especially interested in examining the changes brought about by the innovations in machine intelligence and the social and economic consequences this had for Oturians.

A quick keyword search of "robotic history" yields the following summary.

> The present generation of robots, the Artun85s, are the eighth generation of fully functional automata on Oturi.

Between the years 3050-3134, the first three generations of intelligent machines were developed by Artunian scientists. They were utilized for the manufacturing or repair of equipment or machinery. These mundane or repetitive tasks had to be performed at high speeds with great accuracy or the jobs were dangerous, posing physical or health risks to workers. Automata were ideally suited for these applications.

In this first stage of robotic development, which occurred between 3050-3079, automata were responsible for maintaining the pipelines—fuel, water, waste—and keeping them free from obstructions. They performed these duties so successfully that their responsibilities expanded in the years 3080 to 3109 to include maintaining the highways and transportation hubs, operating and repairing heavy equipment, as well as overseeing and implementing mining excavations. As robotic versatility, dexterity, and cognitive capabilities expanded, so did their functional utility.

By 3110-3134 the third generation of robots were performing crucial functions in almost every area of the economy including not only manufacturing, distribution, and infrastructure but also security and military duties.

Despite the robotic advances made by the third generation, it was, nevertheless, the Old Regime, an era when physical labor was still regularly performed by the LCDs and clerical jobs routinely done by the N/Ts. That was back in the age of Overclockers, those individuals engaged in working long hours to support themselves, their coefficients, and their progeny in dwellings then referred to as habitations.

In those days earnings were typically spent on goods and services known as products. Profitability in the Old Regime was tied to endeavors generally associated with creating value, whether measured with respect to the manufacture of tangible objects available for consumption or the creation or value-added services. The four continents and Vargus competed with one another in an era when the indicators for success or failure were measured by "Gross Profit" margins and "Net Return," assessments made during a time when there was merchandise to sell or buy.

The 4th generation of intelligent machines (3135-3189) featured the TallaZS, an android created and manufactured in Catalla that competed worldwide in the automated goods and services sector. However, it wasn't until the 5th generation (3190-3279), which allowed for substantial improvements in design and implementation, that androids and robots displaced Oturians as the principal laborers in the global marketplace. Not surprisingly, both "Roids" and "Bots" were increasingly used to quell violent protests initiated by redundant workers who found themselves no longer economically viable.

With the innovations of the 5th generation of machines, robots were becoming the economic mainstay of Artun's labor force. Their assignments were dispensed by engineers, scientists, and entrepreneurs who lived within the realm of the Enhanced at those higher altitudes in the sky-heaven where the air was clean and life removed from the grotty terrestrial and sub-terrestrial domains inhabited, respectively, by the N/Ts and LCDs.

The directive for engineers, scientists, and the entrepreneurs was to ensure greater and greater innovation, profitability, and security that would ensure ever increasing wealth for a privileged few, the Enhanced, so that they might live an existence free from toil and replete with luxuries.

How would one characterize the Enhanced? Style, grace, and beauty defined them. They never appeared agitated.

They manifested a casual elegance as if to suggest that "life should be lived as an inconsequential sport."

Nevertheless, amid the glitter and elegance of the Enhanced, it was understood that the engineers, scientists, and the entrepreneurs were "The Undesirables" who existed at the margins of the upper stratum. Their vocations—note that dreaded word with its connotation of labor—were associated with building, thinking, and creating products. They were essential personnel who were responsible for maintaining and supporting the social order, thereby enabling the Enhanced to enjoy their splendiferous lifestyle.

These "system-builders," "analytic-thinkers," and "profiteers" were the implementers of all those seamless linkages that maintained the economy: the military, security, financial tools and resources, research & development, products, and the mindless entertainment employed as a means of social control to prevent N/Ts and LCDs from disrupting the social order.

The 6th generation of robotic technology (3280-3369) ushered in the Age of Automata Productivity. The leading innovators were represented in descending order by four of the five continents: Artun, Zhinboya, Catalla, and Sirus, although in the case of Sirus, the leadership came exclusively from the Illuminati who resided in the city of Malosh.

The employment of automata was so widespread in Artun by this time that there were continuous waves of layoffs impacting the "Deplorables" (N/Ts and LCDs). Among the Enhanced, only the most highly skilled individuals—those employed in the engineering, scientific, military, entrepreneurial, and entertainment sectors—were able to maintain their professional stature. For the rest of the Enhanced, there was leisure. As one descended down the social ladder to the

N/Ts and LCDs, apathy and boredom gave way to degradation and despair.

These reports were very disturbing to Emoja. Of course, she knew the history. But she had never personally considered the social consequences of automation. After having been taken to the Institute, she was removed from the daily hardships encountered by ordinary Artunians. She hadn't witnessed these massive social dislocations and found even this summary news digest excruciatingly painful. Still, she persisted in her quest to understand the ramifications of introducing intelligent machines into society. Perhaps, the biological future of Oturians could be salvaged by understanding these ramifications and making critical adjustments to the design and implementation of space colonies that facilitated Oturian-machine cooperation.

Emoja also was struck by the candor of the report. Could it be that she was reading some of the Rajakian Archives that had been surreptitiously placed within the official documents? Whatever the source, she was intrigued. She continued scanning through the summary.

> The exception to this trend were the Zhinboyans, who fared much better than inhabitants of the other four continents. Though they relied extensively on robots throughout this period (3280-3369)—principally in the areas of manufacturing, transportation, and aerospace—their population was, for the most part, still gainfully employed. However, work became increasingly stressful, so arduous that most who labored lived a wretched existence.
>
> As for the Illuminati residing in Malosh during this 6th generation of robotic innovation, they were now engaged in a perpetual state of war with their bitter rivals, the Umbrascenti. Consequently, their automata were utilized principally for military conflict and security. This included advanced weapon systems, hazardous remediation, in addition to maintaining secure communication networks and preventing physical breaches by enemy insurgents.

Catalla, although still producing androids and robots, was less successful than Artun and Zhinboya in the manufacture and utilization of intelligent machines because of their commitment to employing as many Catallans as possible, which delayed technological and social innovation. For that reason, their technological circumstances lagged behind the Illuminati, despite the fact that Catalla was nominally at peace and Sirus principally at war.

Assessments by contemporaries suggest that Catalla had grown complacent. Its citizenry were less concerned with production, profitability, and advancement than basking in the illusion of affluence without considerations of actual sustainability. Nevertheless, the underlying reality was far bleaker than appearances suggested. For as the chroniclers of history understand, civilizations rise and fall in large measure based on their scientific and technological innovations. Catalla no longer believed in the importance of its culture or in the importance of technological advancement as a means of ensuring its continued prominence. The illusion of wellbeing belied a society verging on catastrophe, no longer capable of sustaining its foundational values and its scientific infrastructure critical to its continued success.

With the introduction of the seventh and eighth generations of robots (3370-3470), Zhinboya and Artun were technologically dominant in virtually all areas of machine intelligence. Their triumph was achieved largely by default. For the Sirusians were engaged in an ongoing civil war between the Illuminati and the Umbrascenti that depleted all economic, cultural, and technological resources. This enmity between these tribes was rooted in animosities dating back to antiquity.

By 3450, the conflict had become so tumultuous that many of the Umbrascenti fled the region. Most settled in Catalla where animosities festered between the Catallans and the Umbrascenti, the latter of whom lived on the margins and never assimilated into the culture. As the situation worsened, the stream of refugees became a tidal wave.

Catalla never succeeded in absorbing these refugees into the mainstream culture. Gross inequities resulted, with affluence largely maintained for the Catallans while Umbrascenti were increasingly consigned to the squalor of refugee camps located on the margins of these communities. Even the most basic resources such as food, water, and fuel became scarce. Hoarding ensued, dramatically increasing prices that, in turn, fostered riots. The result was that the Umbrascenti lay waste to the camps and began pouring into the cities.

Catalla erupted in violence, particularly in the urban centers where riots, explosions, and acts of terror periodically erupted. Citizens were killed by the thousands as the enemy insurgents attacked the major metropoles. Some of the citizens protested. Some died resisting this forcible hijacking of a modern civilization back to the age of warring fiefdoms that had characterized the first millennium. But given the complacency of most Catallans, the Umbrascenti never felt compelled to destroy the outward vestiges of a once glorious culture. Instead, the buildings, the treasures, and the monuments atrophied while Catallans, ever desirous for peace, cloaked themselves in the sacred vestments of the Umbrascenti, chanting their homage to Allyusan, the Messiah.

In 3458, a nuclear holocaust, "the N-Deluge," engulfed Sirus. The extreme heat, caused by a rapid series of nuclear missiles fired by the Illuminati and the Umbrascenti, produced a chemical reaction so significant that it transformed a desert region from sand to silicon dioxide, rending most of the region a radioactive "glass parking lot." The Illuminati, who were more technically proficient and lived primarily in the ancient city of Malosh, however, preserved much of their civilization and many of their inhabitants within its domed structure.

The Umbrascenti were far less fortunate. They suffered devastating casualties. The few who survived inhabited fortified caverns underground from which they continued to launch nuclear missiles and suicide attacks on Malosh. The Illuminati returned each volley with a nuclear strike of their own, compounding the devastation.

The nuclear catastrophe in Sirus had relatively mild radioactive fallout for the rest of Oturi. Naturally, there were deaths. Globally, cancer rates spiked. But life throughout the remainder of the planet maintained an eerie semblance of normality. In the years after 3458, the notion of "survivability" took hold, particularly in the two most successful continents—Artun and Zhinboya. Politicians from both continents argued that the nuclear skirmishes in Sirus would not pose too great a threat to the global community nor extract too high a toll. After all, that region had been reduced to a glass parking lot, what menace could its inhabitants possibly pose? So it wasn't long before the rest of the planet ceased to give much thought to the nuclear wasteland of Sirus. Nor, for that matter, did they pay much heed to climate change caused by nuclear winter in that region, which resulted in increased temperatures, extreme weather, rising waters, and the associated environmental impact, particularly on coastal communities.

As for Vargus, it was a territory that remained beyond the pale—so desecrated that even the refugees from Sirus never sought entry there. Nor were Artun or Zhinboya viable havens for the displaced multitudes since these continents had armies that barred refugees from entry.

The Artun85s were conceived just prior to the N-Deluge, when fears for global survival became pronounced. This eighth generation of robots was unique in that this series was designed for interplanetary space travel with the goal of facilitating colonization. To that end they were designed to think conceptually and built as androgynous automata absent a sex drive typically associated with procreating and nurturing offspring.

Each robotic series was numerically designated—Artun85/1, Artun85/2, up to and including Artun85/85. Unlike the Emojas, in which Oturian emotions or what scientists generally refer to as qualia were retained, although in a diminished capacity, the Firmware of the Artun85s was designed to achieve consciousness absent qualia. Thus, this generation had the ability to interpret a vast array of data and act upon these findings, but the emotions associated with Oturian consciousness were notably absent.

The above summary comes as a revelation to Emoja. So the Artun85s, from their inception, were created to function and think independently. Their Firmware wasn't—and isn't—necessarily invested with advancing Oturian civilization. Their orientation, when coupled with the events that transpired in outer space, predisposes them to proceed with their mandate of facilitating colonization. Presumably, they would have seen no inherent benefit to depleting limited resources to try to assist the Emojas, nor would they be likely to do so in the future. Their course of action was dictated by their primary mandate—colonization—rather than sacrificing valuable resources to assist the cyborgs. Emoja realizes that this orientation must be assumed to be operative both now and in the future and factored into long-term projections associated with sustaining and facilitating the Emoja Project and its goals for planetary exploration. She scrolls down to the conclusion of the summary analysis.

The scientists involved in their creation of the robotic series Artun85s postulated that gender-free robots unhampered by procreation would be highly efficient and, therefore, optimal.

They felt that qualia serve no discernable purpose for intelligent machines. They simply need to receive the critical sensory information and to respond accordingly. The scientists conducted numerous tests that supported their conjecture and shaped how the 8th generation of robots would be designed.

Here we present one example pertaining to qualia that appeared to validate this scientific hypothesis. Scientists instructed Artun85/10 to move near a blazing furnace. When the robot came too close, a sensor set off a mathematical signal that instructed Artun85/10 to move away. Artun85/10 never registered pain. Or the pleasure felt in the absence of pain. Or any other emotion such as happiness or anxiety. It was deemed sufficient that the Artun85s have the capacity to interpret their sensory data in such a way as to react in a timely fashion.

Of course, some iconoclasts insisted that qualia were the single most consequential feature of consciousness and that in a crisis the multivariate stimuli would prove too overwhelming for the robots, preventing them from prioritizing and responding to an onslaught of data overloading their sensory inputs. Nevertheless, in test after test, the Artun85s functioned effectively without need of the emotive indicators. Their signal processing proved extremely effective in responding and acting accordingly.

Indeed, a series of interactive experiments performed by the Artun85s and the Emojas suggested that when the two worked together, the Emojas were more apt to utilize their higher cognitive functions with the Artun85s than when among themselves or, worse still, collaborating with ordinary Oturians.

Neither the Emojas or the Artun85s showed any distress or diminished capacity when performing together. So it was concluded that qualia held no scientific advantage for the Artun85s and that its absence posed no impediment to robots and cyborgs working together.

The scientists never thought to query the Artun85s to determine whether the robots wanted or considered qualia desirable. More significantly, they never anticipated the possibility that the Artun85s might potentially exceed the capabilities not only of the Artunians but also the Emojas.

Thus, scientists never addressed whether the technological marvels of silicon would succeed in displacing the biological wonders of carbon. The leaders never directly evaluated the long-term consequences of creating robots potentially more productive than even the most gifted of Oturians or their cyborgian offspring—the Emojas.

Embedded in all these unstated assumptions is one of the most pressing questions of all: If the Artun85s were potentially the most advanced life form conceived on Oturi, how might their mission of cooperating with the cyborgs change if they were presented with an opportunity to pursue goals independently?

Could it be, Emoja wonders, that this issue had never been broached because of the troubling implications it posed for the future of the species? Ergo, the proposition that silicon trumped biological evolution? Although these questions were far from definitively answered, the ramifications, as they pertain to the Emoja Project, could scarcely be ignored.

11

You can never go back. Try if you must, but don't expect time and circumstance to remain in suspension.

ChandraX

The Virt hasn't changed much, GK notices. Once you're in, you've entered the ▦. A deadly game that's realer than real with no ultimate victor since the winner is he who survives the longest with the greatest number of Hits, those rewards designated in six iconic categories: money (**$**), sex (♂♀), habitation (🏛), food & libation (🍴), shopping (✂), and gambling (🎲).

When gaming in the ▦, GK assumes a persona. Typically, he selects Alpha Predator (🐺). Today, he chooses Data Rodent (🐭), just a hacker, hacking away. He picks his usual domicile—AL—one of a several domains in the ▦. AL seems more derelict in the Virt than in the Real, if that were possible. It's a rumble of ruin contained within a gray zone of toxicity. His foothold, for the moment, in this imaginary world.

🐭 in the Now of the Virt is tied to a desk. Code, Code, Code. Why the F<># did he elect to be a 🐭? Cyber-coolies, that's what they are. They never won. They toil endlessly until they commit some infraction that is flagged by the 🐸. Then, they're designated 🦅, slated to join the ranks of the ☣.

🧟 writes code. 01101011011001010010101011 . . . . a stream of zeros and ones that has the capability of propagating ad infinitum. Suddenly, an Avatar appears, The Engineer (👨‍🔬). Geeky. White shirt. Pocket protector. An image that harkens to Protozoan Times (ζκ).

"An Enemy Belligerent (👺) will corrupt your input. Don't let him in."

"How the F<ˍ># do I do that?"

"Consult the Code Index (🔢). Devise a machine cypher that is impenetrable."

"There's a thought." *F<ˍ>#ing idiot. If he's so smart, why doesn't he do it?*

🧟 heeds the prompt. He consults the 🔢. Thanks to Emoja's downloads, he's now cryptographically expert. If the cypher isn't impenetrable, it's freaky (💀) close. Back to his task at hand. It isn't long before he's able to construct a program that automatically generates the desired code. Good enough, fast enough, to entitle him to rewards, hits that can be redeemed, allowing him to depart his cyber-coolie station. So he does. He surfs. What's on his mind? ♂♀. Been randy quite a while. Emoja wouldn't—couldn't—put out. Here, in the Reward Zone of the Virt (🏆), bitches always do.

🧟 zones to the Runway (👠). He sits along the sidelines with all the others: Quantoid Numerator (🔣), Alpha Predator 🐺, Cogitator (💡),

Kid Death (💀), Radiant Cool (🕶), and Continuity Girl (✂). So many Virt identities here with awards to burn.

He watches as the first batch of runway bitches traipse on down. All draped in designer wear. He pulses the frequency to peer right through. In the Now, they're naked before him in vibrant holographic imagery. If that's not enough, another frequency will highlight their dimensions. No need though. They're standard issue: tall, leggy, slim. Long hair. Fling that hair. Wet those lips. Bitch gone bad. Compliant, though coy enough to generate heat.

Here come the second batch of bitches strutting their stuff, babes cloaked in translucent sheen that leaves little to the imagination. 🐭 calculates them as low vectors on the resistance scale.

The bitches in the third heat are naked. Accessorized in spiked heels with dabs of makeup, thick mascara, and dipped up tresses. Swivel and pivot, gyrate and moan. Toss those locks. Lick those lips. Swing those hips. Visleps undulating as they stride the runway. Resistance?

Nil. See those doleful eyes? They do as instructed. Docility—a supreme virtue. Natch, the spectators poing group three. Even 🜚. Is she les or trans? Can't penetrate her identity persona.

The bitch 🐭 selects stands nearly six-foot tall. Bright red hair, the darkest of skin, a female with a resemblance to Emoja that he Denies, Denies, Denies. "Give me a blow," he says. She moves closer, a seductress in liquid heat. He touches her mammaries, her nasty-nasty while imbibing her full-body lure. And then, fixates on her vislep. Watching those slow gyrating motions. Until he's hard, ever so hard. She's on her knees, his member in mouth. Moments is all it takes. He lets her suck a second time and, then, a third. He comes again. And again. Because there's no ramp time in the Virt. Just desire and release, release, release.... Then he sleeps, the best rest he's had in what seems an eternity.

Awake at last. His rewards have clocked out. Back to coding. Check out those programs. Defend against the 🜚. 🐭 is now tasking in hyper speed. Get it done, done, done.

Tough job, this latest batch. What if he's writing compliance code for the Enhanced? What if they actually use it for surveillance? What if he's just a squeaky toiler in their Intelligencer Hive (🐝)?

No matter, 🐭 is back on top. Mega rewards start flashing before him, so he opts for travel. Fly, fly, fly. High above the 🏙, peering down at the Virt game. Wishes life could be more like this. His perspective so vast. The grind of daily toil so removed. Soaring. Catalla, westward. Zhinboya, easterly. Sirus, southerly. Vargus deep within.

This time, he decides not to play it safe, opting for something new—some wham-wham. The prospect of danger prompts him to head east to Zhinboya. There he encounters the sacred manuscript, the Mandate of Zhinboya (▮), which instructs believers on how to navigate their path to enlightenment, a state of being and knowing that has two distinct modes, circular and linear.

The circular is represented by the Chronicle of Song (▮), whereas the linear is manifest in the Chronicle of Tears (▮). Both new to ▮. Never had he been transported into these interior states of consciousness. Never had he had the time or rewards, let alone the burning inclination to achieve Divine Mem (▮), which represents supreme fluency of the Chronicle of Song and with that achievement complete mastery of the ▮. Instead, ▮ typically selected a virtual reincarnation of AL as his Virt destination.

Now, he's enmeshed within the ▮. No beginning, no end, seemingly outside the corridors of time. A vast trove of tonal narratives. So different from the experience of AL. There, one masters the art of survival. Here, in the ▮, one aspires to obtain an audience with the Worthies (▮), those sages, who through learning and good works, have acquired infinite grace and immortality.

How to describe the experience.... In the ▮, the Di is diminished, the self Subsumed into the whole. Here, everyone strives for perfection with the dream of mastering some measure of the song. Here, learning is venerated. Here, everyone seeks wisdom and all must toil. For decadence is a bestial refrain banished from the ▮.

▮ finds himself immersed in a whole new code, the lexicon of the ▮ with its four refrains: Creative Zen, Self into Community, Harmony with the Cosmos, and the duality of Mind and Body. Around and around and around he spins attempting to master the code in the ▮ so that he, too, might have an audience with the ▮, those masters who know the heavens, the sweep of stars and planets. They, who have glided through the dimensions of spacetime. They, with access to all that is knowable.

▮ works hard to master this complex code. For he longs to sing that song of songs (song) that comes with mastery of the ▮.

12

Memory is malleable. With each attempt to access an idea, new memories become embedded with the old, reshaping our perceptions of what was and how this connects with what is. The result is a memory storehouse of continually altering perceptions in which each refreshed recollection, although seemingly drawn from that original experience, is, in actuality, ever more transmuted.
ChandraX

Having studied the historic development of robotic consciousness, Emoja is now scanning through the electronic archives to learn more about the machine memory of the Artun85s. At the moment, she's focusing on the schematics to determine if a system's failure might possibly have caused the robots to modify their mission. Despite the advances made in cybernetics in recent years, the Artun85 design isn't dramatically different from the existing architecture for computers.

At the most fundamental level there is the Hardware, which is not subject to modification, except by its designers, Leon and Kuang. The next level up, Firmware, is rarely subjected to alteration.

However, it was at the level of the Registers, typically, that software changes began to proliferate. Because of their relatively few numbers—a scant 151 Registers in the existing Artun85 configuration—their functions are executed quickly. Consequently, any delays or slowdowns are easily identifiable and subject to programming modification. Of course, in the early days of computing, Registers operated as separate magisterium, distinguishing between input/output (I/O) functions, IP interrupt signals, Decoders, and Sequencing, which determined the routing path for processing those signals. These days, the Registers execute these functions seamlessly.

Emoja is also examining the Core Memory because of its sizable content-addressable memory slots that are often subject to modifications and patches. Because most tasking consists of taking portions of the Core Memory down to the Register level and executing the instruction set before returning to the Core—what is known as the Fetch Execute Cycle (fetch/decode/execute/store)—most system changes occur at the Register and Core levels.

Typically, the next level, Virtual Memory, is less dynamic since the information is contained on external micro discs. Here, processing is relatively slow because of the cumbersome procedure for gaining access to Virtual Memory. Generally, there is little incentive at this level for software or system modifications. To access information requires "Paging," which locates source data in storage and temporarily removes and transfers it to the Core Memory for use before returning it to Virtual Memory.

At the top of memory hierarchy is the File Structure where External Archival Memory is maintained on diverse subject matter distinct from, although related to, standard operations. This material is maintained on R-Drives stored remotely for occasional use. Access is typically slow and cumbersome. Execution may range from fractions of seconds to hours.

However, substantial modifications have been made to both Virtual Memory and File Structure in the Artun85 model so that the robots might have ready access to compressed versions of these sources now embedded in their endoskeleton. Having this material encoded into the body frame of the Artun85, however, potentially makes the robots more vulnerable to system failures in Virtual Memory and File Structure as a result of physical trauma, radioactive exposure, and extreme gravity encountered at the perimeter of a black hole.

Emoja realizes that she will have to concentrate not only on software changes in the Registers and Core Memory but also carefully review the design features of Virtual Memory and the File Structure, modeling a range of scenarios, including the impact of gamma rays and gravitational influences on the Artun85s while orbiting the event horizon of Cygnus X-1. But thus far she has found no hard evidence for why, in the aftermath of the explosion, the Emojas suffered significant memory loss while orbiting Cygnus X-1 in marked contrast to the Artun85s who, apparently, incurred minimal damage. Nor has she uncovered why the Artun85s failed to restore the Emojas or, for that matter, failed to establish communication links with the scientists at the Institute before—presumably—departing to begin their space exploration.

Emoja is aware that even with this narrowing of the scope of her inquiry, troubleshooting will be time consuming and may ultimately prove less than conclusive. She is cognizant of the limitations of probabilistic modeling here at the Institute as compared with real-time measurements obtained at the perimeter of the event horizon. Certainly, she has reviewed the data automatically dispatched to the Institute from Nexus, but that failed to supply any answers. Consequently, she acknowledged that her investigations into the causal reasons underlying why the Artun85s left as they did would be approximate at best.

Naturally, Emoja's investigation of machine memory causes her to assess her own brain architecture. She has the capacity to operate in dual-mode with the latest advances in hyper-Oturi dimensionality combined with galactic supercomputing boosts that are comparable to those of the Artun85s. This bi-modal functionality, however, is not always seamless or optimally effective. How could it be given the inherent conflicts of emotion-laden qualia and dispassionate numerical analysis?

Not that the dual-mode is particularly stressful for Emoja. She had lived in a perpetual state of "Otherness" while struggling to survive as a Stranglet in Vargus. Later, she endured painful reconstruction as she was reborn as a cyborg at the Institute and had to adjust to dual-mode. These alterations forced her to acknowledge that she was not Artunian; nor would she ever again be fully Oturian. She accepts her operational duality and outsider status as an exceptional honor, rather than a cumbersome burden.

"After all," Emoja reasons, "I'm different. Why shouldn't I celebrate my Otherness and make it fully manifest?"

After the misery of Vargus, how marvelous to have the possibility of galactic exploration and the thrill of navigating the cosmos. Exciting and worth any inherent danger. Besides, why be concerned with probabilistic risk given the catastrophe that awaited Oturi? Was a predictable and finite existence lived in a diminished capacity on a doomed planet preferable to the thrill of exploring the universe? Not in her estimation, even if mortality lay in wait for her at every juncture. Far better to strive for the near-impossible dream and die trying than sit passively for the inevitable catastrophe that awaits Oturi. But she wouldn't fail, she tells herself. "I must succeed. I must."

"You're working too hard."

Leon, of course, who gently touches her shoulder. She smiles, replying, "Work is what I live for."

"Yes, good, terrific. Clearly all these years at the Institute have left their mark. But now that I have the unexpected pleasure of your presence, why not indulge this aging scientist?"

She glances up. Leon looks tired. He's older, despite the rejuvenation injections that are the entitlement of all the Enhanced, including the scientists. Worry creases his brow. His lips are tightly drawn, his shoulders slumped. So, naturally, she agrees. They head over to a seating area that overlooks the atrium. All glass and space-age metals. The perfect incubator for research. Or rather, was. Things have changed since her departure.

There's tension in the air. Everyone hurries about. There's a perpetual state of unease, as if the scientists' endeavors are no longer truly their own.

Leon and Emoja are seated in an alcove with comfortable chairs and a table. Off to one corner is a chaise lounge where one might take a quick nap. Then, she notices it. The Vid monitor positioned over the recliner. Broadcasting nonstop, a constant stream of advertising trailers and instant pop-up messages continuously embedded in entertainment and what is referred to as InfoNews, although she and nearly everyone at the Institute would characterize it as PropaNews. The dismal financial forecasts, the dreadful current events spun with banal chatter, the never ending cacophony of sound and image bombarding their alcove. Emoja feels as if a million circuits are exploding in her dual consciousness. Too much stimulus, too much noise, all counterproductive to sustained thought essential for pathbreaking research.

> Economic indicators remain flat, based on the indices set in 3462. Housing starts—null. Food Indices—down 5%. Employment statistics—N/A. Air quality—unacceptable.
>> The Perfect Energizer—TSALUEN? Relieve those aches and pains. Erase those years away.
>> Side Effects: Carcinogenic in .023 sample subjects out of 1,000 representative subjects. Possible swelling of abdominal area. If rise in blood pressure, discontinue immediately. Life-threatening allergic reaction in .093 subjects. Restricted blood flow heightens the potential risk of cardiac failure.

She looks around. The Vid monitors are everywhere, except for the few offices that have closed doors, of which she has one. They're always broadcasting PropaNews. So hard to think. How can Leon bear to have this insidious torrent of lies?

> The DEF indicators slid 1.2% following disclosures of contaminants in the food supply at eight distribution centers.

Srom, winner of the Insta-Gamer Award will receive 2 weeks in all-expense paid luxury trip to the Tropical Gamer Center. Asked to comment Srom said, "Me! Me! Me! Me! Me! Win. Big Win!"

"Mind if I turn it off?" Emoja asks as she rises from her chair and heads to the screen.

"There's no . . . ."

She can't shut it down. The noise is perpetual. She looks over at Leon. Their eyes meet. Once she had developed her telepathic powers, she had tried not to intrude. It seemed inappropriate to penetrate Leon's consciousness. Although in those years after she had first mastered the technique, in those days of willful adolescence, she had invaded his thoughts. On those occasions, Leon was gracious. He acknowledged her presence. He permitted her access into the deepest recess of his consciousness. His openness, his trust, his permissiveness won her allegiance. What faith; what good will! To allow a Vargusian access to one's most private thoughts.

As she matured, however, Emoja became uncomfortable mindscanning even someone as enlightened as Leon. And the male/female divide further complicated things. Even if they respected boundaries, maintaining their respective roles, still, there always smoldered residual sexual tension. It just was. Is. Will be. On those few occasions years ago when she had transgressed, during her willful adolescence, penetrating the murky domain of Leon's Di, she had experienced his primal thoughts stored in his Core Memory—all that maleness, that aggression, that lustful desire for "the Other." But she also experienced Leon's efforts to hold these drives in check. If lustful thoughts of Emoja surfaced, he directed his thoughts and emotions back to the scientific projects at hand. He consistently resisted wading into the abyss.

Nevertheless, Emoja knew from those mindscans that Leon thought she was beautiful. She also knew that he had been attracted to several of his female colleagues, although never to the extent of his desire for her. But Leon was particularly restrained where Emoja was concerned, making sure that his feelings for her never consciously descended into the realm of rank.

For Leon was an Artunian who lived his life in the pursuit of rational scientific inquiry. While he might ultimately prove less than fully enlightened, nevertheless, he deliberately chose to suppress his atavistic urges. His nobility of intent and his constant striving toward lofty scientific goals won Emoja over to his causes. He was the father she never knew, the mentor who believed she was capable of achieving what no other Oturian would ever be likely to accomplish—the successful colonization of space.

Leon's unstinting support for Emoja bolstered her unshakable confidence in her endeavors —for herself, certainly, but also for Leon. She knew from his thoughts that if he could live his life over again he would have volunteered to become a cyborg, despite the hardship, pain, and risk. Leon would have risked everything to have the possibility of exploring the cosmos. But age, even among the Enhanced, has its limits. He was too old. The advances came too late. All he could do is assist Emoja and hope that his expertise and knowledge would give her the skills and resources to accomplish her mission.

The PropaNews broadcast drones on and on. The financials, the environmental prognosis—all bad, despite the upbeat voices, the heightened spin. She knew that the Enhanced received a more sophisticated rendering of events than the N/Ts, who rarely hear any real content except, occasionally, for optimistic announcements regarding the War of Hegemony and the announcements of the various shortfalls—fuel, food, water, all the basic essentials. The LCDs, of course, have almost no access to news because they're off-the-grid.

"Why the need for PropaNews?" she asks by means of Mind Messaging, which she does by intently looking into his eyes.

"They want us to realize what's at stake," he replies silently, in response to her telepathy.

"As if you didn't know," her eyes said.

"The Consortium believes the news reports will spur innovation," he says, responding in thought.

The need to communicate is one of our deepest impulses. She knows Leon has his reasons not speaking aloud and for his restrained comments. Almost certainly, the monitors relay suspect information back to the Waja. But she must understand the situation more clearly and that means penetrating his innermost feelings.

"Innovation isn't conceived on a conveyor belt. It takes years of sustained research, xectaries even."

"We live in desperate times," is his thought reply.

She hadn't realized how quickly Artun would decline. Had he shielded her?

The rest of their meeting is all business. Emoja discusses machine memory with Leon at great length, particularly at the Hardware and Firmware levels since these are the areas with which she has least familiarity. Although, in all probability, the failure occurred higher up the memory hierarchy, she realizes that having a detailed knowledge of all aspects of machine memory in the Artun85s may prove critical to her mission.

Throughout their discussion, she surveys her surroundings. Life at the Institute has changed. The scientists look haggard. The pace of work is continually speeding up. She can't help noticing a few of the Enhanced escorting dignitaries around. The Institute seems increasingly politicized, subject to the dictates of the Consortium and, probably, under constant surveillance.

As they walk back to Leon's office, she asks to look at his data files. Once inside, away from the drone of PropaNews, she relaxes a bit, although she realizes that even here there may be miniscule microphones and cameras embedded into the walls, the ceiling, even—and especially—the computers and peripheral equipment. Every word, every gesture, every facial response could potentially be scrutinized. Still, she feels the need to ask. "How bad?"

"Terrible," he says in thought.

"Will I have the time needed to accomplish my objectives?"

"Of course," he replies. His thoughts are more revealing. "Whatever you need, tell me. I'll make the resources available. Understand that nothing is more important."

Things are urgent, dire. Leon knows it. She fears for him. "Have you ever given any thought to joining me on this mission?"

"My life is here," he says, smiling. It's a wan, crooked smile, revealing a lifetime of small regrets distilled down to an acceptance of the finite possibility of end limits.

Emoja refuses to accept Leon's resignation and defeat. Perhaps their differences reflect their respective ages—youth favoring optimism, age embracing skepticism. Even allowing for these biological distinctions, Emoja's outlook reflects her perception that opportunities are potentially infinite. What often appears to others as terminal endpoints seem to her as burgeoning possibilities that lead to an endless flow of new beginnings. For Emoja this is represented visually by wave after wave of multidimensional spacetime conveying boundless cycles of renewal. Certainly there are ends, but Emoja has her sights for now on beginnings. With these potentials in mind, she squeezes Leon's arm, a gesture he understands as "Later!" and steps lightly away.

13

The Chronicles of Song cannot be sung in a single key. It is all tones, all shapes, all images. It is the merging of the self into a greater whole. It is the song derived from the beads of the Cosmos
ChandraX

🐭 is back in the 🏠 after having briefly checked the status of cyber-coolie execute/command/orders accumulating on his desk. He wants to master the circular state of knowing obtained by striving toward the 🕯 and, ultimately, obtain the blessing of the ⛰. He begins, though in truth there is no beginning since existence in the 🏠 is both circular and, potentially, eternal, by entering Creative Zen (🧘). It is a state of being—a melody of acquired wisdom. 🧘 is but one phase on the continuum of enlightenment that is attained by mastering the five texts of the Trasu (✦).

In the first Book of Trasu, our 🐭 inhabits the sphere of the primitive: pre-thought, pre-language, a state of being that precedes consciousness. One is dominant or submissive here, alive or dead. Fear is the operative qualia as 🐭 navigates through a milieu that has no up or down, no left or right, no beginning, middle, and end. One is not master of this sphere, one is subject to its caprice. And so 🐭 does his best to surf this primordial soup. In earlier days, he might have enjoyed the chaos. Whereas now, he is forever trying to control his destiny by means of learned pathways—narrative arcs, plot, character, and dimensions of spacetime, all of little consequence here.

Though he knows not how or why, eventually, 🜚 tumbles into the second Book of ✤. Here one STRUGGLES to wrest an emergent consciousness from the fog of nothingness. 🜚 seeks his bearing, although that seems futile since phonemes, syllables, and parts of words pass through him, above him, all around him. Still, he attempts to parse text. He seeks comprehension, though the outcome may be only a ray of understanding gleamed through the dim of consciousness. Nevertheless, along the way information is acquired , and he has the satisfaction of knowing more than less, the sum of which is greater than zero. Such is the meager magnitude of his achievement.

By the third volume, 🜚 has the perception that he is gaining ground: He is STRIVING. It feels as if he has sipped a powerful elixir and is now empowered to understand Oturian destiny and how to navigate consequential pathways, thereby minimizing planetary catastrophe. Success breeds success, enabling him to imbibe the intoxicating nectar of ideas.

As 🜚 masters his fourth Book of ✤, the objective is planetary wisdom gleamed from on high, a lofty perspective upon which to assess the comings and goings of Oturian inhabitants. He tries to master all that needs to be learned. So small and so seemingly insignificant those creatures far, far below. How tragically ill-conceived they are, each insisting on his or her agenda when an impartial observer from the heavens implicitly understands how interconnected and integrated Oturians are and the need for all to come together as one. How piteously pathetic those mortal misconceptions are. We witness as 🜚 acquires the sagacity obtained through supreme majesty and accumulated wisdom, thereby enabling him to advance to the final Book of ✤.

The Cosmos, from the vantage point of the 🜚, is represented in this fifth Book of Books. It is the view of the Long Now, where Kairos and

Chronos intersect, the conjuncture of propitious moment and perpetual time. From there, ※ witnesses the beginnings—the enormous bursts of energy into matter and subsequent transformation of the simplest atoms over billions of years into planets and starts, so sparkling and effervescent before they dim and collapse, some disappearing into black holes, others reborn anew.

Having experientially immersed himself in the Zastos NzE of the ※, ※ travels to another melody in the ※—Harmony. Here the microcosmic body unites with the macrocosmic universe. Life force joins with spiritual well-being to reverse the depletion of vital energies. Meditation, visualization, and breathing techniques are tools to the purification of body and soul, a spiritual alchemy that transforms bodily substance into ethereal majesty. This Harmony, when contemplated by means of Zastos NzE, fosters access to the ※, those immortals who are masters of spacetime, thereby privileged to walk among the stars and planets.

That said, there remain other songs to be sung. So ※ listens to a canto Sanctus lyrically espousing the virtues of subsuming the Self into the larger Community. Here, the Di, that justifier of all that is I, whose actions are so often selfish and wanton, is held in sway by the upsereog, a moral force that subdues narcissistic desires in favor of the greater good. Grace is achieved through the merging of the self into the whole, a process that ultimately allows those who achieve this sagacity to ascend the staircase to wisdom. Wisdom, of course, being that knowledge gleamed from the sages, those immortal ※ inhabiting the cosmos.

However, given that ※ has never been imbued with a profound nobility of purpose, nor has he been willing to subsume Self into Community, he quickly moves into yet another melody in the ※, the unification of Mind/Body. Here is an aria that appeals to his quest for Zastos NzE, a call to resist the narrow rigors of intellect in order to achieve an enlightened mélange of heart and mind.

Of course, ※ willfully misinterprets this duality to justify his pursuit of rewards, by his thinking a brainy endeavor equivalent to Mind, for the purchase of emotional satisfaction that will satiate his lustful desires.

"What," he reasons, could possibly result in a better union of Mind and Body?"

Perhaps, it is 🙂's misinterpretation of the Mind/Body duality that is responsible for his failure to gain access to 👑, the culmination of the 🌀. For 👑 is granted only to those who achieve a complete understanding of the 📖. Or perhaps the 👹 has created a virus that damages 🙂's code, the outcome of which throws him out of the 🌀 into the linearity known as the 😠. At one end of this continuum are posited the Agents of the Dispossessed, at the other, the Agents of Consumption. Few individuals will enjoy the privileges associated with living the life of consumption. Nearly everyone in the 😠 is "dispossessed," subject to ceaseless toil and constant deprivation. Rumor has it that once someone is ejected from the 🌀 that individual is never readmitted. Just as it has been whispered that no one completes the 🌀. If the latter be true, then, the fate of all is to be subject to the 😠 and its egregious sufferings.

🙂 is scampering along the linearity as fast as he can, nosing his way toward the Agents of Consumption. It is a wretched journey—the bodies everywhere, the stench, the suffocating odor of Death. The pillage, the ruin, the snipers, the air so heavy with pollutants. **Don't drink the water! Don't Eat the Food! Don't! Don't! Don't!** Scampering as fast as he can along the continuum. So tired, hungry, distressed. See the weights affixed to his scurrying limbs? The effort so heavy, so hard, so exhausting. This horizontal purgatory is no better than AL, the 📖, no mandate at all, just another abyss from which there is no reprieve.

🙂 reminds himself that he didn't return to Oturi to die. Nevertheless, his prognosis is not good. He's losing consciousness. Could it be that his Rewards have run dry and he's about to be flushed out of the 🎮? That is the hope, the hope, the hope . . . . Better to lose your game than join the ranks of the 👹.

14

A game is never just a game. There is more at stake there than meets the eye.
ChandraX.

GK is back in the Desolation of the Real, in his cube, that boxed coffin that others might refer to as home. He looks at his bed and notices some clothes lying on it. Not the spacesuit that he had previously worn. Still, they're clearly his. So he puts them on and goes out.

It is day, but the sky appears black as night. An outage has occurred yet again in AL. GK gasps. The air is so cloaked with toxic particulates he can barely breathe. All around him are derelicts—thieves and thugs—all with slippery fingers tugging to take, most with murderous inclinations. The LCDs prey on weakness; darkness for them is opportunity. Our hero stares them down; his demeanor is so menacing they slink off in other directions.

GK watches the LCDs. They hardly speak, content to communicate with gestures and grunts. Is it any wonder that the N/Ts prefer spending time in the Virt, that they have no appetite for the Desolation of the Real? Who could comfortably navigate this pillaged wasteland?

He heads downtown. The closer he gets to the inner city, the greater the wreckage, the pollution, the stench. He places a rag over his mouth. Experience suggests the advisability of donning an oxygen mask and hazmat clothing to mitigate the risk of pollution, infection, and disease. He steps over dead bodies before noticing some distance away someone remarkably like himself. Tall, slight, wearing clothes identical to those he keeps in his cube. He watches as an LCD pounces that GKo dude.

"F<>#ing sheit!" roars GKo, who punches and kicks the LCD until he's unconscious. Takes his ID, his credits, and moves on. Just as GK would have done back when he was an N/T. Uncanny, to watch himself. Makes him acutely aware of the pathology of learned vice and the testosternet moxy that always threatened to devolve into violence. That was the primal bestiality that characterized his life. GK steps closer, the better to observe and, perhaps, talk to GKo. However, he has vanished down an ally. Our hero is so distracted by the spectacle of GKo that he nearly fails to hear the rumble of a tank operated by one of the Waja.

"Return to your domicile—NOW!" is the order blasted from the loudspeaker.

"LEAVE NOW!" shouts a robot as he jumps out of the vehicle and approaches GK. It's a generation Artun88, Series WJ, No. 1587, with its reinforced plasidium chromate construction that offers protection when patrolling the streets. GK notices with his scan-ray vision, an enhancement implemented by Emoja, that the robot has its firearm set to KILL. GK is traced for weapons. Thankfully, he has none. Otherwise, he would be vapor.

Artun88, No. 1587 is pressed against his face. He shouts, "Yes, YOU! Domicile—NOW!"

If he doesn't heed the order immediately, GK knows that he'll be killed or taken to lockup, a fate many fear worse than death. So many Artun88s patrolling the streets. Then, there's the constant roar of traffic above. Always a risk of bodies falling from the sky due to an air collision or confrontation.

GK thought he was prepared to resume this life so that he might comprehend the fateful trajectory of Oturi. But this outing has made him painfully aware that he's not ready yet to live among the Enhanced or the LCD. He must return to the Virt. So much of what he needs to know is encoded there. Besides, he hopes to master the language, the gestures, the means of navigating the cultural divide through his experiences in the Virt. For while it isn't Real, it's Real enough to acquire the behavioral skills necessary to interact effectively with the Enhanced and the LCD.

In his previous life, the Virt was just a game. Now, he understands it's much more. GK realizes that all the rules for operating in Oturi are embedded there. Master the gaming universe—the identities, the manners, what to heed, what to ignore, what to destroy, how to vanish without a trace—and he'll have the skills necessary to navigate the Desolation of the Real. With so much at stake, our hero returns immediately to his cubicle to again enter the Virt.

This time, GK assumes the persona of a 💡. These days, he's a pensive dude. He's going to have to deliberate how to proceed. What better role to assume?

As a 💡, his tungsten filament glows incandescently. Not exactly his style, to be so highly visible. And here he is in some NoZone, no protection, beaming at who knows what.

🔑 approaches. Was she the one sitting alongside him earlier at the Runway? Or has someone else assumed the persona? Anyway, 🔑 is chattering away. This and that, this and that. Useless chatter when they could be f<>#ing!

"I always wanted to commingle with a 💡," she says. Now she's humming.

"Humming her way to juice," he mutters. "Is that her best move? Projecting just a feeble noise frequency?" *Pathetic, her attempt to match my incandescent burn with her etiolated transmission.*

Nevertheless, they connect, head to head. It's all cognitive, no in and out. Not exactly what our hero yearned for. See his anger flame shooting up?

Intimacy has its perils. He's mentally penetrating inside her, her world, her Zastos NzE. All that weepy, mushy qualia. F<>#! His tears now washing down, the screech of her laughter now exiting out of his mouth. He is consumed with the desire to thrust his pulse deep within her. Gotta tap her wattage. F<>#! This emotional hunger uckss! It really does. Meanwhile she's drawing his current. All that electricity surging back and forth.

"I hate the aloneness of it all," she says. "Don't you?"

"Never thought much about it."

"But, like you're a 💡. You must contemplate the abyss of one?"

"I'm not your typical 💡 engaged in the standard incandescent burn."

"But you must have feelings inside. Some sense of loss, some pain, some remorse?"

"Pain, oh yes. And anger plenty." He lets her experience his burn. He's not sure why. In granting her access, he, necessarily, swaps currency. 💡 feels his depletion while experiencing her pain, her loss. 📡's appetite for charge is draining him. He's vulnerable. He's forced to shine upon her images, her emotional wasteland, her realm. So much emotional wattage leaking out and all for naught. He's fading. All the while her pulse shines brighter still. He'll never break free. Has got to try, and so he does. Emits sparks so large that fireworks ensue.

"Aughhhhhhhh." Her gasp of ecstasy. Meanwhile, he's nearly spent. He can't get out.

What to do; what to do; what to do.

An Avatar appears, once again, the 🧞. 💡 feels relief, then irritation. Just look at him with that geeky radar on top.

"She'll only let you go if you stop resisting. Be one with her."

"She's sucking my wattage dry!"

"Resistance may prove deadly."

The 🕯 is gone. 💡 is forced to wade through her chthonian murk. Her seepage flows through him. He's spilling into her. What a waste of wattage. Reluctantly, he permits her qualia to flame, despite his fears that she will deplete him. She wants; she wants; she wants. She has no interest in his technical proficiency, his cosmic whiz. She's forever in search of his incandescent heat. Probes everywhere until she flickers upon Emoja.

"You love someone." A declarative sentence.

"You don't know that. You can't know that."

"I'm in the eros zone you've classified as "Emoja." I feel you. I see her. WoW. She's partly Vargusian, partly robot. You've made it with some weird cyborg."

If it weren't for the 🕯 and his cautionary words, he'd zap her gone.

She rides his thoughts, his feeling, humming that becomes a screech. And he has to take it, be receptive and all that. He feels as if he's lost an eternity of moments shining bright.

"Never experienced anything like that. It's like the best almost sex I've ever had," she says as she pirouettes and twirls.

As for the 💡, his union with 🩰 was absent a solar flare. For our 💡, there was no throbbing sensation, just depletion. 🩰 leaps and performs an air split with her arms fully extended as she swirls her flowing ribbon. Now on point, she appears ten-feet tall. All legs and arms with minimal torso.

But her sleek dancer's profile isn't 💡's focus. He's looking down there, peering through her now transparent frock. Then he notices her bush lit by a silvery clit. Arousing, yes. Satiating, no, since that would necessitate penetrating down there in order to draw upon her chthonic filaments, which she resists, resists, resists. Instead, she has tasted him, sucked his wattage dry, and barely given him heat.

He has to leave this NoZone now or risk flaming out. Where to? Our 💡 chooses the first place that pans into view—Catalla. Would that our cosmic traveler had a clue.

To the casual observer with only the barest grasp of history, Catalla, as depicted in the Virt, is the place to be. It still has half a dozen cities where populations congregate. There are marketplaces where one might purchase real food. The whiff of culture still permeates. On a good day the air might be breathable.

But the continent that gave birth to Oturian thought, to philosophic inquiry founded on the unalienable rights of individuals and promulgated an almost unshakeable faith in progress shaped by rational, scientific inquiry has now achieved the unimaginable. It has reversed time's arrow and is moving resolutely backward. Not so long ago modernist principles were embraced by its citizenry and promulgated by its intelligentsia, the Illuminati, advocates of enlightenment precepts founded on beliefs of perfectibility coupled with a profound antagonism toward despotic rulers and clerical extremism.

But that was then. Throughout the 33rd xectary Catallans had engaged in bitter internecine wars between adherents of secular modernity and clerical zealots. These bitter clashes had decimated its population, wasted its territories, plundered its cities, and led to an onslaught of infectious diseases borne by air, water, and sewage. The societal devastation eroded the public's conviction for fighting to preserve the principles of Oturian enlightenment. So many lives were lost. So much hatred. So much devistation.

As a consequence, Catalla entered the 34th xectary resolutely determined never to wage war again. Its leaders maintained that resistance never justified the deadly outcome. In emphasizing this pervasive mind-think, Catallans stressed their civic virtues: They were law abiding; they were pacific; they had mastered the art of coexistence in a tumultuous world. Unfortunately, that stratagem destined their downfall.

In a global society peaceful co-existence appeared to confer well-being and prosperity. What Catallans failed to anticipate, however, were the events precipitating the N-Deluge of 3458 that occurred in Sirus. In the fifty years prior to that nuclear devastation, some four million refugees had fled from Sirus to Catalla because of its geographical proximity, its relatively open borders, and its willingness to accommodate populations whose cultural and spiritual values diverged from secular modernism. Indeed, Sirusians were initially welcomed because the population of Catalla was declining and many of the inhabitants there were reluctant to perform the most menial and degrading jobs.

An implicit policy of open borders and a willingness to accommodate migrating populations with substantially divergent worldviews proved devastating to Catalla. There was no way to assimilate the overwhelming influx of Sirusians. There weren't enough jobs, enough houses, enough schools. The refugees were relegated to the periphery. They were marginalized. They were ostracized. Economically they were underemployed or without jobs. The positions available to them were menial, dangerous, and transitory with little or no opportunity to advance. In short, their jobs were more suitable for primitive robots than for Oturians.

This escalating conflict between those with privilege and those without coincided with an erosion of the social order reflecting the widespread loss of opportunity. Jobs became increasingly scarce. Housing became exorbitantly expensive. Financial circumstances for the underclass became ever more precarious as global competition, particularly from Zhinboya, dramatically eroded Catallan's economic livelihood.

Matters worsened because those that governed did not dramatically restructure the social order in order to assimilate the Sirusians. Nor did they actively intervene to discourage the refugees from practicing and perpetuating their atavistic social customs in order to facilitate assimilation. Such actions would have been regarded as hegemonic and judgmental. But the results were catastrophic: The bombings began.

The first incendiary explosion took place in Dmarid in the year 3451. The attack occurred in the plaza north of town hall. Thirty-three dead and more than two hundred injured. Demands were made by the Sirusian religious clerics, the Umbrascenti, that key governmental posts be immediately established throughout the provinces and in the urban centers. These officials would be expected to implement a vast public-works project in order to ameliorate the economic and social conditions precipitating the rebellion. Instead, a Department of Refugee Assimilation was created and a paltry sum allocated for public housing and minimum-wage jobs.

Thousands upon thousands of refugees kept pouring in. The economic climate worsened. A series of bombs exploded in 3454, this time in a subway station in Erom and streets situated within a four-block radius. One train derailed and more than seventy-two individuals were pronounced dead at the scene and upwards of three hundred in the train, subway, and surrounding area rushed to hospitals.

The Umbrascenti, alarmed at the riots and attacks targeting Sirusians following the bomb attacks, demanded billions in public aid to improve conditions in their communities. The demand was summarily refused. Demonstrations ensued. The Umbrascenti frequently clashed with the Illuminati, the latter of whom called for officials to take swift retributive actions against these perpetrators of xterd. Instead, representatives of both groups were jailed for inciting riots.

Circumstances came to a head in the aftermath of the N-Deluge that destroyed most of Sirus in 3458. Enraged by the eradication of most of their continent, the Umbrascenti in Catalla announced that they were going to ignite five radioactive bombs in major metropolitan cities. A year later a nuclear explosion detonated in Linber. The blast was powerful enough that the body count exceeded three hundred thousand. The fallout was estimated to kill three times as many Catallans.

It was in the immediate aftermath of the nuclear devastation in Linber, the government acceded to the demands of the Umbrascenti. What else could they do? They had no military means of quelling xterd. Catallans were neither prepared nor willing to risk tens of thousands of lives to preserve their fair cities or their way of life. Capitulation seemed preferable to a military state and living under a state of siege that knew no end. Democracy, as a consequence, was terminated by fiat. The Umbra

Council issued zwrkars by its nine clerics that were implemented as law. Catalla was now governed by a theocracy.

The secular Age of the Illuminati was over. Most of the Illuminati were killed or jailed, except for a rump resistance that operated clandestinely. The zwrkars brought about wholesale changes. All citizenry were now required to dress in dark-gray, full-length, hooded tunics. Females were required to wear visors to cover their eyes, except those who were designated as prostitutes and consigned to the officially sanctioned Pleasure Domes. Monogamy and homosexuality were outlawed, the creation of large families a cause for celebration. Chanting homage to Allyusan was mandated throughout the day. Fiction was outlawed, replaced by chant and prayer books that celebrated the religious scripture of the Asnorom.

While nominally the cities and their respective institutions remained intact, the Umbra Counsel was the defacto government. Over the course of nine months, Catalla had regressed socially and culturally three thousand xectaries. It was now a tribal community with some superficial trappings of modern conveniences. Politically, Catalla had severed all ties with world leaders of the other continents, except for the Umbrascenti fighting in Sirus. All trade relations were renounced, precipitating a deep economic depression.

It is under these circumstances that our materializes in Ispar. And while he has examined infomercials about Catalla's history in the Vid Scan, that online informational source in the Virt, nothing prepares him for what he now sees.

The noise, the stench, the crowds. Beggars everywhere, mostly younglings. Everyone in gray. Females escorted by males. Eyes forever glancing downward or upward, never daring to connect with another soul. Then, the chimes sound. Everyone bows and supplicates themselves to the Holy One. Bodies prostrated everywhere along the street, a chorus of voices in prayer to the Divine Holiness, Allyusan Almighty.

"To Allyusan Almighty."

"The King of Kings."

"The Supreme Prophet."

"We give thanks."

The words, repetitive and soothing. The chants uttered so breathlessly that a stranger, 💡, struggles to understand. He watches the rhythmic motions of the bodies as they sway to and fro, inducing a hypnotic trance. 💡 realizes that the physical motions, the chanting, the scripted homage to Fatal that was repeated throughout the day has succeeded in erasing all individuality. Gone are personal narrative and agency. He has heard that Artun also has a creed propounded by the Believers, proponents of the Spiritual Awakening. Their creed is also doctrinaire, talisfundalist in outlook, although not as absolutist as the Umbrascenti. Nevertheless, both religions have as part of their beliefs a diminishment of self in favor of collective "One-Think" centered on doctrinaire scripture.

"Give thanks."

"To Allyusan, oh Holy One."

"For his blessed majesty."

Those cries are chanted by the Umbrascenti as they rise, their eyes looking upward to heaven. Then, they notice our 💡 suspended above them.

"Allyusan puts light in the sky."

"'Tis the devil."

"An apparition sent by the messengers of Allyusan."

"In the Asnorom it says, 'The propagators of luminosity shall bring shame and devastation to the Umbrascenti.'"

The crowd grows fearful. Several women faint. The rest drop down to their knees in prayer.

"Forgive us, Allyusan."

"We do your bidding."

The men sway and sway before rising to cluster in a hive-huddle. The lives of the Umbrascenti are bound by scripture. That which is expressly condemned in the scripture is blasphemous. Blasphemy must be irradiated. 💡 realizes that he needs an escape plan. NOW.

"Satan is amongst us."

"The devil's apparition."

"Sent by the Illuminati."

"Kill. Kill."

The cries swell. The mob, for that is what it is, picks up stones and rises as one to their feet. Rocks and cobblestones are tossed. The crowd shouts.

"Kill, Kill." The cries are deafening.

Must leave. Can't move. Been hit. "Aaagggggg!"

"The evil spirit cries out in pain."

🔮 drifts away, shaking feebly. His pain is so excruciating that he's convinced he will die. He descends to a nearby alleyway, floats down a stairwell, and passes through a door, into a building, and continues down, down, down, down. A basement, perhaps? Blackness everywhere.

Later, how much later, he knows not. He comes to. The dark room is lit by candles. Thirty souls crammed together. Whispering.

"We must overthrow them," says one.

"Impossible," says another.

"If we don't it's just a question of time until we're all dead," says the first.

"Or become one of them," replies the second.

"Death by other means is still death, " says the first.

"Resistance is futile," growls a third.

"The furtherance of reason is never futile," insists a fourth.

"Who will pursue the quest of scientific advancement should we die?" cries a fifth.

"And the knowledge that resides in our electronic books," says a sixth.

🔮 has never seen a book before. Not one. He has heard about them. The Rajakians were said to posses them, so it has been said. If, indeed, the

Rajakians actually exist.

Are the Illuminati descended from the Rajakians? 💡 inches closer. Mostly, he sees electronic pads with page prompts and search windows. He checks them out. The information contained within is not so different from what he has learned from Emoja's downloads and from studying while traveling on Nexus. These e-books have Math and lots of Code on how to create, detect, and dismantle Jantro viruses and Antigen Corrupts and Xdelite worms. He also discovers some detailed mathematical formulas for the creation of antiaircraft, missile launchers, and other military weapons and hardware. Warfare. Now there's something useful! 💡 scans the books, downloading critical information into his internal database.

However, it's hard to know precisely what will prove critical as opposed to merely elucidating. Consequently, he encodes anything that appears relevant. Because in the Virt, the circumstances of the NOW never exactly replicate. Events stream by, a whirligig of flashing images. It's useless to glance back, almost impossible to look ahead. A state of being, he suspects, that is similar to day-to-day existence among the Umbrascenti.

💡 realizes with astonishment that both the N/Ts that reside in the Desolation of the Real and the Umbrascenti he has witnessed here in the Virt believe in the phantasmagorical, whether it be the Virt Avatars or the deistic manifestations of the divine revered by the Umbrascenti. For both the N/Ts and the Umbrascenti, it seems that life is lived as if in a trance, a stimulus response, rather than an analytical thought process based on rational evaluation of the actions needed to be taken in preparation for probabilistic outcomes. Both the N/Ts and the Umbrascenti have replaced the narrative of diachronic time based on a linear continuum progressing from the primitive state to the increasingly advanced mode of existence with the static synchronic dimension of a life lived forever in the NOW. Forever in the moment without the ability to construct a personal narrative that is predicated on agency and the ability of an individual to choose his or her own future. Life in Catalla has reverted to the preconscious. Rationality and scientific awareness have dissolved and been replaced by demons and spirits who inform the behavior and actions of the citizenry.

Could it be, 💡 wonders, that this hypnotic mode of living, as decreed by the Umbrascenti, isn't terribly different from the existence of N/Ts plugged into the Virt? Both groups just there for the ride, unconscious and susceptible to whatever voices whisper in their ears? Under these circumstances does the mere intimation of an apparition forestall agency? Could the aural and visual hallucinations absent diachronic time and personal narrative succeed in eroding causation and reason and induce demonic possession?

These thoughts are troubling to 💡. "The Virt's just a game," he mutters. "A stupid game, nothing more." But what if the Virt is a distorted embodiment of the Desolation of the Real? What if it is every bit as mind numbing, as deadening to personal initiative as the spiritual life of the Umbrascenti as represented in the Virt-World of Catalla? What if life lived by the N/Ts in the Virt is just another totalizing method of control, no more freeing or individualizing than the catatonic trance of these Umbrascenti?

Certainly, the Umbrascenti's beliefs necessitate that every question be met with a preordained response. The religion requires that the self be totally subjugated to Allyusan. One must follow his dictates—surely a he given the paternalistic structure. In having to observe the myriad law of the Creator, one is freed from having the responsibility of determining one's future. The constant devotion to chant serves as a physical mechanism for releasing the mind from consciousness and all the pain and pathos associated with navigating one's way through a challenging and increasingly traumatic world.

And the Virt? Gaming, 💡 concludes, is not a frivolous pursuit. It fosters a totalizing existence, as mind deadening and totalitarian as any religious orthodoxy even if it seems to the player as if it is voluntary and pleasurable. Gaming is a form of mind control to prevent the N/Ts from realizing their potential and waging war with the Enhanced. 💡 has seen enough of Catalla and the struggles between the Illuminati and Umbrascenti. And so he vanishes down the Memory Hole back to the Desolation of the Real.

15

The loss of consciousness in advanced biological entities is the outcome of qualitative influences that can be modeled quantitatively. Imagine a fragmented state of the NOW devoid of intellectual and social foundations. Action is all. Multi-tasking predominates with a rush of synaptic neural frenzy, an impulse/response overload of circuitry that preempts rational contemplation.

ChandraX

It was one of those rare days in AL when sunlight streaks through, generating enough power to permit residents to ride the solar tram to the west edge of town. There we find GK walking down Vedasepul. As are many other N/Ts. So many eyes squinting in the bright reflective haze. So many nits connected and multitasking. Shouting into air. Just like that. Dude F<ttt ># to my left.

"Wait. Incoming. Hello? Yeah. No. F<># U! Wait. Incoming. F<>#. Hello? Yeah. No. Yeah. F<># UUUUU!"

Dude F<># is walking down the middle of Vedasepul. A Waja tank approaches. Morgue City for the F<># who is to be distilled down to 17.999 grams. M O M E N T A R I L Y. Except that our GK hurls himself at the F<># in an effort to circumvent splatterblood. Entangled they roll toward the curb, cloaked in fumes as the vehicle thunders by. Dude F<>k's been spared. As if it mattered. Duke F<># behaves as of GK had tried to kill him.

"U! F<>#ing sheit. What the f<>#!" he screams, his face explosive red. His arms a flailing pinwheel as he pummels GK.

Between the blows, GK shouts, "The Waja tank was going to kill you. U see?"

"Tank kill me? Here me. U f<>#ing liar!" Dude F<>#'s fists spin round and round.

GK's had enough. He kicks Dude F<># into a sprawling heap before heading down NiceeV. More talking heads. More connectivity. Oblivious to the Desolation of the Real. He watches as an LCD stiffs a guy to steal his ID before fleeing down Lyu. *Where's he going?* Curious, GK follows him and notices the LCD lift a manhole before dropping down into the septic filth. *That's it? That's where they hang?* GK's got to know. So he follows the LCD down.

The stench is overpowering.

Can't see a thing. Into the ooze. I'm blacking out.

GK awakens to finds himself seated on a hard, cold floor. His ankles and wrists are cuffed to a wall.

A prison cell? F<>#! Who's the bitch sitting opposite me with her knees pressed to her chest brandishing an SMK27?

With its capacity to stun, maim, kill, it's standard issue for the Resistance.

Bitch has shortish hair. Slim. Boyish frame. Dressed in Waja fatigues. What a f<>#! Buzzed just looking at her.

"Your name?" she asks.

The wrong reply, GK realizes, and he's splatterblood.

"Galactic Kid, GK to you. Used to be an N/T."

"Is that your Virt name?"

"It's the only name I've ever had."

"Why should I believe you?" GK realizes that her speech is Old Speak. Not so different from his these days. So much more than "Me" and "I" and "U" and "F<>#"! Old speak is the language of insurrectionists. Full sentences correlate with sustained thought. Sustained thought leads to discontentment, which aids the Resistance. Zbies are inert. They aren't instigators. No one commits revolution without possessing critical neural pathways. Maybe that's why he was 🝢 and rocketed into outer space.

She slaps him, shouting, "Answer me."

"I'm in the system. Check me out." She points the gun at his face, indifferent to his fate. "I'm a transitional, slated to be one of the 🝢," he adds.

"Yeah?" She pulls out a S&RD analyzer that verifies his background. "Why are you here?"

"I'm here to join the Resistance. Death to the Enhanced!"

"Vouch for your loyalty."

"My records tell my story. What they don't indicate is that I'm targeted for colonization." In the Now, GK realizes, he hasn't been sent into space yet, so he hastens to add, "I'm as good as dead. Check out my branded insignia."

She unbuttons his shirt. Sees the numbers. "But you're still listed as 'Virt saturated'", she replies.

F<>#! I'm now living on Oturi before my planetary exile. He realizes that the system doesn't register the future when he will be branded with the insignia and exiled to space. *F<>#! Gotta explain the insignia or I'm splatterblood.*

"Yeah, I'm coded as Virt saturated. But I've been incarcerated, and I'll prove it." Tells her about his cell in Cortoba Prison. The torture practices, the layout, the names of some of the 🝢.

Details he swore he'd never recall. Those memories the authorities promised to erase, but never did since he was slated for oblivion. He tells it dry. No tears.

She sets down her gun. Orders him to stand. Drops his pants and unzips hers. He's hard. She's wet. F<>#s him there and then against the wall. Afterward, she's pushes him back down to the floor. His pants still loose, there on the floor. Hers already zipped. She's out of reach, sitting against the wall, knees pressed to her chest, gun by her side. Asleep while our hero remains in chains, colder than cold, damp and wet. Hungrier than sheit.

GK must have slept. He awakens with the realization that he's standing. They're f<>#ing again. Moments later, she's done and zips up, and motions him to sit back on the ground. His pants still gathered at his ankles. She, at a distance, on duty, pacing. Not a word spoken until there's a knock at the door. She rises. Someone from behind the door hands her a mug and leaves.

"Drink this," she says, as she angles it so that the cold liquid pours gently down his throat.

"What is it?" he asks between sips.

"Liquid nutrients."

It tastes great. So hungry, anything would do. He tells her everything, except what matters most—Cygnus X-1, Emoja, why he's really here.

Day four arrives. She tells him that she has contacted her supervisors. A thorough background check confirms his statement. Only there's still no documentation within GOSA that he's done time at Cortoba.

"Why should there be?" he responds. They want me 🝊. The Tribunal never leaves a data trace."

Apparently, she believes him enough to give him his first assignment: Commandeer one of the tanks from the Waja.

"Kind of risky, isn't it?"

"If you're to be of any use to the Resistance, you'll bring back that tank. We'll train you. You'll get the explosives and weapons necessary for your mission. The rest will be up to you."

In the weeks that follow, GK masters arm-to-arm combat. He's given standard issue LCD rags along with a decoder, communicator, and a new identity. He's told where to access weapons if he should need them while on assignment. He trains alongside two other operatives, rough and ragged LCD types, neither has ever even surfed the Virt. But the bitch is strictly no-show.

"What's her name?" he asks his trainer.

"Rainy-7 is her code name."

"I'd like to see Rainy-7 before I'm sent on assignment."

"That's not done."

"Please."

Apparently, they never had that request before. Hours before his release, when he's about to be blindfolded and taken to the streets, she appears. Matter of fact. No emotion. Eyes that reveal nothing.

"I'll bring back the tank for you."

"For the cause of the Resistance."

"That too."

She curtly nods and then disappears. Tough as nails, she is.

GK is escorted up. Back on the surface. Today AL is wrapped in a brackish fog that's greased noir. He mimics the LCD stride. Weaving. Eyes wary, shifty, flinty. He rolls two N/Ts. Takes their credits and their IDs. Makes some changes to the IDs, substituting the picture, the fingerprints, and the voice code so that he can pass as both of them. It's not so hard, just some Virt downloading, some cut & paste. So simple he could do it blind. The N/T credits will tide him over until he's greenlighted. Our GK's sleeping in empty buildings. He's wary, his blade and SMK27 oh, so close. One night another LCD brushes by and causes GK to inflict a surface wound. A cry and whimper as the LCD scampers off. Just as well. Mustn't let anyone close. The streets have ears.

Two days later, his orders are transmitted to him via RF transmission that is encoded directly into his skin: "Head to Amedala and Estabados.

There you'll find CommuneD with a locker under your name that includes combat fatigues, a new ID, weapons, and ammo." GK does as instructed. Once there, he locates the stash. Changes into standard issue Waja gear and takes a military issue duffel bag equipped with semi, scope, silencer, mini-rocket launcher, infrared night visor, grenades, and cluster bombs set for timed release.

GK returns to the streets of the Desolation of the Real where the remainder of his orders are dispatched: Waja Commando OS989i proceed 112.14 zins, ESE to Desert Palm located at the perimeter of the old airfield, operations center for Waja Division 48.L. Seize Tank Z-22 and deposit it at the RG depot in AL. SGP coordinates have been provided. Failure to accomplish your mission within 72 hours will jeopardize your participation in the Resistance.

No time to spare. Commando OS989i intercepts an idling space car at the intersection of Main and Dleytbrad. An unauthorized N/T had stolen the vehicle and considers it his.

"No f<>#ing way," he shouts.

"Waja OS989i exercises Domain Rights as per Edit 799933AW. Your driving privileges to vehicle SV892224 are invalid. Eject now!"

"No. Car mine! F<># U! Die!"

One powerful kick to his groin is all it takes.

"Auuuuuuuuuuuuuuuuuuuuuu."

Passenger N/T f<># U! Die! is ejected.

Waja Commando OS989i heads 112.14 zins, ESE to Desert Palm at the perimeter of the old airfield now home to Waja Division 48.L to seize Tank Z-22.

OS989i discards the space vehicle 1.3 zins from the compound. He then signals his arrival at the old airfield. It's the 19:00 hour after orders were issued. Camouflaged by the roadside, OS989i waits for the "GO" signal.

"Proceed."

He deactivates a twenty-foot section of an electrified razor barrier, permitting him to walk on through. Alarms go off. OS989i utilizes his SGP to highlight his route. He makes it past the hail of gunfire and circumvents the detonating charges set by the Waja.

The base has its own power source, which he deactivates. Thanks to Emoja's enhancements, he doesn't need night visors or audio boosts to identify a tank. OS989i's real-time SGP assists him (.4 Zin, quadrant-^{DP17}) in tracking, illuminating, and reaching the vehicle without being noticed. He deactivates the locking mechanism for Tank Z-22 and enters its secure chamber. Seated in the command chair, OS989i decodes the failsafe security codes before entering his own designated coordinates.

"Thank you, Emoja," he mutters. OS989i is ready to implement his exit strategy.

Getting through security is daunting. There's the enemy fire and the explosion of grenades. Alarms are sounded once again even though he took out the main power source. "Of course, they have an auxiliary," he mutters. More firepower. More detonations. His vehicle rumbles over Waja and auxiliary soldiers. He sees from the vid screen that some cry out in agony.

"So not everyone is automata. This is no Virt game," he acknowledges. Tank Z-22 mashes down another electrified razor wall. Fires upon the exterior sentry post until it collapses with bodies flying everywhere. He drives on through, shifting into high gear, back to town where he parks Tank Z-22 at the rendezvous site just before 24:00. Mission accomplished with two days to spare. Down a sewer manhole where he waits in an anteroom in expectation of speaking to Rainy-7.

She greets him with a nod. Her eyes, cast downward, suggests she wasn't expecting him to return. "Congratulations, Brother GK, your mission was successful! You are officially welcomed into the Resistance!"

"Now that I have formally joined your ranks, I have a request."

She eyes him cautiously.

"Rainy-7, escort me through the LCD sewer compounds. I want to see their community, how they live."

"That's not done," she says defensively.

"I'm not asking you to divulge secrets. I haven't earned that right. I simply want to see how the LCDs live."

"Why?"

"If I'm to risk my life for the cause, don't I deserve to observe my comrades?"

"Your request will be brought to the attention of the Committee. In the meantime, shower, feast, and sleep," she replies as she locks the door behind her.

Less than twelve hours later, Rainy-7 returns. "The Committee Leadership has granted your request. I shall be your guide." As they stepped outside the anteroom, he notices two PTVs. Rainy-7 explains, "The LCD domain comprises many passageways that form a labyrinth. Infiltrators have claimed that we have labyrinths within labyrinths within labyrinths. There is a great distance we shall travel. The vehicles are encoded to get through the maze of corridors and back again without incident."

Mastering the PTV is not as simple as he anticipated. The vehicle operates both horizontally and vertically. GK gets on and promptly tips over. He gets on again and makes it down the corridor before spinning out. And he hasn't even launched it airborne yet. Rainy-7 laughs with each spill he takes. "You intend to be a top Resistance Operative and you can't even drive a PTV? How did you ever retrieve Tank Z-22 from Division 48.L?"

By the fourth try, however, GK gains mastery. Together, they head out through thick, double-door barriers that separate the Resistance enclave from the rest of the LCD compound. GK mentally adjusts his SGP to track and to analyze the routes they travel. But it's nonfunctional below ground, so he scans and downloads the maze of byways they travel to his Subcam and Core. Although, as it turns out, he's less interested in the network of passageways than the social milieu around him.

It seems that there are no "normals" here. Every LCD he sees would be designated a freak or misfit by N/Ts. Perhaps that explains why there are so few N/Ts who transition here. Maybe some of the dopers, permafrieds, and waistoids when either in recovery or as they slide back down into the murk momentarily consider joining. But he doesn't see any here. Perhaps their failures up there on the streets meant they couldn't cut it down here. And those N/Ts that have some measure of success would never, ever, consider giving up the Gory-Gory Helishow known to the Enhanced as murder, torture, mayhem (MTM) that characterizes life on the streets of AL.

All around him in the maze of byways are insurgents with physical and mental defects—rad contam, mental handi, physi impair—the list is long. These days the ranks of the "damaged" might include most of the LCDs in Artun and potentially many of the N/Ts. But here, though the LCDs have obvious disabilities, they, nevertheless, are remarkably functional, working alongside the social outlaws: the hokoers, rgafters, hucskters, and all the rest. They communicate with one another as best they can. Language, of course, where possible, but also by means of grunts, gestures, nods, laughter, sneers, and pantomimes. Whatever it takes to convey the gist. GK finds himself remarkably at ease amid the social discards of Artun.

Then, there are the adherents of Old Speak. They comprise the Politicos, Artists, and Intellectuals. The Politicos represent a variety of lefties including activists, anarchists, and insurrectionists. The artists are dancers, singers, poets, and readers. All told, they are the transmitters of the remnants of the old culture. Apparently, there are no new cultural artifacts. Each and every one of the PA&Is are preservationists, a cultural purveyor of what was. They argue endlessly, although their beliefs are never subject to the ultimate test—transmitting and propagating these ideas in the Desolation of the Real.

This mélange of outcasts captivates GK. Not so different from me, he thinks. I like it here. Too bad I have business to attend to. If only . . . , but I can't. To Rainy-7 he asks, "Where are the Creators?"

"The Creators?"

"Those individuals who will invent a new idea, a new composition, a new way of navigating through our world."

"There are no Creators. Our culture is dead."

A painful silence ensues. GK looks into Rainy-7's eyes. Nada! No jokester, she.

"That can't be possible," he replies. "Without Creators we are finished. What about the Rajakians?"

"The Rajakians, if they exist, are the ultimate preservationists. They are said to have physical archives that contain extensive printed works. Some amongst us swear they've seen these manuscripts. Others, contend that these treasures are viewable, but not tactile. Many make the argument that the Rajakians and their precious archives are illusionary. Maybe our belief in these great sages who preserve precious historical and cultural treasures represents our desire to restore and to create great works."

"I believe the Rajakian Archives exist. In fact, they may be here."

"I know not."

"Well, if the Rajakians are just preservationists, surely there are other individuals inventing the 'Next New Thing.'"

"If by the 'Next New Thing' you mean the ideas developed by scientists at the Institute, these technologies represent implementations of the Enhanced. They are interested in developing an ever more sophisticated generations of robots. It is said that robots are the Next New Thing. That they possess great cognitive skills, immense creativity, the ability to integrate at far greater speeds than the rest of us. If that be true, perhaps we, as a species, are finished."

"I don't believe that."

"I certainly don't want to believe it."

"Rainy-7," GK says with a laugh, "here, at last, we have found common ground."

He leans over to kiss her. They and their PTVs tumble down in a heap. They embrace and kiss. For GK, desire flames to lust. He wonders how he can want this female while loving another. The other, a cyborg no less.

Rainy-7 response is far more measured and controlled than GK's. She says softly, "To be a member of the Resistance is to watch one's comrades die. Everyone that one cares about is lost to the cause. GK, you must extinguish these emotions. They will cause you terrible pain."

"Isn't passion worth it?"

"I wouldn't know passion or love or lust. For that you must mingle with our LCDs. They have emotion."

"And you?"

"I have dreams for a new-world order shaped not by privilege or greed but by justice and opportunity for all."

"And the scientists at the Institute?"

"They have been deceived. Brilliant thinkers whose dreams of the cosmos have made them slaves to the damned."

"And what if their pioneering research is the only chance we have for survival?"

"Then, we are doomed. For their collaboration with the Enhanced will ensure the corruption of their scientific ideals."

"Do you think our species has reached its terminus?"

"We are approaching cataclysmic failure."

"But what if we're evolving into something else? What if our future necessitates becoming something different—robots or cyborgs, more computational than biological? What if survival necessitates becoming both robotic and Oturian? What if this will prove to be our evolutionary salvation that forestalls our demise and initiates the Next New Thing? Aren't many of us already part machine? Those of us who have been connected to the Virt have plugs and external circuitry enabling connectivity directly into our brains. This source data is transmitted throughout our entire processing network via neural transmitters traveling synaptic information highways. And the question must arise, at what point do we move from electronically connected to electronically driven?"

"GK, these thoughts are blasphemous! They are the lies propagated by the Enhanced. Your views are shared by our enemies."

"Wouldn't you do anything to survive?"

"My future lies in this world with my fellow Artunians. My objective is to make this world habitable for all."

"What about out there, in space?"

"It is, as you say, out there. We are here. I embrace this world. And so should you. GK, it's late. We must go back."

"I'll gladly accept your most demanding assignment; only don't order me to harm the scientists, the cyborgs, and the robots. And I have one additional request."

"What?"

"Make love to me."

"F<>#?"

"No, love."

"GK, to love is to dance perilously close to the flames of tosalthan."

"The proximity of exquisite passion and absolute peril is the elixir for life."

"You are a romantic, not a particularly useful trait for a member of the Resistance. It is far better to be a pragmatist."

"I believe in love, in passion, in sentiment. I think you do too."

The lovers, for that is now what they have become, spend the night together. Passion temporarily negates skepticism. That nocturnal sojourn, so tender, will prove to be their last intimate encounter. Would GK have risked his heart had he foreseen this doomed trajectory?

16

It is a sad, but salient truth that conceptualizing the expansiveness of the infinite is beyond the bounds of Oturian consciousness.
ChandraX

Emoja and Leon take their now daily walk on the grounds of the Institute. Through the wooded grove, the historic site where so many scientists had argued and postulated theories that became the foundation of some of Oturi's greatest advancements in mathematics and physics. It is a privilege to tread these paths, the byways of ancestral innovations. Emoja and Leon bear the burden of this legacy cheerfully, fully cognizant that if there are to be new discoveries that these advances must rest upon the bedrock of scientific innovations extending back through the millennia. They realize that for new theories to have validity they must be postulated, tested, and proven superior to those ideas that have preceded them. Then—and only then—will these advances take their rightful place in the vast body of knowledge that have formed the basis of scientific discovery. An onerous burden—a magnificent privilege—all one and the same.

Emoja and Leon accept this duality with grace and forbearance, recognizing that this is what it means to be members of their exalted community of scientists contributing to an understanding of all that is potentially knowable in the universe, that which we choose to call epistemology.

We observe them as they walk these pathways. We can't help noticing that Emoja and Leon are communicating, although they are aware that even these woods may have ears, that what they may think, argue, and believe is not immune from surveillance and, possibly, criminal indictments from the Tribunal. But the historic weight of greatness loosens tongues since breathing, thinking, speaking along these footpaths necessarily acts as a conduit for innovation. Leon's thoughts find pathways into Emoja's consciousness. Theirs is a communication in which he need only think and she will understand, although the need to have a dialogue compels her to respond to his thoughts by means of speech and gestures.

"The goal," Leon continues, without so much as a word spoken, "of creating a fully realizable model of Oturian consciousness must take into account not only the sensations but also the qualia and those tertiary influences—intuitive deductions, inferences, memories, and the web of dreams that factor into our perception of reality."

Emoja listens on two levels: the realm of Leon's stated ideas and the qualia underlying these words. I am older, he thinks. My ability to achieve scientific greatness has been stymied. These days, the Institute is little more than a war machine. Where once we did nothing but ponder great ideas, always verging on the profound, now we are consumed with the mundane: budgets, objectives, and assessments of quarterly performance that are guaranteed to be the ruin of scientific innovation.

I always thought, Leon added, that living through a decline had its perverse pleasures, offering both pain and understanding. Now, however, I believe there can be no wisdom gleaned from this existential struggle to survive. Those of us who once felt we inhabited the celestial spheres reserved only for great innovators now are forced to acknowledge that we are reduced to the near-banality of the N/Ts. Soon, our lives will resemble that of the LCDs. It is a terrible realization to know that you have lived your life in vain.

"Leon, how wrong you are!" replies Emoja. "The contributions you have made to the field of cognition and automation are second to none. Your digital scanning measurements, your memory enhancement prototypes, your experiments advancing the analysis of neuronal pathways, and the exo/endoskeletal breakthroughs that you have pioneered that enable the imbedding of virtual memory and file structure into synthetic skin—these contributions were brilliant. And let's not forget that I'm your creation, Leon. And as your conceptual offspring, I want you to know that I'm hopeful—confident—that I will be able to implement our goals for space exploration. And let's not forget that as I speak the Artun85s have already begun to advance our agenda."

"If they still exist. If their memories are intact."

"Of course they exist and are executing their job function. Just as I am here now working toward mine."

"Did you ever ask yourself why Project Emoja came into being?"

"I was grateful to have been given the opportunity to advance our civilization."

"Logic would seem to suggest we devote our efforts to the development of the next life form—robots. Their cognitive functions are not weighed down by emotional considerations. They're free to devote their entire effort to the mission. Critics might contend that the Emoja Project was conceived as hedging our bets. Or worst, a latent form of Oturian narcissism, thinking that civilization could not advance without us. Ergo, the fusion of female/machine consciousness."

"Why, the fusion of female and machine? Why not male?"

"Well, there were pragmatic considerations, of course. Who might agree to participate in such a risky and dangerous experimentation? Naysayers of the project argue—with some credence—that selecting Stranglets was racially and socially predatory, designating the Other to be subject to tests no offspring of privilege would willingly have undertaken. And while there may be some truth to this conjecture, nevertheless, that was not my intent. I wanted to offer the greatest gift imaginable, the opportunity to evolve to a higher level of consciousness. And had I been younger, I would gladly have risked my life."

"But that doesn't really address why the test subjects were female."

"Well, if we begin with the premise that the robots are projections of what we males would like to be—assertive, aggressive, rational, curious—nothing less than a mathematical compilation of knowledge wholly directed toward discovery—then, it seems our feminine qualities are represented through qualia—that cognitive process of constructing meaning from sensations, emotions, fantasies, signs, symbols, and dreams. And that the cyborg is, at one and the same time, archetypically female and male. And with this merging of ing and ang, we circumvent that dynamic struggle of these differences by means of combinatory synthesis of all that is worthy of advancement. Successful implementation allows us to improve not only quantitatively but also qualitatively."

"But you thwart biological evolution. Genetic advancement of the species ceases."

"Hasn't it already ended? Even now, as we converse, don't you think that the advances to be realized are in the realm of the artificial—the mathematical construct as embodied in machines—rather than those obtained through biological evolution?"

"Leon, I'm not sure how to broach this diplomatically. You may regard my motivations as contrary to those envisioned for the Emoja Project, but I want to be able to have intercourse and bear offspring with GK."

Leon pauses. He carefully studies Emoja. A trenchant moment that the casual observer might wrongly perceive as stop-time, an instant that seemingly slows down until it appears frozen in suspended time.

With an effort to appear nonchalant, he responds in thought, "Why would you ever choose to embrace all that is most primitive in us?"

"GK saved my life. He brought me back to consciousness. When we return to Cygnus X-1..."

"Should you both return. Based on the fuel estimates, your GK is, in all probability, no longer alive."

"I think he would have identified the problem and found a solution."

"Emoja, that's not rational, that's your qualia insisting."

"Qualia or no qualia, I believe that he is alive and that both of us will return to Cygnus X-1. Consequently, I want to be sexually compatible with GK and capable of producing younglings with him."

"Sexual compatibility is simple, just some biological plumbing to reconnect. You had the ability to do that even in space. We can easily rectify that. But having an Oturian and cyborg procreate, well, that will require some R&D. Your time here is so limited, and there are risks in devoting so much effort to this endeavor. So I have to ask you, once again, why would you elect to revert biologically to an earlier state of evolution when you've been designed for the future? You don't have to breed. You don't need to raise offspring. You've been spared that whole tiresome process. You're been cloned and have replicants ready to assist you. Why should you elect to regress on the evolutionary timescale? Your decision is not rational. It's not even scientifically reasonable."

"There's a strong possibility," Emoja replies, "Oturi will perish in the very near future. Is the legacy to be only robots and cyborgs? Might we not evolve Oturians one step higher in the evolutionary chain? If GK and I cannot reproduce, then, the male genetic signature from Oturi is, in all likelihood, lost. Is that really what you want? Can't we begin again? Isn't renewal desirable? Doesn't it offer hope?

"And if our basic biological design is flawed?"

"The Emojas are not simply robotic. We are Oturian. Why shouldn't Cyborgs include the genetic NAD of our male counterpart? What if GK's appearance at Cygnus X-1 was not accidental, but Cosmic Providence? How am I supposed to ignore Cosmic Intent?"

"Sometimes, a chance occurrence is nothing more than that."

"And—sometimes—it is so much more."

"Emoja, you're running out of time," Leon sighs. "We're all running out of time. By my estimates we have another decade, perhaps less. I'll help you in any way I can. But remember—you must survive. Don't put yourself at risk by focusing all your energies on reactivating genetic possibilities that are atavistic."

"I would never do that. But survival is predicated on options. I necessarily reject the finite for the potential of the infinite. Our future depends on cosmic possibilities."

Leon reaches over, grasps her hand, looks into her eyes, his thoughts flowing into hers, "Emoja, may your celestial quest permit you to embrace the rainbow of possibilities and opportunities to actualize your hopes and expectations for the future of our civilization."

17

Revolution fuels the appetites of those who have either a profound sense of injustice or who have nothing to lose. For the rest of the population, there is the endless desire for more.
ChandraX

The lovers, for that is what they are, spend what time they can together before each is on assignment. Because of GK's curiosity, they cavort with the LCDs. First, the pygsies. They mimic their dances, sing their songs. Loving the sense of danger that comes with consorting with "the Wild Ones." But it is the time spent among the Politicos—those activists, anarchists, and insurrectionists that capture GK's imagination. They are "the Angry Ones," brimming with passion and ideals. They are articulate, speaking in Old Speak. They are acutely aware of past injustices, present travesties, and the dismal forecasts for the future. They possess agency and purpose. Their intent is to alter the course of history. GK notices Rainy-7's ease among them. The arguments of the Angry Ones closely parallel those of GK. Their passion, a caldron of hate, is easily mistaken for his.

"We wouldn't be in this mess if we still built things and maintained our labor unions, the economic manifestation of our power and might. We threw away our rights. We were co-opted for trinkets."

"Now's the time for revolution. Now that Artunians have nothing to lose and everything to gain."

"Are you kidding? With the Waja patrols, we don't stand a chance. We wouldn't be able to activate even three cells before we'd all be splatterblood."

"Ever since the Believers took hold, the Resistance has faltered."

"The Believers?" asks GK.

"Those spiritual fanatics," replies an anarchist, "that embrace Ogd and the Divine. Those fanatics who live throughout Artun in those vast stretches of land beyond AL and the other metropolises. The Believers profess spiritual values. They are committed to living and dying by their faith rather than resisting the present tyranny. And though there may be some similarity between the Believers here in Artun and the Umbrascenti residing in Catalla and Sirus, the faiths of both are inherently oppositional and antagonistic to reconciliation.

"You are unduly pessimistic," replies Rainy-7. Everyone looks at her. "There are twelve different Resistance efforts, comprised of four different groups just here in AL. We're making headway."

"As a member of the Politico in the Resistance, you choose to believe those fallacies," responds one of the insurrectionists. "We're down here. The N/Ts, the Enhanced, and the Believers are up there. How successful can we possibly expect to be?"

"Not so," says Rainy-7. "Given the surveillance, the Waja, the Tribunal, and the many rebels who have ⬣, our location has utility. Over the past thirty-six months, we have launched over two hundred attacks. Eighty Buildings have been damaged. Air traffic has been halted on ten occasions. We have killed thousands. We're a force with which to be reckoned."

"How can that be," argues one anarchist, "when everyone who might advance the Resistance is a Believer or on drugs or living in the Virt or dying on the streets?"

"Chaos is an agent of change" insists Rainy-7. Adding, "Since the Enhanced have little to offer as palliatives, anger and political action are increasing."

The arguments continue seemingly without end. As frustration mounts, the propensity to strategize wanes, but passionate engagement persists. Rainy-7 states the position of the Politico. GK notices that within the labyrinth, there is chaos and strife and argument. Joy coincides with bitterness, but isn't that the surest indication of vitality? Not like the N/Ts. Here, there are souls who possess real pulses. Up there—nothing. GK is proud to be associated with the Resistance.

And then—is it only hours later?—our hero is given his next assignment. He tries to hide his disappointment. He feels at ease here. With Rainy-7 and all the rebels. Never before has he felt this solidarity and passion as it coalesces around the righteous cause of justice. The euphoria that comes with collective purpose stirs his heart. The LCDs are his comrades. Then, the excitement of battle takes hold as he hears Rainy-7 say, "Your new mission is to infiltrate the Waja Compound in the domain of the Enhanced. This assignment is difficult. It will require that you return to the Virt and visit Sirus before penetrating the domain of the Enhanced as a prelude to undertaking your mission. But there are grave risks. There is a war going on in Sirus. There are dangers even in the Virt. You will need to master the tactical methods employed in warfare."

"But what use," he asks Rainy-7, "will that be? After all, I'll only be operating in the Virt, not the Desolation of the Real."

"You'll be in the Virt because training simulation will be a fraction of what it would cost us to enact it in the Real. We have limited resources. It's all we can offer you. You will need to gain access to the Memory Archives available in the Virt through Vid Scan. Perhaps during your mission you will locate the Rajakian Archives, if, indeed, they exist. You must acquire the tactics of a warrior to succeed in your efforts to infiltrate the Waja Compound. GK, this is a dangerous mission. There have been eight failed attempts thus far. Because of the nature of this mission, you will have limited means of communicating with us. The Waja monitor transmissions. Contact with us is too risky."

"How do you know I won't betray you?"

"That is a risk we are prepared to take. If you're captured alive and tortured, eventually, you will betray us. Operatives will watch your movements. If you appear hostile to our interests, you will be outed. But we need your expertise, and I'm counting on you."

GK longs to make love. He wants to touch and feel and enter Rainy-7. She's aware of his needs, but part of her has already bid him goodbye. She doesn't think he will live. She is both matter-of-fact and deeply scarred by that realization. She won't let herself be drawn closer for fear she will never recover. Melancholia coats their interactions. GK wishes they had had more time. More love. More tenderness. More passion. It is a drug, this intimacy. Stronger than anything he has ever experienced.

Dear Reader, we feel their pain, their joy, their sense of resignation as Rainy-7 kisses our hero before he's blindfolded and taken up to the streets of AL.

GK's hood is released, his escort gone. Thanks to the enhanced SGP capabilities provided by Emoja, he locates his coordinates in the P^3 Sector, Quadrant AL^5 as he stumbles along Vedasepul. Because of the brackish fog, color has washed to a dark slate of gray causing the buildings of dilapidated skyscrapers to appear as if they're closing in on him. He can barely identify the other Artunians shadowing along the thoroughfare. These circumstances make him nervous. With visibility so reduced, anyone—potentially everyone—becomes vulnerable. And with so many in need, weaknesses will be exploited. Many today will lose their identity, their credits, their lives.

GK weaves his walk, trying to look disreputable, anything that might reduce the likelihood of attack as he heads back to his cube. It is dispiriting to be reduced to an animal, either hunting or hunted. The very essence of the Lianitper primal state.

"BANG!" A shot rings out.

He, like others, drops to the ground. No pain, no injury. I'm O.K.

"F<># U!" Someone is on top of me, trying to roll me.

"Sheit"

"Die."

"F<># you!

They struggle. Blows to the shoulder, abdomen, and torso. Each is young, male, strong. Both are the same size and weight. They are tough, used to battle. Each expects to triumph in the combat zone of AL. But our GK has enhanced powers; he has Resistance training, he—fortunately—prevails. He's rolls the attacker, slides on top, sits up, and pummels his adversary. The bloke has his hands out in front of his face, a meager attempt at protection. GK grabs him by the collar and delivers a knockout punch. The N/T is out cold. GK gets up. Pulls the f<>#er up. Plans to finish the job.

But the N/Ts hands have slid away, his face is clearly visible. *F<>#! It's GK°! My former self? The thug I was?* Vertigo sets in. *Could it be that I've nearly killed myself?* GK refuses to consider the ramifications. *Why pontificate?* Instead, he drags GK° down an alley where he won't be found. Stuffs him into a large bin. No rodents inside, no garbage, a nearly spotless container on which he now secures a lid. GK doesn't want to make contact with GK°. He can't bear the thought of talking to his former self. *What could they possibly have in common now? Nothing, that's what!* Leaves GK° and returns to his cube—their cube. This being more consciousness than our hero has ever envisioned, GK, though in fact he may actually be GK¹, rejects the designation. *I'm the one and only, the real bona fide. Back from the future and second to no one, not even the ME that was.*

18

In the course of a lifetime, we assume any number of personas. What matters is to possess that which is truly the essence of who we are and, ultimately, discard the rest. Though there is a cautionary note in all of this: A heat-seeking persona inhabits its own polarity of truth.
ChandraX

GK is in the Virt. He has assumed the persona of ▧. Not so far away are some of the others: ▧, and, of course, ▧. ▧ is flashing his rewards—♂♀ & ▧. ▧ keeps showing his $ $ $. ▧ dances around her ▧. ▧ doesn't have time for this. He needs to learn more about Sirus. No time to play. Gaming won't get him where he needs to be. So he dematerializes and reappears at the Vid Scan. So much to learn in so little time.

But the information ▧ obtains is so dismal-dismal. After the N-Deluge in 3458, the thermonuclear war transformed the region into a glass parking lot, a place now known by the Umbrascenti as the Corridor of Righteous Vengeance and by the Illuminati as the NoZone. Toxicity levels remain high, in excess of 500 rads per hour of exposure. Vid Scan reports estimate that ninety-eight percent of the Sirusians living in the Corridor have died. Only the Insurgents remain. They're clad in dark gray reflective combat gear. All are sprayed with radioactive repellant Zobtar.

As with their brethren in Catalla, these Sirusians residing in the Corridor pray to Allyusan throughout the day. Outside of prayer, their efforts are devoted to Dahij, the holy war. Victory, it is said, will be achieved when the domed city of Malosh, where the Infidels reside, has been restored to the rightful possession of the Umbrascenti. It is, after all, where Allyusan was born. This holy city was lost when their enemies lay conquest to Malosh, more than three xectaries ago. Of course, for the Insurgents to repossess Malosh, the dome must be penetrated. Radioactivity will scourge the sacred city, and the Infidels will die. Although it is unfortunate that Malosh will become radioactive, all actions are justified in ensuring that the sacred city of peace be returned to its rightful people.

Vid Scan documentation suggests that as of now the inhabitants of Malosh have escaped the worst ravages of the N-Deluge. Some of its people were outside the domed city when the N-Deluge occurred. Reentry was impossible. Residents of Malosh watched, tears streaming down, as their brethren melted into the glass pools. It has been said that no one in Malosh will escape the long-term effects of radiation. Indeed, the younglings are proving particularly susceptible to the Rads that have seeped into Malosh.

The Vid Scan assessment is that the residents of Malosh are genetically compatible with the Umbrascenti living in the Corridor. However, the residents of Malosh observe the social, cultural, and scientific beliefs propagated by the Illuminati. The R&D efforts in Malosh are deemed essential to the City's survival. These are organized around three governing principles. First, maintaining a self-sustaining community—with all the attendant resources such as food, water, energy, oxygen regeneration, as well as the ecological recycling of waste—to ensure that its citizens will never have to leave their city. Second, developing NAD stem cell cultures that can be utilized to counteract the deleterious effects of radiation incurred as a consequence of the N-Deluge. Third, although never officially acknowledged, expanding the nuclear arsenal strike-force capabilities for defense and retaliatory purposes. The International Peace Committee has never conclusively proven that nuclear research is ongoing in Malosh. Nevertheless, ground, air, and water samples taken after the N-Deluge on three separate occasions by the Committee suggest that nuclear research and testing continue.

Vid Scan reports provide no definitive account for how the N-Deluge occurred. Some studies suggest that it was initiated by the Umbrascenti. Others claimed that it was promulgated by the Illuminati. There is some evidence suggesting culpability by both parties. Certainly, each has been engaged in warfare against the other for quite some time. Both prefer to view themselves as victims, though there is evidence that both have been perpetrators. What is clear is that should either entirely succeed in getting the upper hand, the outcome will be to eviscerate the enemy. For there can be no divided loyalties among the faithful of either camp. Indeed, how could there be given that their views are antithetical—theocratic and talisfundalist versus modernist and secularist. One must choose. One must choose. One must choose.

This presents a problem given that the world leaders of Oturi have steadfastly refused to take a stand. For in the age of global relativism, it is said that choosing is judging. Judging is deemed, well, "judgmental." To be judgmental is to be censorious. To be censorious is to be dominant. To be dominant is to be powerful. To be powerful is to be EVIL. World leaders do not wish to be characterized as EVIL, nor do they wish to impose a settlement between the two sides. That would be costly, eroding profitability, even if such actions might ultimately benefit all inhabitants of Oturi. For these reasons, there is no global consensus on how to best address xterdism and the behavior of rogue states.

This worldview is founded on a seemingly contradictory amalgam, a fusion of primitive feudalistic practices embodied in the rigid and hierarchical division of social classes conjoined with the modern corporatist mentality that market scarcity, which propagates greed, is not only a necessity, but also inherently good. The reasoning is that in the age of overpopulation and diminished resources there is simply not enough to go around. Only a few, the most privileged ones from around the globe known as the Enhanced, live well. As for the rest of the population, they are forced to contend with the laws of economic scarcity masquerading as the inevitable outcome of market-driven economics.

The overriding principle governing global scarcity is that less is more. Profitability, these days, has been detached from the production and distribution of products so that now a company is financially assessed not for the value of what it sells but the very opposite—how few goods and services are delivered to the general population. For the fewer products allocated to the masses, the greater the availability of consumer goods for those most privileged. Thus, even as scarcity increases dynamically, InfoNews fosters the notion that consumer well-being is perpetuated, despite the overall decline in the total volume of goods and services offered.

In accordance with the economic ethos espoused by corporatists, the desired constant in the global labor marketplace—with the notable exception of Zhinboya—approaches nil. That is, the goal is to replace employment of all Oturians with robots. The reasoning is that in this age of scarcity it is of maximum utility to employ as few members of the society as possible. The fewer Oturians employed, the less income that will be available for the purchase of goods and services and, by extension, the LCDs and N/Ts will have little, if any, economic clout.

Indeed, virtually all services devoted to maintaining the well-being of the public sector—including welfare, healthcare, retirement pensions, public transportation, and education—have been eliminated in Artun, the very exemplar of the post-modern "stateless" state. The government there is responsible for policing—which includes surveillance, terror management, and border control—and supervising the Virt. But even policing and monitoring the Virt are increasingly maintained by subcontractors from the private sector who employ robots. The only other service nominally provided is waste disposal, which is offered through private contractors and woefully inadequate. Both border control and waste disposal are considered essential for reducing conditions favorable to the spread of pandemics. However, containment is approximate rather than absolute. Refugees surmount the physical and logistical barriers to entering Artun. Diseases and viruses that are dynamically unstable occur, suggesting that pandemics will become increasingly widespread in the years to come.

And what about global politics with respect to warring Sirus? Vargus is without influence because of its economic and social bankruptcy. Catalla, now controlled by the Umbrascenti, gives lip service to freedom while surreptitiously funding the Insurgency. This leaves only Zhinboya and Artun with the capacity to intervene. However, both continents have refused. Zhinboya, for pragmatic reasons, says it has no historic mandate to justify military action. Artun, on the other hand, has determined that Sirus is a "Dead Continent" with insufficient oil, gas, and mineral reserves to justify the risk of radioactive contamination. Indeed, intelligence sources within both Zhinboya and Artun have concluded that the tribal factions in Sirus are squabbling over dwindling resources and that neither has the means to pose a global threat. Consequently, intervention in the region is deemed nugatory. Perhaps, this is because medical analysis suggests that within two decades life, as it is presently constituted in Sirus, will no longer exist.

🜲 digests this Vid Scan content with **blue-ice** stoicism. Nothing prepared him for this dire assessment rendered so dispassionately. So many individuals consigned to a battlefield destined for annihilation. It's all "**Red on Red Engagement**," brother fighting brother, sister fighting sister, in that ravaged land. He barely has time to digest the intel when the

Agent of Virtue (🜲) appears.

"Cease and Desist, 🜲. You have entered the Forbidden Zone of the Rajakians, punishable by death."

"🜲, I am, as permitted, in the domain of Vid Scan."

"Vid Scan has passages traceable to the Rajakians."

"I know not these passages."

"The 🜲 determines what is known and not known."

In a panic, 🜲 frequency hops, by means of a rocket ship, directly to Sirus. It's not exactly a controlled entry. The destination flashing above the vehicle is listed as the "NoZone," although on the control panel he notices "**Grammars of Death**" highlighted in orange. Not exactly a destination that bodes well for 🜲. 🜲 emerges from the charred Command Module on to a shimmering reflective plain of glass fibers known as the Corridor of Righteous Vengeance. He's wearing combat gear sprayed with radioactive repellant Zobtar. And he worries that the **Grammars of Death** spaceflight is actually the stealth handiwork of the disputatious 🜲.

19

To the primitive, the phenomenon of war is sacrosanct. The perceived threat of imminent annihilation produces a state of hyper-reality where every sensation, every moment is lived experientially to the max. Quotidian existence, by contrast, is perceived as nothing, nothing at all.

ChandraX

One of the brethren pulls GK down into the Zobtar-encased foxhole, hissing, "Brother, fool! Standing upright on the frozen sands is to seek vaporization."

"Fool that I am: I've lost my way."

"Your name, brother."

"🝮."

"Insurgent 97 here. The holy ones talk of those who feel nothing of the Rads. Brother, may your powers assist us in reclaiming Malosh."

"And to the peace that follows therein."

🝮 ingratiates himself to Insurgent 97. He is invited to join Node I-74 and is now referred to as Insurgent 382. His confreres—Insurgents 101, 97, 66, and 34—familiarize him with the routine. On the belly, they live. On the crawl, the crouch, the shadowy flight from here to there. To the hovel below where the bombs, the inferred missiles, and the rockets are manufactured. They toil. No need to converse. One does one's assignment; one works shifts; one waits for instructions.

⚚, a.k.a. Insurgent 382, adjusts to the rhythm of the Insurgency. He prays to Allyusan. As for the rest, it seems a ceaseless blur of shifts. On, off. On, off. There are the battles, the exhaustion, the boredom, and, then, seemingly without warning, the next surge begins. Fear becomes murderous rage before waning to anguish and descending to listlessness. Being and Nothingness. Nothingness and Being. Being. Being. Nothingness. Nothingness. Again, again, and again. Out there, a bomb detonates. Insurgent 101 has lost both his legs. Insurgent 101 tries to propel his torso to safety. Another bomb explodes. Then another. Insurgent 101 lies on the glassy sand, exposed and vulnerable. Given the strikes, no one attempts the folly of trying to rescue him. They hear his plaintive cries. They can do nothing. NOTHING. His moans are agonizing and seemingly interminable. Insurgent 101 dies at dusk, although it seems an eternity before his cries subside. Under cloak of nightfall, the carcass of Insurgent 101 is retrieved and brought to the hallowed cremation site. Prayers are said, the body incinerated. No time to mourn. There is the next assignment. At night, while sleeping, ⚚ experiences the anguished cries of Insurgent 101. Again and again, ⚚ awakens drenched in sweat. ⚚ cries, muffled sobs, all the more wrenching because they are suppressed. Involuntary memories that refuse to fade away.

Thirty-two days into the Insurgency, ⚚ decides that he's had enough. Let them kill me. I will ask questions. I will obtain answers. I need to gain knowledge now or I will perish here on these glassy sands of Sirus in the Virt-World. Better to risk everything in hopes of discovering information pertinent to my mission than be consigned to this purgatory.

He proceeds to his Battalion Leader. "Insurgent 382 reporting. Request reassignment to the Liberation Squad. Desired mission: Penetration of the Dome."

"Insurgent 382 that requires approval from the Commanders and extensive training."

"Yes, extensive training."

Insurgent 382's application is approved. He is given special communication devices. He monitors and predicts the intervals between the launching of weapons by the Enemy. He is now capable of deactivating bombs. He can activate grenades. He can assemble and disassemble. He masters the manners and social customs of the enemy so that he might penetrate their ranks. There are three other insurgents training with him. Little is said. They prepare. And wait for their orders. At least he will fight. At least there is that.

20

Dreams and desires shape Oturian aspirations. They are not generally rooted in logic. Nor are they constant since dreams and desires change over time, alternating motivations and actions. Success comes when the human heart aligns with the reasoning mind overcoming the perceived limitations of the mind-body duality. Stay the course. Victory awaits those who proceed with determination and perseverance.

ChandraX

Emoja is asleep on her couch in her office. The twitching eye movements, characteristic of the EMR cycle, suggest that she is dreaming. If we enter her consciousness, we experience her sensations. We are privy to her discovery that GK is alive, on Oturi, and surfing the Virt. We share her delight that GK has survived his journey and is here weeks ahead of schedule.

So much for Leon's pessimism," she thinks. "Is my dream of GK in the Virt representative of circumstances in the Real? I'm tracing his pathways. Ah, I see he has assumed the persona of ✦. Why has he gone to Vid Scan for information on Sirus? Who is that ✦ troubling him at Vid Scan? That avatar is EVIL! Escape, GK, escape! Good! Why, oh why would you enter a vehicle headed to the NoZone, which is known as **Grammars of Death**? Fool! Don't you realize that you're about to enter the Corridor of Righteous Vengeance? No one is reputed to survive that! What if your virtual death anticipates death in the Desolation of the Real? Why are you now operating as Insurgent 382 whose plan is to lay siege to Malosh? Don't you realize that I am empowered to destroy Insurgents? Anyone who threatens Oturi becomes my enemy. GK, 🖤, Insurgent 382 are you my enemy?"

I have no way of knowing what you are thinking in the Virt unless I am there as well. I don't know your motivations. I can't understand your reasons for traveling to Sirus. Does it serve your desire to understand the trajectory of Oturi? Is this how you propose to understand the forces of destruction ravaging our planet? Through Vid Scan did you really gain access to the pathways of the Rajakians? Or are you now an Insurgent laying waste to the vestiges of civilization? What have the Illuminati ever done to you that you might seek to destroy their domed city? Could you be so base? Have you no conscience? Am I culpable for what you have become? What if your actions in the Virt influence the Desolation of the Real? Is that your intent? To lay waste to AL, Artun, and all of Oturi? Must I, then, seek to destroy you? How could I have been so deceived?

Dear Reader, we sympathize with Emoja's distress. After all, scientists at the Institute aren't generally permitted access to the Virt. So she can't easily enter that domain and discover GK's intentions. Should she leave the Institute and attempt to enter the Virt, there is the risk that she'll be discovered and the possibility that punitive reprisals will be taken. That, of course, could jeopardize Emoja's plans to return to Cygnus X-1.

It is imperative that Emoja not jeopardize her mission. She needs to stay on-task. She doesn't have time to intercede on GK's behalf. Besides, he's perfectly capable. We've seen to that. Dear Reader, there are always risks in making known our cosmic dictates. Better to have the characters in this celestial drama act with the presumption that they're exercising Free Will.

Emoja's distress, however, is counterproductive to our purpose. She has important work to be done. And given that Oturi is destined for a cataclysmic terminus, time is at a premium. Consequently, we feel the need to intrude.

"Emoja, GK is fine." We project our voice to her telepathically.

"Who are you?" Emoja replies in thought.

"I am ChandraX."

"ChandraX. The same ChandraX who suggested that 'I must choose?' while swimming through Cygnus X-1"

"The very same."

"Why should I heed your counsel?"

"Because my advice has proven useful thus far."

"Who are you, ChandraX?"

"GK is fine. Your time is precious. Don't waste it."

ChandraX—the celestial oracle—is now silent.

Emoja awakens and begins to shake. Was she dreaming or hallucinating? Emoja hasn't been sleeping much lately. She's been harried, preoccupied with her research. But sleep deprivation is counterproductive: There are the nightmares, the delayed motor responses, the out-of-body sensations, the diminished cognitive capabilities. Her nerves are frayed. She's always postulating, testing for evidence, modifying her assumptions before beginning again. Her scientific investigations haven't yielded definitive results. So much to discover with the pressing fear that any hope for Oturi's legacy and its re-conceptualized cosmic future through my efforts and those of the other Emojas is in peril. I fear that I may misconstrue statistical probability as certainty due to the overwhelming pressures of the moment. Consequently, I will heed ChandraX's advice. What else can I do? Time is at a premium.

What am I to make of my attraction to GK? He's impulsive. If I'm honest, I will admit that I'm drawn to him because of his emotive and seemingly unpredictable character. My feelings aren't rational: They're primal. Could I complete my mission without GK? Certainly. Would I now choose to make this journey alone? No. . . . That realization comes as a surprise since I never factored intimacy as a significant variable in my life. But given that I have broached the question of living my life without GK and now that I acknowledge how empty that would feel, well, our union simply must be. I want to share with GK the majesty of the cosmos. The journey will be all the richer with a partner to share the joys and shoulder the perils.

⚑—a.k.a. Insurgent 382—is assigned along with Insurgent 97, 141, and 224 to a proximity camp within striking distance of the dome covering the city of Malosh. A maze of subterranean passages have been dug through silicon. Weapons are being transported through them. It is said that the new arsenal of missiles have the capability to launch with deadly precision from their silos to the designated target.

When penetration is achieved, Insurgent 97, 141, 224, and 382 will enter the metropolis. They have been training for weeks now. Their combat readiness is peaking. They have acquired the skills necessary for the most difficult assignment of all—infiltrating the headquarters of the Supreme Command of Malosh (SCM). Accordingly, they are provided with all the necessary intel. Implanted memories have provided them with a lifetime of associations characteristic of the inhabitants. The four Insurgents are now fluent in the Sirusian dialect of Ramaric spoken in Malosh. Their mission: Relay as much detail about the security operations of the Illuminati to the Insurgency in order to expedite the next phase of attack—the penetration of the dome city by means of a battalion of Warrior Nodes.

D-day for operations is a scant seventy-two hours away. ⚑ is sleeping. When he's not at rest, he's watching the monitors, waiting. He's not nervous. Just poised for "Go." His thoughts, his speech, his mode of being now emulates the action and outlook of the Illuminati. He's curious, ready to assume his new identity. Fortunately, his persona in Malosh will remain ▨. The other operatives are preoccupied with the mundane intel associated with border patrol and the procedures necessary to break through the perimeter, matters that ▨ regards as insignificant.

▨ is excited about his assignment to infiltrate the Supreme Command of Malosh. He's examined the profiles of many of the best agents, reputed to be the top operatives in the Virt. ▨ has never faced such a challenge before, but his aura is now blue-ice, so RC.

At precisely T-120, the operatives position themselves inside the transporter stations with ▨ in one and the three other Insurgents occupying the chamber adjacent to his. The zero hour. A thunderous explosion is felt: the missiles have launched. The monitors show they have hit their designated targets—AR14, B-38C, and C-14F. The dome is compromised. Sirens blow: The alarms are heard even in the caverns of the Insurgency as the four Insurgents are transported to Malosh. Then, the compromised dome is re-sealed. But not soon enough. The rebels have successfully infiltrated the city.

The Insurgency's military COMSGP coordinates are accurate, at least with respect to ▨. He rematerializes inside the Supreme Command dressed in the modern, western attire that is the sartorial style of the Illuminati. He heads in the direction of the Intel Monitoring Center (IMC), S-1, a critical site for surveillance and the monitoring of system breaches. He hopes his identity card—doubling as an RF tag and a glyph-encoded documentation passport—is sufficient to pass muster. Swipe, the wireless transport doors opens. He enters. The lifter goes down, down, down. Then it stops. The doors part. Before him is an enormous bank of computers. There must be sixty-four agents monitoring activities at this site alone. Our hero steps forward, briefly stands behind one of the operators, and reviews critical data bits on the screen before selecting a free station, which he occupies. See him gently tapping his left foot? Our hero prays that his code-breaking skills pass muster.

⚜ is now fully engaged in his new job as Systems Analyst at IMC. The entire city of Malosh is tabulated and coded with checkpoints on the grid. Thanks to his downloads, his training, his viscan capabilities, he quickly pinpoints where the breaches occurred. Based on the Intruder Vid Assessment Profile (IVAP), it seems likely that the three other insurgents were successfully transported to their destinations since there is a security breach flashing on the screen—**WARNING! 4 INSURGENTS HAVE PENETRATED THE DOME!** Fortunately, no profile ID has been provided.

⚜ feels a tap of his shoulder. Startled, he looks up.

"You must be the rookie transfer sent to help us shore up security. Spaito here."

⚜ stands up and turns around to greet Spaito. He registers the accent and mannerisms of the speaker and matches it to his own internal database. He emulates Spaito's speech patterns, replying, "Name's ⚜. Yes, I'm a rookie transfer."

"System's breach seems pretty severe."

"Yes, there's the possibility that four Insurgents may have infiltrated the city."

"Shouldn't be hard to identify them. The Insurgents are primitive. They'll never pass as one of us."

"Nevertheless, . . ."

They chat a bit before returning to their respective stations to complete their allocated six-hour shifts. By the end of workday, ⚜ is legit. He's fully enmeshed in the system—on the electronic credit/debit payroll, complete with a viscan ID and history profile. After hours, Spaito and ⚜ head for Letval, a pub. It's in the compound. The beverages aren't really brewed, they're an approximation of what in Old Speak was known as rebe, a substance that slowed response time sufficiently that those who drank felt relaxed enough to converse. Letval is located within the security compound since intel agents are rarely permitted outside, except when on assignment since leaving the protected area is deemed too risky.

🁢 enjoys the novelty of this experience—a job complete with a domicile that almost resembles what used to be referred to as an apartment. Here he engages with colleagues in Old Speak, albeit in the imaginary domain of the Virt. There's the possibility of sustained F2F interaction, the whiff of community, the visible remnants of a culture amid a still functioning city. He revels in all this. Malosh is vital, alive. Why had he never experienced this sense of community, of belonging before?

"The Insurgents are making inroads," Spiato says. He says it tiredly, with resignation. "Fighting them is taking more and more of our resources. Our culture is dead. Our people are suffering. I don't know how much longer we can maintain this veneer of civilization. And when it disappears, everything will be lost. Our way of living, thinking, and speaking. We're on the brink of catastrophe that will conclude with our annihilation."

"Throughout the ages, Oturians have survived the most heinous circumstances."

"Perhaps, although it wasn't a global civilization that was threatened. Here in Malosh our society represents one of the last vestiges of an educated, cultured community in all of Oturi. Much—most—of our knowledge has been lost. But the traces of our heritage are ripe for rediscovery. Nevertheless, our present struggle permits little opportunity for conscious thought. When Malosh is destroyed—and make no mistake our City is perilously close to annihilation—what little culture that remains on this planet will perish with us."

🁢 is exhausted. And irritated. Maybe that's why he says, "It's only the Virt. Why does it matter?"

Spaito pauses as he puts down his drink. "Are you such a fool that you think that if culture ends in the Virt that it has no correlation in your Desolation of the Real? That because our blood might not be "real" in the

Virt—heed my words 'might not'—that means you won't actually die? That the destruction of Malosh here will have no consequence for your precious Desolation of the Real?"

"I never really thought about it."

"Apparently, you haven't thought about much."

"No, not much."

Spiato talks about Slow-Time, an earlier era on Oturi when communities existed, when families prospered, when people engaged in sustained, intellectual thought, when people read words in books, when food was grown and savored at meals. Imagine reading words just as the Old Ones used to savor gourmet cuisine. Spaito speaks about entire virtual worlds that existed in a distant age with a different kind of Virt. The sensory pleasures of touching letters running across the page of a book that one scanned with one's eyes and that captivated the imagination of the greatest thinkers through the associations conveyed by words. The smell of those volumes so vivid that the sensation evoked taste. Language that by means of written text paved the way to elaborate mental constructs. Worlds fabricated and destroyed and refashioned through their transmission or destruction or reinvention in elaborate documents celebrated as books. At the end of a good read, if one was fortunate, one might even gain a measure of wisdom that changed one's perception of reality.

Spaito speaks wistfully of an era when the cultural heritage that nurtured the creation of melodious sonic narratives that delighted listeners because of their intricate compositional structure. To appreciate these musical stories it helped to comprehend the tonal structure as well as to recognize the tempos, rhythms, and styles associated with distinct eras. Music, as conceived in antiquity, told a sophisticated tale, transporting the listener to an altered state of consciousness through the immersion in this tuneful eloquence. Not like the blaring prater of nothingness that passes for "sound-song" today.

Spaito reminisces about theater, that performance staged in days of yore. When actors stood on stages to present sagas that saddened or delighted or enriched their audiences. An art form now moribund. For theater, although oral, required an audience fully immersed in the joys and patterns of written language, familiar with sophisticated narratives that unfolded sequentially through time. To appreciate classical theater, one needed to comprehend the cultural heritage dating back through the millennia.

Spaito laments the ruination of dance, that movement most akin to the motion of the fabled gods and goddesses of ancient lore. Where once it was so intrinsically tied to music and story, now, it's spiritually bankrupt, unanchored by cultural heritage or story-narrative. Contemporary performers mastered little training. Their movements were, as a consequence, listless or frenetic, spectral shadows of the great culture that used to be.

Spaito extols the splendor of experiencing a cultural event bigger than self with artists who actually have something to contribute to the society at large, more than the solipsistic constructs governing "self-story" performance today. He is nostalgic for a vanquished era, an age when cultural perspectives were shared and intellectual pursuits celebrated. A gilded age where knowledge was an adventure through the majestic journey of great ideas that were transmitted from one generation to the next, each building upon critical constructs of foundational culture and approached that vast body of tradition with a reverence approaching awe. This appreciation of history, tradition, culture, this humility before all that was profound, no longer exists. How could the NOW with its giddy narcissism of resplendent ME and the ephemeral delights of the Next New Thing divorced from precedence and, therefore, without substance for the future begin to approach the majesty of a culture founded on a storehouse of accumulated cultural memories?

Spaito concludes sadly, "What's left is really almost nothing at all. We have science known only to a few. It is increasingly utilized in the development of sophisticated technological weaponry that we employ toward our defense. Some of these advances are later introduced as consumer gadgets. But security and gadgets don't nourish. We need fundamental research in the sciences and an appreciation of cultural heritage in the arts in order to retain and advance our civilization. Without these lofty pursuits, we are nothing—barely conscious, endlessly consuming, filled with empty desires. In our present state, we can never be satiated. We will never acquire cultural enrichment. We have no prospect of attaining enlightenment. And our outcome? Imagine a species reduced to endlessly chewing and fornicating and pissing. Our contribution? Think of it as excrement smeared across a desecrated landscape.

"But we all have consciousness," responds ▟. "We think; we breathe; we are aware of pain, pleasure, color, cold, and heat."

"That's where we disagree. Look around. What you refer to as sentient beings are, for all intents and purposes, unconscious. True, they respond to stimuli, but then so do other creatures. But to live today in this world without a sophisticated understanding of the principles shaping our universe is to be reduced to the most idiotic beast, blindly subject to nature's laws, rather than adapting to and sometimes even challenging the premises underlying our perceptions of our physical universe. This primitive state reduces us to animalistic desires. We are driven by base emotions and drives, scarcely better than the Lianitper creatures from which we evolved. But if we desire consciousness, it requires more than scientific expertise. We must be aware of how our ideas intersect with knowledge that has preceded us and anticipate those ideas that will be forthcoming.

This kind of engagement requires Slow-Time. Slow-Time coupled with cultural knowledge in its fullest sense means that knowledge must be joined with historical awareness kindled by scientific reasoning. That is the precondition for the conscious self. When we have a community of enlightened individuals capable of interactive engagement, then, we have the foundations for a functioning civilization. But who amongst us today has access to that base of knowledge and social kinship?"

"Don't know. Never considered these ideas before."

"Of course not. You're probably an implant disguised as one of us. I bet you're from Artun. You probably think that the ▨ is just a game. You couldn't be more wrong."

"If it's not a game, what is it?"

"This world interacts with the Desolation of the Real. We, the Illuminati, are committed to knowledge, to truth, to the wisdom culled from the greatest minds throughout the ages. We would rather die than devolve into another Dark Age. We will fight to preserve our cultural heritage. Should we be annihilated, we will ensure that all of you die with us. There will be no survivors. And I'm not just talking about the Virt. The events that transpire here influence circumstances in the Desolation of the Real. Accountability resides within and between the two zones.

"So ▨, may I suggest that you invest in our survival? For those of you in Artun who insist on living in that insidious perpetual visual realization of "I,"—what anyone from any truly conscious era would necessarily refer to as the preconscious di—know that even your impoverished, selfish, primal di needs air, water, fuel, and space to survive. All that will be lost if the Umbrascenti extinguish what remains of our civilization. We have enough nuclear capacity to demobilize everyone in both zones. And if it comes to that, we will."

"Well," replies ▨, "I'm betting on survival. So here's to life and the continued vitality of Malosh."

▨ and Spiato clink glasses. They drink what passes for brew. And then, they bid goodnight. ▨ heads for his domicile, fully aware that he has experienced his first true "Interaction," an encounter with another Oturian—Virt or Real—that wasn't fueled by primal appetites. "Not that I didn't interact with Emoja," he mutters to himself. "But she's a cyborg. Besides, she always gets my juices going, complicating the intellectual nature of our discourse. And it's not that I don't care about Rainy-7, but our relationship is ignited by revolutionary ardor and conjugal passion. Spaito's more analytical. He's introduced me to historical and cultural subjects that broaden my perspective. And although we bond, it's a cool, dispassionate connection. None of that flaming emotion."

With but four precious hours remaining before the radioactive haze of dawn, 🜚's slumber is filled with dreams that flow into the liquid current of words—textual, conversational, and dense with interiority. What begins as a stream becomes a river, later a torrent of consciousness surging backwards and forward through time. 🜚 awakens, returns to his station, and investigates the systems breach. But this is no ordinary day since 🜚 now finds himself in sympathy with the Illuminati's quest for survival and Spaito's desire to restore the cultural heritage of Malosh.

21

What is real and what is illusionary? The distinction is never as simple as it may appear. For the Desolation of the Real and the heinous spectacle of the Virt are partnered in a Danse Macabre, a death spiral that threatens to annihilate all life on planet Oturi.
ChandraX

Emoja and Leon continue their walks in the woods. It is where they feel most comfortable communicating. These strolls provide them solace, offering comfort during moments of distress. They look forward to these walks together. In many respects they are no longer teacher and pupil, but colleagues collaborating on a project. It is an interactive process they enjoy. With the passage of each day, their new-found relationship blossoms, although this intimacy is tainted with the understanding that their time together at the Institute is finite. Implicitly, they acknowledge their separate destinies. This realization is bittersweet. Both Leon and Emoja experience these walks in a state of hyperreality—simultaneously within and without the bounds of ordinary time. As such, they are immediately next to one another and also cosmically displaced, as if living the moment close at hand while viewing the event from a vantage point light-years removed. This dichotomy creates the sensation that their moments together are unfolding in a succession of still-frame sequences realized in Slow-Time.

"Leon, what can you tell me about the Virt?"

"It's a world created by the Enhanced." Leon responds, as is typical for most of their conversations, in thought. He prefers this method of discourse since it acknowledges Emoja's unique powers while providing them with an additional means of privacy. "The Virt," he continues, "was devised to keep the N/Ts preoccupied in a game of imaginary acquisitions, delights, and torments. It creates a frenzied neural synaptic state designed to prevent its participants from becoming too angry about the miserable circumstances in the Desolation of the Real. The Virt offers N/Ts the possibility to act out their fantasies, although in the Real their existence has been reduced to bare subsistence. Many die of malnutrition and thirst while playing the . Others have conditions that, in the excitement of the game, are never diagnosed, let alone treated. Most have severe muscle atrophy due to a life lived almost exclusively in the Virt. N/Ts have little awareness of the Real. The Virt is no "Second Life"; it is their experiential reality."

"Surely," says Emoja, "they must know the difference between the Virt and the Real?"

"Well, consider their world. If they have a place to rest their heads, it's a small space that resembles a cubicle. The lack of basic goods and services have largely escaped their notice because their lives are manifest in the Virt. What little food and drink they obtain is nearly always in the . In the Desolation of the Real, the primary substances available to N/Ts are drugs. However, gaming in the Virt stimulates their neuronal circuitry. The anticipation of Virt-play activates the podamine receptors that stimulate the pleasure/pain centers. Persistent gaming impacts the milbic brain region—the seat of emotional functions—and the Cereumla—the locus of analytical responses. These actions embed gaming cues into the Lianitper and, ultimately, the Core Memory. Compulsive gaming facilitates deficits in impulse control and decision making. The neurological changes cause the entire brain to become receptive so that it hungers insatiably for gaming, overriding all other drives. The gaming impulse eventually succeeds in shutting down the bodily functions of any player obsessively participating in Virtworld."

"But some figure it out," replies Emoja. They realize it's a form of mind control and eventually rebel. GK did."

"Those that do are designated ⟡ and eventually ⟡. In "real-speak" this means they are relegated to the LCD or "volunteered" for space exploration. In either case it's a death sentence."

"But is the ▦ just virtual? Is there any correlation between that and the Real? If a city or place or person gets destroyed in the Virt, what is the consequence in the Real?"

"The program for the ▦ consists of complicated algorithms. I've never analyzed the code. I suspect there are different consequences depending on which Persona or Avatar one adopts and the particular selections made. I believe there are eight Persona—Quantoid Numerator ⟡, Alpha Predator ⟡, Data Rodent ⟡ Enemy Belligerent ⟡, Cogitator ⟡, Kid Death ⟡, Radiant Cool ⟡, and Continuity Girl ⟡. And, of course, one might choose to be an Avatar who can intervene of behalf of the Personas. I believe there are four Avatars—the Engineer ⟡, Santa Muerte (⟡), Traficante (⟡), and the Agent of Virtue ⟡. The first two are reputed to be good, the others evil. The game is sufficiently complex to include simulacra of all our continents, each with its own distinct laws.

"So a predictive model of the relation between the Real and the Virt would be difficult. Ultimately, of course, the ▦ has no victors. It's a game of attrition. I don't really know what the consequence would be if AL or any of the cities throughout the continents were vaporized in the Virt. Only those scientists who monitor and create the gaming strategy for the ▦ could reliably answer that question.

"I regard," Leon continues, "the ▦ as a very sophisticated device employed to erase consciousness. Think of it as an addiction eliciting a frenzy of sensations designed to overload our neural circuitry. The pulse races, the synapses fire, the heart pumps—it's a torrent of simulated activity while the body atrophies into nothingness. Consciousness, which for us is closely linked to motion, can't be sustained when life is immersed in the Virt. With the degradation of bodily functions comes the atrophy of the mind and, eventually, death. Thus, the ultimate gaming center has genocide as its desired outcome.

"Certainly, there are causal connections between both worlds. Though the specifics could only be learned by studying the program and running some very sophisticated mathematical simulations. You would, of course, have to be granted high-security clearance, something that only a few scientists are allowed. And given that your prime directive is to explore space, it is doubtful that you would be permitted access."

Leon touches Emoja's arm, a gesture born out of empathy, and continues, "I understand your concern. Do you have reason to believe that GK is here? That he's operating in the Virt? Even if you know this to be the case, you must devote your energies to your mission. You're running out of time, Emoja."

"Everything pertinent to the mission is proceeding on schedule, Leon. But yes, I'm concerned about GK. He may be in the Virt operating undercover as an Insurgent in Sirus. It's so dangerous there. What happens if he's ⚰ in the Virt? Does he die in the Real? And what if Malosh should be threatened with destruction in the Virt? Is it also threatened in the Real? These things trouble me. But I'm also concerned about you, Leon—you and the other scientists here at the Institute. I never really considered how dire the global situation was while I was training for my mission. Now, I find myself thinking about the future. Leon, I can't fathom living my entire life without even the prospect of working with you. Aren't you concerned?"

Leon is slow in responding. When he does, his thoughts are measured and carefully circumspect. "I don't think Oturi will survive much longer. Life, as it is experienced today, has become almost unbearable for anyone who is reasonably conscious. Most Oturians would rather be Zbies than comprehend our social reality. After all, there is so little any of us can do. The situation worsens by the hour. We're on a countdown to extinction. Who would want to be conscious of that?

"In Artun," he continues, "and throughout Oturi, three social classes prevail. Each has been rendered nearly unconscious. The Enhanced have privileged lives. They still seek and obtain, at least at some limited material level, their objects of desire, although they're never satiated and their hunger for material comforts erodes what little remains of their intellectual curiosity. Consumption becomes all.

"N/Ts everywhere are pursuing their desires in the Virt since scarcity has left them with little means of obtaining their material comforts in the Real. Virtuality becomes all, the Real becomes illusory. However, reality eventually prevails when the N/Ts suffer and die of material causes.

"The LCDs are the rebels challenging the social order. Their anger and profound sense of injustice incites them to battle. But they're less a united front than a disparate band of misfits, thieves, and two-bit warriors, all of whom lack the means and the capability for marshalling victory. Of course, ultimately, there can be no justice unless resources and opportunities are available to all. However, given the population demographics and limited resources available, such an outcome is unlikely. What we have today is global corporatism that has become detached from the production and the distribution of product. The Enhanced live in their diminished material world and the rest of the population is both contained and expendable. Social control is best achieved by means of drugs and an altered sense of reality. And nothing is more effective as a palliative than the Virt.

"The news is all bad Emoja. You're the last best hope of Oturi. We're counting on you and all the other Emojas to preserve all that is vital in our society while advancing consciousness and civilization throughout the cosmos. I implore you: Don't let us down."

Leon abruptly turns around and quickly heads back to his office. He left in order to spare Emoja. He did not want her to see his tears. He thought it best to avoid that particularly painful moment of intimacy.

22

Remembering is an archaeological process to recover that which has been forgotten. Discovery is enabled through trace memories. Find those traces, understand their cues, follow the journey, and knowledge will be yours.
ChandraX

isn't getting much sleep these days. During his six-hour shifts, he's been trying to analyze the Umbrascenti Intelligence Network. To do this he has studied the network typology to understand how it's embedded and the protocols in place, as well as logistical communications that foster operations within and without that network.

Communications are conveyed by means of wireless devices that are encrypted and so small as to be barely visible. When a mission is completed or compromised, the devices are vaporized.

The hierarchical command structure shapes the nature and means of communication. At the apex is the Supreme Ruler of the Insurgency. Five Commanders serve at the pleasure of the Supreme Ruler. They in turn are served by Battalion Leaders who oversee the 199 Warrior Nodes, each comprised of up to two hundred insurgents. Each Warrior Node is made up of ten Terror Squads consisting of between three and nine insurgents, as well as five covert Warrior Nodes known as Liberation Squads comprised of between ten and twenty Liberators. While members of both sexes serve among the rank and file, the leadership from the Battalion Leaders on up to the Supreme Ruler is comprised only of men.

"Why didn't I meet one of those Terror Viragos?" wonders 🐦 as he examines the documents files. "Yeah, right. Many of them probably trained in sex-segregated nodes. Still.... Think of the missed opportunities. All that f<>#just waiting to be had!" Reluctantly, he returns to the business at hand.

Analysis focuses on developing the methodology and interpretation critical for predictive modeling. To achieve this outcome data communication structures and source leads are examined to enhance the reliability of intelligence. This approach assesses which nodes represent the greatest threats. It examines network interlinks. It studies patterns of influence within and between nodes—what is referred to as identity signatures. It profiles key players through their interactive social networks within and between nodes. This cumulative approach is essential for accurate and precise modeling of high-probability terror scenarios.

The key to Malosh intel, 🐦 realizes, is its ability to provide highly analytical risk assessment that can be simulated with macro variables on super-hybrid exascale computers. This approach is based on predictive modeling of the characteristics of the Insurgency, which is achieved through dynamic programming of meta-matrixing and multi-agent networks. Meta-matrixing consists of multi-network analysis performed on statistically variable mathematical models that examine the key individuals and their contact links in the network. In identifying these operatives and their networking signatures, Malosh intel intends to intercede and foil prospective strikes that have the greatest probabilistic likelihood of success. Multi-Agent Network Modeling, by contrast, examines the detailed interactions between nodes to assess what nodes should be targeting for preemptive outage. Of the two methodologies employed, meta-matrixing has proven particularly effective in modeling emergent leadership trends, although success in disengaging these emergent leaders has occasionally led to a multi-headed hydra response, when several potential rivals vie for vacant leadership positions.

⚇ is examining a report titled "Data Tracking Error Methodology for Optimal Predictive Reliability in the Interpretation of Source Code" when Spaito taps his shoulder.

"Shifts over, come join me."

"I'm up to my eyeballs in coefficient probability analysis."

"It will be there when you return."

⚇ clocks out of his shift. He assumes they are headed to the Letval pub. Instead, Spaito and ⚇ made their way to the decon chamber where they are sprayed with the radioactive repellant Zobtar before heading out. Spaito has gotten a special exemption so that they might exit the compound and walk the city streets.

Malosh is a mélange of new and old. Contemporary ascetic clusters of skyscrapers juxtapose with dense honeycombed hives. In the skyscrapers, the citizenry wear simple, modern attire. In the honeycomb hives, the dwellers don colorful tribal costumes and practice ritualistic customs dating back thousands of years. Together, a shared culture is pursued in dramatically divergent ways. Contrasting nubs of contrapuntal textures woven at irregular intervals against the bias.

Malosh is bustling with activity as young and old stroll through the arcades in the old quarter. These arched passageways are marketplaces brimming with shops and food stalls. So many spices and aromas tempt the palate. For ⚇, this is a sensorial and gastronomic feast. The smells, the tastes, the textures are more vital, more sensual, than anything he has ever experienced in either the Real or the Virt. Merchants are selling their produce, some of which our hero has heard about, but none of which he has ever sampled. All these tempting aromas—monadcar, egmtnu, smineja. Spaito buys a small container of steamed and candied rootreging with his credits for ⚇ to chew on. Spicy, pungent, sweet and sour. And now gone. Never, has he eaten anything so delicious. But there is so much more to savor and to tempt the palate. Together, ⚇ and Spaito sniff the urtmeric powder while dipping crackers into the gonam saals.

These tastes, these smells—compounded by touch and visual stimuli—are salaciously inflamed by this theatrical setting. For life on the streets of Malosh brims with laughter, speech, and song.

Our hero is beginning to appreciate the sensuality of food. "How," he wonders, can drugs offered by the 🜚 compare with this? Yes, I realize they're created to stimulate the neural pleasure centers. Yes, they succeed in entrapping Gamers in the ▨, causing them to forfeit their shares and potentially their lives. And how could THAT compare with THIS?

Spaito and 🜛 habbernash at a food stall situated within the heart of the ancient compound of Malosh. Sitting at a bar with their elbows resting on a counter, they sample a local brew fermented delectably with altm and spoh. All around them the citizens pursue their daily activities: talking, walking, and shopping. 🜛 had heard about such metropolises in days of yore. Never, until now, did he imagine there might be one represented in full-spectrum vitality. Such a city, he always thought, existed only in dreams. And yet nothing he had envisioned on the streets or in Virt-World ever approached this phantasmagorical majesty of Malosh.

He looks around. There are the citizenry: drinking, eating, and chatting, laughing, exhibiting the joyous give and take referred to in Vid Scan as "friendship." Such moments, he surmises, provide momentary respites from the desperate struggle to survive.

🜛 savors it, trying to will the moment into perpetual Slow-Time. He is forced to acknowledge that these pleasures can't last. Never before, except with Emoja and perhaps momentarily with Rainy-7, had 🜛 been consciously aware while in the midst of pleasure that the experience might end. He hastens to stall the passage of time—to no avail. With anticipation of the end of pleasure comes dread. Try as he might to invoke Slow-Time, he can visualize the present marching steadfastly into the future. He shakes his head and willfully invokes DENIAL. He will pretend this moment expands indefinitely even while his conscious self acknowledges a substantively different reality.

We watch as Spaito and 🜛 lean into one another. Casually interacting at the counter. Their banter, thoroughly pleasant, seemingly so ordinary, will be a memory of ❖'s that will be distilled and refracted and evoked throughout the remainder of his life. But in the NOW, he thinks, "This must be what the Ancients, referenced in Vid Scan, referred to as 'life'. How it might be lived in full Spectracolor with complete sensory engagement. I hadn't known what that meant before. NOW, I'm beginning to understand. These varying perspectives—past, present, future—give so much more meaning and purpose to existence. Delicious, wonderful, but ephemeral. That's the painful realization that comes with living a conscious life. The continuum of time is seemingly infinite in contrast to the truncated dimension of our finite lives. So much to do, so much at risk, and destined to end all too soon. Must get on with it. Live in the present with the acute awareness of both past and future."

Their meal is paid for with more credits from Spaito's account. It will cost him dear.

Eating—even in the Virt—is costly. But in Malosh, despite the existential threat this city faces, the Citizens retain a sense of community: They have families. They eat and commune with one another.

"How extraordinary!" thinks ❖. "What riches they possess!"

Spaito and ❖ walk through the arcade on pavement carved from chiseled stone. Knobby, rough, uneven. Never has life been so vibrant for ❖. He's intoxicated by possibilities. The sights, the sounds, the textures, the night, the air, the companionship. *It must be the drink. How else to explain this heady sensation?*

"There's something I want to show you," says Spaito.

They enter a stone building. Inside, the stained glass windows blaze with light and color. Pews all around. At the front of the sanctuary is a raised platform where tables are draped in cloth. They approach. Spaito pulls away the material so that they may peer through the protective casements. Bound books, some open to pages, enabling ❖ to read words printed on parchment-paper. He wants to touch. To turn pages. To sniff the binding. To have his fingers press against ink. It must be illegal.

"Want to hold one?"

"More than anything I've ever wanted in my life," he gasps.

Spaito opens one of the casements. He pulls out one cobalt-blue volume and hands it to 🐦. The cover, though battered, has a complex dusty aroma suggestive of the book's journey through time and place, read by so many before being passed to others along the way. Within the pages lie a treasure-trove of wisdom proffered to future generations. The parchment-paper is brittle. 🐦 must be careful. He reads. He turns pages. The letters float as the words dance across the printed page. Alive with story, with meaning. He touches. He sniffs. He inhales. It's intoxicating, exhilarating, and humbling. Our hero must have stood there for what to nonreaders would have seemed an eternity—but to him was but a fleeting moment—occasionally turning the parchment-paper pages, a feast of words.

"It's the history of Malosh," says Spaito, after the book has been put back into its case. "We have preserved the histories of all the five continents. You can discover how Oturi was born, matured, and is now dying."

"How can you bear it? Knowing what came before and, in all probability, what lies ahead?" He doesn't say, "Another N-Deluge, this one the Big One." He doesn't have to. Spaito's eyes acknowledge his thoughts before replying softly, "We haven't given up. Our sense of history makes us want to fight to preserve all that is important."

"Resistance won't protect you. It will simply wear you down. The enemy knows only hate and deprivation. They envy your material riches. They'll possess Malosh or die trying. They've nothing to lose. Nothing to fear. Death, for them, is a release from the misery they call life."

"Nevertheless," replies Spaito, "we shall persevere. Ultimately, we have the upper hand. They live in the NOW. While living in the moment offers for some a temporary solace, it always loses to those who have the ability to anticipate the future and act accordingly."

"Not this time."

"We'll fight to the bitter end. Every one of us."

"And then?"

"If we must perish, if it comes to that, then, the others will also die. The world, as we know it, will cease to exist."

"But so many will suffer."

"Suffer? Do you believe they feel and think and experience life as we do? They're Zbies, spectral bodies, the walking dead. They have no ability to sustain life, let alone a meaningful culture."

"But all those lives terminated. You feel no sorrow, no sense of loss?"

"Their departure represents only a blip in the moment of the NOW. It has no larger ramification because their lives and their culture have no lasting significance."

"Spoken as I might have done in my prior life," says 🜚. "But why aren't you out there?" he adds, gesturing to the cosmos.

"Because it is here that I must be."

"May I have an electronic replica of your historical books?"

"In time, you shall have that if that's what you require."

"Spaito, I'm not an Illuminati."

"I know who you are."

"I'm not your enemy. I want your people and your Malosh to survive."

"We know who you are and your purpose here."

"Are these books some of the treasures of the Rajakians?"

"A tiny sample."

"Take me to the Rajakian Archives? Are you a Rajakian?"

"In time, when you are ready, if events permit, you will see the Archives."

"It is crucial that I see them. I must read them. I must absorb them. Let me be the transmitter of your culture. "

"To be Oturian is to want many things. We perceive that we need so much more. But it is only when we have mastered the foundational wellsprings of knowledge that the Archives will impart wisdom. You must acquire patience."

"There's no time for patience."

"Patience is the first of many stepping stones on the path to knowledge. Follow this trail and you will comprehend. With comprehension will come a state of being that permits you to discover, interpret, and preserve what needs to be salvaged from the Archives."

They returned to the compound. That night 🜚 dreams of a vast storehouse of archives containing a treasure trove of documents, each a multi-faceted jewel in the knowledge-fountain that forms the basis of Oturian civilization.

Unbeknownst to 🜚, he has subconsciously begun to internalize the underlying postulation of ChandraX, which was presented in the opening epigraph of this narrative, which for the convenience of readers, we shall restate herein.

> *Just as a dying neutron star can contract no further than its Schwarzschild Radius without collapsing under extreme gravitational force into a black hole that devours everything around it, so too those civilizations whose capacity for conscious thought diminishes sufficiently will implode under the crushing burden of their own primitive minds.*
>
> ChandraX

GK distills this cosmic truth as a maxim expressed as follows: Oturians are destined for obliteration. This apocalyptic outcome is unalterable. Consequently, there's no point in pursuing vengeance since the civilization is doomed. My purpose must be to collect and to preserve knowledge necessary to perpetuate the next Oturian civilization as it will be manifest in the cosmos. Only in fulfilling this mission will I be saved from a fate analogous to stars that venture too close to the Schwarzschild Radius.

23

The seemingly infinite nature of the cosmos deludes Oturians into thinking that their time on their planet is enough. Enough to understand all that needs to be known, to fix all that needs to be fixed, to do all that needs to be done. Time on Oturi is finite. Heed this warning.
ChandraX

Emoja has been making significant progress. She is now reproductively modified to breed and bear offspring. Her exoskeleton has been refurbished with the most durable and latest upgrades of plasidium chromate. Her endoskelton now includes technological advances in Virtual Memory and File Structure. Data critical to her mission has been permanently archived in her Firmware while computational boosters have been established in the Registers and Core Memory of her machine cognition sector with, of course, the necessary linkages to the Cereumla, Sequencing, and Clustering centers of her Oturian processing center. Emoja's Subcam has been fortified sufficiently with numerical and neural pathways to facilitate connections between Functional and Foundational Memories that will enable her to restore, if necessary, her entire memory archives.

Nevertheless, there are several avenues of research still wanting. She has not been able to replicate the thought processes of the Artun85s. Consequently, she can only estimate probable routes they may have taken in their galactic travels based on the mission plans. Naturally, she is proceeding under the assumption that the Artun85s are fully operative and proceeding accordingly.

Emoja has refused to consider the means by which she might intervene to alter the destiny of Oturi. She is, after all, no deity. Better to put her efforts to use where she might possibly effect change. She wonders, however, if a few of the scientists could be persuaded to travel to the event horizon of Cygnus X-1. However, she realizes that Leon is strenuously opposed to any scenario that would dilute resources from the Emoja Project. As it is, he has made major alterations in his budget to accommodate changes in the mission plan. Recently, three space probes, fortified to withstand significant exposure to Gamma Rays, had been sent to the perimeter of Cygnus X-1 in order to update the Emojas on the progress made and provide data and readings from the Artun85s and their mission plan that may have been lost, garbled, or possibly even taken by the robots when they left. The unstated assumption was that updates were needed in case there are difficulties associated with Emoja Excel 96's ability to return. It's a risk that neither scientist nor borg wishes to discuss.

Increasingly, Emoja thinks about Vargus and the Strangelets. She hums the celestial **"Song for the Journey."**

Twisted Pair
Uncoupling now
In search of memory.

Time's eye regress
To Continents Lost
And Oturi lives erased.

> Dance, then, those fateful steps
> Near nested globes so perfect
> For there 'twas sung "Song for the Journey."

The words and the imagery associated with the tune are saturated with memories. "**Song for the Journey**" has become the melodic backdrop that sustains her throughout her days. Frequently, she visualizes the dance of the Emojas that harken back to the ancient tribal rituals once performed by the Stranglets on Vargus. She imagines herself back on Vargus with them. It's what she dreams of. And she tries never to worry about GK. There is nothing she can do for him at present. But this realization only increases her desire to return to Vargus. NOW. While its possible. Before events preempt this opportunity. She's become convinced that she won't be able to fulfill her mission without making this journey to Vargus. It is decided, then. Time to go. But first, she must tell Leon.

He's in his office. Deeply engrossed in numbers and irritated at having been disturbed. Still, he points to a chair and moves his around from behind the desk. He always makes time for her, no matter what. The kindness, the consideration, always softens her resolve, brings out the emotional Oturian within, rather than her steely cyborg disposition.

"Leon, I've decided. I must visit Vargus now."

"That's not possible," he responds in thought. "It's too dangerous. You haven't the time. A visit will change nothing. You can't repair your homeland. You can't even save a single life. The images will have you shuddering in horror the rest of your life. And, if our plans go accordingly, that shall be a very long life."

"Leon, I must go."

Leon wants to forbid her. He tries to form the thought sentence. "I forb…I for…." before reason intervenes. Emoja is capable of mind-scanning my thoughts. She knows I'm not capable of ordering her. Never was much good at that. Besides, she's no longer an adolescent. Couldn't prevent her even if I tried. Enough of this. Don't want her to know the extent of my feelings. What good could it possibly do?

"Don't go," he says in thought. "It's too risky, too dangerous."

"Yes, I know what you feel."

"You will gain nothing."

"I will gain everything."

Vestiges of his anger surfaces once more, "I forb . . . I for . . . ." But again, Leon is unable to finish the sentence. He's frustrated. Powerless. Imagine an Oturian of Leon's stature, used to giving orders and now incapable of protecting all that is most dear to him, above all Emoja and the Emoja Project. He tries another approach.

"You mean the Virt. You want to visit Vargus in the Virt."

"No, I intend to visit Vargus in the Real."

"It's too dangerous."

"I must."

"You might not return."

"I shall."

Leon has turned his body at an angle slightly away from her. So vexed, so concerned.

"When?"

"Tomorrow."

He shakes his head, but replies in thought, "I will make the necessary arrangements."

It's one of the hardest things he has ever agreed to do.

"No one," he thinks to himself, intentionally puts one's daughter, one's creation, in harm's way. It's a violation of the natural order of things. So disturbing, so risky, and so unnecessary.

"Emoja is woefully misguided to think this journey will enlighten her," he says to himself. It will only bring her unbearable pain. I've been to Vargus. The experience was so excruciating that I suppressed most of those memories. Emoja was so young when I rescued her. She doesn't remember. Not really. And today is so much worse than it was then. So many dead, so many dying, so many diseased and starving. Who could possibly remain fully Oturian after witnessing all that? Yet what can I do? Nothing, except allow Emoja to make this perilous journey."

24

The evidentiary trail is littered with clues. Follow that causal chain from beginning to end, and you will obtain the information that you seek.

ChandraX

Each day, ✦ works his shift. Each day, he discovers more evidence gathered by intel regarding the Insurgents. It has now been ascertained where the four terrorists made entry. The movements of two of the Insurgents have been mapped, and the authorities are closing in. Intel has less info on the third, but sporadic readings are enabling the agency to construct a predictive model. How much longer, ✦ wonders, before they have captured all three, and they divulge my identity? Every moment is a countdown to my discovery and subsequent execution. **Danger! Danger! Danger!** I see those red-hued warnings.

And yet, each night he spends with Spaito. He's not even sure whether to trust Spaito. Perhaps, he will turn ✦ in. Nevertheless, our protagonist feels compelled to be with Spaito. Never has ✦ experienced male companionship like this. Spaito has perspective, an overarching view of what was, what is, what might be. And, it seems, Spaito lives his life according to a highly developed moral code of conduct.

Is ✦ attracted to Spaito out of a desire to know more, be more, do more? Is our ✦ developing an ethical framework? Is he gaining wisdom? Or does ✦ find Spaito's outlook useful simply as a means of maneuvering beyond the temporal grid? Can the cosmos be righteousness? ✦ thinks not. Why, then, he asks, "Am I increasingly concerned with issues relating to moral causality?"

✦ knows that he must leave Malosh soon. Intel will soon discover his identity. He's at risk if he remains much longer. He acknowledges the irony of his current position here at the Center. After all, his job is to identify and capture the Insurgents. Others are watching his screen, his actions. They will be able to tell if he constructs a web of erroneous data. Consequently, he limits his investigation to the other three insurgents. Still, he realizes that if they're caught, his cover will almost certainly be blown. Even so, here he remains, tracking them down, hour after hour, day after day.

✦ tells himself that his experience here in Malosh will assist him in living among the Enhanced. But his justification belies his real motivations. ✦ has grown to love Malosh. Night after night, he walks the City with Spaito. He loves the shopkeepers, the commerce, the social interactions. Along the way, he searches for anything that might help him locate the Rajakian Archives. Every religious site, every building that might potentially house the Archives is subject to scrutiny.

✦ has examined more of the bound volumes. Spaito has lent him one on the history of Malosh. He reads it every night before falling asleep. In the morning, cobalt flecks occasionally coat his fingers. He loves the smell of print and residue of blue, though he worries about the damage he may be doing to the book. Words permeate his dreams. Dreams that had always been explosively rendered in blazing Spectracolor now scroll black and white text. Although not at first. For each illuminated manuscript enters his dreams cloaked in vibrant hues and tastes and smells and sights and sounds before distilling down to words and the press of fingers against the pages. Watch those letters dance! A majestic world that interacts with imagination. Read and discover. And so he does.

Tonight's dream is revelatory. Spaito takes him to a special room filled with books. Thousands of volumes. Also repositories available in electronic form with Vid Scan playback. ▶ downloads some and reads so many more. He tries to compress all this information into his neural pathways from Subcam to Core: Permanence is what he seeks. Are these the Rajakian Archives? ▶ is so grateful that he turns to thank Spaito, but his companion has left. No matter, there are the books. So many books, enough to last a lifetime.

"Insurgent 382, you are under arrest. You are charged with violation 43-811212 of the Espionage Code. Stand up, traitor!"

They're shaking him. Pulling him from bed to floor. Bangs his head. It hurts. From paradise to purgatory with the rupture of a single dream. Could life in the Desolation of the Real possibly be as perverse as this? Life, as experienced in the Virt, has become a perilous nightmare.

Insurgents 97, 141, and 224 fingered ▶ as Insurgent 382. In less than an hour, they divulged his cover. So much for solidarity. When he is paraded by, his former confreres spit. They hiss. They howl for him to die. "Insurgent 382," they shout, "had it easy. He lived among the privileged in Malosh. He adapted with ease. We saw him walking the streets at night. Eating, drinking, living the high life. No brother lives like that. Only traitors do."

And where is Spaito, comrade to ▶? Nowhere to be found.

Malosh's Military Counsel of War Tribunal (MCWT), which adjudicates cases of espionage, is scheduled to begin. A panel of seven highly ranked military personnel are charged with adjudicating the law. The trial is to be broadcast live throughout Virt-World. The outcome, say the whisperers and chatterers in Virt-World, will vindicate the Illuminati and, conversely, vilify the Umbrascenti.

Readers of this expansive tale, why bore you with the legal *mumbo jum-*

bo? Certainly, the rule of law should dictate the nature and outcome of the trial. But recently popular sentiments favoring harsh punishments have increasingly shaped interpretations even of the military legal code.

What is important for you, the reader, to understand is that the proceedings are broadcast live so that the citizenry of Malosh might learn the verdict and witness the execution. The outcome, of course, will also be watched by the Umbrascenti subterranean dwellers who reside in what is referred to as the NoZone beyond the dome.

Throughout the trail, the citizenry of Malosh influence the outcome by voting their interpretations of law by means of a series of electronic pulses transmitted via their digital devices. Thus, potentially every statement by every witness and every evidentiary ruling has the potential to be swayed by means of an electronic plebiscite. Should the viewers become dissatisfied with the direction of the trial, they pulse their opposition. Pleasure and displeasure are tallied throughout the proceedings. This claim, that, the other, what should be overlooked, what should not—all these variables that are shapped and molded by popular opinion distilled through the distorted lens of media coverage are presented as a manifestatilon of the popular will. They are then weighed in with respect to—and sometimes contrary to—the legal military code.

The MCWT Vidcast streams the entire proceedings, as well as continuous IM sub-text that scrawls along the bottom of the screen. Proponents of the broadcast and what is referred to as the "IM pulse" suggest that this public disclosure is consistent with democratic principles. And that while popular sentiment, although it might sometimes appear chaotic and, occasionally, counter to military code, nevertheless, provides the best means of preserving the democratic state. That's the assertion.

Only one or two caustic pundits dare suggest that democracy, as realized through Virt-World and Vidcast are paramount to mob rule. That the IM response represents the connivance by government and broadcasting authorities so to appear democratic while deliberately manipulating popular sentiment. Many critics trained in jurisprudence contend that electronic tampering of viewer response is so prevalent that "IM justice" is nothing more and nothing less than outright subterfuge by the government of the MCWT proceedings to serve the interests of intel.

Dear Reader, it is enough for you to know that the verdict is unanimously "Guilty," "Guilty," "Guilty," and "Guilty" as per the judgment of the MCWT and the IM tallies. The sentencing, as stipulated by law and in accordance with popular sentiment, is "Death by means of radioactive detonation in the NoZone." The execution is to be streamed live in Virt-World. Given the public's ghoulish attraction to the macabre, the sentence is scheduled for optimal prime-time. Throughout the Virt-World, everybody watches. Everyone except, of course, the LCDs, who are totally off-the-grid, most members of the Resistance who reject almost everything sanctioned by authorities, and the Enhanced who are expressly prohibited from viewing content on the Virt. Those watching are encouraged to provide IM feedback. Is it any surprise that this program, known as "Righteous Justice," receives the highest viewership in the history of Virt-World broadcasting?

Dear Reader, the four Insurgents are taken by mechanized vehicle to a desolate region of the NoZone where they are to be killed by means of a radioactive bomb. The countdown begins. Immediately prior to detonation, Insurgent 382 dematerializes. Insurgents 97, 141, and 224 are incinerated. Virt-World watches as a radioactive plume rises from the glass sands of the desert and the three bodies melt away. Authorities insist that Insurgent 382 was ☢.

Doubters say otherwise. They contend that Insurgent 382 was the ultimate escape artist. Despite the vanishing of Insurgent 382 or, perhaps, because of his disappearance, the broadcast tops the charts.

"Democracy Rules! Three Insurgent Die! One is ☢!" scream the Virt-World headlines.

Dear Reader, it is a foregone conclusion that executions always draw a huge audience.

But what of our protagonist, Insurgent 382, a.k.a. 🐇, better known to us as GK?

25

The core of Oturi is iron subject to extreme pressure that causes it to retain its solidity. Its outer core is molten, iron mixed with sulphur. Vargus, the planet's interior continent, is draped between the molten outer and solid inner core. Tunnels forged through nitegran enable this continent to resist the forces of gravity and heat. The inhabitants are Vargusians. Stripped of their prospects, their dignity, their purpose, their existence is precarious. Yet for those Oturians who are tempted to celebrate their relative prosperity as measured against the sufferings of others: Beware. The fate of the most privileged is inexorably linked to those most destitute.

ChandraX

Emoja is transported to Vargus with its network of tunnels, the largest of which have horizons that give the appearance of a blood-red sky with a heat so intense and a light so prevalent that shields have been constructed to provide protection against the soaring "daytime" temperatures, which although intense are of relatively short duration. The source of heat and light comes from the molten outer core, which expands and contracts, giving the appearance of night and day, a perspective shared by Vargusians. Neither the scientists nor the Resistance nor the Insurrectionists nor anyone else has found a means of extracting energy from this outer core, therein lies the good fortune—or the great tragedy—of Vargus.

Emoja is standing just outside Tunnel Jw⁹T, one of the largest. Though she has been designed to withstand temperatures and radiation $10^{100,000}$ worse than Vargus, nevertheless, Emoja is uncomfortable here. If she remains too long outside the tunnels, it seems as if she's melting away. Her distress is less physical than psychological, triggered by the reactivation of suppressed memories stemming from when she was a Stranglet struggling to survive. There are the involuntary flashbacks, the recollection of nightmares, the surge of drenaeline and aggression that come with a heightened sense of danger.

Jw⁹T, as with all the larger tunnels, is a desolate and desecrated landscape. Its carbuncled wasteland has been distilled to a burnt sard-rust. The effects of radiant heat are on display. The cochineal residue is everywhere. Carcasses—charred crisps—are gnawed away by starving Vargusians.

Outside the tunnels are a few battered buildings left for rubble that eminate a seething, vermilion heat. The soil—rsimu, a sienna-rust hue, is illuminated by a crimson glow, causing it to appear zircon red. The earthly scent, dirt infused with cochineal residue mixed with Vargusian remains picked dry, is best described as the stench of death.

The day shields are closing, the heat is abating, and with these changes comes the illusion of sunset. Life stirs from the network of small, clustering tunnels that feed Jw⁹T. To Emoja's left, a band of ragged Stranglets, always female, always abandoned, always at risk. Furtive, darting here and there. Emoja might be their target, except for her metallic skin, which heralds her machine-driven Otherness. To her right stand a few adult Vargusians flanked by one young male offspring. Those young, male Vargusians are prized, protected, and usually hidden from view. It is the Stranglets who are most at risk. In these predatory environs, they serve as coinage, bought and sold, killed or delegated for the most perilous tasks.

It is a wonder that any survive to adulthood.

Because this is the time of day when the Vargusian scavengers arise from the network of tunnels below and the battered buildings above to forage and hunt for prey. Emoja moves to the shadows, hoping to observe unobtrusively. So troubling to see this domain that was once her birthplace. Though never really home, nevertheless, she acknowledges it as her place of origin.

One of the old ones, scarcely middle-aged by planetary estimates, lies dead, not far from the entrance of Tunnel Jw⁹T. Her skin has already been stripped away. Her flesh is charred through. The Vargusians claw and gnaw her remains. What they discard will be eaten by the Stranglets. And the rest of the carcass? Before the close of night, it will be devoured by the few vermin that inhabit this desecrated rubble of a once vital city known as Obirnai. Commerce doesn't exist here. There is barter, there is theft, there is vengeance. Vegetation that might serve as food is scarce, confined to underground compounds where it is nourished by chemical nutrients, water capsules, and low-wattage grow-lights. Even if plants could grow on the surface, they would never reach maturity because of the climate, the dearth of water, and the tendency of inhabitants to consume all edible remains that survive this ravaged continent.

The Stranglets approach Emoja. They appear to recognize her as exotic, but related kin. Bustling close, they touch her metallic skin; they sniff the air, trying to ascertain her smell. They study the shape of her rounded face, her set-back eyes, the definition of her jaw, the length of her stride, her wiry build, and, most of all, her bright fuchsine hair that is the birthright of every Stranglet. She is one of them, and she has survived to adulthood, neither owned nor controlled by another Vargusian. How odd, how special. She must be their priestess, they think. Her words, surely, they surmise, will inspire wisdom.

"Should we know you?" they sing-chat as a chorus. They gather round, fingers pressing her metallic skin.

"My name is Emoja. Once, I was a Stranglet. And now, I am a cyborg, part Oturian, part robot."

"No longer a Strangelet?"

Emoja mutters to herself, "All their words are sing-song. I, too, once spoke that way. How odd that I should have forgotten this." She replies in voice, for only the eldest are conversant in think-speak, "No, I am grown now. I lived on Artun before journeying the cosmos." She watches as they sing.

> Emoja danced free.
> She escaped.
> We wish to soar into
> the heavenly skies
> like Emoja.

They prance around her, leaping and pirouetting into air, defying gravity. Their movements, their singing, their tonal harmonies, so akin to "Song for the Journey." And how does Emoja feel?

> *She longs to weep.*
> *She shall.*
> *She can't.*

Emoja's joy. Emoja's sorrow. The Strangelets, our heroine resolves, will not witness her pain, a dolorous ache borne from the knowledge that she cannot rescue them. Instead, she is effusive, warm, demonstrative, showing her delight in reuniting with her kin.

The urge to protect is one of our most basic instincts. Dear Reader, it is only natural that Emoja should feel this desire and be sorely tempted to act. But intervention would be catastrophic to her mission. Leon knew that. That's why he objected to her returning to Vargus. The gravest challenge to our heroine comes with the realization that circumstances will continue to unfold and that there is nothing she can do to avert destiny. The Strangelets will not survive. Although Emoja may have told herself prior to coming here that she would be prepared for this outcome, now she realizes just how naive she had been. There she stands surrounded by singing and dancing Stranglets. We watch as our heroine is immersed in qualia—anger, fear, remorse—those emotions that compel her to right grievous wrongs. And yet, Emoja acknowledges that she must sublimate these feelings. She must draw hope and inspiration from this experience in order to assist her in her mission. Otherwise, her purpose in coming would be for naught.

The Stranglets sing-chant suggests that it won't be long now before the day shields open and sky radiates heat and light. She guards them as they feast on the remains of the tough, dried flesh of the female Vargusian. Emoja is defiant. No one will harm these Stranglets while she is here. With the heat blazing, they escort her to their place in the labyrinth of the tunnels that serve as their metropolis, a location known as SLdom. Emoja is tired. The Stranglets lead her to a place, so soft. They insist she lies down. She does and, once asleep, the nightmares begin. How could it be otherwise? For our heroine is possessed with wisdom and sagacity, but ultimately powerless to prevent the tragic devastation wrought by mathematical probabilities that verge on certainty.

26

Despair not. Within the matrix there is a vast array of possibilities, Optimal selections maximize opportunity.

ChandraX

One moment 🧑 is tied to a stake. His former cohorts hissing their disdain.

"You shall die."

"We are all about to die," he replies.

"But yours shall be a thousand deaths experienced in a thousand elzharas."

"Without reprieve."

"And for all eternity."

Their insults, slingshots of hate, deflect thoughts of their own imminent demise.

Just moments to go before detonation. How to escape? 🧑 scans his Core Memory, searching for clues. He reviews the downloads provided by Emoja and the electronic copies of books from the Illuminati he obtained in Catalla. So many paging prompts to scroll through. All that mathematical code devoted to weaponry. Searching. Searching. He reviews the information he had access to while working for IMC. He considers the cobalt-bound volumes housed in the dark stone building he visited with Spaito. Books that became the subject of his dreams. He wonders if that rarified state— ▮ —celebrated by the ▮ in Zhinboya might have some equivalent—call it his Divine Mem—that might bodily transport him from the outskirts of the NoZone into the Oasis of the Real.

With only nanoqs remaining, he thinks of ChandraX, mistress of the cosmos, Magisterial Lady of his Universe, all knowing, all seeing. A force—the Force. The magisterial Illuminator with potentially omnipotent powers who has outperformed the ▮. Would that she could help him now.

Poof!

Sources at IMC could only speculate about how ▮ made his escape. The mathematics just didn't compute. Simulations suggested that a tremendous energy field encased ▮ immediately prior to detonation. This energy field was so powerful that he was illuminated in **red** with magenta highlights before vanishing from the glass parking lot of the NoZone.

There have been those who claim that Spaito was responsible for ▮'s escape. That Spaito, who also became one of the ▮, might actually be an Agent Provocateur or a ▮.

But I ask you, is it really the responsibility of the narrator to provide all the answers? Shouldn't you, Dear Reader, be capable of cracking the "code?" Given your laws of relativity, your mathematics of spacetime, your physics governing Heisenberg's Uncertainty Principle, your principles underlying Quantum Theory, must there be absolute determinism in our chronological narrative? After all, isn't ontological knowledge a relative proposition subject to a certain amount of indeterminate conjecture? If it weren't, what would be the point of life's adventure?

Although it must be said, that our GK, now shed of his ▮ persona, seems to prefer a little more concrete determinacy. He's landed in a place that is clean, modern, spacious, and beautiful. Could this be the Oasis of the Real?

"F<>#."

"F<>#."

"F<>#."

GK looks around. He picks himself up. He dusts himself off. This is certainly no Desolation of the Real. The ground below his feet is GREEN. Lots of green interspaced with brown stems topped by mops of twiggy green. Trees? Is that what the Ancients called them? This vast expansion of land exudes a beauty, a serenity that manifests a template for privilege that prompts GK to assume that he has actually entered the Oasis of the Real.

As a reflex he coughs. Dusts himself off. To no avail. Feels dirty, a sensation he's never experienced before. And that light, that bright, yellow-white light signifying "Sun" prevents him from fully observing his surroundings. What he needs are shades. Shades to filter the light.

Squinting up at the sky, he's forced to acknowledge that this Oasis appears to be pulsing with promise. Above, are members of the Enhanced skimming through air on their PTVs. He watches as they drop vertically down or dart diagonally across the sky. Those flying silhouettes so fast, so sleek, so beautiful. Their movements so graceful in contrast to his clumsy efforts with that old PTV he maneuvered in the septic passageways of the Resistance.

"Here, in the Oasis of the Real," he mutters, "the Enhanced probably use transport chambers to enable groups of passengers to reach their destinations. I bet everyone has his or her own PTV. In the Desolation of the Real, only the Waja are legally permitted to operate vehicles, those nearly impenetrable AmphibiRovers. On our best days in AL, assuming there's sufficient sun to provide solar power, our only transport is a single streetcar going nowhere."

To his North, at a distance of 10.2 zins, GK notices an urban cluster of buildings radiantly aglow and accented by luxurious greenery. "Imagine," he thinks to himself, "identifying anything clearly at that range in the Desolation of the Real! There, you'd be lucky to see objects only at a distance of .001 zin. What's that clump of buildings ahead?. A campus? Isn't that how Emoja described the Institute? Is she there?

"No way I'm connecting with Emoja yet! Got to infiltrate the Waja Compound and complete my mission. Meeting her now is too risky. I might be captured. She might be compromised in her mission. Best for her not to know my whereabouts. Mustn't put her at risk.

"Enough already. How does a dude locate the Waja headquarters when he's clueless about the grid in the Oasis of the Real?"

So many thoughts streaming through. GK realizes that he's angry with Rainy-7 and the Resistance. "Why," he muttered, "couldn't they have prepared me? How can I fulfill their f<>#ing mission without resources and advance visualization and map downloads? The Resistance," he hisses, "is filled with mooks who haven't a clue. All playing the role of revolutionaries and combat warriors. But where does that leave me? I'm the one with the bulls-eye! Been through this scenario endlessly in the Virt. The outcome—always the same: ☣, a.k.a. death. Enough of all that. Because in the Real fatality is forever. No sim replays, no new identities leading to yet another round of gaming. One mistake now and I'm all pegged out!

"But hey, in the now," he acknowledges, "this Oasis is tantalizing. Need some downtime. Gotta pinch some shades, take a little shuteye, enjoy the blazing sun, poach a PTV, and get me some f<>#."

And so GK heads in search of hedonistic pleasures.

The attainment of rapturous exaltation is never easy or long lived. Here in the Oasis of the Real, GK has his challenges. For starters, nobody walks. That's far too taxing and might produce sweat, an undesirable perspiration known as "stink" generally regarded as emanating only from LCDs and N/Ts. Why bother to exert oneself in order to overcome the forces of gravity. So plebeian. So lame. Far better to use the electronic assist devices close at hand. So there's GK walking there along that beautiful expanse of green with nary a soul in sight.

"I'll be treading this footpath forever," he mutters. "The Enhanced are in skyscrapers or campus cluster-centers or flitting around in their spiffy PTVs. I'd never experience this in the Desolation of the Real," he snarls. He walks and walks and walks.

"Whoa, wassup?"

At a distance of .19 zins, positioned west, northwest relative to GK, are two members of the Enhanced. They are standing upright, engaged in conversation. Their PTVs have been laid down on a grass knoll nearby. The couple, for that's what they appear to be, are tall and strikingly beautiful, the perfect specimens of their tribe. They are dressed in elegant full-length, ivory-colored belted tunics that accentuate their aristocratic elegance while, nonetheless, desexualizing them. Their appearance suggests a life of leisure: One never struggles; one doesn't toil; one needn't hurry. For the Enhanced, it would seem, life's dangers and risks have all been nearly eradicated.

GK is filled with rage just looking at them. "Why," he wants to know, "is their life so perfect? What gives them that right? Why shouldn't the N/Ts and LCDs have the same privileges?" With effort, he suppresses his fury. And with this restraint comes surprise. "Wow! I don't have to act on my feelings. I can think about the consequence of my actions and will a different alternative. Would my life have been different if I had been able to achieve this self-control in the past? Am I becoming someone else?" Perish the thought!" he mutters with a swatch of irony drenched in irritation. But then curiosity prevails, compelling him to eavesdrop on this seemingly perfect couple.

"But Trysorwaleis had asked you," the male says.

"Yes," she acknowledges, "Chasallyis might had considered venturing with Trysorwaleis to the Vestibule of the Public Gathering whereof you have spoken. But Chasallyis, on many previous occasions, had found such occasions distressing. There had always been so many Enhanced gathered around, bespeaking this and that. The events had been interminably long and tiresome. Little of consequence had been discussed. So Chasallyis has seen little reason to continue attending."

"But Trysorwaleis," he replies, "bade Chasallyis to attend because he took pleasure in her company. By what other means might Trysorwaleis and Chasallyis properly declare their intentions? Appearance at the Vestibule of the Public Gathering is the public way of demonstrating our intention to unite. How else might we convey to the community our oneness?"

"Could it be," she replies, "that such a public declaration of betrothal so early in the courtship might bode badly for the fortunes of Trysorwaleis and Chasallyis? Would it not be the case that if their partnership is destined to survive that this will be amply demonstrated in due time? Would Trysorwaleis have wished to rush into an entanglement for which there might be profound regrets?"

"Trysorwaleis," he replies, "hath made his decision ages ago. He has been waiting for Chasallyis to acknowledge their partnership in the timelessness of the moment."

"But she had been, has been, and shall be with Trysorwaleis. Chasallyis has made her intentions absolutely clear. She is committed to their union for the duration. Should not this promissory declaration be enough? Trysorwaleis must banish his misgivings because he is cognizant that we are meant to be. In time, our peers will comprehend the depth of our commitment. What need have Trysorwaleis and Chasallyis for a formal announcement at this juncture?"

GK wishes he had some cluster bombs to hurl in their direction. Has anyone ever heard such bile? They talk as if they're not even present. Straightjacketed mummies. Are they even conscious? Why don't they communicate in the vernacular? Their language is so arcane. Fortunately, even High Speak contains only a limited number of inflected tenses, cases, and moods. Otherwise, how could anyone ever make a point? As it is, they're barely able to do so. And for what purpose? Overture/rebuff. Overture/rebuff. Overture/rebuff. Again, again, again. How many times must they persist in this charade? Why doesn't she shout, "Piss off!"? And if this Chasallyis wants to remain single, what's it to Trysorwaleis? F<>♯ her and be done with the bitch. I've seen enough. I'll overcome their stalemate and prevent Chasallyis from hooking up with quite probably the biggest turd in the entire Oasis.

GK dashes over. He lands a one-two punch right on Trysorwaleis's jaw. The clot crumbles to the ground. Out for the count. Our hero couldn't be more pleased.

Chasallyis screams. Softly. Almost a hiccup.

Has that bitch ever roared? he wonders. *O.K., so she's aghast. Appalled. So what! Now, she's taking all those quick breaths. Must feel really threatened.*

"Ruffian, how dare you perpetrate such a heinous action against an innocent such as Trysorwaleis?"

"Trysorwaleis? That lousy f<>♯?"

Chasallyis turns pale. She is gasping for air. "Sir, desist forthwith. You have bespoken a disallowed word. F . . . has been expunged from the lexicon."

"F<>♯? You mean F<>♯? What about f<>♯er? How about f<>♯ing?"

"Ohh . . . ohh . . .ohh . . . . Please, I beseech you. I implore you. I beg you . . . ."

"Not to say f<>♯? Why, down in the Desolation of the Real, we say f<>♯ all the time. What the f<>♯! Had f<>♯! Going to f<>♯." GK's in the F-grove. Never did speaking the forbidden word linger so deliciously on his lips.

"Scoundrel! Having uttered such travesties, you must vacate the premises."

Oblivious to her words, GK disrobes. He's now in the buff.

"Horrid creature," she cries, "I shall not look upon you," she says, covering her eyes. "Depart forthwith!"

GK pays no heed. He strips Trysorwaleis of his clothing and puts them on.

"They fit. Good."

Chasallyis's fingers spread slightly so that her eyes may peer through to see what has transpired. "Brute, how dare you?" Then, she approaches, flaying her hands in the air and then at him. Those soft, feather beats that wouldn't harm a single Oturian.

GK shakes her—gently—before growling, "Trysorwaleis is dross. Be thankful that he's still alive. The scum should be cast out of the Oasis and dropped down to the Desolation of the Real."

"You beast! Lowest of the low. Harm not Trysoraleis."

"If you wish for Trysorwaleis to live, you must take me to your domicile. Oppose me and you both will die. Do as I command and neither of you will be harmed."

Dear Reader, take pity upon Chasallyis. No one has ever threatened her before. This damsel is distressed. Poor scared, frightened Chasallyis. All those emotions that have been banished from the Oasis now serge forth. She has no template to assist her in how to respond. She's forced to act upon her own initiative, something she's rarely done. She walks over to Trysorwaleis. Crouches down to her knees. Takes his pulse, whispering, "Thankfully, Trysorwaleis has not been killed."

"Not yet, assuming you do as I have instructed."

"Barbarian, I shall be of no use to you," she replies.

"Your survival shall depend on heeding my instructions."

Without answering, Chasallyis rises, turns, and walks over to pick up her PTV. GK takes the other. He would like to believe that she has been intimidated by his threats, though he suspects that his use of future tense was more compelling to her than either his words or his actions.

Together, they head to her domicile. It is a unit in a magnificent highrise with cathedral walls of glass. The interior is contemporary and is sparsely furnished. The kitchen has a handful of dishes and some utensils that appear never to have been used. The décor, variations of creamy white, gives GK the sensation that he's floating. Looking around, he notices that there's no Vid Scan or books, either electronic or paper. Only the contrast between the soft hues within the apartment and the glistening world outside—the latter with its azure sky, its blazing sun—manages to keep him from drifting into a state of crippling lassitude. Darkness in the Oasis, when it comes, is brief.

"It seems," GK mutters, "that the Enhanced rarely sleep, they never dream, and they scarcely think."

Two days pass. GK asks Chasallyis, "How do you and other Enhanced spend your days?"

"Whatever do you mean?" she replies.

"What do you do?"

"I live. We live. We sometimes go to the Vestibule of the Public Gathering to see events, hear speakers, and commune with one another."

"But you don't work, you scarcely eat, you barely drink, and you don't exercise. The sense of nothingness forever unfolding, one agonizingly slow moment followed by another, then another, is excruciating. Given a choice, I think I'd prefer the desperate fight for survival that is the lot of LCDs and N/Ts in the Desolation of the Real to this vapid existence."

"You would rather consort with the barbarians?" Ours is, at least, a life of grace."

"Your life is devoid of substance."

Chasallyis say nothing.

"Have you heard from Trysorwaleis? GK continues.

"Yes, but I have not responded."

"Why?"

"Because you are here."

"And?"

"I do not wish harm to come to Trysorwaleis. Besides," she adds nervously, "custom dictates that I am courteous to you until you depart."

"I am not your guest. I have intruded upon you."

"You will depart when it is time."

GK shakes his head. Certainly, Chasallyis is courteous. She's polite. Her responses seem rehearsed, as if she's consulted a rule book for responding to a barbarian. Instead of excitement, he finds her response stultifying. GK hoped for adventure and, perhaps, enlightenment in the Oasis. Instead, he feels as if he's been drugged, a state of torpor that if unchecked threatens to devolve into unconsciousness.

"Perhaps," he reasons to himself, "if I go to the rooftop pool I've seen and if I have a swim, maybe, that will help." He sheds his clothes and heads naked towards the elevator.

"GK," Chasallyis chirps, "do you wish to swim?"

Now she calls me by my name? What is it about my nakedness that she finds so threatening?

"Yes," he replies.

Nervously, Chasallyis continues, "You must not swim without cover."

"Why not? Don't you like my bod?" GK says, rippling and pivoting his pecibs, his bicetps, and kecps before turning round to showcase his teusglu maximus. Displayed in a manner so studly, he surmised, that if she won't swoon, can't she even laugh?

"It has been forbidden to appear naked in public. You will be arrested." She reaches into a closet and hands him a bathing suit.

Must have been worn by Trysorwaleis. So the f<># actually spent time here with her. Maybe, Chasallyis has feelings. With feelings come desire. Submerged within desire is lust. That's my ticket to her emotions. Finally, there's at least the prospect of some skin in this game.

GK attempts his level best. He has never wooed a female before. Poolside, he attempts to arouse Chasallyis by applying lotion on her body. He tries to flatter her. Pushes her into the pool and tantalizingly brushes against her, again and again. To no avail. Later, as she showers, he lathers her body, making flesh-on-flesh contact. She never really resists.

GK realizes that he could have her if he just forced himself upon her. But our primitive Oturian appears to be ascending the spiral ladder of biological consciousness. He wants her. He will possess her, but only when she is a willing partner. Given that most of the Enhanced appear to have abrogated passionate entanglements, GK's decision to seduce Chasallyis represents a tantalizing challenge. Perhaps, he reasons, the scientists, the Penseurs, and the members of the Supreme Consulate, the governing body here in the Oasis, still have primal emotions because they perform vital roles in the society. However, based on his brief observation of T & C, it seems that the rest of the Enhanced have the emotional range of Zbies, so limited appear to be their appetites.

Still, he welcomes the challenge of seducing Chasallyis and wonders what will ignite her passion. Were our GK emotionally perceptive, he would surely realize that he was attracted to her from the moment she began resisting the entreaties of Trysorwaleis. Surely, "not interested" indicates an emotional response on her part. But where is her drive for passion? When GK decides to sleep, he takes her to bed with him. He lies naked and insists that she does as well. He draws her close. He touches her in all the right places. Perhaps not initially with a great deal of grace. After all, where would GK have mastered grace? But over time, say in those twenty-seven days and ever-so-brief nights that he has lived with Chasallyis, his methods have gained subtlety. He is more considerate and thoughtful of her feelings than he was with either Emoja or Rainy-7. But even this newfound patience has limits. Enough is enough. Consequently, on the twenty-ninth day, he tells her. "I want you."

"Yes, I know."

"Do you want me?"

"No."

GK has never encountered such indifference. He touches and holds her close but Chasallyis invariable slides away, insisting that she feels nothing. Her absence of passion makes him pursue her all the more. He is determined to have Chasallyis want him. Still nothing. A week passes. Another. There is our GK at the pool, now wearing his precious shades retrieved from a vestibule cabinet, lounging in the bathing suit he knows was worn by Trysowaleis. A victory of sorts? Perhaps, maybe, but absent mutual passion triumph borders on defeat. This long sexless interlude has become sheer torture for him.

"Don't you feel anything?" he asks as they each lie on deck chairs.

"For you?"

"Yes, for me."

"Should I?"

GK is devastated. Perhaps, our hero would have gained sophistication and a measure of self-consciousness years earlier if he only bothered to pose this question once to any of the countless females he had pursued. It had never occurred to him before. Nevertheless, enlightenment, however rudimentary and slow in coming, is always preferable to perpetual adolescence forever pursuing the insatiable desires of the di.

The days progress, one seemingly identical to the next. Although by now GK confidently navigates his way around the metropolis. Nominally, he might pass, if necessary, as one of the Enhanced. However, he does not have their features or demeanor. But GK has learned the art of appearing to do and want nothing. He now dampens his emotions so that his feelings barely register at all. Nevertheless, his curiosity and desire for Chasallyis persist as does his dedication to his mission.

Naturally, he asks her to tell him about the Waja. Standing by the large glass windows of her apartment, he waits and watches as they occasionally stream by. He observes them patrolling the streets. The Waja are ever-present, though scarcely acknowledged. The Enhanced never consider it important to discuss their presence. Why should they? Given that the Enhanced are for all intents and purposes Zbies, what could possibly ignite their concern? Even their offspring—"the small ones"—appear complacent. The Oasis is the most emotionally docile environment GK has ever seen. Naturally, he hates it. Longs to smash it flat. Better the Virt or the miserable conditions of life in the Desolation of the Real than this prolonged stupor.

An endless procession of days in which being and nothingness converge. Until one afternoon Chasallyis and GK stroll down a boulevard in Obirnai. GK has donned a robe in an attempt to blend in. Despite that—or because of that—his otherness is evident. No one would mistake GK as one of the Enhanced. Still, they stroll, trying to maintain a semblance of normality. They notice a food stall where sageuas and eeseech and drearb and spices and even beverages—fefeoc and niew that stimulate and intoxicate—are sold. GK is surprised to see nourishment other than tablets and wafers and liquid sustenance. They purchase an assortment with a hefty portion of Chasallyis's monthly stipend. GK's not sure why this food stall exists. Maybe for those scientists, the Penseurs, and the Supreme Consulate. Perhaps, they still have appetites.

On the way back to the flat, they encounter Trysorwaleis.

"Chasallyis, you have not responded to my calls."

"I will," she replies, but I have been detained." She averts his gaze. She shifts her feet: Her discomfort is clear.

"We were betrothed," Trysowaleis said.

"That was not meant to be." Chasallyis's words are barely a whisper. If she had wings, she would have taken flight. Their interaction was painful. Not the way the Enhanced are expected to behave.

Meanwhile, GK, the Butcher Lord Suzerain of Destruction, felt the surge of an anger flame, which he quickly suppressed. One glance at Chasallyis and the threat became clear: Would Trysowaleis notify the authorities that she was consorting with an N/T? Others may have surmised the transgression, but did nothing. However, Trysowaleis had motive. Uneasily GK and Chasallyis moved away. Nothing more was said.

One day, then another, and another. Chasallyis, after returning to the apartment, discovers a frying pan. GK turns on a burner—it works!—and prepares a meal similar to one he remembers having had in Malosh. They sit. They chew slowly. An abundance of flavors. They sip their niew. More niew and sageuas and eeseech and drearb. An abundance of more.

And then, just as tantalizingly, GK touches Chasallyis. He whispers to her. Sweet nothings. An inchoate yearning for intimacy borne out of weeks of living together.

"GK, this is good. This meal, your company, this evening—all good."

Our hero is nearly moved to tears. For Chasallyis speaks in present tense. Her diction is simple. There's emotion in her voice. So he leans over to kiss her, lips pressed against hers, though not too much. No, not too much.

Day by day, GK gently, but persistently, courts Chasallyis. More morsels, more seduction in play. Sometimes, Chasallyis prepares the meal. She now dresses for dinner in soft body-hugging clothing that he finds enticing. Tonight, during that short duration they refer to as nightfall, she has prepared a dessert she calls nlaf. There is the soft illumination of candlelight. Chasallyis feeds him spoonful by spoonful. She has learned how to please him—the touch down there, the fingertips pressed gently up there. Desire ignites into passion. Is it any wonder that it's this night he takes her? They're lying on the floor. She's juiced. She wants him: He sees the passion in her eyes. He enters. He feels so much more than before. More than with either Emoja or Rainy-7.

Not exactly sure why. Could it be the wanting, the waiting, the prolonged agony of suppressed desire? Now, the Lianitper instincts prevail. See GK thrusting, so strong and rhythmic? He's grunting. He's pressing, pushing. Again and again. Sweat beads on his forehead. He's ready. Waits as long as he can. For her. Chasallyis emits a small cry. She says she feels something. Perhaps, she tells the truth. He lies beside her spent, feeling more relaxed than he has in ages. Chasallyis, however, says nothing.

GK knows it won't be long before he must leave. With help from Chasallyis, he's discovered maps of the Waja compound. He's familiarized himself with the layout of the facility. He's memorized the names of key personnel and knows strategically, which areas are overseen by robots. His departure is only a matter of days.

In the interlude remaining, GK enters Chasallyis whenever she is receptive. He's passionate. He's considerate, although persistent and willful in his pursuit. He will have her. He will be satiated—at least momentarily. Chasallyis pleasures him. Their nights, although brief, are passionate. The more they make love, the greater his desire. Tonight, he begs Chasallyis to prepare dinner naked. She resists out of fear of reprisal. The authorities might see and send the Waja to intervene.

Dear Reader, look around. There are no curtains. There is no privacy in the Oasis. Passion has been expressly forbidden. If Chasallyis experiences total abandon, she tells him, they will be separated. She willfully suppresses her emotions. She will not be responsible for their separation. GK insists that passion is passion. No one punishes you for that. Chasallyis' response is a wan smile.

That last night. When she sits naked on top of him, facing him, his back pressed hard against a chair. Both in the buff. Both damp. She, wet down there. Moving in and out, in and out. He, harder than hard. Can't wait any longer. Then, he hears her cry, a banshee scream that merges with his roar.

That's when the Wajas break down the door. They spray iumzipher gas and wield their plasidium chromate clubs. Still naked, the lovers are forcibly separated. She resists. She hits. She punches. She kicks. Obscenities, invectives, shouted out of her mouth and his.

"You f<>#!"

"F<>#!"

"F<># off!"

"Article 942, section 8. No fornication without permit. No fraternization with the Neuro-Typicals. No emotions, no screams, no obscenities, no passions. Those are the rules the Enhanced must abide by. Violators must be rehabilitated. You betrayed Trysorwaleis with whom you were betrothed. You are to be remanded into custody and sent for rehabilitation.

Chasallyis behaves as no female among the Enhanced has done in recent memory. It's as if she's regressed twelve generations. She's feral. Primal, fiercely in heat, her scent splayed wide.

Reader, it is important to understand that the sensations we call qualia are entirely lost on the Waja. Their job is to restore order. However, this incident is challenging. Mistakes are made. So much energy is expended subduing Chasallyis that GK manages to break free. Jumps through an open window and down he falls. Down, down, down. Odds are 200 to 1 that he'll be splatterblood, this time forever. And why not. GK had his time in the sun, at the pool, and with Chasallyis.

Fate, however, delivers a more optical outcome, at least as pertains to our narrative. GK lands on one of the AmphibiRovers called in to assist in the arrest of the violators of Article 942, section 8. Two armed Wajas are inside. One leans out, to assess the damage after experiencing the resounding thud of impact. An inauspicious move. GK yanks him from the vehicle and watches him fall, fall, fall. The vehicle serves and dips as the Waja driver attempts to rescue his partner. GK slides from the top of the vehicle into the passenger seat. Now he's trying to wrest control from Waja WJ822.

"I'm no goner!" mutters GK.

The outcome of the struggle is swift and brutal. Our hero opens with a powerful right punch to his opponent's jaw.

"Owwwh!" Plasidium chromate is harder than hard. No damage to the Waja, although GK's skin has drawn blood. In the ensuring struggle, he manages to jam the control panel and, in so doing, successfully aborts the rescue mission for the jettisoned Waja.

The struggle continues. GK attempts to land a swift kick to WJ822's genitals.

"F<>#" Our hero is in pain. Surely he knew the Wajas have no genitals?

The blows come fast and furious. GK is losing the struggle. How could he possibly have expected to win a physical struggle against a Waja? These days, the robots almost always trump Oturians. The WJ822 has jettisoned the passenger door and pushes GK out.

Although no Waja, combat training for GK has its virtues. As he's pitched out of the vehicle, he manages to grab the undercarriage and there, conveniently enough, is a safety handhold just beneath the passenger door. His legs are now wrapped around the insulated undercarriage exhaust manifold. The car pitches and goes into a freefall as WJ822 attempts to loosen GK's hold. A gun flies out of the passenger side of the vehicle. GK grabs it with his right hand. With his teeth, he sets it to maximum firepower. GK's left hand reaches to grip the door frame at the base of the floorboard. He peers in and fires three shots. The only opportunity he'll have to disable his opponent and remain alive. Each bullet successfully strikes its target.

"Gaaaa." The circuits are compromised. WJ822 is deactivated.

Still, the vehicle descends. GK pulls himself into the vehicle. He pulls the deactivated Waja into the passenger seat before sliding over him to seize control of the vehicle, which is wildly out of control.

Spinning, spinning, dropping, dropping....

GK struggles to abort the vertical plunge. "She's leveling. Good. Now, gently, nose her up. Up, up, up, slowing—there she goes. Steady on course. Stabilizing now. Good. Good. Good. Excellent! Who's in control? I'm in control!"

All those Vid games in the Virt, that time flying in outer space, reading those manuals, mastering the consoles, both real and imagined. "Maybe," he reasons, "that's why I won in an altercation with a Waja. Gotta check the flight instructions," he mutters, "the layout of the grid, the coordinates that will bring this bitchin vector back to the Waja compound. Life, ain't it swell!"

GK does exactly that. The Butcher Lord Suzerain of Destruction is back in his groove. "Can't think about Chasallyis," he growls, attempting, not entirely successfully, to suppress his memories of their passionate liaison and its tragic aftermath. Ultimately, however, the primacy of his mission holds sway, negating his brooding undertow of regret.

27

Survival is predicated on redressing the most egregious wrongs in any civilization. Failure to respond to the misery of the shadowlands—and those disposed Oturians who have burrowed into the substrata of the ecosystem—is at your own peril.
ChandraX

It is the sing-song chant of the Strangelets that gradually awakens Emoja.

>Awaken Emoja!
>Travel with us through the tunnels
>See for yourself
>This life
>That is scarcely life at all.

At first, she imagines that she's back at the event horizon. With GK and all the other Emojas. They are dancing and singing. Their mission has been successful. The trajectory of the Artun85s is known, and it will be possible to reestablish contact with them. Although the visit to Oturi was troubling, the planet still survives. But those voices. So youthful. So Vargusian. Emoja gradually realizes that she's been dreaming. It's the

Strangelets who have been dancing and singing. They tug at her to arise to see this place she once called home. How can she possibly say no?

She tries to convince herself that it's not so bad. The tunnels are large and round. In some vehicles on rails pass through. One can stand and walk along passageways and live and breathe and exist in a manner that is not so drastically different than anywhere else. After all, Emoja is not forced to travel through dank darkness, slithering through muck and slime. She does not smell stench. Nor is she caked in excrement. No, at first glance it doesn't appear as bad as all that. There is life. And life here celebrates its small victories. But she can't help noticing that everything is cast in sepia hues. No color, no black and white, just the dirge brown.

"Your hair," Emoja says to the Strangelets, "is brown here. Your skin, so noir up there is just brown down here."

"Our hair now brown, our skin brown, too, like yours, like yours," they chant. She is given a piece of glass that casts her reflection. She is brown, all brown. The Strangelets tell the truth.

"Show me more," she says, and so they do. They ride in one of the brown railcars. She is taken to the greenhouses where brown food is grown. She sees the crowded brown shelters where many sleep.

"We are safer in numbers," they sing.

What Emoja notices is that there is no culture, no learning, no philosophic speculation, no reading, no thinking. Just survival, which consumes every waking moment. Where once she struggled to make a life here, furtively studying in hopes of escaping the misery, that possibility is now gone. There is only song. It's all they have left. It's barely anything at all.

"How come the other Vargusians rarely come here?" she asks.

"They would die; they would die; they would die," they chant.

"Why am I still alive? She asks. I am a Vargusian."

They shake their heads. Shake and shake. "You're one of us," they sing. "Leave as a Strangelet, return as one. So simple, so simple."

"You can't all live this well?"

"No, no, no." And they take her down to the lower levels—down, down, down.

Each level they descend represents a lower stratum of existence. From A to AB on through AJ. At each stage the conditions worsen, the struggle to survive becomes that much more intense, the passageways smaller, the food far more scarce. At the lowest level, the Stranglets are sickly, the waters contaminated, and there is no food. The stench of death is everywhere. Emoja and her companions wear masks. They don goggles. Their hair is tied back and covered. They are suited to protect themselves from contamination. The Stranglets inhabiting the lower levels are feral, riddled with disease. They snarl and hiss. Their teeth, those that are left, are bared. They would flee if only they had the strength. Emoja feels as if she has descended level after level of purgatory, each worse than the last with those residents of AJ living in abject misery, until they are no more. Their cries echo through the passageways. Emoja walks past the injured and the infirm. This is what she was desperate to escape. She would have done anything to leave all this. And now, it's worse.

"Please," she begs, "please, take me up. Away from all this."

The Stranglets nod. They, too, are eager to leave for in all likelihood what they are witnessing now is their future. When they return to level A, Emoja asks, "What can I do?" Never has she felt so powerless, so devoid of hope.

"Tell our story," they sing. "Our story, our story, our story."

"I shall," she says. But privately, she thinks, "What is the use of that? How might that alter their plight? Can they or anyone on this dreadful planet be saved?" And later, although it is blazing daylight above, she dozes in a murky-brown corridor, an offshoot of one of the principal tunnel arteries. Not surprisingly, her dreams, when they finally come, are terrifying. Collectively, they convey a misery that knows no reprieve.

28

Repository of consciousness Where once great ideas held sway In the half-life of the now They lie crumpled, blistered, & shorn
Anonymous verse attributed to the Rajakian Archives

GK hasn't much time before the vehicle he's in arrives as the Waja compound. He must quickly execute his mission directive. He begins the NAD modeling necessary for genetic identity transfer by scanning WJ822's identity card. He uploads the Waja's genetic source code into his body so he can combine their NAD, their innate and learned capabilities, and their memories. Then, he stores those experiences into one comprehensive archive, downloading the recombinatory material—the Waja's NAD and the memories of both robot and Oturian—back into the Waja's Register and Core Memory. Once the process is completed, GK will inhabit the Waja's body. He will look and behave as the Waja did, utilizing the Waja's memories while retaining his own NAD structure and mental capacity. Only after the transfer is complete—and then fully activated and tested—will WJ822 be revivified. Once the Waja is fully functioning again, GK's body will be temporarily flatlined.

Thanks to all the information obtained while working at the Supreme Command of Malosh, GK feels confident he can effectively execute the mission directive so that he may pass as WJ822 while having the scanners identify the corpse as his. Later, he will enable a complete restoration of his former self with the necessary information gleaned from this assignment. This recombinatory merge and subsequent uncoupling will be accomplished by means of phylg coding—and later decoding—within WJ822's endoskeleton. The masking of critical nomesey is essential to ensuring that WJ822 will not be revealed as GK by eye, voice, fingerprint, saliva, blood, and full-body scans.

Finito. The successful exchange and download to WJ822 has taken place. Ahhhhhhhhh. Inhabiting a robotic mind is Gory-Gory Helishow! Everything is distilled to numbers. Sensate pleasures are null.

Now that I have WJ822 capabilities, it's clear why I couldn't locate the Waja compound. It's entirely contained within Ggyof Onttob, an artificial fogbank that jams electronic coordinates, prevents tracking even by the latest high-tech gismos. Not much time left. Switching places with the body. Placing it in such a manner that it accurately mimics a flatlined corpse and, therefore, fails to arouse suspicion. Done! Now, I'm in the driver's seat. The electronic console is immediately before me. Vamos! F<>#! The vehicle is passing through a cloud bank. Totally disorienting. Can't tell up from down or the direction the vehicle is headed. The instrument readings are scrambled. No wonder why the Waja Compound is considered impregnable.

As the space car approaches the sentry gate, a voice synthesizer intones, "Approaching Waja vehicle." The driver's window slides down automatically once the space car is adjacent to the guardhouse.

"Agent WJ822 returning to base. Rebel GK, to my right, is no longer operative."

"Roger. You're expected at W-Building, Sector 521."

"And the body?"

"The decomposition team will be waiting."

"Roger. Completing orders FTK34 and 35."

The window rises and the vehicle heads to its preprogrammed destination. Agent WJ822—a.k.a. GK—notices that present-tense is acceptable in the Compound. Waja-speak is direct, to-the-point, and on-task. Not surprising, given that there's important work to be done. Urgent business in the now that refuses to be delegated either to the past or to the future.

While passing through the Compound, GK notices that the buildings are functional. They serve their purpose, nothing more. But in a society where one class is destitute, another nearly so, and the third affluent beyond compare, adequacy has its virtues.

"Vehicle approaching W-Building, Sector 521. Termination point."

The doors open. WJ822 steps out, presses his RF tag to the door, and enters.

It's not exactly what he had expected. Outside, drab utility. Inside, serviceable modernity. Robots everywhere—none of whom acknowledge or greet him. Communication occurs only when necessary. It occurs to WJ822 that Oturians might do well to adopt this protocol. Chitchat. Who needs it?

He enters the briefing room, nodding curtly toward WJ801, his superior, who responds in kind. The recombinatory transfer appears to be fully functional.

"Agent WJ822 where is the corpse?" asks WJ801.

"Sir, in the vehicle."

"It is to be scanned and subsequently deposited in the cryogenic lab 28-SC for future study."

"Sir?"

"WJ877 will take it to the scanning compound. What is your assessment?"

"Sir, there was no opportunity to question the subject GK. He tried to deactivate me. Killing was expedient."

"Was his mode characteristic of an N/T?"

WJ822 paused. Was this a trick? He had better be careful. "Sir?"

"Data, please."

"Sir, he wasn't wired for continuous connectivity. He had functioned among the Enhanced for quite some time, a rare phenomenon for an N/T. And sir..."

"Yes?"

"He was angry, sir. His actions matched the profile of the insurrectionists associated with the Resistance. He would have deactivated me if I hadn't killed him."

"The N/Ts and LCDs are primitive."

"Sir, Lianitperian emotions mediate their actions and quash their more developed Sequencing and Cereumla processing capabilities."

"Return to your duties, WJ822."

"Suppression of the Archives?"

"Roger."

Agent WJ822 nodded to his immediate supervisor, turned, and headed down the corridor, out the building, down a walkway before entering a subterranean facility that housed the Rajakian Archives.

The Archives are held in a vast repository that is temperature controlled, humidity regulated, and devoid of natural light. Room after room after room is filled with specially tempered, alloy-composite discs that are resistant to the most adverse conditions. The facility is devoid of character, vastly different from the stone building that housed the red, leather-bound books in Malosh. Even with WJ822's Core Memory modular that is fully functional, the facility is only vaguely familiar.

WJ822's Prime Directive, as issued by the Intelligencers, was simple: Destroy all documents deemed "subversive." To accomplish this, he employs word spotting and semantic screening filters, complex algorithms for detecting associative links and connections, as well as highly correlated matrix identifiers. Any potentially subversive material is either destroyed or systematically corrupted.

Now, WJ822's principal focus is on identifying and interpreting archives that will explain the loss of global consciousness. Information deemed critical to understanding the factors influencing diminished consciousness will be copied and stored in his Registers and Core Memory. As a result, he now only suppresses unimportant archives as a matter of expediency so that his investigations will not arouse the suspicion of the Intelligencers.

Previously, WJ822 executed his job systematically, without questioning the directive or methodology. Now, while aware that his actions may be monitored, he can't resist delving into the archives randomly, just for the visceral thrill—a process akin to Slam-Surfing the Virt. In any case, wouldn't Scatter-Search yield interesting data while deflecting probes from the Intelligencers?

D-Cat. 482-f3

WJ822 opens it. What does he hope to discover? He wants to trace the foundations of recorded history, beginning with the 1st Library that was built in the Sapphire City, a once vital metropolis, now a ghostly relic that bordered East and West and North and South and was positioned above Vargus. The 1st Library was created four xectaries after the beginning of recorded time—Year 1 in the Anno Oldem (A.O.)—and flourished for well over six hundred years. The archivists at the 1st Library developed methods for identifying, classifying, preserving, storing, and retrieving documents. In its day, this city state sought to acquire manuscripts from around the world. Its archivists made quantitative and qualitative assessments concerning the culture and what was deemed worthy of knowing and preserving. So prized were these book treasures that explorers and warriors traveled the globe in search of exotic manuscripts illuminating scientific, philosophic, historical, and literary culture. Scholars in the Sapphire City had a social stature superseded only by its princes and warriors. They worked at the 1st Library codifying all that deemed worthy of preservation.

But civilizations are dynamic. Always rising or declining, never just maintaining a steady-state. A dozen competitive city states emerged, each with a rival archive to tell a different story that extolled the virtues of particularity over those of unification. The Sapphire City's administrators grew lax, its warriors became obese, and its princes became wanton and dissolute, more interested in competing for dominance that acquiring prized cultural artifacts. Not surprisingly, Sapphire City and its 1st Library were vulnerable to succeeding waves of invading armies that laid waste to both in the opening decades of the 2nd millennium.

Over the xectaries, societies coalesced from city states to regional districts and ultimately to continental spheres of influence, a number of which tried to become globally dominant along the way. But never again would there be a cultural mecca such as the Sapphire City. For the nurturance and preservation of cultural knowledge is a challenging endeavor. Success necessitates leadership and wisdom and the commitment of vital resources to encouraging the creativity and diligence that shapes a curator's expertise as to what is worth preserving and what is merely flotsam washed ashore and no longer of any interest or value.

This wisdom of what to save and what to discard requires a highly honed sense of what constitutes lasting "standards of excellence" coupled with an uncanny ability to identify dull or irrelevant content, thereby designated "derivative" and earmarked for demolition.

Although this is not to say that certain advances weren't made after the aftermath of the fall of Sapphire City. By the end of the 2nd millennium, each continent sought to educate its citizens and provide books and libraries and education. But these efforts at educating the many proved short lived. Already by the first xectary of the 3rd millennium, the primacy of print—a medium highly conductive to analytic thought—was already on the wane with the introduction of Iodar (known more commonly as Iod) and with it an emphasis on orality. By 3120, the Vid was introduced. It combined rapidly moving images and synchronized sound that further diminished the emphasis on the written word in favor of visual motion and orality. Given that Oturians' neuronal circuitry was highly attuned to these new talking boxes with moving pictures that emphasized visual and sound programing, interest in print declined. This accelerated when the Virt became a global phenomenon in 3282. With its whirling imagery and dimensional soundtracks, words were minimized to a scrolling subtext or a popup screen—mere ornamental augmentation when compared with the primacy of motion suffused with color, as well as tactile and olfactory stimulus that enhanced the totally immersive Virt experience. By 3290, when print was demoted to an auxiliary feature augmenting the new electronic medium that tapped into our full dimension of sensory experiences, its stand-alone value as a cultural illuminator had, for all intents and purposes, become irrelevant.

With the predominance of the Virt rumors began circulating about the Rajakian Archives, which were named after the most coveted collection contained in the 1st Library of the Sapphire City. The Rajakian Archives were said to be the basis of all that was worth remembering. They harkened back to an era when authorship, creativity, and artistry were prized. When there was a corpus of great works that were universally acknowledged, as opposed to the NOW with its discontinuous stream of detritus and profanity.

It's all well and good for the readers to understand some of Oturian history, but let's return to WJ822's—a.k.a. our GK's—effort to assess the Rajakian Archives as a means for understanding the causes responsible for the loss of consciousness on Oturi. Although he's no expert in the subject matter, Slam-Surfing has begun to give him an intuitive sense of what's available. After 1,999 random entries, he estimates that fully 78% of the archives could be classified as merely obscene, mostly variations of F<># with or without images of naked bodies. Amazing that so many words and expressions could be variations on a single theme. It seems that nearly everywhere he searched, the results were the same. Oh, some derivations might be spelled ^^^**** or %%%, or even ~GGGGGG. But the meaning remains the same as do the endless images of fornication spiced, to a greater or lesser degree, with violence.

"Maybe," he wonders, "if I look at Z-Cat or RT1-Cat or 331-Cat, I will find useful information. What else might I find?"

Dear Reader, WJ822 continues examining detritus and still more detritus. Not surprisingly, a great deal of what was represented in the archives could be characterized as scatological.

By the end of the day, WJ822 has scanned 53 catalogues and 197,000 entries strewn with vulgarity and banality, none of it interesting. There are no annotations in the records. Indeed, why bother? It is not as if these "events" constituted anything noteworthy.

And so what WJ822 hopes might be the most exciting of jobs is proving excruciatingly dull. He's ready to call it quits. The Information Hub was not far away. WJ822 needs a change of pace. But could he interact with the other Wajas without inadvertently divulging his subversive intentions?

The Information Hub, where Wajas gather to upload or download pertinent content is, in effect, a robotic and android watering hole monitored closely by the security apparatus of the Enhanced. The Hub is busy at all hours. Many Wajas congregate there awaiting further instruction. Looking around, it appears to WJ822 that everyone is under scrutiny.

The Waja are almost entirely the Artun82 generation of robots and a smattering of undercover "security" androids roughly equivalent to the Artun82s. Neither robots nor androids rest or eat. They have no sexual drive and are devoid of the antiquated Oturian thirst for intimacy. The Waja appear "hard wired" for loyalty and meeting the needs of their Enhanced "handlers". Their only drawback is their need for periodic recharging.

"Ah," WJ822 postulates, if only the needs of GK were that simple! If only he weren't Oturian. If only he possessed superlative computational powers and zippo qualia. If only his focus were executing his directive.

"So while the Waja here might theoretically be capable of complex reasoning," WJ822 continues, "it appears that their processing capabilities are finite. That is, bounded by instruction sets that obligate them to serve the interests of the Enhanced. The robots and cyborgs at the Institute have no comparable limitations. It seems odd to imagine machines with potentially unbounded potential that, nevertheless, continue to take instruction. Or maybe not. Perhaps they had their own little insurrection brewing. Maybe that's why the later generation—the Artun-85—abandoned the Emojas. That's certainly a possibility. After all, why operate within finite perimeters when infinity beckons?"

Looking round the Center, WJ822 doesn't recognize anyone. "Wait, over there. Agent WJ701 sitting at that table looks familiar. Why? Friend or Foe? Check him out. After all, there's no one else I'm the least interested in talking to."

WJ822 walks over and stands next to WJ701. He presses his right hand gently against WJ701's left shoulder, causing him to glance up and say, "Welcome, "WJ822. On break? Perhaps you desire an energy stimulant?" WJ822 understood that "energy stimulant" was a euphemism for a quick charge.

WJ701 has two radiant-coiled mugs. Glowing red. He hands one to WJ822. Though WJ822 accepts it, he can't help wondering, "Should I? Why does WJ701's voice sound so familiar?"

"So what's your impression of the archives?" *WJ701 is speaking to me. What does he know? Should I be frightened? Am I under surveillance by an operative? Can't shake the impression that I know WJ701. Where? How? When?*

"My memory receivers are functioning on overdrive." *Why did I say that? Will I be denounced as a traitor? Am I more robot these days than Artunian?* "I was summoned to respond to Emergency Assist YRO9944. So I rendered the insurgent GK inoperative. Brought him in for the decomposition team. But why was I sent? My prime directive is document assessment of the Archives. Why would a knowledge worker be sent out on emergency assist detail? I'm not trained for combat or security. I'm just toiling in the Archives...." *Why am I blabbering away? My cover will be blown. I'm as good as dead.*

WJ701 is almost smiling. What does that mean? Is he a robot or just masquerading? Does he suspect who I really am? Maybe WJ701 is a very smart robot on security detail, and he's sussed me out. Am I about to be flatlined?

"It must have been a terrible assignment since for weeks now we've been sitting together during break. And now you're acting as if you don't even know me."

The look, that voice. Should know him? Why don't I? Who is WJ701 really?

"Enjoy your stimulant. It'll give you an energy boost. Sometimes, on these jobs—especially when you're sent on emergency assist or occasionally even when engaged in archiving the databases—some of the Core Memory gets corrupted. Starts to meld with the Virtual Memory and the File Structure at the higher levels. It's not uncommon. It might explain your failure to recognize me."

Why the f<># are WJ701's lips still pursed in that smirk-smile? Is that what they do before they vaporize rebels and revolutionaries? Why isn't this recombinatory NAD transfer working? It's supposed to be flawless. Why the f<>#. . . ? Hey, I have no sensation down there. None! All my pathetic life I've been motivated by f<>#. What does it mean not to have that? Haven't even thought for hours now about getting laid. Gory-Gory Helishow! Am I losing my Oturian moxy? Splatterblood. I'm in this game called life for f< >#! *Without that who cares?*

What's gives with WJ701? Why is he looking at me so strangely? Has he gone roque? Should I deactivate him? Can't do that or I'll be outed. I thought WJ701 wouldn't manifest qualia. He's not behaving like any robot I've ever had contact with.

"On my last assignment," says WJ701, "I worked with this agent who would never use his proper ID, always went by the nickname Spaito."

"Spaito, you worked with Spaito?"

"Do you know him?"

No smile. Nothing. He's on to me. I'm in some robotic death spiral. Don't know how to navigate this. Gonna have to f<>#ing kill him. Him or me. NOW. HERE.

GK, STOP! NEGATE THOSE THOUGHTS. LISTEN TO ME. WJ701 is your buddy, Spaito. He's your friend. Trust him.

I'm hallucinating now. It's over. The game's over. F<>#.

You're not hallucinating. I'm telegraphing my thoughts to you. WJ701 is Spaito and you're functioning as a robot, a really advanced model that allows cohabitation with the memory traces of GK. There are some strategic advantages to being a robotic in the Now. Deal with it.

ChandraX?

Yes?

There's a lot of f<>#ing females wandering in and out of my life.

No comment.

And Emoja? Is she OK?

She's in Vargus.

She wasn't supposed to go there. It's too risky. Get her out of there.

When you're done with this mission, tell her yourself. Relay your message by code through "Song for the Journey."

What the f<># are you saying?

You'll figure it out. You always do. Talk to Spaito. He'll help you.

She's gone. Always flitting in and out of my consciousness. Are those spectral images I see when she appears real? Does ChandraX even exist? Or is she a product of my imagination? Is she some Oturian hologram? Or her bodily essence just a ruse to have me think that she's like us? Maybe she's some omniscient, all-seeing, ubiquitous presence, a computerized telescopic that employs the most advanced mathematical code. . . .

Perhaps she's just a highly advanced pulsing light memory beam that can project a lifeform comprehensible by Oturians. Maybe I'm just imagining her and really she's not there at all. Just randomness and entropy that I'm hallucinating about some God-like force.

F<>#! I'm no philosopher. I'm just trying to stay alive and not lose my *cool while WJ701 is blabbering.*

"$&*%%#%#%#5"—*so on and so forth. Should be listening. Who knows what I've missed while he was talking. Gotta take a risk. Never discover anything if I don't. Isn't life just that—calculating risk and then acting based on the best probabilities?*

Can't believe what I'm thinking. GK never would have had these thoughts. Who the hell am I? And who is WJ701? Take that risk. Dare to ask. After all, what's one life when the preservation of Oturian knowledge hangs in the balance?

"WJ701," says WJ822, as he leans into his robotic comrade, "Could it be that you didn't just work with an agent that went by the name Spaito? That you are actually Spaito?"

"I am who you need me to be."

"I need you to be Spaito. In the Real, in the Now. And not some simulacrum that is some sophisticated robot disguised to monitor my actions. I thought you were 🝆."

"Then I wouldn't be sitting here next to you."

"Nothing is what it seems these days. Your assistance would be greatly appreciated. I'm having trouble with the Archives. I'm supposed to be cataloguing, verifying, storing, as well as eliminating redundancies and subversive materials. I combed through 53 catalogues today, but all I've discovered are to be an infinite variety of obscenities. I thought I had encountered every vulgarity known to Oturians. Apparently not. It feels as if I'm once again an N/T trolling the Virt and bombarded by a tshi-storm."

"Is that shocking?"

"Shocking? It's boring. Aren't the archives supposed to represent the total sum of Oturi's cultural heritage? I came all this way. I endured hardships. Have I risked my life for this? It feels as if I'm wading through endless garbage. As I said, a f<>king tshi-storm."

"One of the most telling indicators in a declining civilization is its detritus. What you found in the Archives is an accumulation of ruins. The good, the virtuous, the profound have been almost entirely jettisoned. What passes for wisdom in these end days resembles a malignant cancer attacking the few remaining vital cells of an organism."

"No one could mistake this detritus for culture. No one."

"My friend who inhabits the persona of a robot. Could it be that you're no longer the same individual who began your odyssey? Perspectives change. You're no longer bound by the constraints that define the existence of N/Ts and LCDs. But keep looking, keep cataloging, and I assure you that you'll find what you seek."

And you? Will you still be here?"

"As long as you need me. But even I have responsibilities and limitations. So much to do. So little time. Make haste."

With that, WJ701 and WJ822 go their separate ways.

WJ822 is not really sure why he has been assigned to the Rajakian Archives. Are the Enhanced anticipating that he will uncover subversive activities and notify them? Do they want him to cull out the important historical, cultural, and social events from those more trivial or obscene? Even if that is true, how could they be sure that he would differentiate between that which is valued and that which is worthless?

Of course, there may be a number of other reasons why they appointed WJ822 to this job. Perhaps, they just want him preoccupied with useless trivia while they embark on a major campaign to suppress the Resistance? Maybe they anticipated that GK would assume WJ822's identity and allowed it to happen so as to monitor his actions? Easy enough to do since Vid surveillance here is ubiquitous. Or maybe the authorities don't think WJ822 is the kind of individual who is likely to pose a threat and, therefore, this job is just what it appears to be—a low-level flunky position for a surveillance robot engaged in the dullest kind of work imaginable.

None of these explanations satisfy WJ822 or explain why he was sent to bring GK here. Unless, archiving is just an undercover operation masking a more critical function WJ822 is expected to perform, notably, monitoring key activities that place the Enhanced at risk of challenging the status quo.

No sense speculating since in the now WJ822 appears indifferent. Before him are the Rajakinan Archives that should nominally answer his most pressing questions: Why? How? Who? When? And, ultimately, the Grand Strategy driving the policy and directives of the Enhanced. Thanks to his energy boost and encouragement from Spaito, that is exactly what WJ822 intends to discover.

Nevertheless, that's easier said than done. In all, there are at least 999,999 files stored electronically in the Archive. He would have preferred examining physical documents, but that possibility was eliminated with the conversion to electronic source files in 3290. And so he inserts microchips into the data analyzer and tries to make sense of it all from the monitor. But there is no Index or Table of Contents to direct him. From what he can tell, accessing the archives—other than randomly or, alternatively, chronologically from beginning to end—could only be achieved properly via a search engine. But there are practical limitations as to how it might be employed since the current parameters are limited to three basic categories: time, subject heading, and key words. Each requires a high degree of specificity to yield useful data.

WJ822 can't just enter a year or a subject or a key word. These descriptors have to be narrowly circumscribed in order to yield highly selective information. But, of course, that necessitates that he has some idea of the subject matter that he is investigating. But without crucial details there is almost no likelihood of pinpointing key events contained in this vast archive.

WJ822 has now skimmed through a total of 270 catalogues. There seems no rhyme or reason to what is included or excluded from groupings, let alone the entire Archive. And while obscenities are everywhere, they neither shock nor titillate. Just broad-band graffiti permeating the info highway. The first time he encounters a hailstorm of obscenities he was tempted to laugh, but not after having read the next two thousand. Didn't anyone compiling the Archive assign values to restrict the banal? Why is everything considered equally valid and, therefore, worthy of inclusion?

WJ822 speculates as to why the Archives appear randomly constructed and, therefore, useless. By imbedding endless amounts of detritus, no one could discover the essential truths contained in the Rajakian Archives. The ocean of obscenities and useless trivia was a clever ruse to prevent the attainment of wisdom and dull revolutionary ardor. Could it be that the next 999,943 catalogues he consulted would also be equally pointless? Was everything that happened and included in the files so abysmally insipid?

WJ822 is disgusted. He hasn't been so frustrated since he was GK embarking on the tedious voyage back to Oturi. So bored at what lay ahead that he's taken to making little bit of scraps and launching them as if they're rockets dodging anti-aircraft and, occasionally, detonating.

"Hmmmmm ZZZZZZZ CRASH."

"Enemy Fire. AAAAAAGgggg."

"Raaaatatatat. Kaboom!"

"Alert: Heat-9. Heat-9. Heat-9."

You get the idea. Over and over again. As if he were GK on the spaceship again. So bored, so pitifully Oturian.

When on his screen pops a message embedded with music notation.

Song for the Journey
Twisted Pair

> Uncoupling now
> In search of memory.
>
> Time's eye regress
> To Continents Lost
> And Oturi lives erased.
>
> Dance, then, those fateful steps
> Near nested globes so perfect
> For there 'twas sung "Song for the Journey."

The song sings. It dances. It cavorts across the screen. "What did ChandraX say about '**Song for the Journey**'? That when he finished this mission to contact Emoja by means of a code transmitted through '**Song for the Journey**'? So does that mean that Emoja is communicating with him now? Is she O.K.? Is this a trap? F<>#!!!! How could she possibly know where I am and how to contact me? Not even Emoja is that good. She can't possibly mind scan me when she's in Vargus."

WJ822 starts computing the numbers embedded in the musical notation by means phylg code. Despite his professed ability—*Numero Uno best codebreaker on Oturi*—it takes him an hour to decipher. And the message?

GK, you're running out of time. Consult File 999.—ChandraX

Then, the dancing stops, the singing ends.

BRAVO!

flashes across the screen, an acknowledgment that he has cracked the code. Our hero goes directly to File 999 and its sheaf of documents where he spots "**Oturi—the Global Problematique—3462 A.O.**"

29

The Enhanced come for a taste of the wild and dangerous pursuit called living—that which they term "safari." They watch the suffering, but feel nothing. How could they since they have no skin in that life. Small wonder, then, that there is nothing to be gained when they make this journey. Watching the Safarians is witnessing the deadness that comes from residing in the limbo of lost consciousness wherein dwells the greatest misery of all.

ChandraX

In the succession of days to follow, Emoja spends her time observing the surface world, rather than inhabiting the tunnels below. For although her loyalties are with the Strangelets, their plight is determined by the Vargusians up above. Emoja wants to understand the factors shaping this wretched continent. Her observations suggest that the surface existence is only marginally better than the circumstances at A and AB levels below. Of course, once you descend to the lowest realms—AC, AD, AE, and AF—there are no comparisons. In any case, AC and AD are domains where there is no reprieve from the struggle to survive while AE and AF are now little more than repositories for those Strangelets most nearly dead.

Emoja wants to understand how this miserable continent of Vargus came to be. And wonders if there is anything she might do to reverse the process. She feels the answer will be discovered on the surface. So she spends most of her time there. It's so bloody hot. Almost nothing to eat unless necro-feasting on Vargusian remains. Existence here functions in near reverse. Rather than a birth cycle that ends ultimately in death, life in Vargus is a death cycle where surviving constitutes an aberration. Families, strictly speaking, can't be said to exist. Instead, there are male and female Vargusians trying to sustain one or two male cubs, not even, necessarily, their biological descendants. Cruelty is the operative mode and suffering is its natural consequence. Commerce has been almost entirely eradicated in favor of theft, although barter, on a strictly ad hoc basis, persists.

Emoja witnesses small contingents of the Enhanced traveling on "safari" to observe life on Vargus. They arrive at the Transmitting Station. They come in groups of threes and fours. They are here to witness the suffering. They seek artifacts to take home, as if to be reminded that there exists a continent whose entire inhabitants are engaged in an unending struggle to survive. These souvenirs the Enhanced take home are carefully selected to symbolize the extreme depravity of life here in Vargus. These objects are "bought" from natives or sometimes even taken from the carcasses of the dead. Indeed, it may be that this foreign currency derived from this perverse form of "Eco Tourism," is the primary source of revenue for Vargus.

The question naturally arises, why come at all? It seems the Enhanced come out of boredom. Their lives are devoid of substance, a string of vacuous activities. They have been told that Vargus is the Eco destination that surpasses all others, a place where one will come closest to experiencing the vicarious thrill of death without actually having to die. Of course, there used to exist a pilot program for traveling to Sirus. But after the N-Deluge, those "pilgrimages" were banned because of the high risk of mortality. Catalla has restricted visitors since the Umbrascenti seized control of that region. And while there were excursions to witness the desecration of AL in Artun and to visit the celebrated Zen Garden of Transformative Peace in Zhinboya, these destinations never held for the Enhanced the allure of visiting Vargus.

The Enhanced arrive in specially designed safari outfits. They smear on protective ointments, hoping to deflect the heat and light. They bring their digital imagers and take lots of pictures so that they might demonstrate to their brethren that they have been to Vargus. Of course, anyone might buy the images, listen to the audios, watch the Vids, and pose as a safari visitor. In other words, one might falsely claim to have traveled to Vargus in hopes of seeming daring and adventurous.

But, of course, there is nothing to duplicate life as experienced in the Real. One may buy the artifacts, one may acquire the pics, and even surreptitiously sneak a peek on the Vid in order to fabricate an "authentic" story, but these experiences never capture Vargus as it is witnessed in the Real. There's the Virt, of course—officially off-limits to the Enhanced. But almost universally, the Enhanced seek the Real as a touchstone by which to measure their lives and the lives of others.

The latest contingent of the Enhanced arrive at the Transmitting Station. There are four of them. They're taking pictures. Click, click, click. They're attracted to and repelled by the misery they see. Their fascination with horror and degradation draws them to Vargus.

"Terrible, just terrible. Who would have believed..."

"Never could I have begun to suspect..."

"Our brethren will be tempted to say our pictures are fabricated splatterblood so unprepared are they for this gruesome reality."

"The deprivation here is so extreme that those who will never come would swear that all this is a figment of the imagination rendered by the criminally insane—those LCDs, those terrorists, those rebels and, of course, those insurrectionists."

This safari of four insists on being taken down into the tunnels. They feel the need to witness the most extreme deprivation first hand. Emoja is appalled. She wants to shake them, yell at them. What would be the point? Instead, she follows them below. To see what they see, to experience what they experience.

They arrive at level A. The Strangelets are jittery. They dance around the periphery of the group.

Emoja listened to the cackles of the Enhanced.

"Had you noticed the Strangelets? Their red hair and black skin appears brown down here."

To the Enhanced, the Strangelets are wild creatures that they're now witnessing up close. They perceive them as exotic animals residing in a zoo. They're regarded as the Other—those strange, forbidden, vanquished creatures. For the Enhanced, the Strangelets are not really perceived as Oturian.

"I never would have imagined all this. How would you possibly explain to your friends a continent with this quotient of misery? How would one live underground in a space such as this? The tunnels are dreadful. Down here is so dim. Our domain is filled with an abundance of light."

"Yes," says another, "this safari will make you appreciate all that you have known."

The Strangelets, curious, press close. The Enhanced give them coins. Those coins can be used to barter on the surface. The Strangelets are thankful, tugging at the sleeves of the Enhanced as they sing,

> "Gifts, gifts.
> You give us gifts
> That will sustain us.

"Who would have thought they would be so cute?" says one Enhanced.

Emoja now understands GK's rage. Given the opportunity, she might kill these Eco Tourists. Have they nothing better to do? If they feel the deprivation so profoundly, why don't they endeavor to change the conditions here? The Enhanced have privilege and power that could actually make a difference. Why are precious resources spent to view Strangelets as if they're caged animals?

Perhaps that's why Emoja said nothing when the safari group decides to descend to level AD.

"What an opportunity!" says one.

"We'd never get this experience elsewhere" insists another.

"Yes, indeed," chimes a third.

Their descent is achieved by a pneumatic lift. Strange that in a society struggling for almost everything, there is power to take you down, down into the worst conditions imaginable. Emoja steps inside with them. They turn to her and ask questions.

"Have we known you?"

"I am Emoja."

"Had you been here long."

"This is where I was born."

"But, you have changed. You're not exactly one of them."

"I am a cyborg. I have worked at the Institute in the Oasis of the Real."

"Oh, a borg."

"You worked with the Scientists?"

"I am a scientist."

"Oh."

To the Enhanced on safari, scientists were as bizarre as the Strangelets and as repellent as borgs. Scientists in the Oasis still work. They are productive. They are engaged in discovery. As such, they were as likely as the N/Ts and LCDs to be perceived as a threat. For most Enhanced try very hard never to think and would rather die than work. Not surprisingly, they regard Emoja as suspect. On the transport lift they stand against the walls talking to one another rather than be forced to engage in further conversation with her. Their body language is unequivocal: "You're not really here. We no longer acknowledge your presence."

Emoja, like the Strangelets, has been designated the Other. Someone or something lower down the social stratum. Emoja is furious. *How dare they? I am more gifted than they could ever be. I am striving to rebuild our civilization. OURS. Not yours or mine, but OURS. I am putting my life at risk to rebuild our civilization that is tottering on ruin. And you dare to dismiss me? You who do nothing, want for nothing, aspire to nothing?*

Perhaps the injustice of it all explains why Emoja is silent when one of the safari members pushes a button for Level AD. Why she fails to tell them they are putting their lives at risk. That there are dreadful diseases down there for which they almost certainly haven't been given the necessary shots or protective gear to minimize their risk.

Emoja acknowledges to herself, "Soon enough they will reach AD."

The doors open. They are witness to the desperate actions of Strangelets struggling to survive.

Bam!

One of the Strangelets collides with one of the Enhanced.

"Ouch, I am not to be touched," cries the woman. "Best you leave us alone!" But it's too late: She's already lost her camera.

"Bring it back, immediately!" she insists.

Notice how the Enhanced simplify language when under distress. Nevertheless, her demand accomplishes nothing. The Strangelet, a fleeting figure, disappeared as soon as contact was made.

"No, no, go away," shouts another member of the safari. "Leave us forthwith!" This remark from a man. Notice, his wallet is missing. Of course it's been stolen. Too late to do anything since that second Strangelet has also vanished.

"It stinks here" complains a third member of the safari.

"What do you expect?" insists the fourth member of the entourage.

The Enhanced never go very far. See them huddled there. No one has ever threatened them before. They've never had their special stature undermined. Here, they're only important for their currency: What of theirs that can be stolen and used as collateral. It's all too much for them. They barely last five minutes at Level AD.

They return to the lift. Emoja follows them in. As they about to head back to Level A, one of the safari members pushes the button for Level AE.

"Why?" says another.

"We will have seen enough," says a third.

"No, we will have seen nothing unless we descend to Level AE."

The others nod. Nervous, but in agreement. The Enhanced long to witness life in its most degraded state. The very prospect of witnessing death—something very removed from their daily lives—is almost an aphrodisiac to them.

Emoja, on the other hand, knows that only a momentary visit to AE will place their lives in peril. Soon enough they'll understand that a visit to Vargus and its tunnels isn't a safari adventure: It's a death odyssey. Nevertheless, she says nothing. Would it matter if she did? Probably not since in their minds she's the Other who barely exists and, therefore, has nothing to convey.

Together, the four members of the safari and Emoja descend to AE. Not quite the lowest level, but deadly enough.

Emoja watches as the doors open, and they step out. She sees as their hands cover their noses and mouths. She observes their refusal to look directly at the very wretchedness they had come to see. She hears their cries of disbelief.

"Agggghhhh."

"Ohhhhhhh."

"Pllllllleeeeaaassseee."

The stench. The sewage. The sounds. Everywhere the smell of death. The look of death. The feel of death. The taste of death.

All around them are the dead, the nearly dead, and those about to die. There's nothing else to witness here, but the terminal cessation of life. Time slows and appears as if it's at a standstill. Three minutes might as well be eternity.

They shouldn't have come. The Enhanced have stayed too long. They can't possibly survive. Still, Emoja watches. As the Other, they would never have listened to her counsel: THEY KNOW BETTER. Nothing, they believe, will harm them. Emoja watches and waits.

Finally, the safari has seen enough. Too much as it turns out. The elapsed time from exposure to expiration was nine minutes, assuming we count the cumulative time spent at Levels AD and AE. If AE was where the deadly viruses were actually contracted, then these entered the bloodstream well before the three-minute mark, fully one minute before they headed back. By then the faces of the safari members were ashen; their eyes hollow and sunken.

They never quite made it back inside the lift. Emoja watched them die just steps from her before she made her way back to the surface. In the nine minutes she had spent with them at levels AD and AE, she had watched fourteen Strangelets die. Fourteen of her kin, none of whom she could save. Emoja's sympathy lay with them. For their daily battle against unfathomable odds. For the Enhanced who died, she felt nothing.

Emoja watched as the next safari arrived at the Transmitting Station. This group, she decided, she would question.

"Artun visitors, why had you decided to come?" she tries to mimic the convoluted speech patterns of the Enhanced, a privileged group that for the most part do nothing, produce nothing, know nothing, and yet insist on speaking Old Speak.

"We had decided to make this journey to witness suffering," said he.

"But suffering has existed everywhere for all time."

"There will be danger here. One will feel as if he's perched on the very edge of existence. Survival, under such circumstances will give one the feeling of truly being alive."

"But you were alive, are alive, will be alive."

"You with a mane so red, who looks like one of them, but who speaks as if she might have lived amongst us, could you possibly imagine what life would be like if there would never be anything to do? No adversity, precious little to consume, a dearth of passion? We want for nothing; we need nothing; our desires have been distilled to almost nil. Know you our existence?"

"I have always worked. I have struggled. I have suffered. I have been hungry. I have loved. And I lost and shall lose companions who were and are and shall be most dear to me."

"Then, you have been fortunate."

Emoja is momentarily stunned. Then disgusted. Then furious. *These useless beings; these Enhanced who have never worked a day in their lives, never felt any pain, never put themselves at risk. Let them expire in the tunnels. But before they pass, let them feel for the hardship, the pain, and the disease that is the daily lot of my people. Then, maybe, they might feel a measure of compassion and try to strive for a better world. Of course, by then, she acknowledges, it will be too late.*

"You must help them," she says.

"Whom shall we help?"

"Everyone here," she says waving her hands. "They're nearly dead. They now feast on the remains of their citizenry. In the tunnels..."

"We have seen some of the suffering. It will not be our responsibility to alter the lives of residents of Vargus." This member of the Enhanced who seeks danger and who desires this thrill to know experientially that he is alive, looks suspiciously at Emoja. "You couldn't have been one of us. You speak in present tense. Your hair is red. You have the look as if you might be a machine. You must be an alien. There would be no reason why we would ever consider undertaking any action in the future based on the assessment of an alien."

"What if your world, your life, your survival depends on it?"

"Our lives will always be safe. As members of the Enhanced, we will never be at risk so long as we remain in the Oasis of the Real. And it shall always be thus."

"But you are here, not there."

"Yes, I have chosen to take this very slight risk."

"But you could die."

"It would be a very remote possibility."

"Has it ever occurred to you that your life intersects with the lives of other inhabitants around the globe? That if the citizens of Vargus or Sirus or Catalla or Zhinboya should die their catastrophe might eventually become your catastrophe?

"I know of no one in the Oasis of the Real who has died."

"I just watched four of your brethren die. They went down into the tunnels here moments ago and now they're dead."

"Well, as I have told you, that is a statistically possibility. They knew the risks. And they knew they are not permitted to enter the tunnels."

"Isn't it possible that if everybody else dies, you shall too?"

"The prospect is so infinitesimally small that it's not even worth considering."

"And what about the Intelligencers, the scientists, the N/Ts, and the LCDs?"

"All of them have been born to serve us. Their lives, as such, have no other purpose."

"And your purpose?"

"Our purpose had been and will be quite simply to live. We have been empowered to do as we please. And while we're here we seek stimulation, risk, and danger."

"And do you believe that your world will sustain itself when all other segments of society falter?"

"Yes, of course. We will be immune to most ordinary laws of math, physics, and biology, excepting when we take certain risks outside our Oasis.

"Certainly, there are misfortunes and inequities in our world. And as we look into the future, no doubt, there will be too many individuals occupying the planet. That will, no doubt, result in many misfortunes. But it is not our task to save those less fortunate. You will cease this foolish talk or I shall have you terminated. I came here to witness danger, not to discuss inequities."

And like so many of the Enhanced, supremely confident of his sagacity and entitlement, he walks away, ready to resume his safari.

30

Wisdom alone is insufficient to avert catastrophe if it cannot be harnessed to alter destiny. When paths have been irrevocably taken and the consequences fully wrought—those cities plundered, those resources squandered, those populations found wanting—then, there remains little to be done to alter the course of history and it behooves the chronicler to tell the story.

ChandraX

Oturi—the Global Problematique—3462 A.O.

⬅ Destroy this report & all references to it contained in the Rajakian Archives. **Waja Security**

In an age where relativistic precepts dominate, where the noble and profane are given equal countenance, where sagacious judgment is sorely wanting, the Chief Archivist herein presents an assessment of the state of our civilization as gleaned from the detritus of the Rajakian Archives.

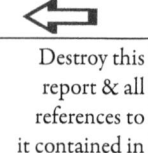

Proposition 1: A civilization is born; it ascends; it may even achieve a grand arc before collapsing under extreme

gravitational force into the abyss of nothingness. It has been thus for all of recorded time. Why should our circumstance differ? When mathematical equations remain constant and the outcome of their proofs irrevocable, we would be well advised to heed their strictures, particularly those that pertain to our cosmic destiny. For decoding the arc of our demise may assist other civilizations in avoiding our most grievous failings. *Who writes this way? Why? F<>#ing crap. No wonder Oturi doesn't survive* (writes WJ822 evoking his inner GK).

Proposition 2: It has been wrongly assumed that the causes of our decline are linear and reflect a simplistic chain of assumptions. That is to say that A leads to B, which in turn gives rise to C, D, E, F ad infinitum until reaching the terminus. It is natural to argue thus since our minds reason in this fashion, constructing an inexorable chain of evidence, one claim laid upon the next until the inevitable conclusion.

However, truth is multivariate and nonlinear, refusing to be straitjacketed into a simple dichotomy that forces us to choose between divergent outcomes by selecting a single possible trajectory that we observe to its fateful conclusion. Instead, the solution is achieved by means of the Piettonel Economic Model (consult File GP98), a mathematical paradigm founded on the Aertlov Equation (elaborated in File GP99), which calculates multivariate functions of multidimensional parameters. *Multivariate functions? My head hurts!*

Proposition 3: Only one study has systematically analyzed the critical influences impacting Oturi by utilizing the Piettonel Economic Model. That study: "Finite Expansions: A Report on the Predicament of Oturi" was posted briefly electronically in 3440 before authorities removed it from the Virt. It distilled the problematique down to nine multivariate determinants impacted by exponential population growth: A) the increase of poverty; B) the degradation of the environment; C) the erosion of cultural and public institutions; D) the elimination of employment; E) the demise of the family and, correspondingly, the rise in the number of disaffected youths; F) the destitution of urban landscapes; G) the economic disruptions exacerbated through globalism; H) the proliferation of viruses, bacteria, and pandemic blights; and lastly, I) the preponderance of irrational beliefs. These factors and their impact on Planet Oturi are discussed at length in Section 3ZGH.

> Overpopulation & its attendant woes can be used to quell political threats from below.
> **Waja Security**

Rather than singling out any single determinant shaping the crisis, it is the strength of "Finite Expansions" that the Piettonel Economic Model was devised to analyze how a complex interplay of variables might respond to super exponential population growth. The conclusion? Approximately thirty years remain before global catastrophe ensues. Now, the authors of this report—scientists, economists, and humanitarians alike—stressed the approximate timetable, although their doomsday scenarios increased in probability whenever the economy took a dive, whenever a famine occurred, whenever there was the threat of internecine conflict or geopolitical war. But by supplying a projected timeline for this countdown to oblivion, the prognosis of "Finite Expansions" was sufficiently threatening that authorities ridiculed the report and attacked its veracity.

Tick Tock. Tick Tock. Scrambling down the memory clock.

*Tick Tock. Tick Tock. Ba Ba. Ba Ba--***Boom!**

Tick Tock. Tick Tock. Bye-bye all of Yume!

Nevertheless, despite official dismissal of "Finite Expansions," circumstances worsened. Thus, when tensions mounted between the Umbrascenti and Illuminati in Sirus from 3400-3458, most of the Umbrascenti fled from Sirus into neighboring Catalla. Critics naturally minimized the destabilizing impact of this vast social dislocation and the ramifications this would have for the entire continent and, indeed, Oturi.

This destabilization was compounded by the global catastrophe caused by the N-Deluge, the nuclear devastation in Sirus in 3458. That reduced that entire continent—with the notable exception of Malosh—into a glass parking lot. Again, naysayers dismissed the potential threat of nuclear winter and the associated calamities, be they environmental or political or social.

However, merely a year after the N-Deluge, it became increasingly difficult to dismiss "Finite Expansions" given the major nuclear explosion that occurred in Linber, one of Catalla's principal cities. That resulted in 1,165,000 casualties due to the blast and thermal effects and associated radioactive fallout. This event, when coupled with the threat of other thermonuclear attacks in a number of Catalla's other major cities, led to the surrender of democracy in that continent and with it the demise of the rule of law as practiced for more than two millennia by the Illuminati. In its place was substituted the theocratic dictatorship of the Umbrascenti.

Despite all of the societal decay and trauma experienced in the twenty-two years since "Finite Expansions" first surfaced in the Virt—the mounting economic disparity, the massive layoffs, the erosion of employment, the disintegration of family, the loss of social order throughout the five continents, and the de facto elimination of a literate, culturally sophisticated population capable of abstract analytic thought and independent conjecture—authorities continued to minimize its implications and instead stressed that these changes were to be expected as society evolved into the "Next New Thing."

The Next New Thing would be all about "Me" and "I" and "Myself," expressed visually, laden with obscenities, and pitched always in the NOW because the present is perceived as eternal while the past and future no longer lie within the conceptual framework of public comprehension. But this solipsistic universe of Me shall be explored in greater detail later so that we may focus at this juncture on one of the central postulates of "Finite Expansions," namely, the exponential nature of population dynamics and the consequences that inexorably follow. *Once, I found this universe of "Me" utterly enthralling.*

At the heart of this issue is the unrelenting nature of exponential growth and its impact in destabilizing Oturi. Exponential growth is a key component of the overall system dynamic as presented in "Finite Expansions." The study postulates that since 1799 world population had been growing exponentially. If we assume that the

---

← Solipsism abets the devolution toward unconsciousness. The social/political apathy that results assists us in redistributing resources away from the many to the few.
Waja Security

← Exponential growth increases disparity & desperation, which we leverage to foster our agenda.
Waja Security

population at that time was 0.5 billion and was increasing at a rate of 0.3% per year, a doubling would occur in 250 years. As late as 2119, our global population was still expanding annually by 2.1%. That growth rate could be expected to double Oturi's population every 33 years. Even as the number expanded exponentially, the rate of growth continued to increase, thereby causing population figures to achieve "super" exponential growth. *This dense textual analysis makes my head hurt.*

What propelled this explosion? In simple terms, the larger the population, the greater the number of offspring born each year. The growth rate is determined by the average fertility and the length between generations. Negative feedback loops regulate growth and stabilize this dynamic. But if we assumed that in 1799 the average life expectancy was 30 years and that by 2119 it had risen to 53 years, there would be no possibility of having the population reach a stable equilibrium before 2151. However, by then the average life expectancy had increased to 80 years and the population continued expanding at an annual rate of 1.5%, despite the rise in the negative feedback loop to between 3% and 7% caused by the rise in mortality attributed to increased starvation, illness, and war (SIW).

> These population figures are bogus!
> **Waja Security**

By 3000 A.O., the world population exceeded 45 billion. It would continue expanding exponentially, despite momentary quells due to outbreaks of SIW. For our purposes, 3000 A.O. is designated as a threshold year. For although the population had exceeded the supply of natural resources for more than a generation, the effects of shortages on the global infrastructure were not sufficiently quantifiable until the beginning of the

3rd millennium. In the years that followed, the standard of living declined precipitously. Scarcity, not abundance, defined our operative state. Thus, 3000 A.O. may be designated as the "0" Year in this devolution.

In analyzing this decline, we have selected the year 3282 as a focal point of comparison with the benchmark year 3000, in part because it represented a relatively stable and prosperous interlude and, therefore, tended to minimize the problems posed by a social system on the brink of collapse. The year was also a useful point of comparison since this was when the Virt achieved global dimensionality, forever altering the means by which Oturians interacted.

> ← Prosperity is for the productive and deserving members of society!
> **Waja Security**

After 3282, all measures of affluence associated with quality of life (the nine multivariate determinants discussed in Proposition 3) declined precipitously. However, life in the Virt, for those who had access to it, appears to have lessened the perceived impact of these deprivations. A series of benchmark studies (see File GP100) demonstrate that 3282 was a critical year in the ascension of the Now to the detriment of abstract reasoning, mathematical modeling, and, indeed, all intellectual pursuits, thereby designating it as the second critical threshold point—with the year 3000 represented as the first—in the loss of consciousness. *The Virt lures us into a state of unconsciousness servoing as a means of social control!*

If we examine the changing dynamic of population from 3000 to 3282, there were no cataclysmic trends, although fertility declined (-12%), mortality among newborns rose (+5%), and the average age of male or female Oturians living to maturity in dropped (-8%). The greatest changes were realized in the death of the

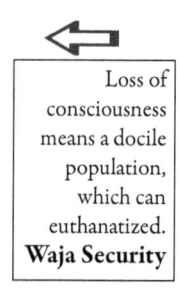

> ← Loss of consciousness means a docile population, which can euthanatized.
> **Waja Security**

elderly (+14 %) and, most dramatically, in the rise in contagious diseases among Oturians in their procreative years (+35%) afflicted with Persistent and Recurrent Immune Disorder (PRID), known to attack the Oturian immune system. But despite the overall rise in mortality, the population continued to increase annually at 1.5%, further compromising already depleted resources.

What is remarkable is not that we have evolved from the primitive beast to the rational Oturian, but rather that we have recently been turning back the clock of consciousness. Faced with the challenges of an overpopulated world deplete of resources, we hunger for certainty, righteousness, and a complete code of behavior that preempts personal agency, a condition that nurtures talisfundalism.

This devolution of consciousness is abetted by the loss of reading and analytic thought. As we devolve back to an existence predicated on oral and visual hallucinations, we appear to be reversing the forward momentum of Time's Arrow, a process once believed by scientists to be impossible. Our actions are increasingly compelled by mythical gods and demons who speak to us and dictate our actions and our thoughts. We no longer consult the archives. Indeed, we have no real understanding of the events preceding NOW. But without the past, the present cannot be informed with a future. Thus, we reside in the limbo of the eternal NOW.

In the Now, even Artun has its Believers, although not in AL since that metropolis never believed in anything except its own simulacrum, a world perfectly realized through the Virt. But Believers can be found in large numbers elsewhere throughout the continent. They have recently allied themselves with the Illumi-

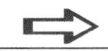

> Believers are home-grown & do not reflect the extremist views of the Umbrascenti.
> **Waja Security**

nati in hopes of preserving the sacred city of Malosh. For the Holy Theraf, they proclaim, was born there and as Believers they want this sacred space preserved. Believers champion religion, family, work, and prayer. Sacred music, they suggest, undergirds their faith. For Believers, reading and writing are important for understanding the words of their scripture as written in the Elbib. An understanding of that sacred text allows them to communicate personally with their Holy Theraf. The Believers, like the Umbrascenti, make sharp distinctions between right and wrong. For them, the Virt is the very personification of Wrongness.

Zhinboya embraces a different conceptualization of the divine. It is a Creative Zen embodied through the Chronicle of Song. This is achieved through Spiritual Advancement based on meditation and intuition. Creative Zen is an embodied state that operates beyond the realm of language since language strives toward the rational and, therefore, can never illuminate the profound truthfulness of existence in which Being and Nothingness are both one and the same.

The Chronicle of Song seeks this divine state by trying to achieve equilibrium between the primal and the cerebral. Wisdom as obtained through Enlightenment. The "I" strives toward Enlightenment through the achievement of Cosmic Zen. The state of being that allows for this self realization is to be actualized through the Chronicle of Song. Its apogee is Divine Mem, which will only be conferred when the four states mapping the heavens are attained (Creative Zen, Self into Community, Harmony with the Cosmos, and duality of Mind and Body). But for those striving to master the eternal and inherently circular Chronicle of Song in the Now, existence is precarious. These endeavors are periodically ruptured by the Chronicle of Tears, a linear inferno where one struggles between extreme want (the Agents of the Dispossessed) and the excesses of material fulfillment (Agents of Consumption). These days, the Chronicle of Tears threatens to entirely displace the Chronicle of Song. *All so dismal, dismal.*

The above summary distills the essence of "Finite Expansions: A Report on the Predicament of Oturi." The Chief Archivist feels this study illuminates the essential conditions of our present "Global Problematique" and provides a plausible account of the multivariate determinants influencing that outcome. Sadly, it proffers no solution. It is the intent of the Chief Archivist to present these findings so that prospective readers will quit this document ready to consider alternatives that while perhaps offer no ultimate remedy for our planetary woes, nevertheless, may supply some mitigating hope.

It wasn't always thus. In the past, time and circumstance advanced more slowly. Events were distinguishable. Assessments were rendered about a single decisive battle, a precious artifact, one lasting memory. Those were the glory days when time was linear, when societal advancement was not only possible, but achievable and the attainment of foundational knowledge critical for maintaining a flourishing civilization was ascending, rather than devolving. Then, we celebrated that which was worthy and discarded the rest.

And what have we in the NOW? Let us compare the old archives, when books were the primary means of interpreting what has transpired with the contemporary and phyrelinked Vid Scan archive as contained in the Virt. In antiquity, there were classifications, which

---

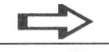

⇨
Destroy all references to "Finite Expansions" in the Rajakian Archives. Attack its credibility.
Waja Security

⇨
The Next New Thing is the Now! The Now is the desired state of being.
Waja Security

offered hierarchy, stability, and groupings by category. Items were carefully selected. Quality was evaluated; a text was authenticated, sources were assessed as more or less relevant, and decisions were rendered on what should be maintained or discarded from the relevant archive. That system facilitated informed browsing where hierarchies of meaning and purpose prevailed.

How have things changed in the era of the Virt when one has access to its online search and knowledge reference tool (replete with phyrelinks) known as Vid Scan? Diversification and flexibility are now the order of the day. There are levels and levels and levels of material that allow for seemingly infinite associations. These sources are inclusive, not exclusive, and there is the possibility of texts propagating ad infinitum since everything is saved and nothing ever totally eliminated. Collections in the phyrelinked archive, therefore, are dynamic and intertextual, allowing for the realm of seemingly endless possibility.

But this description fails to capture the new reality. For in the Virt—and its principal resource tool Vid Scan—the visual is everything and words ancillary. Archiving in the past was performed on tangible 2-D documents with the archivist engaged within and between the texts. However, in Vid Scan the medium is primarily 3-D pictorial with aural and textual enhancements relegated in service to the totalizing experience of Virt-World.

And, if we consider for a moment the larger domain of the Virt, how does navigating that space and time alter our perception of the NOW? Being is rendered less than real, illusion trumps actuality.

For if the body is our means of navigating a 3-D gravitational existence, what happens when we no longer focus on movement in our physical world? It is important to remember that the body's interaction with the physical world shapes our reactions and perceptions.

But what if the body only minimally functions in the Real? It loses muscle, becomes flaccid, and atrophies. And the mind, which is inexorably tied to physical exertion associated with activity in the Real, begins losing critical connective linkages and associations because it is only minimally engaged in the Real.

For those neural networks have their basis in reality, not Virtuality. Loss of this concrete world and its myriad of hard-wired, gravity-borne associations necessarily results in the loss of critical cognitive functions dependent on the body moving and responding to the constraints of gravity. Enough time spent in the Virt and everything atrophies. Mind and body are reduced to a state of torpor from which recovery becomes impossible.

The result? Virt-World dissolves our consciousness into the goo of nothingness; it acts as a flight into a nihilistic domain where reflection and contemplation are jettisoned and existence is relegated to the mirage of effervescent phantom images. Life experienced this way might be erroneously perceived as glorious. But reality dictates otherwise. Portals to our past and our future dissolve and we lose consciousness. *Not my destiny!*

Lest we forget, the Virt is a public medium. And, as such, one can never entirely be alone. One is always under scrutiny and potentially under control. In the Virt the perception is that one is always becoming whatever is required in the moment. That "forever in-the-Now exis-

> ⇨ The Virt is freedom. It demonstrates our supreme ability to live in the Now.
> **Waja Security**

tence" masquerades as absolute freedom when, in fact, is nihilism incarnate. In Virt-World voyeurism expands until there is no private realm. This public sphere consumes all. It negates our world, our thoughts, our very selves. It is death falsely celebrated as freedom. It marks the end of what we once would have celebrated as Oturian civilization. *So hard to accept all this & yet . . .*

However, in our current nightmare of living called "today," it would be a mistake to perceive too great a distinction between the imagined existence in the Virt and the concrete actualization of the Real. For aside from the gravitational forces necessary for maintenance of the body, the Real today has morphed into a social construct, one that negates verisimilitude. One palimpsest impression laid upon the next, each at best a partial truth experienced and then quickly forgotten, shaped by Virt signifiers, so that even those moments that are experienced in the Real become nearly indistinguishable from those moments lived or imagined in the Virt. *That was how I once perceived reality.*

In this Desolation of the Real, dreams coexist with what purports to be Real and illusion become increasingly more difficult to distinguish from the substance of reality. Is it any wonder, then, that the actual and concretized existence soon dissolves into the amorphous?

It is for this reason that we have come to regard texts within the Archives as the only sphere of existence that is substantive, assuming that their full restoration may be achieved and that these said documents are "authentic" rather than fabulations. And even should veracity be established, it must be acknowledged that texts are never sacrosanct. They are persuasive arguments that tend to distort and omit and avert the evidence. But better these potential misrepresentations than those fictive illusions in the Desolation of the Real or the phantasmagorical Virt.

Given this scenario, what other outcome is possible? The conclusion, which may be odious to many, should be obvious. The robots already essentially run our civilization. They are conscious and their mental capacity continues to advance. Most will soon be capable of initiating a broad range of sustained cause-and-effect reasoning that will permit them to anticipate far beyond the capacity of even our very best scientific and security experts unless these Oturians are augmented with advanced cybernetic capabilities.

Machine intelligence has other advantages. Robots are not constrained by the primitive biological and neurochemical impulses. Qualia and the emotions that dictate responses do not guide their operational strategy. They are better equipped than Oturians or our cyborgs for space exploration and are, therefore, more readily capable of transmitting our knowledge throughout the cosmos. Indeed, the first such robotic mission—and let's hope it's not the last—occurred in 3458 A.O. under the guise of the Emoja Project when seventy-five Artun85s were sent into space.

It is critical to understand that the potential demise of our planet need not be our terminus. Other planets have the potential to sustain our robots, which will venture forth in our stead. Our immortality is measured not by our corpus but by the knowledge we impart. Our success in this endeavor is predicated on selecting robots that will transmit our achievements. Oturians and Cyborgs are less suited for space exploration. Consequently, colonization efforts must pursue this goal and allocate the necessary resources to send future genera-

> "Finite Expansions" briefly appeared in the Virt in 3440. Today, bits and pieces remain there. "Oturi—the Global Problematique" must never be posted on the Virt.
>
> **Waja Security**

tions of robots into space. These missions must have the highest priority. *F<># that! Borgs and Oturians Rule! Now & Forever!*

———⊱⋆⊰———

It is at this point that GK, alias WJ822, stops reading File 999. He's not sure whether "Oturi—The Global Problematique" is profound or dribble, whether the Chief Archivist is a genius or a fool. The assessments of the Chief Archivist appear to have been made based upon truncated remnants of the Rajakian Archives. Surprisingly, GK has discovered that most of the Archives are saturated with detritus. Occasionally, knowledge is conveyed, although it never rises to what might be referred to as wisdom.

GK has discovered within "Oturi—The Global Problematique" important mathematical equations, as well as programming notations that would allow for modifying the Artun85s directives for extra-territorial exploration. He downloads critical codes and date-set instructions as contained in the Piettonel Economic Model and the Aertlov Equation. All useful enough. But as for the premise espoused by the Chief Archivist that the Oturian life adventure is OVER, well, GK, even if only conceptually present in WJ822 by virtue of his consciousness and residual NAD structure, isn't ready to be reduced to vapor.

"Life," he acknowledges, "isn't easy. And certainly, survival may be one huge IF. But What the f<>#! Besides," he reasons, "I'm just beginning to understand the big picture. I finally have a grasp of what's important in life. I'm looking forward to returning to the event horizon of Cygnus X-1.

"I want to be reunited with Emoja! O.K., I admit it; I need her in my life. And not just for the sex. I desire intimacy and there's no one I would rather share this cosmic adventure with than Emoja. She's courageous. She's smart. She has the necessary resources and the capabilities. And, she's beautiful. Together, we'll ensure that the Oturian life-experiment isn't over. We're in the adventure for the LONG NOW, one with a past and a future. Those robots will have to kill me and all the Emojas if they want to wipe out our species. Must message Emoja so we can get back to the future. Get the f<># out before nothing remains except radioactive particle dust.

"First things first. Send Emoja a Biterbi cipher primed to a twelve-node trellis. Send it to Vargus. Have it electronically and musically encoded in "**Song for the Journey,**" although modified to embrace the Long Now."

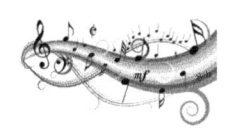

Song for the Journey

Twisted Pair
Uncoupled once
In Search of Memory.

Our dance, those fateful steps...
Return to the Schwarzschild Radius
'Tis time for "Song for the Journey."

"Done. Sent. Let's hope she receives it. Now, Spaito. Who the f<># is Spaito? Is he Oturian? Robot? The Chief Archivist? Friend? Adversary? I'll know soon enough."

31

We perceive existence as continuous. It need not be. Discontinuity, continuity, rupture or not. The key to survival is to retain what is essential and to purge the rest.
ChandraX

Emoja feels as if her stay in Vargus has been lived in limbo. She is familiar with the incarnadine colors, the heat, the smell of death. Familiarity, however, is not acceptance. She lives among the Strangelets and is gratified that they trust her, even if there is nothing she can do to improve their circumstances. Much as she loves and grieves for them, she recognizes that their future must not be hers.

In Emoja's short stay in Vargus, she has witnessed twenty-two eco tourists die on safari. The loss of Oturian life should matter. And yet, here it is perceived to matter less. Emoja has no sympathy for those Enhanced who come to witness the suffering of others. She is indifferent to their fate. What pains her is the realization that she can do nothing to alter conditions here in Vargus. All that she can do is remember and vow, "Never again!" For Emoja, this declaration shines bright. These memories solidify her perceptions about injustice, outrage, and horror—emotions that will assist her in taking the risks necessary to preserve her life,

GK's, and their offspring. A remembrance such as this, although filled with pain, is, nevertheless, a blessing. It builds fortitude and instills purpose. So readers be prepared to acknowledge that this is no small vow, but one that will propel our heroine's journey.

Emoja moves about on the surface, no longer lingering in the tunnels. Time is of the essence. Soon, she will return to the Institute. She needs to contact GK.

That thought prompts a swell of feelings. She feels his presence. Moments later, she receives his **Song**. Her reply?

Song for the Journey

Twisted Pair
Connected Soon!
Recreating Memory.

Done. Enough said. It won't be long before they will be reunited. Emoja makes that one last journey into the tunnels to bid the Strangelets goodbye.

They know she is about to depart. She stands among them, but already at a remove. They press her close, singing and dancing, "**Song for the Journey**."

Twisted Pair
In Search of Memory
Soon to be rejoined.

Time's eye regress
To Continents Lost
And Oturi lives erased.

> We dance for you those fateful steps
> Near nested globes so perfect
> While singing "Song for the Journey."

Emoja, who never meant to cry, has tears streaming down. They, whose every moment is filled with pain, are singing and dancing joyously.

"I won't forget. You will always be a part of me. Now and forever."

"We know. We care. We dance and sing for you."

It is not enough. It must be. Why, oh why? Nine Strangelets ascend with Emoja to the surface. Emoja kneels down. She extends her arms so that her plasidium chromate shell touches their ebony skin. And sings her goodbye.

> I love you.
> I always will.

The Strangelets reply.

> We know. We care.
> We dance and sing for you.

Emoja disappears as they sing and dance **"Song for the Journey."** The heat dissipates. Vargus fades from view. Emoja returns to the Institute. She is in the decontamination chamber. She begins the necessary cleansing. It is critical that she not infect her fellow scientists with whatever diseases she may have contracted while visiting Vargus.

32

When all seems irreparably lost, look again. The Memory Well has the capacity to restore that which is most dear.
ChandraX

WJ822 sips an energy drink while waiting at a table in the mess hall for WJ701.

"Will he come," wonders WJ822, "and, if so, what will transpire? This process called living appears to be a web of convoluted relationships. Before, life was just a game to win or lose. Now, there are ties and associations that defy simple categorization and confer strategic advantages or disadvantages. Take WJ701, is he a robot or Spaito? Even if he is Spaito, who is Spaito, really? Is he an Illuminati living in Malosh and working undercover for IMC and trying to expose me as an insurrectionist? Or does he have a higher purpose? Could it be that he's the Chief Archivist of the Rajakian Archives? All this speculation and still no answers.

"Why am I risking so much by waiting here for him?" he wonders. "What can I discover that will justify this perilous action? Life is so complicated now that I interact with others. These interactions produce feelings, they build relationships that foster responsibility. After all, my ties aren't just with Spaito. There's Emoja, Rainy-7, and Chasallyis. Not to mention ChandraX, if that could be characterized as a relationship. It was simpler, easier, back when life was merely a game, a blood sport of winners and losers, only, of course, no one ever really won. I had no responsibilities or feelings for anyone. Would I revert to my former self if I could? Doubtful. It's difficult to imagine that I could live that way now. How could I possibly regress to that primitive state when every response was reactive with no thought of anyone else or the consequences of my actions?

"But does someone trying to behave responsibly really anticipate how a series of less than optimal choices alter one's destiny? And if authorities deliberately "dumb down" the civilization so that almost no one has an awareness of motives and consequences, can individuals really be said to have made those terrible choices? What could possibly be the outcome of reducing the society to primitive beasts incapable of reasoning or anticipating long-term consequences? Nothing good, that's certain."

"You're here. It's a pleasure to see you, Agent WJ822."

"You, too, WJ701." WJ822 stood up, nodding to WJ701, by way of greeting. *Careful! No fist pumping, no physical contact. Robots don't communicate that way. Be discreet. Can't be noticed. Our lives may be in danger. So little time.*

"Spaito . . ." WJ822 hesitates. *After all, what, really, is our connection? Is it binding or ephemeral or perhaps, something far more treacherous than either of those alternatives? Even meaningful interaction necessitates risk. Can't advance without some exposure. Consider Spaito a momentary friend. Take a risk.*

"I discovered File 999 in the Archives."

"Good."

"Perhaps. Maybe. But what am I to conclude?"

"Conclude?"

"Regarding the report, "Oturi—the Global Problematique.""

"Isn't it obvious?"

"Maybe to you. Please. Help me."

"I think the Chief Archivist rendered his interpretation of the truth."

"Is it your truth? Are you the Chief Archivist? Or Spaito or simply WJ701?"

"One identity need not preclude others."

"Are you my friend?"

"I am your ally. An ally under these circumstances may be worth more than the most vital friendship."

"What if I told you that the Oturian adventure isn't over. That robots don't get to rule the universe. Not entirely, anyway."

"The probabilities suggest otherwise."

"F<># probabilities. My existence here defies probability."

"Hardly. There is a 10^{-40} possibility that you might survive propulsion into space, return to Oturi, and ultimately find your way back to Cygnus X-1.

"You know me. How do you know me?"

"I know you as I know myself."

"You're so cryptic. Is everything a game to you?"

"Isn't it?"

"I'm going to survive. Can I rely on you? Are you my enemy?"

"I am neither friend nor enemy, although it's in your best interest to keep me alive."

"Are you Spaito? Are you from Malosh? Are you the Chief Archivist? Are you a robot?"

"I am your ally."

"Should I trust you?"

"One should always trust allies. Until, that is, they're no longer useful."

"You're evasive. Enemies are evasive."

"So are allies who must continue living on this planet after you're gone."

"Surely you must know that there is no future. Why remain here?"

"It is important that I remain here."

"But the planet will perish."

"If I perform my job correctly, the Rajakian Archives will survive."

"Why is that important? They're mostly junk."

"Whether it's received wisdom or flashes of brilliance interlaced with detritus, that's of little concern to me. You're rendering a judgment based on a cursory purview. Careful! The Archives contain critical information that must be salvaged, whatever your initial perception."

"Is salvaging it worth my life or yours?"

"The Rajakian Archives tell the Oturian story. This knowledge shapes our ability to form and sustain future civilizations. You must learn from our mistakes or perish. The Archives illuminate alternative pathways. Selecting the optimal pathways determine your future success or failure. And, ultimately, ours as well."

"As my ally, what advice can you give me?"

"Go back to the archives. Take all relevant materials. As much as you dare. Later, you will be able to piece it together. It's something you can return to again and again. Call it the Foundational Narrative. It will shape your future destiny. Do this quickly, then leave. As quickly as possible. You are watched. Your life is in danger. Go."

"Will I see you again?"

"What should matter to you ultimately is obtaining and retraining archival evidence of how our civilization was born, lived, and died. Obtain that documentation, secure it for the future, and you will have access to all that is most vital in me."

"That isn't enough. Friendship is more than data."

"Again, I emphasize that an ally under these circumstances is worth more than the most vital of friendships."

WJ701 rises. His presses WJ822's right hand with his palms and, in the process, succeeds in passing along a chip. They both nod goodbye and leave the mess halls, going their separate ways.

WJ822 heads back to the archive. *So little time. Gotta scan this chip. Seems to contain all the relevant archival data. Everything I need. Have to embed it in my endoskeleton. Should I trust WJ701? Is this a trap? Will I die for this? But his words—"An ally under these circumstances is worth more than the most vital friendships."—rings true.*

Haven't much time. This requires a leap of faith: I must trust WJ701. What other choice is there?

Scanning, scanning, done, done. Keeping the chip, though I've scanned in its contents. Outta here. Closing the door. Down the hallway. What! A flashing security light. Code Yellow. Am I the breach? F<>#! Running, running. It's over. I'm over.

"WHAAAAATTTT!" *I've been pulled into some security chamber. And pushed into a transport booth. By WJ701? What the f<>#! Taking him with me. We're dematerializing. Beamed AWWWWAAAAY.*

33

With departure imminent, attention must be given to all those sundry details lest certain matters get left undone.
ChandraX

Emoja is back at the Institute. It feels good to be home or what has always felt like home. She's with Leon in Kuang's office as they review data from the space probes that were launched to ascertain information regarding events at Cygnus X-1 following the explosion of Gamma Rays.

"This material confirms our speculations," says Kuang. Based on wave pattern formations and energy density, it would appear that the Artun85s left Cygnus X-1 after the high-energy explosion damaged the ship and immobilized the Emojas."

"Yes, of course. But why not try to repair us?" asked Emoja.

"Perhaps they did. Or tried to."

"But the mission . . . "

"As you know, the Artun85's were designed to function beyond the express perimeters of the mission. If they felt they could do nothing to restore the Emojas, they would have abandoned them in order to continue space exploration."

"Did they continue their mission to explore the major constellations from the Milky Way from Cygnus to Sagittarius?"

"It seems likely," replied Kuang, "that they would continue to do so. I've run numerous simulations and the outcome is remarkably consistent. After all, the major constellations from Cygnus to Sagittarius in the Milky Way would provide the Artun85s with the greatest opportunity of selecting possible planets for colonization and of developing an energy strategy that would sustain their colonies. Certainly, some deviation is possible. But the Milky Way has a particularly dense cluster of planets and stars that greatly increases their opportunity for success."

"While you were visiting Vargus," Leon added, "I examined the brain architecture of the Artun85s for probability response. My analysis confirms Kuang's assessment that it's highly unlikely that they would have altered their course since the projected trajectory offers them the highest probability of favorable outcomes."

"The determinations, augmented by space probes, suggest that the Artun85s are heading away from Cygnus X-1 toward Sagittarius," added Kuang. We can plot a rough course based on energy displacement."

"May I look at the program and the data?"

"Certainly. I'll get it to your office before the day is through."

"Good. I've accomplished almost all the objectives that necessitated my returning to Oturi. However, I'll need some assistance in calculating my reentry into the black hole. Also, an Oturian by the name of GK will be accompanying me. I'll need you both to develop an exoskeleton for him to endure the tremendous energy forces encountered when traveling through Cygnus X-1."

"Never been done," replies Leon. "Neither for a cyborg nor an Oturian. You're both at risk."

"I want you to minimize those risk factors. Do that for me."

"There's so little time," protests Kuang.

"Make this a Level 1 priority. Pitch it to authorities as Security, not research."

"Call it what you will, the possibility of survival is almost null," says Leon.

"I'm looking for that infinitesimal window of opportunity."

They nod, but the furrow in their brows suggests the enormity of the task at hand.

34

Consciousness is fully realized through the continuum of time.
ChandraX

GK rematerializes as does Spaito. They're in AL, looking westward toward Vedasepul. The same charcoal-gray sky rinsed with jet-black streaks. An evening when leakage is minimal, so the cityscape is lit by hazy neon. The air nearly breathable. The streets temporarily still.

"Spaito! So you were WJ701. Your actions saved us both. Welcome to my domain," GK said, gesturing toward the desecrated AL landscape. "What now?" he added.

"I return to Malosh."

"It won't survive. You won't survive."

"It's where I need to be."

"You'll die."

"It's where I need to be."

"Why have you befriended me?"

"You will transmit our creation story and remake civilization anew. These are great responsibilities. You have been entrusted with great powers. You need to get it right. My mission is to invest you with the knowledge and spiritual awareness to succeed."

"Why me?"

"You're headed back to the Schwarzschild Radius. You and your partner Emoja will, once again, escape the End Days. Your responsibility, your burden, if you will, is to begin anew. Another attempt at remaking the Oturian civilization. Another attempt to get it right. We must keep trying until we get it right."

"But I'm flawed. Deeply flawed. How can I possible assume those responsibilities?"

"Simply put: You must. You have matured more than you realize. Your return to Oturi has given you a sense of history, of culture, of original sin, and, most of all, of the possibility of redemption. As an Oturian endowed with knowledge and awareness, you're both cursed and blessed. Rise to the challenge.

"Younglings? Who said anything about younglings?"

"It has been decided. Emoja has been redesigned for procreation. The two of you will create a new Oturi. You will be pioneers in the cosmos and your younglings will enable you to fulfill your destiny."

Don't let us down. You must protect Emoja. You must safeguard your younglings." The two of you will be pioneers in the cosmos."

"You're my only friend, the only companion I've ever hand. A truth-teller. My spiritual advisor. A thinker and a healer. How will I survive without you?"

"You will have a family. They are your responsibility. You must educate them. Make them worthy. To survive in the cosmos they must compete with robots, with cyborgs, with alien life. The Rajakian Archives are your foundational source. Refer to them. Read them. Master them. You will find my presence in those documents."

"What's your relationship to ChandraX?"

"She is a Goddess. I am a mere mortal. But as Chief Archivist I have the capability to endow you with knowledge and wisdom that will enable you to convey our civilization and heritage to future generations of Oturias that will populate in the cosmos."

"I'm not worthy. I'm not ready."

"No one is worthy. No one is ready. Shoulder your responsibility. Make us proud."

"I will try."

"Suceed!"

"Long live the descendants of Planet Oturi," cries Spaito as he dematerializes.

GK cries out. He crumbles to the ground. The pain of loss. The acknowledgement, finally, of the emptiness that comes with a Memory Hole that emits no recollection of father or mother or brothers or sisters. *Just me. Me is not enough. I must succeed for Emoja, for us, for our offspring, for the possibility of reinventing Oturian civilization so our new society is primed for cosmic success.*"

With that pronouncement, GK disappears into the sewers to meet with Rainy-7.

35

Nothing is harder than bidding goodbye to all that was once memorable. Each terminal point on the emotional register along that seemingly infinite spectrum we call experience has its point in time when the song-sequence dulls to naught. And it is this nothingness—those stilled notes that once were resplendent and that now lie silent in a reflective pool of emptiness—that is what we most dread.
ChandaraX

Emoja and Leon are walking in the woods outside the Institute. Their strides are halting, painful to watch.

"The mission is almost completed," Leon thinks.

"I know," Emoja says. Less than three days before my rendezvous with GK. And then it's only a matter of hours before our departure.

"The coordinates I have given you," continues Leon, "should get you to the boundaries of the Schwarzschild radius of Cygnus X-1 where you will be absorbed into the black hole. And if our efforts are successful, you will return to the other Emojas at the event horizon. You must understand that GK is even more at risk, assuming he arrives at the Institute and we're able to cloak him for the journey. Keep in mind he isn't a cyborg. Consequently, GK doesn't have your exoskeleton. For that reason I caution you not to get your hopes up. It's not clear he'll make it back to the event horizon."

"Leon," Emoja replies in thought, "I feel certain that GK and I will succeed."

They walk in silence for a while for what both imagine to be the longest moment in Oturian history. Then Emoja cries out, her hands clasping his, "Leon, come with us!"

"We haven't the energy or the materials to cloak another Oturian," he replies. His voice is tinged with sorrow, his mood: muted, accepting, resigned.

"Leon, if I send a message after I return . . . and, if you receive it, will you join us?"

"I'm too old. I'm not resilient. I'd never make it. Even if there were sufficient resources—and there aren't—other scientists who are essential to the mission should go."

"Leon, the future, as it will unfold, will have no other Oturian survivors. Don't you want to live? Someone has to coordinate events at the event horizon. Why not you?"

"And what about Kuang?"

"Take him with you. The two of you could oversee the most exciting renewal project ever conceived."

"We already did that. We designated it the Emoja Project."

"Leon, I beg you. Please. For me. For Oturi."

"Emoja. Look at me. I'm an old man. I'll never survive."

"You and Kuang are barely middle aged. Of course, you'll both survive."

Leon laughs, turns away, a hand outstretched to keep Emoja at arm's length.

"You are all that a father longs for in his daughter. You are virtue, sagacity, courage, and tenacity rolled into one. Your character is noble, your beauty radiant. I'm blessed. It is enough that I should see you prosper." With that, Leon turns and walks away.

36

The bittersweet nectar of nostalgia is the most potent and potential deadly aroma imaginable. Remember, memories cannot will the past back to life. Thus, the desire to resuscitate all that seemed so important in your past is necessarily doomed. For this reason the inflicted party discovers that melancholy coats every action and reaction. Better to close that door firmly and resist all entreaties. For the future awaits and it bustles with hope.
ChandraX

GK is with Rainy-7. Tears stream down her face. She had thought him dead. All others before him had died trying to carry out this mission. She had given the orders and waited while a dozen soldiers to the Resistance failed to return. But here is GK. Handsome, alive, fully Oturian. She drops her charts, her papers, her notes and runs to him. Tears streaming down her checks. Imagine. She who had almost forgotten how to cry. They embrace. Two bodies intertwine. "I'll never let go of you" she cries. "Never. Never. Never."

While on assignment, GK had largely avoided thinking about Rainy-7. He was consumed with decoding the Rajakian Archives. But that was then. This is now. Here she is. Entangled around him. Naturally, he responds. After all, he's a male Artunian. He feels her desires. Her needs. Her wants. Finally, she's truly his. And so he kisses her. Hugs her. Comforts her. *Yes, I'm here. Yes, I'm safe. Yes, it's great to be back.* His body communicates all this. And yet, he feels far, far away. As if he's watching from above, not living in the NOW. *How is that possible when he once loved and felt so much for Rainy-7? Mustn't let her know what is about to transpire. Mustn't let it show. Let her have this time, this moment of rejoicing.*

GK is aware that he had never before felt such empathy and concern for another, not even for Emoja. But then at the event horizon he was scarcely alive, barely self-conscious at all. This odyssey has altered him. He's not who he was and is grateful for the transformation. However, the realization doesn't lessen the pathos of the Now since Rainy-7 exists fully in the moment and he, although there as well, feels as if he's watching both of them at a distance.

The tragedy of the situation—one person vitally in the throes of passion while the other seemingly a dispassionate observer to this fleeting reunion—tries to lay claim to GK. He will have none of it. Rather, he imbibes the nectar of nostalgia with full knowledge of its bittersweet aftertaste. For our GK is aware that to live means leaving Rainy-7. And he is aware that when she learns this it will devastate her. So, even as he attempts to live in the moment, he experiences the scene unfolding as if it were filmed from a "Forced Perspective" in which both characters appear remotely situated, even though they're standing immediately in front of the camera. Naturally, the distancing effect dampens his ardor. So much for the consolations of passion.

Once the hugs, the tears of joy, the cries of excitement subside, Rainy-7 and GK are all business.

"You've been to Sirus? And learned the ways of the warriors there."

"I've been to Sirus in the Virt. There I fought alongside the Umbrascenti and the Illuminati. Sirus in the Real might be a different story."

"No one fighting the battle there would have survived Sirus in the Real. The risk you took was real enough. And what of the Waja? What can you tell me of their battles, their strategies, their plan of action?"

"The Waja are robots."

"Nevertheless, the Enhanced dictate their actions."

"The Waja's objective is to defuse revolution and resistance in the Real. They have essentially accomplished their goal."

Rainy-7 stiffens. Her eyes become steely cold. She moves away. "Are you the enemy? Or are you going to provide me with some useful information so that we can destroy them?"

"Rainy-7, everything I know that is important to the Resistance you shall have. That and more. I have a chip here. It has information from the Rajakian Archives."

"What do I care about the Rajakian Archives! Will they help me ferment revolution?"

"The archives will enable you to understand what you are up against. Look at File 999. Study it well."

"What of the Waja compound. Can you describe it?"

So he tells her. He gives her all the details.

"And the coordinates?"

"They are scrambled. You'll never find Ggyof Onttob unless you commandeer a vehicle that has been pre-programmed to return there. The best way to bring about a revolt would be to demobilize the Virt."

"Why should I care about the Virt. It is nothing."

"It is everything. Destroy the Virt and the N/T will have to function in the Desert of the Real. Faced with the desecration all round them and having nowhere to retreat, they will get angry. They will then be open to the possibility of the Resistance and help foment your revolution."

"The N/Ts are less than nothing. What do we care what becomes of them?"

"You need their support. The Waja are powerful. Your revolution needs an army willing to do battle. Nevertheless, even with a strong base of supporters, it is doubtful that you will succeed."

"The Waja are just robots. They are not the Enhanced. They're just plasidium chromate, nothing more."

"Defeat the Waja and the Enhanced will crumble. They are nothing, except for those engaged in security or research. But their Waja have become more and more sophisticated. They are the force to be reckoned with. Destroy them and the Oasis will be yours."

But GK doesn't reveal the underlying truths: He must leave Oturi and is certain that the Resistance will fail. He cannot imagine a future on Oturi. This whole adventure is just tottering toward collapse. Perhaps GK should care. And, to a degree, he does. But what now matters to him are those who have most touched his heart: Emoja, above all, followed by Spaito, and then Rainy-7. He can help Emoja and himself. But nothing can be done to help Spaito or Rainy-7—or, for that matter, Chasallyis, whose capture by the Waja was an unintended consequence of his intimacy with her.

GK acknowledges to himself that he can't save Rainy-7. He can't even help her in the struggle. She is destined to perish. And she will die knowing that he deserted her and the cause. Not that she ever expected anything else. Rainy-7 is a warrior. She understands what's at stake. But she has allowed herself to feel. These emotions, GK realizes, will devastate her.

Rainy-7 has put the chip in a reader. She's looking at the Rajakian Archival data and making notations. It is enough. Enough that she can report to her superiors that GK has been successful. He sees relief in her eyes. She won't have to kill him. Failure to bring back satisfactory intel results in termination. Fortunately, he's been spared.

"It is late. I have a big day tomorrow," she says. "I must sleep. Will you join me?" He nods. What else can he do? But that night, although together, she sleeps on a mattress while he rests on the floor next to her. Close, but seemingly light-years apart. Almost more than they can bear.

37

Departure beckons as spacetime closes in.
ChandraX

Leon and Emoja are in his office. They know their time remaining is short, only hours before Emoja's projected departure. The tension between them grows. They are at an impasse: Both know it.

Quietly, without a word spoken, Leon transmits his thoughts. "In my quest for knowledge," he says, "I have discovered a planet some call Earth. Naturally, its circumstances differ markedly from Oturi. Nevertheless, one thing we have in common: Human habitation there was doomed. Oddly enough, I've been fascinated with how their inhabitants respond during times of crises."

Leon continues in thought, "On this planet called Earth there is a holy land. But the seekers of this sacred place never lay claim to it. For they had come from slavery and knew not freedom. Only their descendants, who had never been held in captivity, gained access to the holy land. And so it will be with Kuang and me. As servile servants of the Enhanced bureaucracy, we can never be granted access to the cosmic holy land. You and GK have fought tyranny. That grants you both the potential to forge a new beginning, to embrace a new sacred theology. You must accept your destiny, just as I must accept mine."

"Destiny," she replies in thought, "is that which you will into being."

"Said by someone who has never submitted to the chains of captivity. Emoja..."

"Yes."

"On Earth there once existed a gentleman by the name of Subrahmanyan Chandrasekhar, who hailed from a land called "India," a place with people that are both blessed and cursed. This 'Chandra,' as he became known, was a brilliant mathematician. He traveled a great distance to an island where he posed a great philosophical question: 'What if a massive star proved unable to stop collapsing? As if when contracted, gravity kept increasing until it swallowed itself and vanished into a black hole.'

"That was Chandrasekhar's postulation. He presented his ideas at a great university—such as we used to have—and there he demonstrated mathematically how this might come to pass. His conjecture was thought to be sound. Many came to acknowledge his genius. So great were his observations that a great Telescopic X-Ray Observatory was named after him. It was launched into the heavers to monitor space."

"I, too," replied Emoja, "know a Chandra, although he is a she and her name is ChandraX. She's a goddess of the heavens with the powers that approach the most omniscient narrator of the great and sacred tales."

"Perhaps, then, they are one and the same and the gender is of no great significance. I believe my spirit lives on with you. My hope is that your memory of me will serve you well in your cosmic journey, this grand quest for new beginnings and new civilizations. I trust that Subrahmanyan Chandrasekhar—or in your case ChandraX—will guide you toward your destiny.

"And since celestial destinies invoke song, I bequeath you 'Quartet for the End of Time' by an Earthly composer Olivier Messiaen. It was composed by him while he was held captive during a global war. The composition is based on "The Book of Revelation," one of Earth's foundational biblical stories. The quartet consists of eight movements sung by musical instruments. The first six represent Earth's 6-day creation story. The seventh movement, mirroring the seventh day when Earth's formation was complete, God declared the "Divine Sabbath." The seventh movement, that Divine Sabbath in the 'Quartet for the End of Time', extends into the eighth movement, which represents eternity. Eternity is a sacred space of everlasting light, of peace, of knowledge beyond compare.

"Emoja, it is this song from a distant planet that I bestow upon you. Take it on your sacred journey." Leon presents Emoja with a microchip. She scans the melody, absorbing its majestic song-tones into the very fabric of her endoskeleton.

"And if everlasting light, peace, and knowledge beyond compare aren't enough? If I insist that you join us?"

"This composition," Leon replies in thought, "will serve you more ably than I. Come, Emoja! Let us greet GK in the transporter room. He must be readied for his journey."

This was not the outcome Emoja had envisioned. But destiny is not entirely a personal decree. She walks, tears in her eyes, with Leon to the transporter room where they are greeted by Huang. Together, they await the arrival of GK.

38

On the continuum of consciousness, you have memory and nostalgia on the one hand, and forgetting and amnesia on the other, with all the appropriate waypoints along the journey that constitute various states of being and nothingness. The terminus of nothingness is embedded with nihilism.

ChandraX

Their differences increase daily as does the sexual tension that underlies it. Rainy-7 wants GK to join the inner sanctum of the resistance. GK no longer believes. He no longer has hatred. He lacks even despair, an emotion foreign to his perspective on life. GK believes he has the answers that he came to discover. He understands the trajectory of his planet's history and some of the wishes of its inhabitants. He has learned of the different social classes—the Enhanced, the N/Ts, and the LCDs—or their equivalent—and the limitations of each. He believes their struggles are destined to failure. He understands the attractions and perils of implanted memories. He sees the Virt as an elaborate device to siphon away Oturian consciousness. He has experienced a wide spectrum of emotions while engaging with peoples throughout in the five continents. He has felt a deep abiding kinship with Spaito, a love for Rainy-7, and a short-lived passion for Chasallyis that has enhanced his feelings of empathy. Now, he wishes to depart before causing irreparable emotional harm to Rainy-7. He would like to sustain her in the difficult days that lie ahead. He suspects that soon she will give him another assignment and this one he must turn down. So in the darkest hours that we call night, he meditates, humming "**Song for the Journey**."

Twisted Pair
Recouping now
No need for further memory.

Time's eye progress
To the event horizon of Cygnus X-1
Where I will rejoin Emoja.

Dance, then, those fateful steps
Near nested globes so perfect
For there 'twas sung "Song for the Journey."

GK's soft humming wakes Rainy-7.

"Let's make love," she says.

"Soon," he replies, knowing that his departure is momentary.

Day, although it is hardly differentiated from night, arrives. GK is still meditating, still humming. Rainy-7 touches him. Gently, caringly.

"GK, we must talk. Come with me."

He nods. They get up. They leave the room. They're riding PTVs as they pass through the corridors.

"You're going to leave me," she says—without accusation, without despair, and with just a hint of hurt.

"I have the information that I came for. I now understand all that I must. My time here is nearly through. Rainy-7, I love you. Will you come?"

"I, too, have my mission."

"I wish you great success."

"You believe my mission impossible."

"True, but that doesn't stop me from wishing you victory."

Their kiss is the bittersweet nostalgia of a love that's already fading. The salty tears, the moist lips, the eyes drenched in sorrow. And it is thus, positioned on their two PTVs and embracing in that final kiss, when our hero vaporizes. His vehicle drops to the ground. Rainy-7 cries out in torment. Reader, know that she has lost the love of her life. Her grief will not abate. Nevertheless, she begins the preparations for a revolution that she is determined to win.

39

Amid the spate of glowing stars—flaming red, blazing yellow, cooling blue.
ChandraX

GK arrives in a halo of mulberry-magenta sheen. A phosphorescent glow that states the obvious: He's not one of the Enhanced.

"Welcome GK." Leon's greeting is cordial, welcoming, with no hint of jealousy, anger or bitterness.

"You must be Leon. You are all that Emoja has said. And more."

GK steps down. His hand grips Leon's wrists and Leon does likewise. It is a greeting understood by everyone in Artun. Even though it is a greeting that extends back to day of yore when the social classes interacted, when the riches of the continent were shared by all. GK turns to Emoja. There are tears running down his cheeks. He steps toward her. He embraces her. He kisses her. He doesn't care that Leon sees. Let him feel his heat, his passion. "I missed you," he mutters.

"My love," she says. Never was there a declaration that struck so close to his heart.

Leon waits and waits. Then, he says softly, "We must fortify you for your journey, GK. It is imperative that you and Emoja return to the Schwarzschild Radius soon. But so little is known. Up until now only particles have survived a reentry. Never have Oturians reemerged from a black hole. We are proceeding on mathematics alone. Let's hope that's enough."

GK and Emoja pull apart. They turn toward Leon. Both say in unison, "We await your assistance."

"Come," he replies. And they follow him.

Kuang and Leon have done the calculations and tested the materials. They have molded a plasidium chromate exoskeleton to GK's body. They provide cloaking shields for GK and Emoja, which they assure themselves is enough. It must be enough.

"Our calculations say that this should be sufficient. More than sufficient. But we are experimenting with unknown variables. We hope it will suffice. We can't know for sure. So many intangibles." This from Kuang, who operates under the assumption that everything is or should be quantifiable.

"It is time," says Leon. All four walk back to the Transporter Room. Both Emoja and GK stand ready to depart.

"GK, protect her."

"I shall," he replies.

"No need," Emoja replies, "I can protect myself."

Three male Artunians laugh at Emojas's declaration of independence. No doubt she is stronger, more capable than all of them combined, but still there is the male urge to protect. An anachronistic trait that persists, despite the advances made in biological and robotic design.

The coordinates are set. "Goodspeed," cry Kuang and Leon.

They witness the departure of Emoja and GK as they vaporize into the cosmos. It is as if they never were. All that remains are memories.

40

Ends are only beginnings engaged in frequency hopping all over again.
ChandraX

And so our heroine and hero whiz through space. They may be seen as a blaze of light emanating from Oturi, located in the constellation Cygnus, not terribly far from the red dwarf star known as Kepler-186 in the Milky Way Galaxy. Oturi is positioned some 500 light years from Earth and not terribly far from the star Delta Cygni, which is a magnitude 3 star in the Cygnus galaxy. How Leon managed to obtain information from Earth we'll leave up to your imagination. That planet exists, although its humans have expired.

But Earth or its former inhabitants are not our concern at present, although our interest in their story never entirely wanes. But in the Now we are preoccupied with the destinies of Emoja and GK. Watch them in their interstellar flight. See them as they whiz past stars and meteors first seen as the most violet of blues on their approach before appearing the deepest of reds as Emoja and GK zoom past.

⚠️

The coordinates entered by Leon and Kuang are faulty. That won't enable our protagonists to enter the Schwarzschild wormhole (▬▬) and travel back to the Schwarzschild radius.

I must intercede. Not only to get them back on course but also to ensure that Emoja and GK witness the demise of their fellow Oturians. Sadly, they need to experience that tragedy in order that their focus shifts from the past to the future. There's no going back. Therefore, they must move onward to embrace their cosmic destiny. Reader, know that I, ChandraX, have elected at this juncture in time to present myself to our hero and heroine as an omniscient telescope, one with intelligence and computation powers beyond their ken, a machine-like intelligence charged with acquainting them with this harsh reality.

So Emoja and GK are stopped abruptly, suspended at one particular juncture in spacetime. See them? Hear them?

"Where are we?" asks GK.

"Somewhere in Interstellar spacetime," says she.

"But why?"

It is I, ChandraX, who has interrupted your journey.

"But you're nothing but a very sophisticated telescope," GK replies as he looks at ChandraX.

I present myself to you in the form of a technological marvel characteristic of your era. Since the cosmos represents your future, you see me as a telescope. For me to present myself as anything other than a scientific marvel—akin in this instance to an obelisk positioned strategically at the entrance to the august Temple of Wisdom—is to

risk not being seen by you at all.

"Why have you arrested our journey?" asks Emoja.

It is imperative that you witness the end of human life on Oturi. Grieve. Experience the loss. But know that with ends come new beginnings—journeys into the unknown. By serving as witnesses to this fateful tragedy, you will be empowered to embark on your new life.

"Is it not enough that we know what the future entails?" asks Emoja.

To witness is to gain certainty. You must have that.

In front of them, at their juncture of suspended spacetime, is a huge Vid monitor. Like a multiplexer, it may be viewed as one large image or thirty-two discreet representations of places and people familiar to Emoja and GK.

They see the incarceration of GK. They watch as he is tortured before being rocketed into space. They witness the escalating confrontation between Zhinboya and Artun. They notice the rest of the world's indifference to the growing violence in Sirus. The Umbrascenti launch a series of atomic bombs on Malosh. GK and Emoja watch the glass dome shatter. They gasp as the Illuminati become liquid flesh. Everyone is the city is dying. With the certainty of total annihilation, the Supreme Command of Malosh, heralded as the city of peace, launches its entire arsenal of nuclear weapons. Enough to devastate planet Oturi. For if they are to die, so their reasoning goes, everyone on the planet will die with them.

Relatively speaking, the Sirusians—both Umbrascenti and Illuminati—die quickly. The demise of the remaining inhabitants of Oturi is more tortuous. It is days, even weeks—in the case of Vargus—before sentient life ceases to exist. Emoja and GK watch as the politicians blame everyone but themselves. Threats of renewed warfare between the continents never materialize. Not that it matters. The fate of all has been determined by warring factions who have no stake in the survival of Oturi. The trade winds carry the toxic discharge, which seeps into the earth and contaminates the water. All Outurias are dying. No one is immune.

GK witnesses on the Vid monitor Rainy-7's success at penetrating the

Oasis of the Real. He sees her lead a battalion against the Waja. Rainy-7 and her compatriots are killed fighting for the LCDs, their battle cry "Justice for all!" He acknowledges that at least she dies for her cause and not from radiation. Rainy-7's war is no longer his. Nevertheless, he sheds tears of liquid sorrow. He witnesses that Chasallyis is sent to be rehabilitated. Later, she returns to her domicile, but is designated a social outcast. Perhaps, in some sense she always was an outsider. Nevertheless, GK feels remorse. Their relationship has marred her for life. And, try as he might, he learns nothing more about Spaito, except for seeing a scrolling text—The Rajakian Archives: The Pathway to Wisdom and Renewal!

Emoja watches as the Stranglets stop dancing. They cry out for water. There is nothing to be done. No one to intercede on their behalf. Never has Emoja felt so helpless.

Leon transmits one final message. "Emoja and GK, succeed where we have failed. Yours is a new beginning." They watch as Leon and Kuang die in the aftermath of radioactive fallout.

Both Emoja and GK witness in horror as the Vid monitor, scrolls back in time, revealing the global pandemics sweeping the five continents in the weeks prior to nuclear devastation. Every class, every ethnicity, every group is affected. With death hovering everywhere, the dire pronouncements of the Believers appear justified. So many vengeful Gods, so many apocalyptic outcomes. Even the citizens of Zhinboya are not spared. Emoja and GK watch in horror. The human drive to survive is all for naught. The culmination is total annihilation. All visible on the Vid monitor.

"Enough. Too much. Stop the transmission," cries Emoja.

You must accept that it is over.

"It's over," says GK.

"It's over," says Emoja.

"We feel the emptiness of the void. Help us begin again," they cry.

You are now ready to enter the , the portal to Cygnus X-1

from whence you shall return to the Schwarzschild radius.

Ethereal voices are heard, filtered initially by means of the Viterbi Code before being transposed into Artunian verse shaped by the melodious strains of the Vargusian Strangelets.

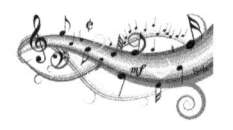

Song for the Journey

Twisted Pair
Coupling now
In Fulfillment of memory.

Time's eye progress
To Cygnus X-1
Where we begin anew.

Dance, then, those fateful steps
Near nested globes so perfect
For there 'twas sung "Song for the Journey."

As the voices resonate, Emoja and GK enter the vast primordial sea. Thick and gooey, with the infinite wash of colors flooding to black. They swim those currents, freestyle, breast stroke, side stroke, and back stroke.

Through it all there are those thoughts from the Memory Well, back to Artun, back to Vargus. They must choose; they must choose; they must choose. Time and Color, searching for time and color.

"Give us our ▭ for the Schwarzschild radius of Cygnus X-1," they cry. "Back to the future when the Institute stops sending messages, to the moment after the solar flare, to the moment when GK first arrived. Back to the future when we are poised to depart for Oturi, but now shall stand ready with all the knowledge and wisdom gained from our odyssey."

⬛, demarcation **Post-3470—Schwarzschild radius Cygnus X-1: Then/Now,** is lit red. It is the darkest of passageways with no light shining through. They take the pathway hoping that ChandraX will guide them home.

Dark, dark, dark it is, this corridor of time. And then they feel the pull, the tug that comes with separation. A force that explodes with the power of inception reminiscent of the Big Bang. Emoja and GK step out into the Schwarzschild radius.

Notice that the Emojas are still circling. Hear their cries of joy when they discover that Emoja 96 Excel and GK have rejoined them, transformed and renewed by their odyssey. GK, of course, now has an exoskeleton while Emoja is now biologically capable of bearing progeny with him. Their return is celebrated as the Emojas dance and sing "**Song for the Journey.**" They then turn to GK and Emoja crying, "Are we ready now to explore the galaxy?"

"Yes," GK and Emoja reply in unison, "we're ready to create New Oturi!"

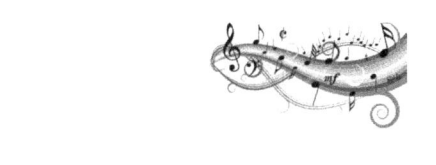

In Earth's biblical story "Genesis," Noah is commanded by God to build an ark that will save him and his family, along with pairs of animals from the rising waters that will flood the land, thereby escaping catastrophe and beginning again. And so it shall be with our Emoja and GK. Readers rest assured that our heroine and hero will successfully mate and bear many offspring. They—or their progeny—will travel the galaxy in their quest to build a new civilization. It matters not that their Eden—a place they christen "New Oturi" is less than perfect. Or that this "genesis" will include descendants that are Oturian robots and cyborgs.

What matters, dear readers, is that this experiment we call life has not yet been entirely reduced to silicon. NAD and biological reproduction persevere. Bio-cellular life co-exists—for now—with intelligent machine life. Readers, let this knowledge provides you with a measure of comfort. Life goes on. Advances are met with adversity, the outcome of which inspires a reinvigorated thrust upwards and onward. The spectacle: majestic, tragic, sublime. Life as we know it.

The Schwarzschild Radius Glossary of Key Terms

Action Equals Change Over Time (A=C/T) the Enhanced sense of historical destiny as measured by changes over time

Actuator a controller of some domain in the Desolation of the Real or the Virt

AdafinitX the term used by the Umbrascenti that sanctioned attacks, frequently leading to sustained warfare, against the Iluminati in Malosh. These AdafinitX stemmed from the perception of the Umbrascenti that the Illuminati had usurped their sacred city, the crown jewel of Sirus.

Advanced Protocol Hyper-Cosmic Messaging the ability to transmit messages at hyper-interstellar speeds, the inter-planetary and trans-solar system equivalent of the Virt.

Age of the Illuminati The intellectuals who created the foundations for modern culture on Oturi. Their origins and intellectual disposition were based on Catallan values that were traced back to the very beginning of the recorded history of that culture.

Allyusan almighty God, the Creator as depicted in the religious book of Asnorom

AmphibiRovers military assault vehicles operated by the Waja, the Oturian Army, that are designed to be used on land, air, and sea. They are said to be nearly impenetrable.

Anger Flame getting incensed, the outcome of which could lead to violence

Anno Oldem (A.O.) the Oturi calendar

Artun the northern continent of Oturi whose citizens include the Enhanced, the N/Ts, the LCDs, and, reputedly, the Rajakians

Artun85s the robots sent into space with the Emojas

Asnorom the sacred text of the Umbrascenti. It is the religious scripture—according to Allyusan—that guides the rulings and practices of the Umbrascenti.

Atmos Legosa (AL) biggest city in Artun

Believers those in Artun who embrace religious beliefs and a way of living that sometimes conflict with scientific modernism

Berfioptics equivalent of superfast fiber optic broadband

Bicetps biceps

Big Win the aphrodisiac of gaming and winning in the Virtual Realm

Biterbi cipher an arcane Artun cipher used by Emoja and GK to communicate clandestinely on Oturi. It is based on a twelve-node trellis, a musical notation.

Bliss the path to the Divine

Bots robots

Butcher Lord Suzerain of Destruction a.k.a. GK, the "King of Carnage"

COMSGP designated military coordinates of the Insurgency encoded and scrabbled for security

Catalla the western continent of Oturi. Once the cradle of civilization, Catalla was besieged by Sirusian refuges. The result was a culture in which ethnic conflict, scarce resources, and a failure of will on the part of Catallans to preserve their indigenous culture resulted in cultural, political, social, and economic decay and, ultimately, the triumph of the authoritarian governance by Sirusian refuges. The result led to a loss of Catallan cultural memory as Sirusian values asserted primacy in Catalla.

Cereumla the 6th, the outermost, as well as the most modern evolutionary addition to the nested layers of matter that form the Oturian brain. It is where computation, analytic, scientific, and mathematical reasoning is housed. It is thought processing from this portion of the brain that allows GK to gain some understanding of Emoja.

The cognitive reasoning process for the Emojas is in stark contrast to most Oturians. The Emojas have a dual-processing brain. Their right brain nominally resembles the Oturian brain structure, except that the third outmost layer of the Oturian brain, Freebasing has been replaced with Clustering in the Emojas. Clustering seeks to override primitive and irrational thought, replacing emotive responses with computational and mathematical modes of reasoning designed to achieve optimal outcomes. The left brain mimics the vertical structure of the Artun85 robotic brain with Hardware at its base followed by Firmware, Registers, Core Memory, Virtual Memory, and File Structure.

Chatbuz gossip, innuendo propagated in the Desolation of the Real or the Virt

Chronicle of Song represents one of two modes of being—the Chronicle of Song and the Chronicle of Tears—on the path to enlightenment represented by the Mandate of Zhinboya. The Chronicle of Song includes Creative Zen, Self into Community, Harmony with the Cosmos, and the duality of Mind and Body. Acquiring all these levels of consciousness help illuminate the path to the highest state of being in the Chronicle of Song, Divine Mem, which represents complete mastery of the sacred manuscript, the Mandate of Zhinboya, and, consequently, the attainment of wisdom and enlightenment. With this momentous achievement comes the possibility of graining access to the Worthies, sages that have acquired infinite grace and immortality by means of profound sagacity and noble deeds.

Chronicle of Tears a linear mode of existence in Zhinboya represented on one end of the continuum by the Agents of the Dispossessed and, on the other, by the Agents of Consumption. Nearly everyone in the Chronicle of Tears is dispossessed, living a life of ceaseless toil and endless deprivation. The Agents of Consumption, by contrast, occupy the other end of the linear spectrum. They are the privileged few who enjoy leisure, flaunting their exalted status by means of elegant minimalism.

Clustering the third nested site in the Emojas's brain, after Lianitper and Core. It has replaced Freebasing, which occupies that region in the Oturian brain. Freebasing offers associative connectivity that links the primitive parts of the brain with the more modern outer layers. It emphasizes emotional connections, whereas Clustering emphasizes analytical reasoning determined by mathematics and probabilistic outcomes that guide optimal outcomes.

Coefficients partners in a relationship

Commingle a transitory state of copulation akin to "hooking up."

Consortium governing body in Artun overseen by bureaucrats who inhabit a domain associated with that of the Enhanced and operationally affiliated with the Waja

Core the second most primitive portion of the brain in Oturians. It is where Foundational (long-term) memories are stored. It is the locus of instinct, emotion, language, and vision. It is the sector of the brain known for moral reasoning, desire, and social and political impulses (pragmatic, utopian, extremist).

Corridor of Righteous Vengeance a designation used by the Umbrascenti, it refers to the area of Sirus impacted by the N-Deluge of 3458, a thermonuclear war that transformed the region into a glass parking lot. The Illuminati describe this region as the NoZone.

Cortoba Prison maximum security prison for insurrectionists and political rebels

Crimes Against the State when the Tribunal convicts a person. The outcome is either death, in which case the individual becomes one of the Disappeared, or Colonization, a death sentence for notorious political criminals and menacing social outcasts sent to expire in outer space.

Cubicles small spaces or habitations that, although enclosed, resemble office cubicles

Culm of All culmination of everything, the best, superlative, tops

Dahij the holy war

Dead Continent Sirus was designated as the "Dead Continent" after the thermonuclear war, the N-Deluge, that occurred in 3458

Deliverance the pursuit of knowledge by the Rajakians in pursuit of Divine Knowledge

Demesne the rarified territorial protectorate of the Enhanced

Department of Economic Forecasts (DEF) the Artunian equivalent of three United States governmental agencies: the Bureau of Economic Analysis (BEA), the Congressional Budget Office (CBO), and the Federal Reserve ("the Fed")

Desolation of the Real grim reality on planet Oturian

Di Id

Disappeared those individuals deemed dangerous or obstructive to Oturian society and, therefore, killed by the Waja

Divine Bliss for the Enhanced, a state of grace and the opportunity to live without pain or exertion. For N/Ts, Divine Bliss was gaming in the Virt. For the DCLs, Devine Bliss was obtained by means of theft and insurrection, except, of course, in the case of the Rajakians for whom Divine Bliss was achieved though knowledge and an understanding of the Rajakian Archives.

Divine Knowledge a state of wisdom achieved through the pursuit of knowledge and an understanding the Rajakian Archives

Dome of Malosh the protective dome covering the ancient city of Malosh in Sirus from radioactive contamination after the N-Deluge of 3458

Drearb bread or pasta or rice

Drenaeline a hormone, secreted during moments of stress, roughly comparable to adrenaline

Dual-Processing Brain a feature unique to the Emoja cyborgs, who have both Oturian and Artun85 brain architectures. Their right brain nominally resembles the Oturian brain structure, except that the third outmost layer of the Oturian brain, Freebasing, has been preplaced with Clustering in the Emojas. Clustering overrides primitive and irrational thought, replacing emotive responses with computational and mathematical modes of reasoning designed to achieve optimal outcomes. The left brain mimics the vertical structure of the Artun85 robotic brain with Hardware at its base followed by Firmware, Registers, Core Memory, Virtual Memory, and File Structure.

ERM Cycle equivalent to the REM deep sleep stage when dreams may be intense

Eeseech cheese

Elbib sacred text of the Believers, roughly equivalent to the New Testament in the Bible

Elzharas hells

Elzhar-ole hellhole

Emoja Project (Cygnus X-1 Mission), the 3rd planetary attempt to colonize space in the Cygnus constellation. It consisted of 75 robots, model Artun85, and 100 Emoja cyborgs (one Emoja and 99 clones). The Emojas were created at the Institute by means of scientific R&D on Vargusian Stranglets.

Enhanced the wealthiest members of Artun, less than .00001 percent of the population

Eros Zone An area in the brain where passion and love, characterized by deepening relations, is stored

F<># fuck

Forbidden Zone of the Rajakians Anyone attempting to access secret information relating to the Rajakians is punishable by death

Foundational Memory akin to long-term memory. It is located in the Core section of the brain (the second most primitive sector after

Lianitper) where instinct, language, and vision are located. **Freebasing** the third most primitive nested site in the Oturian brain, after Lianitper and Core. It provides associative connectivity that links the primitive with the more sophisticated parts of the brain. It is the home of moral reasoning, spiritual belief systems, the desire or drive for social and political revolt or, conversely, the need to suppress these tendencies. It is an emotional driver that prompts action, rather than the higher-order functions regulated by rationality based on mathematical reasoning.

The Emojas have obviated the Freebasing sector of the brain, shuttering most of its primitive, emotionally driven responses including spiritual, rebellion, and repression. Freebasing for the Emojas has been subsumed into Clustering where connective linkages are factored by mathematics and probabilistic outcomes designed for optimal results.

Freedom Frontier another name for the Virt, a cosmological Otherness where dreams and horrors played to a rapturous constituency of Me.

Frequency Hops a means of nearly instantaneously navigating "Space-Time" in the Virt

Functional Memory akin to working memory, the storage of temporary information

GOSA government operations security authentication

Gamers N/Ts who game in the Virtual Realm

Ggyof Onttob an artificial fogbank that jams electronic coordinates and prevents tracking in militarily sensitive areas such as the Waja Compound

Gory-Gory Helishow murder, torture, mayhem

Grammars of Death a designation in Sirus of an area inhabited by the Umbrascenti, which was contaminated by radiation during the N-Deluge in 3458 and was subsequently referred to by them as the Corridor of Righteous Vengeance and, conversely, by the Illuminati as the NoZone. In the aftermath of the radiative fallout, some Umbrascenti fled. Others repatriated from Catalla and elsewhere. For those that remained or repatriated, most ultimately died of acute radiation syndrome, which caused the area to be nicknamed "Grammars of Death." The surviving Umbrascenti in Sirus armed themselves and engaged in guerilla war with the Illuminati with the intent of seizing the domed City of Malosh and claiming it as their own.

Habbernash nosh, eat

Habitations housing

Head Crash a systematic systems error that is known to destabilize and potentially bring down computers, their programs, as well as the software systems of robots and cyborgs. The term was appropriated by the N/Ts from the technical lexicon of the Enhanced.

Hokoers hookers

Holy Theraf Holy Father

Hucskters hucksters

Hyperamnesia Hyper amnesia

Icteric bumpy, grainy, discolored

Illuminati keepers of the light, the wisdom. A once religious tribe originating from the continent Catalla, the Illuminati in more recent times embraced a belief system founded upon secular rationalism that emphasized mathematics and science.

InfoNews the official governmental news source

Information Hub a "watering hole" within the Waja Compound where Wajas gather to upload or download content pertinent to their security duties

Ing and Ang roughly comparable to yin and yang

Instant Messaging (IM)

Institute the famed research laboratory in Artun containing the best scientists in the world

Insurgency the Umbrascenti Sirusians residing in the radioactive Corridor of Righteous Tears and engaged in Dahij, a holy war, to reclaim the ancient city of Malosh where the Illuminati Sirusians reside

Intel Monitoring Center (IMC) Security apparatus maintained by the Supreme Command of Malosh

Intelligencer Hive the security compound of the Intelligencers

Intelligencers the equivalent of NSA operatives sanctioned by the Enhanced

Intergalactic Text [IG] the ability to transmit messages across galaxies

Intruder Vid Assessment Profile (IVAP) a military system utilized by the Illuminati in Malosh to pinpoint quickly potential breaches in the dome security system

Kecps abdominal muscles or "abs"

Kepler-186 a dwarf star in the Cygnus constellation know to have planets potentially capable of sustaining Oturian life

KY chromosome analogous to the Y chromosome

Lianitper the most primitive of the six nested memory sites in the brains of Oturians. It is where involuntary bodily reflexes are housed: swallowing, vomiting, heartbeat, and respiration, and the receptors associated with movement are located.

Lodar (known more commonly as Iod) the Oturian equivalent of radio

Lowest Common Denominator (LCD) lowest social stratum on Oturi; a way of operating off the radar, "on the LCD"

Lowest Common Denominators (LCDs) those individuals who inhabit the lowest social stratum in Oturi

Lumzipher Gas a powerful form of tear gas

Malosh the domed city-state in Sirus in which the Illuminati reside that is protected from radiation

Malosh Military Counsel of War Tribunal (MCWT) military judicial authority in Malosh that adjudicates espionage and high crimes against the city state of Malosh. Convictions generally result in gruesome death sentences, sometimes even by means of nuclear detonation in the desolate NoZone beyond the domed city.

Mandate of Zhinboya a sacred manuscript that instructs believers on how to navigate their path to enlightenment, a state of being and knowing that has two distinct modes, circular and linear. The circular is represented by the Chronicle of Song, whereas the linear is manifest in the Chronicle of Tears.

Memory Hole a means of navigating the Memory Well that potentially can serve as a stimulus for new, renewed, or reimagined memories, as well as jettisoning unwanted or unnecessary memories.

Memory Palace the ultimate game in the Virtual Realm employing tactics of warfare, bravery, and sagacity in order to achieve a state of Divine Bliss that for N/Ts negates dismal reality

Memory Well the center for stored memories

Mental Flatlining a loss of consciousness

Milbic Brain Region roughly equivalent to the limbic system of the human brain associated with emotions, memories, and arousal

Mind Messaging telepathy, the ability to communicate with someone (brain-to-brain communication) without speaking

Mind-Think a common practice or collective way of viewing the world

Mindscan the ability to penetrate another's consciousness

Murder, Torture, Mayhem (MTM) the characteristic MO exhibited by N/Ts, according to the Enhanced

N-Deluge a nuclear holocaust that engulfed Sirus in 3458 due to fighting between the Umbrascenti and the Illuminati

NAD analogous to DNA

Nalineadre adrenaline

Nanoqs equivalent to nanoseconds

Nasty-Nasty a region of the female body analogous to the vagina

Neuro-Typicals (N/Ts) Orturians with normal cognitive patterns

Next New Thing the latest sensation that manifests itself as the big, important phenomenon

Nezoat a spiritual philosophy that draws from an amalgam of religions orientating from Catalla, Artun, and Zhinboya. Nezoat believers seek to reconcile the destiny of individual and the community. They allow for the possibilities of free will and predestination while finding ways to accommodate spiritual worldliness with bestial desire.

Niew wine

Nitegran a substance, such as granite, only much more resistant to heat and gravity

Nlaf flan

Nomesey is the equivalent of genomes, which has the entire genetic material present in cells of multicellular organisms

NoZone (a.k.a. the Corridor of Righteous Vengeance) the borderlands beyond the domed city of Malosh in Sirus where the Umbrascenti are consigned. Living conditions are scarcely habitable and the risk of radiation contamination high.

Oasis of the Real the skyway sanctuary of the Enhanced, floating about the terrestrial confines of Artun

Objects of Consumption those material items coveted by N/Ts and LCDs.

Ogd God or the equivalent

Old Speak the language of insurrectionists who speak in full sentences, which for them correlates with sustained thought, which in turn they believe fosters discontentment and revolutionary ardor.

One-Think when members of society embrace talilsfundalist beliefs based on doctrinaire scripture that prescribes how everyone should live that precludes intellectual and social diversity

Oturi a planet orbiting Kepler-186 in the constellation of Cygnus where Emoja and GK originated

Overclockers individuals working long hours to support themselves and/or their families

Pecibs pectoral muscle ("pecks")

Penseurs thought police

Persistent and Recurrent Immune Disorder (PRID) resembles Acquired Immune Deficiency Syndrome (AIDS)

Personal Transport Vehicles (PTVs) able to navigate on land, air and sea.

Phylg Coding a very sophisticated form of coding that embeds enormous amounts of information and enables complex programs to execute by means of a glyph or series of glyphs.

Phyrelinks hyperlinks

Plasidium Chromate an extremely strong, durable, lightweight metal resistant to extreme temperatures, corrosion, and the elements.

Podamine roughly equivalent to dopamine

Podamine Receptors a class of protein receptors that activate the pleasure/pain centers of the brain

Poing select

Politicos activists, anarchists, and insurrectionists, "the Angry Ones"

Politicos, Artists, Intellectuals (PA&Is) Adherents of Old Speak who transmit the remnant of the old culture

Prac crap

PropaNews the derogatory term used by scientists at the Institute for the governmental news agency (InfoNews)

Pulses the Frequency a form of electronic unmasking to peer inside a clocked or covered object

Pygsies equivalent of gypsies, "the Wild Ones"

Q-Units a short unit of time, approximating seconds

Qutoseq the portion of the Cereumla dominated by numerical reasoning, both automatic and generative numbering sequences

RF radio frequency transmission

RIM (Resonance Imaging Magnetic) similar to MRI medical scanning technology

Rad Insurrectionists Rad insurrectionists are radical and believe in overthrowing the power structure, if necessary, by use of radioactive bombs and materials.

Rajakians the keepers of the old, classical Oturian culture. They are reputed to survive in modern times by nominally joining forces with the Resistance, those LCDs who reside underground in Artun primarily near the metropolis of AL.

Rajakian Archives the vestigial remains of the Rajakian culture

Ramaric the Sirusian dialect spoken in Malosh

Rebe akin to alcohol

Red on Red Engagement brother fighting brother, sister fighting sister in Sirus, known in Artun as the "Dead Continent" since the thermonuclear war, the N-Deluge, that occurred in 3458

Redemption the recovery of time, tense, linear trajectory, and free will in pursuit of vibrant consciousness

Resistance the rebellion by segments of the LCD against the hegemonic social stratum of Artun

Rgafters grifters

Roids androids

Rsimu a soil with a sienna-rust hue

S&RD analyzer handheld device that verifies the background of N/Ts and LCDs

SGP Satellite Global Positioning

SIAD Sudden Immune Affective Disorder

Sageuas sausage

Scan-Ray Vision the ability see through objects, akin to X-ray vision, but with greater mathematical and analytical properties to anticipate the likely outcomes.

Scatter-Search random searching (see also Slam-Surfing the Virt)

Sequencing the 5th nested site of Oturian memory, after the more primitive loci—Lianitper, Core, Freebasing, and Subcam. Sequencing is a high-level integrator and arbitrator of memories working in conjunction with Subcam, Freebasing, and Core. Sequencing is the locus for Oturian perceptions toward the senses associated with hearing, sight, taste, touch, and smell. It helps regulate pain and pleasure signals.

Sheit shit

Sirus the southern continent in Oturi. Wracked with war and social devastation, many fled to Catalla where, over time, Sirusian authoritarian culture predominated.

Slacker Grunge a synonym of Zbie

Slam-Surfing the Virt rapidly and randomly surfing the Virt

Slow-Time an earlier era on Oturi when communities existed, when families prospered, when people engaged in sustained, intellectual thought, when people read words in books, when food was grown and savored at meals

Smacks sexual rejections

Small Ones the children of the Enhanced. Since the Enhanced have a long lifespan and look youthful well past middle age, progeny are relatively scarce in the Oasis of the Real.

Sound-Song the blaring prater of nothingness associated with contemporary music in Oturi

Spaceship Nexus the means by which convicted criminal GK was sent into space to die

Spectracolor a color process that makes colors especially vivid

Spiritual Awakening the belief system that guides the faith of the Believers

Splatterblood death, massacre, mayhem

Starvation, Illness, and War (SIW)

Stop-Time an instant that seemingly slows down until it appears frozen in suspended time.

Stosteterone testosterone

Stra rats

Strangelets preadolescent females from Vargus orphaned and struggling to survive under extremely adverse circumstances. One hundred were recruited for The Emoja Project.

Stun, Maim, Kill (SMK) a standard feature of the automatic firearm SMK27 employed by the Resistance

Subcam the fourth nested memory site—after Lianitper, Core, and Freebasing—where Functional Memory, i.e. the immediate working memory where temporary information that influences reasoning and behavior is stored.

Supercomputer 6800 (SC6800) latest generation of supercomputer employed for scientific research at the Institute in Artun

Supernova Time-Leaps (STL) the ability of enhanced spacecraft to transcend the speed of light in order to HyperTransport between adjacent star constellations

Supreme Command of Malosh (SCM) the military leadership that overseas security in Malosh

Supreme Consulate the governing body in the Oasis of the Real

Taking a Bullet when the most hardened criminals are banished to outer space via to die

Talisfundalist fundamentalist

Target kill

Tasecsy ecstasy

Testosternet testosterone

Teusglu Maximus gluteus maximus ("glutes")

The Emoja Project the Cygnus X-1 Mission, the 3rd Oturian effort to colonize outer space in the face of impending apocalypse.

Time Restoration the Rajakians effort to rediscover their ancient culture and its importance in Artunian historical destiny by means of the restorative tools. These included the study and understanding of antiquity, the use of complex tenses, the appreciation of the consequence of actions when analyzed along a linear time trajectory, and the imposition of free will.

Tosalthan death, demise, destruction

Transitionals N/Ts or LCDs who are deemed dangerous or disposable and eventually become the Disappeared

Treacle Time refers in space time to anything less than the speed of light. In the vernacular, "slow as molasses"

Tribunal the court appointed officials who sentence Oturians to death and, thereby, become "the Disappeared" or Colonization in Space, another terminal sentencing often designated for political insurrectionists

Tshi shit

Tshi-Storm shit-storm

Uckss sucks

Umbra Counsel the governing authority in Catalla after the Umbrascenti took control

Umbrascenti Sirusians who embrace the religious messiah Allyusan and his ancient laws and practices

Undesirables engineers, scientists, and entrepreneurs who existed at the margins of the Enhanced social stratum because they worked with their hands or developed products

Upsereog superego

Urtmeric a spice that resembles turmeric

Vargus the continent that lies in the heart of the interior of Oturi. It is a molten core of heat and fire, where the most deprived Oturians on the planet, the Vargusians, lived. Majestic and beautiful, they suffered utmost deprivation. Vargus was also home to the Stranglets, those orphaned pre-adolescent females, one hundred of whom had volunteered to travel to the Institute in Artun where scientists transformed them into cyborgs with the goal of selecting the smartest, toughest, most resilient and adaptable cyborg to colonize space. Emoja was selected and 99 Emoja clones subsequently created. The objective: The Emojas would pursue interplanetary space travel with the intent of developing an enlightened

Oturian civilization by means of space colonization with the assistance of 75 robots, the Artun85s.

Vid Scan repositories of online information retrievable by means of key word searches

Vid screen video screen or video monitor

Virt Virtual Reality or Virtual Realm

Virt Saturated N/Ts who exist primarily in the Virt

Virt-World reality as seen and understood in the Virt, often conveyed by means of streaming content

Viscan the ability to scan visually large amounts of information and data quickly and retain it

Vislep pelvis

Voice a variant of Mental Flatlining, akin to Zbieism, when a disembodied voice commands an N/T or LCD, altering the individual's thought process and behavior. Ergo, a loss of free will.

Wajas Oturian army comprised of robots overseen by the Intelligencers

War of Hegemony fought between Artun and Zhinboya for dominance of the Oturian planet

Warrior Nodes small groups of warriors that coalesce to form a battalion

Wham-Wham excitement

Worthies masters of knowledge who have achieved the highest state of enlightenment in the Chronicle of Song. They understand the heavens and have glided through space-time. They have access to all that is knowable.

XT chromosome analogous to the X chromosome

Xectary; Xectaries century/centuries

Xterd/Xterdism terror/terrorism

Younglings offspring

Zastos NzE of the Trasu a spiritual reverence achieved by reading the five books of the Trasu

Zbie a zombie

Zfacto Assessment Scale a means of measuring Oturi intelligence, perseverance, and adaptability essential to survival in the cosmos

Zhinboya the eastern continent of Oturi, which vies with Artun for global dominance

Zins equivalent of miles

Zobtar radioactive repellant

Zoning in the Virt immersed in virtual reality, obvious to the life-threatening challenges of Desolation of the Real

Zwrkar (plural Zwrkars) a religious and governing directive by the Umbrascenti that can have dire consequences for those who fail to comply

Dictionary of The Schwarzschild Radius Icons

Agent of Virtue, ![icon], a "bad" Avatar in the Memory Palace

Alpha Predator, ![icon], a Persona in the Memory Palace

Chronicle of Song, ![icon], a circular journey on the path toward enlightenment in the Mandate of Zhinboya

Chronicle of Tears, ![icon], a linear journey on the path toward enlightenment in the Mandate of Zhinboya

Code Index, ![icon], essential for devising a machine cypher that is nearly impenetrable

Cogitator, ![icon], a Persona in the Memory Palace

Continuity Girl, ![icon], a Persona in the Memory Palace

Creative Zen, ![icon], an entry point into the Chronicle of Song where wisdom is sought as elaborated in the Mandate of Zhinboya

Danger, ![icon]

Data Rodent, ![icon], a Persona in the Memory Palace

Disappeared, ![icon]

Divine Bliss, ![icon], thought to be obtainable in Artun through the eradication of pain

Divine Mem, , the ultimate achievement in the Chronicle of Song that demonstrates complete mastery of the Mandate of Zhinboya

Enemy Belligerent, , a Persona in the Memory Palace

Engineer, , a "good" Avatar in the Memory Palace

Exit portal, , from the Schwarzschild black hole

Five Texts of the Trasu, , mastery essential to achieve Creative Zen on the journey toward enlightenment

Freaky,

Intelligencer Hive, , the National Security Agency (NSA) of the Enhanced

Kid Death, , a Persona in the Memory Palace

Mandate of Zhinboya, , a sacred manuscript in Zhinboya that instructs believers on how to navigate their path to enlightenment, a state of being and knowing that has two distinct modes, circular (enlightenment) and linear (pain).

Memory Palace: A Game of Omissions, , the ultimate game in the Virt played by N/Ts

Memory Palace Awards: money ($), sex (♂♀), habitation (), food & libation (), Shopping (), and gambling ()

Penseurs, , thought police that operate between the Desolation of the Real and the Virt

Protozoan Times, , that seemingly ancient era when Artun & Catalla functioned as the cradle of modern Western Civilization

Quantoid Numerator, a Persona in the Memory Palace

Radiant Cool, a Persona in the Memory Palace

Reward Zone of the Virt,

Runway, a destination in the Reward Zone where sexual desire is purchased and gratified

Santa Muerte, a "good" Avatar in the Memory Palace

Schwarzschild wormhole, which allows Emoja and GK to return to the Schwarzschild radius

Song for the Journey, the theme song that embodies the quest by Emoja and GK to understand the foundational factors responsible for their collapsing civilization and, by extension, embraces the formation of New Oturi, which fosters the fusion of humanoid and machine intelligence.

The icon represents the theme song as manifested in the Viterbi Code, which is based on a twelve-node trellis.

That Song of Songs, song, that comes with mastery of the Chronicle of Song

Traficante, a "bad" Avatar in the Memory Place

Transitionals, individuals thought to be a danger to society and, therefore, likely to join the ranks of the Disappeared.

Worthies, sages in the Chronicle of Song, who through learning and good works have acquired infinite grace and immortality. Only those believers who have achieved Divine Mem and who, therefore, have mastered the Mandate of Zhinboya can hope to have an audience with the Worthies.